W9-CZX-440

NIGHT SHIFT

NIGHT SHIFT

A Novel

ROBIN COOK

THORNDIKE PRESS
A part of Gale, a Cengage Company

LIBRARY OF CONGRESS CIP DATA ON FILE.
CATALOGUING IN PUBLICATION FOR THIS BOOK
IS AVAILABLE FROM THE LIBRARY OF CONGRESS.

ISBN-13: 978-1-4328-9955-4 (hardcover alk. paper)

Published in 2022 by arrangement with G. P. Putnam's Sons, an imprint
of Penguin Publishing Group, a division of Penguin Random House LLC.

Printed in Mexico
Print Number: 1   Print Year: 2023

To Jean, Cameron, and Primo, my Nuclear Family

PROLOGUE

New York City
Monday, December 6

Dr. Susan Passero, an internist at the Manhattan Memorial Hospital, known colloquially as the MMH, ushered her forty-first and final patient of the day, Florence Williams, out of the examination room. It was nearly 6:00 P.M. She said a warm goodbye and encouraged Florence to keep up the good work adhering to her rather complicated medication schedule. Returning into the room, Sue took a deep breath, readjusted her Covid-19 mask, and sat back down at the computer terminal to finish the required entry. Like most doctors, she despised being so chained to the demands of the electronic health record because of the interference it invariably caused between her and her patients, yet she knew that modern medicine demanded it. When she was finished and had dutifully checked all the necessary boxes, she washed her hands for the thousandth time that day, pocketed her stethoscope, and headed out into the clinic proper.

As per usual she was the last doctor to finish seeing the scheduled patients, so the clinic was all but empty. At the far end the housekeeping crew was already starting the daily cleaning. Sue waved to them since she was on a first-name basis with several, and they waved back. Up until then it had been a normal, busy Monday, and Mondays were always the busiest day of the week since on top of the scheduled visits, a number of the patients who'd come into the Emergency Department over the weekend often needed follow-up.

Sue Passero was a big-boned, athletic African American woman whose body habitus still reflected her accomplishments in the collegiate sports of soccer, basketball, and softball. Mindful of her appearance, she was wearing a silk dress under her white doctor's coat, her hair in a contemporary short, spiky style. As an outgoing person she was friendly to everyone at the hospital, particularly food service personnel and the cleaning people. Despite being a board-certified internist with subspecialty training in cardiology, she was never tempted to assume a holier-than-thou attitude with the other hospital employees like some narcissistic doctors she knew. The reason was simple. Out of necessity through high school, college, and even medical school, she'd worked at just about every low-level academic medical center job, including cleaning monkey cages. The result was that she sincerely appreciated everyone's input. At the same time, she was demanding. No matter what someone's work entailed, they had to give one hundred percent, which was the way she had always approached her duties.

"All done!" Sue called out to Virginia Davenport after leaning into the scheduling secretaries' office. Like Sue, Virginia was always the last clinic secretary to leave for the day. In her role as the most senior clinic employee, she took her job seriously, which was why she and Sue clicked and worked well together.

"Here's your patient schedule for tomorrow," she said, leaping up and handing a printout to Sue. Virginia was a tall, slender woman with an oval face framed by tight blond curls and punctuated with dark eyes and very white teeth.

"Thank you, girl," Sue said, taking the paper like a handoff to a relay race sprinter as she moved quickly down the hallway. Now that she was done seeing patients, she wanted to wrap up the day, get in her car, and head home to New Jersey. As she hustled down to her tiny office, she glanced at the schedule. It looked like any other day of late, with thirty patients on the calendar, although that would invariably balloon up.

"I also printed that article about the medical serial killer that you asked me to," Virginia said, running to keep up with Sue. "And here are the phone calls that came in while you were seeing patients that need a response from you."

Without slowing, Sue took the phone messages and the article, glancing at the latter. It was a *New York Times* piece from October about a Texas nurse who had been found guilty of killing four postoperative patients by injecting air into their arteries. Entering her office, Sue slipped behind her desk and sat down. "You are a dear," she said, looking up at Virginia, who had followed her. This final interaction between them was part of their daily routine before Sue's departure. "Did you happen to read the article?"

"I did," Virginia said. "It would be hard not to, seeing the title. It's horrific that people are capable of that kind of behavior, especially in the medical profession."

"What scares me about this particular case is that the nurse's motivation was to keep certain patients in the intensive care unit so he could get more work hours. Can you believe it? I mean, it's a new one for me. I can sort of understand, in a sick way, the so-called mercy killers who mistakenly profess to be saving people from pain and suffering. I can even intellectually understand the scarier hero syndrome, where misguided sociopathic fruitcakes are trying to burnish their image by putting patients in jeopardy to get credit for supposedly saving them." As she was speaking, Sue pulled out a large blue folder from between two bookends. Opening it, she slipped in the article to join a number of other similar ones.

"It's a terrifying thought, no matter what the motivation," Virginia said. "The hospital is supposed to save people and certainly not kill them. I tell you, the world seems to be getting more and more crazy."

"Any of these calls demand immediate attention?" Sue asked, holding up the list of names and phone numbers. "Or can I call on my way home?"

"Nothing earth-shattering," Virginia assured her. Although trained in psychology and social work, rather than in healthcare per se, she had learned over the ten years she'd worked in the Internal Medicine Clinic to recognize true medical emergencies. From experience Sue had learned to trust her. "Has the MMH ever had such a problem?"

"Interesting you should ask. I'm afraid the answer is yes. About fifteen years ago, my friend Laurie Montgomery, in her inimitable style as a medical examiner extraordinaire, outed a nurse here who was being paid by a shady organization working for a health insurance company to kill postoperative patients who carried the markers for bad genes."

Virginia knew Laurie from having set up numerous lunches and even an occasional dinner date for her and Sue. The two doctors were old friends from their college days and had gone to medical school together.

"Why?"

"To save the insurance company money. With their genetic baggage, the involved patients were destined to need lots of expensive healthcare."

"Oh, my goodness," Virginia said, covering her mouth with her hand in dismay. "That's awful. That's worse than the Texas nurse. How many patients were involved?"

"A half a dozen or so," Sue said. "I don't remember exactly. It was bad, and I've tried to forget the details but not the lesson. It was an awful reminder of how much business interests have taken over medicine. Especially with private equity trying to eke out every last penny of compensation."

"That's unfortunately true," Virginia said. "And mentioning business interests reminds me that you have a Compliance Committee meeting tomorrow at noon."

"Thank you. I appreciate the reminder, and if that's it, I'm out of here." Sue slapped the surface of her desk, stood up, and pulled off her long white coat. The fact that she had another committee meeting didn't surprise her. As a particularly dedicated member of the MMH staff, she felt it was her duty to volunteer for multiple committees. Currently she was a member of the Mortality and Morbidity Committee, the Infection Control Committee, and the Outpatient Reorganizing Committee, as well as the Compliance Committee. On top of that, she was vying for a seat on the hospital board. Luckily Virginia Davenport was willing to assist with all this added work.

"You are all caught up," Virginia assured her, heading for the doorway. "Drive carefully on your way home. See you in the morning."

"Same to you on the subway." Sue exchanged her white coat for her winter coat, which was hanging on the back of the door to the hallway. Picking up her mobile phone, purse, and the list of patients whom she needed to contact, she followed Virginia out into the hallway, where they parted ways. Sue was intent to get out of the high-rise garage before the rush of cars coming in for the night shift starting at 7:00. Although most of the employees came by mass transit, enough private vehicles were involved that it could be a minor traffic jam.

The route required taking the pedestrian bridge from the outpatient building to the main building and from there a second pedestrian bridge to the garage. Although a few of the night-shift personnel were arriving, as were some visitors, it was not nearly as busy as it would get between 6:30 and 7:00. Sue found her car where it had been parked that morning by the valet service in the doctors' section, which was already mostly empty, as was usually the case. As she approached her beloved BMW with its heavily tinted windows, she reached into her coat pocket and fondled the electronic key fob, pressing the door open button in the process. The car responded by turning

14

on its interior as well as outside lights.

Sue opened the driver's-side door and tossed her purse into the passenger seat before slipping in behind the wheel. As she always did, she hung her ID lanyard on the rearview mirror. She reached for the starter button, but her hand never made it. To her shock and horror, a cloth hood was thrown over her head and pulled down around her shoulders. As she reached up to tear the hood away, an arm came around her throat, yanking her back against the headrest with such force that her back was arched away from the seat. Letting go of the hood, she tried to pull the arm away using both hands while crying out in utter terror. Unfortunately, her voice was muffled due to both the hood and the compression on her neck. In the next instant she felt a stabbing pain in her right thigh.

Gritting her teeth, Sue managed to pull away the arm encircling her head enough to take a breath. But then a second arm came to the aid of the first, dislodging one of her hands and repinning her head back against the headrest, again restricting her airway.

Out of sheer desperation, Sue tried to bite the arm that was around her neck, but her efforts were restricted by the cloth hood. The attacker responded by upping the compression of her neck and increasing the hyperextension of her back. As forcefully as she could, she then tried to dig the nails of both of her hands into the restraining arms, but as she struggled to do so, she suddenly became aware of losing strength. It was as if the muscles in her arms and neck were becoming unresponsive. At first, she thought it might be a kind of fatigue from making a superhuman effort, but it progressed relentlessly. Rapidly her hands lost their grip on the arms encircling her neck. Then, even more frightening, she found herself struggling to breathe.

Marshaling her last ounce of strength, Sue tried once more to cry out, but no sound escaped her lips, and with an agonizing roar in her ears, she lost consciousness . . .

CHAPTER 1

Tuesday, December 7, 6:45 A.M.

Without making it obvious, Dr. Jack Stapleton put muscle into the mild hill climb on West Drive in Central Park where it bordered the reservoir. It had given him a bit of satisfaction to overtake and pass a small, tight covey of younger, serious cyclists on their imported road bikes, all of them clad in skintight, fancy duds emblazoned with all sorts of European product endorsements and wearing clip-in, expensive bike shoes. He, of course, was on his relatively new US-made Trek bike that was every bit as fancy as the others, but his dress was far different. He was wearing his usual brown, wide-wale corduroy jacket, blue jeans, and an indigo chambray shirt with a dark green knit tie. Instead of bike shoes he had on Nike kicks. His only concession to the forty-five-degree weather were gloves and a scarf.

As he had done practically every morning

since he had arrived in New York City to begin his new life and second medical career as a New York City medical examiner at the Office of Chief Medical Examiner, or OCME, Jack was using his bike to commute from his home on the Upper West Side down to the east side of the city. It was a far different mode of transportation than when he'd been a conservative, midwestern ophthalmologist. Back then he drove a Mercedes to his office every day, attired in a glen plaid suit with carefully polished shoes.

The current pacesetter of the group of well-heeled cyclists responded just as Jack envisioned. It would have been demoralizing to have a middle-aged, possibly blue-collar individual pass them, so he stood up and began a chase. There was no way for the cyclist to know that Jack probably rode his bike more often than they did. Nor did they have any idea that Jack also played demanding pickup basketball on a near-daily basis, weather permitting, and was accordingly in tip-top physical shape. The rest of the cyclists followed the lead of the pacesetter, standing up and pumping furiously.

Meanwhile, without making it obvious by remaining sitting, Jack increased his own effort such that his lead slightly increased despite the more obvious efforts of the pursuing bicyclists. Several minutes later, as Jack crested the hill and began his descent, he stopped pedaling and allowed himself to coast, which permitted the clot of pursuers to finally catch and overtake him to regain their sportive dignity.

Under more normal circumstances Jack would have continued the impromptu race all the way to the south end of the park, where he'd exit on his way to work. But on this particular morning, his attention switched from aggravating the "serious" cyclists to musing about the Brooks School that he was passing to his right on Central Park West. It was where his son, JJ, was enrolled in the fifth grade. As if it were yesterday and with understandable chagrin, Jack could remember his disastrous visit there two years earlier, when Laurie, his wife, asked him to go to talk to the school authorities in her stead about their concern that JJ needed to take Adderall for ADHD after JJ had gotten into a few tussles on the playground.

What made Jack an inappropriate substitute for Laurie was that he was absolutely convinced there was nothing atypical with JJ. Combining that reality with his belief in some kind of conspiracy between the pharmaceutical and education industries, both of which seemed in his mind to be overly eager to start kids on what was essentially speed and turning them into nascent druggies. Unfortunately, Jack had made sure that the Brooks School knew exactly how strongly he felt. As a result, he had succeeded in alienating the school authorities, who threated to expel JJ. Ultimately, Jack had agreed — along with Laurie's insistence — to have JJ at least evaluated by a psychiatrist, who agreed with the diagnosis, but luckily by that time it no longer mattered. The evaluation process had taken long enough that it was apparent to all that JJ was not exhibiting any more playground shenanigans. As a result, the school's insistence on medication fell by the wayside — that was, until last week, when JJ had had another fight during recess. Suddenly the whole issue had resurfaced, and it was the reason Jack was now on his way to the OCME so early in the morning. The night before, he had been harangued by both Laurie and her mother, Dorothy, who were both championing the use of ADHD medication. Awakening way before the alarm and not wishing to be again subjected to more pressure before rethinking all the pros and the cons of the situation, Jack had decided to leave the apartment before anyone else was awake.

Jack's normal route would have taken him to the southeastern corner of Central Park, but because of the dramatic uptick in bicycle use in Manhattan due to a combination of frustratingly heavy vehicular traffic, the Covid-19 pandemic, and E-bikes, bike lanes had majorly proliferated. The result was that his commute was significantly faster and safer, although Laurie doubted the latter. Now Jack exited the park in the southwest corner into Columbus Circle. From there, he used the dedicated bike lane to head south on a combination of Broadway and Seventh Avenue all the way to 30th Street. Conveniently, 30th Street also had a bike lane, although it wasn't as safe since it was merely painted on the pavement alongside the parked cars. Jack's destination was at the corner of 30th Street and First Avenue, where the old OCME building stood, which still housed the autopsy suite.

As Jack rode east on 30th, his thoughts went back to Dorothy's role. He recognized she evoked serious ambivalence in his thinking. In relation to his daughter, Emma, who had been diagnosed several years earlier with autism, Dorothy had played a positive role. She had taken it upon herself to

21

organize and then manage the complicated interviewing, choosing, and scheduling of the behavior therapists, speech therapists, and physical therapists who were responsible for Emma's impressive progress. But even Emma's improvement was not without some controversy. Jack was inclined to enroll Emma in a specialized school for children on the autism spectrum that was close to the Brooks School. But Dorothy disagreed and so far had convinced Laurie to her point of view.

Worse than the mild disagreement over Emma's situation was Dorothy's continued anti-vaccine stance, since she still insisted that it had been Emma's MMR vaccine that had caused her autism, even though the possibility had been scientifically proven false. Worse still, her anti-vaccine feelings had extended to the Covid-19 vaccine, and no matter what Jack or Laurie said, Dorothy refused the jab. Making her intransigence that much worse was that Dorothy had all but moved in with them to take over the second guest room right after her husband, Laurie's stern cardiac surgeon father, had passed away three months ago, in September.

On several occasions Jack had tried to broach the issue of establishing some appropriate time frame for Dorothy to move back to her spacious Park Avenue co-op, but Laurie wouldn't hear of it. It was her belief that Emma was benefitting greatly from having her grandmother constantly around and that Dorothy was still much too fragile to move back to an empty apartment.

All in all, Jack was feeling a bit like the odd man out, especially with Laurie acting more and more like the chief both at work and at home. Not wanting to force the issue and possibly cause a disruption in the fragile home environment, Jack looked to work to occupy his mind and emotions. He needed to scare up some kind of difficult case to monopolize his thoughts. It had worked in the past; investigating a chiropractic death had helped him deal with JJ's diagnosis of neuroblastoma when the boy was an infant. One of the definite benefits of being a medical examiner was that every day was different and there was always the possibility of confronting a perplexing circumstance. He and Laurie certainly had proven that over the years without an ounce of doubt.

After waiting for a green light to cross First Avenue at the corner of 30th Street, Jack rode down along the old OCME building that had long ago overstayed its usefulness. When it had been built more than a half century ago it had been state of the art. Now it was hardly that. A new autopsy building with offices for the medical examiners and the Toxicology Department was sorely needed. It was supposed to be built near the new high-rise OCME building four blocks to the south but had been held up by budgetary problems. It was one of his wife's main objectives in her role as the chief medical examiner of the City of New York, and she was counting on the new mayor soon to be sworn in to give it the green light.

Turning in at the receiving bay where bodies arrived and departed, Jack rode between the parked ME Sprinter vans, hoisting his bike up onto his shoulder as he climbed the side stairs up onto the platform. Then, walking the bike, he passed the security office and waved to the guards, who were busy in the process of changing shifts. Jack did the same passing the mortuary techs' office. Off to the left, where the Hart Island coffins for unclaimed bodies were stored, Jack secured his bike and helmet with a cable lock to a standpipe. He was the only one who used his bike to commute to work, and there was no official bike stand. Nearby was the darkened, isolated autopsy room for decomposing bodies.

Eager to see what the night had brought

in terms of new cases, Jack mounted the stairs one floor, passed through the sudden infant death syndrome room, and entered the part of the ID area where the day began for the OCME. It was a little after seven in the morning.

CHAPTER 2

Tuesday, December 7, 7:10 A.M.

"Good morning, Jennifer," Jack said with more alacrity than he felt. In contrast to some of the other forty-one medical examiners, Jack did not make it a habit to project his inner mindset and mood to others, mainly because he was a private person. Dr. Jennifer Hernandez was one of the relatively new medical examiners on staff, and it was currently her turn to be on call for the week, meaning if one of the medical examiners was needed during the night to back up the forensic pathology fellow, she was the designee. It was also her role to come in early, go over the cases that had come in during the night, confirm the need for each to be autopsied, and then divide them up between the medical examiners. "Anything particularly interesting today?" Jack added as he approached the desk where Jennifer was sitting. He tried to act casual.

"I just got here two minutes before you," Jennifer said. "I haven't even started looking at them." In front of her was a modest stack of folders containing the workups done by the medical legal investigators, or MLIs, highly trained physician assistants who went out into the field, if necessary, to investigate all deaths thought to be possible medical examiner cases. The police and hospital supervisory personnel were all highly cognizant of which deaths were required to be reported to the OCME by law and which weren't. Although the previous day's haul was extensive since it included the entire weekend, today's cases were modest in number. Jack estimated no more than about twenty.

"Did you get any calls during the night from the pathology fellow or the MLIs for any problems?" Jack asked, trying not to sound too eager. Cases where the on-call ME participated were invariably more challenging and interesting.

"I didn't," Jennifer said. "I gather it was a fairly quiet night. Mostly overdoses."

Jack inwardly groaned. He wasn't surprised. They were seeing on average five overdose deaths a day, which were more depressing than intellectually stimulating. There was no forensic mystery involved, only the social question of what was happening to society to foment such an ongoing tragedy, above and beyond the appearance of fentanyl in the drug world. "Do you mind if I take a look?" Jack asked. He was sensitive to not be too pushy with his seniority.

Jennifer laughed. "Be my guest," she said, gesturing to the stack of folders. It was common knowledge among the MEs that Jack often arrived early to cherry-pick cases to find the most challenging. No one denied him because everyone knew he was the kind of workaholic who always took more than his share of cases, even the routine ones. Jack was the opposite of a slacker, especially when he was stressed out like he was at the moment.

"Oh, no!" a voice cried. Both Jack's and Jennifer's head bobbed up as Vinnie Amendola breezed into the room with his ever-present *New York Post* tucked under his arm. He was a slight, dark-haired, and unshaven man who was dressed in a hooded sweatshirt and baggy sweatpants, looking slouchy despite being the most senior mortuary technician at the OCME. In contrast to his appearance, he was impressively knowledgeable about forensics. Having worked closely with Jack for many years, they were a well-oiled team. "God! I hate to see Dr. Stapleton here this early," he moaned, rolling his eyes skyward while slapping his paper down onto the side table between two upholstered easy chairs as if angry. "Damn it all! It means I'm going to be stuck in the pit all day listening to his bullcrap. What could I have done to deserve this?" *The pit* was the nickname for the autopsy room among all the mortuary techs.

"I hope you didn't get all dressed up for us," Jack quipped. Lots of sarcastic barbs was the bulk of their normal verbal interaction.

"Let me guess," Vinnie said as he collapsed into one of the chairs. "Problems on the home front? In-law difficulties? Am I getting close?"

Jack grimaced. Vinnie knew him much too well. "Things could be better," Jack admitted without elaborating. "What I need is a challenging case."

Vinnie immediately got the message and didn't tease further. Instead, he changed his tone and said, "Okay! Anything promising?"

"I haven't yet had a chance to look," Jack responded. "How about getting the communal coffee ready?" Making coffee in the morning was one of Vinnie's self-imposed jobs, as he was usually one of the first people on the day shift to arrive.

"All right, already!" he said, pretending to be irritated.

Jack redirected his attention to the stack of folders, hoping to hit pay dirt, but his optimism quickly dimmed. As Jennifer had warned, the first three were run-of-the-mill overdoses. Although he was certainly aware each was its own personal tragedy, particularly the third case, which involved a fifteen-year-old boy, none of them would be enough to dominate his mind at least for a few days or even for a week, which was what he was hoping to find. But then, like an unexpected slap in the face, the name on the fourth folder jolted him. It was *Susan Passero,* the name of Laurie's oldest and closest friend, who also served as her general medical practitioner. Jack also knew her, and he certainly respected her as a first-rate internist as well as personable, socially committed, and a dutiful mother. Although Laurie usually saw Susan solo, mostly for lunch at least once a month, Jack and her husband, Abraham, known as Abby, had on occasion had been included with the women for dinner or to attend some sort of cultural event.

With his pulse quickening, he emptied the folder and hurriedly searched through the contents for the MLI's investigative workup.

As he did so, he hoped that the body downstairs in the cooler would turn out to be a different Susan Passero. As he snapped up the workup, Jack's worst fears were realized when he read that the deceased was a physician on the staff of the Manhattan Memorial Hospital who had died suddenly in apparent good health, which was the reason it was deemed a medical examiner case.

Jack sighed loudly and involuntarily stared off into the middle distance, already worried about having to call Laurie and give her this disturbing and shocking news. With all the stresses and strains that were happening at home and those associated with her relatively new role as the chief medical examiner — running the largest ME office in the country, with more than six hundred employees and a yearly budget of $75 million — this added emotional burden was potentially going to be horrendous.

"Something wrong?" Jennifer asked, sensing Jack's reaction.

"I should say," he answered. He glanced at Jennifer, who knew Laurie well. Jennifer was the daughter of Laurie's late nanny, and Laurie was largely responsible for Jennifer's career choice as a physician and a forensic pathologist. Jack held up the MLI report.

"I'm afraid this autopsy case is one of Laurie's closest friends."

"Good lord," Jennifer said. "What happened?"

He went back and read more of the workup. "She apparently died in her car in the MMH's garage. She was found slumped over the steering wheel by a nursing supervisor named Ronald Cavanaugh, who was coming on shift. He described finding no pulse, and with the help of another arriving nurse alerted the ED while starting CPR."

"Cardiac, probably," Jennifer said.

"That's what the ED physician ultimately thought," he said. He looked back at Jennifer and shook his head. "Wow! What a tragedy! This is going to be one hell of a blow for Laurie. Besides being a friend, the woman was a committed doctor, a doctor's doctor, as I'm sure Laurie would agree."

"Who was the MLI?" Jennifer asked.

"Kevin Strauss," Jack said as he went back to reading.

"He's good."

"I agree," he mumbled.

"If you are going to have a heart attack, I guess a hospital is a good place to have it," Vinnie said as he was making the coffee.

"But not in your car in the garage," Jack said.

"Did the ED send a resuscitation team?" Vinnie asked.

"Within minutes," Jack said. "Apparently they made a lot of effort because the nursing supervisor and the other nurse said that the patient initially showed some signs of improvement when they started CPR."

"Did they ever get a pulse?" Jennifer asked.

"No, no pulse was obtained either in the garage or in the ED where she was moved while the CPR was continued."

"I wonder what they thought were signs of improvement."

"It doesn't say," Jack said.

"Any history of cardiac issues?"

"Apparently not," he said. "What she did have is type 1 diabetes, which I didn't know, and I don't believe Laurie knew, either, which is surprising for as long as she and Sue knew each other."

"Well, sudden cardiac death is certainly not unknown with type 1 insulin-dependent diabetes," Jennifer said. "And I actually did hear about this case last night."

"How did that come about?" Jack asked, looking up from his reading.

"One of the ID team called me with a problem," Jennifer said. "The husband of the patient was the one who came in to make the ID, and he was understandably very upset and let it be known that he was firmly against an autopsy. He demanded the body be released immediately to his designated funeral home. I ended up talking to him and tried to calm him down. When he would finally listen, I explained to him that it was not possible for the body to be released because his wife had died suddenly, in apparent good health, and that we were required by law to determine the cause and manner of death. I made sure he understood that an autopsy was needed."

"I find all this really surprising. Was the name of the husband Abraham Ahmed?" For a few seconds, he entertained the idea that maybe this case involved a different Susan Passero, but the idea was dispelled when Jennifer confirmed the husband's name.

"Good grief," Jack said. "I'm shocked. Did he offer a reason for not wanting an autopsy?"

"Yes. He said he was Muslim and that he didn't want to delay burial."

"My word! You live and learn. I've spent some social time with the man and had no idea Abby, as he likes to be called, is Muslim. What did you tell him?"

"I told him most likely an autopsy would

have to be done, but I assured him it would be done quickly and with full respect for the body. Because of a previous case I read up on Islamic attitudes and sensitivities toward autopsies. I knew that in this day and age, it is not as clear cut as he was suggesting. I read it's not mentioned in the Koran."

"Was he satisfied?"

"Not particularly," Jennifer admitted. "He was obviously put out about the situation. I encouraged him to call back this morning, saying he could talk to whoever does the case."

"Have you decided who you will assign it to?"

"I was thinking I would do it myself," she said. "For one thing, it's my understanding that Muslims prefer the same gender do the autopsy as the deceased, and since I've already spoken to the husband, it makes sense."

"Oh, boy," Jack commented vaguely with a shake of his head while nervously running a hand through his modified Caesar cut. It was turning out to be a much worse day than he'd bargained for. "Well, I think I'd better call Laurie right away to get her in the loop, but I'm not looking forward to it. She's going to be one unhappy lady, and because of a few other issues on the home front, as Vinnie correctly suspected, I hate to be the messenger."

"Sorry to hear. Would you like me to do it?" Jennifer graciously offered.

"Thank you, but no," he said. "It's nice of you to offer, but I've got to step up to the plate. I kinda immaturely bailed out this morning and need to face the music." Jack never minded mixing his metaphors.

Jennifer picked up the phone that was on the opposite end of the desk and moved it over in front of him. Jack waved it off, saying he'd use his mobile but wanted to wait until he reread Kevin Strauss's investigative report more carefully. He knew Laurie would have all sorts of questions, which he wanted to be able to answer.

"Want some fresh coffee for fortification?" Vinnie called out without a hint of sarcasm from where he was standing by the coffee maker.

"Please," Jack responded as he began rereading and committing to memory Sue's most recent blood chemistries, particularly her glucose and cholesterol levels. As he went through the whole report, it was obvious that Kevin had had an opportunity to go over Sue's entire digital health record, which included being diagnosed with type 1 diabetes as a child. What Jack was most interested in determining was if there had been any history of cardiac issues whatsoever. There had been none, though, and a relatively recent routine ECG had been entirely normal.

"As per usual, the MLI did a bang-up job," Jack commented to no one in particular when he finished. He then pulled his mobile out of his jacket pocket and retreated to one of the upholstered easy chairs. Vinnie brought over a steaming mug of coffee and set it on the side table. Jack acknowledged the gesture with a nod as he pulled up Laurie's mobile number on his phone's screen and then, after a sip of his coffee, tapped the screen gently to put the call through.

CHAPTER 3

Tuesday, December 7, 7:32 A.M.

"Okay, what's the story?" Laurie answered after the first ring. As Jack fully anticipated, it was plainly obvious from the tone of her voice she was irritated. "Why in heaven's name did you get up and leave without so much as a note on the fridge? Do I have to deal with *three* children when two is more than enough with everything else going on?"

"Okay, okay," he said. "I'm sorry."

"Are you already at the OCME?"

"No, I stopped in at the St. Regis for their lovely French toast," Jack said, and immediately regretted it.

"This is no time for sarcasm, my friend. You are in the proverbial doghouse, so don't make it worse."

"You're right," Jack said, controlling himself. "Yes, I'm at work. As an explanation, not an excuse, I'm feeling a little like the odd man out when you and your mother

38

gang up on me about JJ's Adderall issue and Emma's schooling."

"Neither of those issues has been decided," Laurie said.

"I beg to disagree, according to your mother," he said, "but listen, there is another issue here that you need to know about for multiple reasons. Are you prepared for a shock?"

There was a distinct pause that Jack allowed to continue and took a sip of his coffee as he waited. He felt it was important for her to have a moment to put aside her pique about his leaving that morning without a note, which Jack was willing to admit had been a bit adolescent.

"Is this a shock in relation to the OCME?" Laurie questioned finally. Her voice had changed, sounding more like the chief medical examiner.

"No, it is personal," he said. "I hate to be the messenger, but your dear friend Sue Passero is downstairs in the cooler needing to be autopsied."

"Good lord!" Laurie responded. "That's awful news. What on earth happened?"

"Apparently, she suffered a terminal event in her car while still in the MMH garage."

"Most likely a cardiac issue, with her history of diabetes," she suggested.

"I didn't know you knew, but that would be my guess, too. I didn't know she was diabetic until I read the MLI's report."

"Sue kept it a secret," Laurie said. "She didn't want to be treated any differently because of it, and she swore me to secrecy. I didn't know until we were in medical school."

"I suppose I understand. I'd probably do the same."

"Poor Abby, Nadia, and Jamal," Laurie said sympathetically. Nadia and Jamal were Sue's children, both of whom had followed Sue's lead into medicine and were currently residents, one in surgery and the other in internal medicine like his mother. "This is going to be a terrible shock for them, but more so for Abby as the stay-at-home dad. He'd put his career on hold so Sue could pursue hers."

"Well, maybe this can be an opportunity for him to go back to selling insurance, if he is inclined."

"I sincerely doubt it," she said. "Not after thirty years of being a househusband."

"Abby came in to make the ID," Jack said. "Surprisingly, he apparently made a stink about not wanting an autopsy done, and Jennifer Hernandez had to be involved to explain why it was necessary."

"Did Abby give a reason?"

"Yes, he said he was Muslim."

"That's surprising."

"That's what I said."

"He did grow up in Egypt, so he probably was raised Muslim, but I had no idea he was practicing. Sue never mentioned it, nor did he. How did Jennifer handle the issue? Did she have to come in to speak with him?"

"No, she spoke with him by phone while he was here making the ID. She managed to get things ironed out, but Abby wasn't a happy camper."

"Well, let's get the post done quickly," Laurie said. "Speed and a timely burial are really the issues for Muslims. But an autopsy needs to be done. And I'm sure Nadia and Jamal will want some answers even if Abby doesn't. You do the post as your first case and be quick about it."

"Why me?" Jack complained. A cardiac event with a type 1 diabetic wasn't going to suffice for what he had in mind to appease his anxieties. It was too forensically routine. Besides, he was reluctant to autopsy someone he knew socially. Such a circumstance had happened to him two years earlier, when Laurie had him autopsy one of the New York University pathology residents who had been rotating at the time through the OCME for a month of forensic training, and it had been a bit unsettling, which had surprised him. After all he'd been through personally, including feeling responsible for losing his first family in a plane crash, he thought he was immune to other peoples' problems.

"Do it because you are there, because I can count on you to be discreet, and because you are probably the fastest and the most thorough prosector on staff. If Abby is truly religiously concerned, the faster it is done the better."

"I was here early trying to find a challenging forensic case," he said. "Doing a routine post is not going to cut it, so to speak."

"Why on earth do you particularly need a forensically challenging case today?" she asked petulantly. She was now one hundred percent the harried CEO and not the marital partner.

"Why is the sky blue?" Jack questioned superciliously. "Don't ask me unless you are willing to drop the Adderall issue, at least be open to discuss school for Emma, and, perhaps most important, propose some sort of a timetable for your mother to move back to Park Avenue. On top of everything else, we really shouldn't tolerate her continued anti-vaccine stance and her refusal to get the Covid vaccine."

"Let's not bring up my mother while we're on the phone!" Laurie stated, in a tone that precluded further discussion. "Not now! Besides, it's only been three months since my father passed away. She's doing the best she can, and she has been invaluable for the progress Emma has made. I'm sure you recognize that. I'm heading out the door as we speak and will be there shortly. Get Sue's autopsy done, so I'll be able to speak to Abby, Nadia, and Jamal."

It took him a moment to recognize that she had disconnected as he had begun speaking to bring up Jennifer's point about his not being the correct gender to do Sue Passero's autopsy. When he realized he was talking into a dead phone, he pulled it away from his face and glanced at it to check if she had really hung up on him. Shaking his head in frustration, he was beginning to seriously rue his encouragement of Laurie to take on the job of chief medical examiner when it had been offered to her. At the time he had thought that she would change the chief's role to give the MEs more investigative freedom, but it seemed as if the role was changing her.

"I heard part of that," Jennifer said. "What was her take?"

"She wants me to do the post on Passero and get it done quickly. I tried to bring up the gender issue you mentioned, but she hung up on me. Do you mind if I do it?"

"Of course not," she said. "Laurie's the boss."

"Yeah, right," Jack added. He stood up. "But can you do me a favor? Can you try to find me a case to follow this one that might provide a bit of forensic challenge?"

"Funny you should ask," Jennifer said, holding up a folder in her hand. "This one might fit the bill. It's a supposed suicide with a contact gunshot wound in the left temple."

"That hardly sounds exciting," he said.

"True, but Janice Jaeger thinks otherwise."

Janice Jaeger was one of the more senior and hence experienced night-shift MLI investigators, someone whose work Jack particularly highly respected. On numerous cases that she had investigated, she had anticipated his need for additional information so that it was available before he even knew to request it. Over the years she'd developed a sixth sense for what information was ultimately required to button up a difficult case.

"That sounds intriguing," Jack said. He walked over to take the folder. "What was it that sparked Janice's interest? Do you know?"

"I'm not sure, but she underlined that it involves a thirty-three-year-old female who was found naked."

"Hmmm. Interesting! Was there a suicide note?"

"Apparently not."

"I'll take it," Jack said without even looking at the folder's contents.

"It's yours," Jennifer said. She picked up the next folder in front of her and slid out the contents.

He turned to Vinnie, who was hidden behind his beloved *New York Post*. After finishing with the coffee making, Vinnie had repaired to the second easy chair to commit to memory the day's sporting minutiae. "Let's go, big guy!" Jack said, trying to marshal his own enthusiasm. "We have to bang out this case in record time to satisfy the big boss."

As Jack retrieved his mug of coffee, he noticed Vinnie hadn't budged. As he'd done a hundred times over the years, he snatched away the mortuary tech's paper and quickly exited the room, which elicited a string of curse words from Vinnie as he leaped up and followed. It was a ritual that they had repeated over and over, week in and week out. Even on more normal days, Jack was an early bird, eager to start work, and he always had to build a fire under Vinnie. Part of the routine involved Vinnie bellyaching that they were the only ones in the pit for at least an hour until other, more civilized people arrived well after 8:30 A.M.

"Okay," Vinnie said as they waited for the rather slow back elevator to arrive. "Tell me, why did you jump on the suicide case? A contact temporal suicide wound sounds pretty routine to me."

"Simply because the woman was found naked," Jack said as he stepped into the car, holding the door open for Vinnie. "Women who kill themselves are never naked. The fact that this one was, means something is rotten in the state of Denmark, and we need to listen to the dead woman to find out what it is."

"No shit," Vinnie remarked, wrinkling his forehead in apparent disbelief. "Although I can't imagine the issue is going to come up very often in normal conversation, it is an interesting tidbit to know. I have to say: You can learn something every day in forensics. It never stops."

"That's exactly why I love being an ME," Jack said. "Back in my previous life as an ophthalmologist, before I saw the light, so to speak, every day was like every other day. In many ways, I didn't know what I was missing. It's also nice that you don't have to worry about screwing up because the patients are already dead."

Vinnie laughed uproariously despite having heard the joke more times than he could count. He was a great fan of dark humor.

Jack and Vinnie went into the locker room together and changed out of their street clothes, putting on scrubs, face masks, face shields, and other protective paraphernalia for working in the autopsy room. While Vinnie went into the pit to get everything ready for the case, including instruments and sample bottles and the like, Jack took a quick moment to scan Janice Jaeger's investigative report on the suicide case. There was no doubt it was going to be forensically interesting, hopefully just what the doctor ordered as far as he was concerned. The deceased was the wife of an NYPD officer, and the gun was the husband's service weapon, not an infrequent circumstance. The woman was found in bed, and it was the husband who called 911, supposedly after hearing the fatal shot.

While Vinnie was busy in the autopsy room, to speed things up Jack went into the walk-in cooler to get Sue's body. Although the other MEs insisted on a sharp separation of their duties and those of the mortuary techs, Jack was more egalitarian, especially early in the morning when he was eager to get underway. The big walk-in cooler was a relatively new addition to the morgue and had been installed in the same area where the old bank of body drawers had been. The body drawers were the ones seen in movies and TV shows from which bodies would be pulled out on rollers. Although such storage was visually interesting, as a whole they take up too much space and were ultimately inconvenient, especially in mass-casualty situations. Instead, a large cooler that could accommodate more than twice the number of bodies with easier access had been designed.

Conveniently, all the shrouded new arrivals from the previous night were already on individual gurneys near the entrance. He needed to locate the correct body, which he knew wasn't going to be difficult. All he had to do was raise the covering sheets enough to check out the respective faces. He certainly didn't have to check the ID tags on the corpses' toes. When he did find Sue on the fourth try, seeing her face gave Jack pause, more than he expected. Even in death, she was a physically impressive person.

For a moment Jack just stared at her. Her usually carefully coifed hair was plastered against her forehead and her face was paler than it had been in life. Her mouth was also distorted by an endotracheal tube and her red silk dress had been cut open to expose her chest where a few ECG connectors were still in place, all remnants of her having been through a major resuscitation attempt in the Emergency Department. "Sorry, my friend," he whispered, his breath visible in the chilled air. Seeing her there in the cooler reminded him how fragile life was.

After replacing the sheet, Jack maneuvered the gurney out of the cooler, across the hallway, and into the autopsy room, which had been upgraded to an extent since his arrival at the OCME but still held remnants of its outdated self. There was no doubt that the largest, oldest medical examiner institution in the United States was in dire need of a new autopsy suite.

Vinnie had made great strides in getting ready with his usual efficiency, and Jack's favorite autopsy table was ready with everything laid out. It was table number eight at the far end of the room, and Jack headed in its direction. He much preferred this table because its location far from the entrance meant he was less casually interrupted by fellow MEs coming in to do their cases. Jack wasn't asocial in any way. Far from it. It was just that he liked to maintain his concentration with the fewest interruptions as possible. As Laurie had suggested, he was the fastest prosector on staff.

After the gurney came alongside the table, Vinnie pulled off the sheet. He then helped Jack lift the body onto the table.

"Wow!" Vinnie said with a grunt. "She is one solid lady."

"She was quite an athlete in her day," Jack said. He walked over to the X-ray view box and glanced at Sue's film, which Vinnie had already put up.

"X-ray is all clear," Vinnie called out. Over the years he'd become expert at reading X-rays to the point of occasionally catching small details that Jack might miss.

Jack nodded, then returned to table eight. Vinnie had a camera ready, and Jack took a few initial photos, and while he was doing so, he noticed what looked like a small bloodstain on the dress near Sue's right hip. Pointing to it he asked, "Does this look like blood to you?"

"Could be," Vinnie agreed after bending over to take a closer look. "It wouldn't be surprising, either."

"Get me some scissors anyway," Jack said. He knew that body fluid stains, including blood, were certainly an occupational hazard for a doctor during a normal day in the clinic, but Sue was meticulous. Once he had a pair of dissecting scissors, he cut out a square of fabric containing the stain. He put it in a sample bottle that Vinnie held out. With that accomplished, they removed both the black Burberry winter coat whose arms had been cut open lengthwise during the resuscitation attempt, and then the red dress. Next to go were the underclothes. For thoroughness, all of it would be saved for a period of time as standard practice.

Once the body was completely naked, Jack and Vinnie together did a thorough external examination that included the entire body, talking as they did so to point out everything and anything abnormal. The only things of note were multiple injection sites on her abdomen and both thighs, some obviously older than others, as would be expected with an insulin-dependent diabetic. One on the right thigh appeared to be the most recent, with even a small amount of surrounding bruising. Jack took several close-up photos in his usual obsessive-compulsive, detail-oriented fashion. Later, when they removed the endotracheal tube after ascertaining it indeed was in the proper position in the trachea, Vinnie noted a laceration of the upper frenulum between the gum and the lip.

"It probably occurred during the intubation in the ED," Jack said. "But good pickup!"

While Vinnie held the upper lip away from the teeth, Jack took a photo of the defect. Then, after removing the intravenous catheters, they were ready to go.

"Let's not dillydally," Jack said as he reached out toward Vinnie while glancing up at the wall clock. The tray with the instruments and all the sample bottles was on Vinnie's side of the table. On Jack's side was the camera and a pad for notes and diagrams. Picking up the scalpel, Vinnie jokingly slapped it into Jack's hand the way he'd seen it done in movies during operations on live patients. They both laughed at the routine nature of what they were about to do, a procedure that normal people would find ghoulishly cringeworthy.

CHAPTER 4

Tuesday, December 7, 7:55 A.M

Now that the autopsy proper had started, Jack and Vinnie worked efficiently and silently. Since they could anticipate each other's moves and instinctively knew what had to be done, there was little need for conversation. With the scalpel in hand, Jack made the usual Y-shaped incision, starting at the points of both shoulders, connecting over the sternum, and then running all the way down to the pubis. It was done in two rapid, decisive strokes. When Jack was finished freeing up the margins, Vinnie exchanged the scalpel for the bone shears, so Jack could cut through the ribs to free up and remove the sternum. With the body open like a book, exposing most of the major organs, Jack proceeded to take the usual fluid samples from the aorta, the gallbladder, the urinary bladder, and the eyes with a variety of syringes that Vinnie

53

silently handed over.

"Okay," he said, more to himself than to Vinnie, when all the toxicology samples had been obtained and he was looking down at the heart nestled between the lungs. "Let's see what went wrong with the ticker."

With forceps and scissors, Jack opened the pericardium. So far everything appeared entirely normal, yet he wasn't surprised. Often fatal heart attacks, even massive ones, weren't grossly visible, nor were sudden ruptures of heart valves until the organ was opened. Back to using the scalpel, he freed up the heart by cutting through all the attached great vessels and lifted it out of the chest cavity. Gingerly he placed it on a tray Vinnie presented. Stepping down to the foot of the autopsy table while carrying the tray, Jack used a combination of large dissecting scissors and a long-bladed knife to open all the chambers.

"Looks pretty damn normal," Vinnie commented. He had joined Jack, watching intently.

"You got that right," Jack agreed. "The pathology is going to be in the coronary vessels." Meticulously he began tracing out the complicated arborization of the heart's arteries using more delicate dissecting tools. He worked quickly but painstakingly, looking for the telltale signs of atherosclerosis or plaque lining the interior of the vessels, a condition frequently suffered by diabetics, which could cause the vessel to occlude suddenly, thereby denying a segment of the heart its needed oxygen and nutrients. When it happened, it was called a heart attack.

"My word!" Jack said with surprise as he continued working. "I don't see any plaque whatsoever. The vessels look like those of a normal teenager." In the recesses of his forensically oriented mind, faint alarm bells began to sound. With no cardiac pathology, the idea that Sue's death was natural was being seriously called into question, thereby awakening the possibility of it being accidental or, worse still, homicidal.

"You said she was athletic," Vinnie said.

"True enough. She was also chief of internal medicine at an academic medical center. She knew how to take care of diabetes and her general health, and she practiced what she preached."

When Jack was finished with the dissection of the heart and Vinnie had bottled and labeled all the histology samples, Jack returned to his position on the right side of the patient. Moving on, he palpated the lungs before removing them. As he did so, he sensed they were a bit heavier than expected, which was confirmed when he weighed them. "Curious," he mumbled.

"How much?" Vinnie asked.

"Two-point-four pounds," Jack said.

Stepping back down to the foot of the autopsy table, Jack made use of the same tray he'd used to dissect the heart to make a series of slices into the lungs. "Mild pulmonary edema," he commented as he looked more closely.

"Does that surprise you?" Vinnie asked.

"Not really," Jack said. "It's mild and non-specific."

"Does it make you more suspicious this could be a drug-related death?"

"Not really," Jack said, but he wondered if Vinnie could be correct. Pulmonary edema of varying degrees was invariably present in the rash of drug overdose cases the OCME was being barraged with. Jack would have to wait in Sue Passero's case, as ultimately toxicology would supply the answers if her passing was drug-related. Jack was still surprised and even troubled by not finding any visible pathology with the heart, which he had hoped he could offer Laurie, knowing how disappointed she was going to be if there wasn't some specific explanation that she could provide for the family. Although there was a slight chance histology might come through showing significant microscopic pathology, Jack sincerely doubted it was going to happen, and even if it did, it would take days. Such a surprise had never happened to him, where he had not been able to anticipate what the microscope showed.

"Let's move on," Jack said, regaining his place at the table while taking another glance at the clock. The next organ system to be removed was the digestive system, and he began by opening the stomach, which was empty of food contents. As Jack was quickly palpating his way down the digestive system before removing it, he heard the door to the autopsy room bang open. Turning his head, he saw Laurie enter, pressing a face mask over her nose and mouth. In violation of her own rules of autopsy room apparel, she was dressed merely in a long lab coat over her colorful dress.

Laurie was hardly a fashionista or clotheshorse, but she had always made it a point to dress in a feminine style and made sure her voluminous, shoulder-length auburn hair was clean and pulled back out of the way. When she had just finished her forensic pathology training and started at the NYC OCME, women were a distinct minority in the field, and she felt obligated to proclaim her gender. Now that she was the first female chief medical examiner here, she felt a similar responsibility since she was paving the way for others.

As soon as he saw his wife enter, Jack pulled his hands out of Sue Passero's abdomen and folded them over his gowned torso. He watched her approach and could tell her eyes were glued to the disturbing sight of her long-term friend flayed open on the autopsy table. Out of respect, he stayed silent, waiting for her to speak. Vinnie did the same.

After a pregnant pause, Laurie audibly took a deep breath through the mask she had clasped to her face and lifted her eyes up to meet Jack's. "I thought I was prepared for this image, but I wasn't," she confessed. "Maybe I was secretly hoping there was some mistake of identification. Obviously there wasn't. What a loss for everyone who knew her."

"I agree," he said soothingly. "She was a doctor's doctor, the kind of doctor we all imagined before we went into medicine and learned that unfortunately not everyone in medicine joined the club for the right reasons. But, be that as it may, prepare yourself for a surprise. The heart is grossly entirely normal. More than normal. It's like the heart of a youthful athlete. Not an ounce of atheromata visible, and I went through most of the coronary system, practically down to the capillaries."

"None?" Laurie questioned. "Are you sure?"

"None," Jack echoed. He pointed toward the dissected heart still on the tray at the foot of the table with both lungs. "Take a peek."

"I believe you," she added quickly. She didn't want to have anything to do with the nitty-gritty of her friend's autopsy. "That is surprising, since her death certainly had to be a cardiac issue. I suppose we should keep in mind a channelopathy with a fatal arrhythmia."

"She had no cardiac history whatsoever," Jack said. "Kevin Strauss, who's thorough, as you know, was the MLI, and he obviously went through her entire computerized health record."

"Well, a channelopathy is still possible," Laurie said.

"A channelopathy is possible but certainly not likely with no cardiac history. We'll have the DNA lab look for the usual markers, but it's definitely a statistical long shot. We'll also send all the usual samples up to Toxicology to have an idea of her glucose level and the like. She did have pulmonary edema. Not a lot, but a little with the lungs coming in at two-point-four pounds."

"Sue always had her diabetes under control," Laurie said. "She was obsessive-compulsive about her sugar levels. Pulmonary edema? You are not considering a drug overdose, are you?"

"Not particularly, but we have to touch all the bases, so we are sending all the usual samples up to John in Toxicology to see what he comes up with. And there is also the slight chance of a massive stroke, but I doubt it."

"I doubt it, too, and Sue wasn't taking drugs," she said definitively. She took another sighing breath through her mask while hazarding a final glance at her friend's corpse. "I was so hoping to have something concrete to offer as an explanation to Abby and the kids when I make my call."

"Just like I'll be wishing I had something definitive for the damn death certificate, which I'll be responsible to fill out and sign. Without a clear-cut cause, I'm going to have trouble calling it a natural death."

"I'm confident you'll figure it out," Laurie said. She started to leave but then turned back. "Thanks for doing the case and doing

60

it quickly. I appreciate it. You are partially forgiven for leaving this morning without so much as a note. Don't do it again."

"Aye, aye, sir," Jack said while saluting with his gloved hand.

Laurie eyed him and paused as if she was about to say something else, but she didn't. Instead, without another word, she turned around and left. The swinging doors out into the hall squeaked as they closed behind her, and except for the water running along the autopsy table and making a sucking noise at the drain, a heavy silence reigned.

Vinnie eyed Jack, and Jack stared back at him. "I'm not sure the boss liked your salute," Vinnie said at length.

"You are probably right," Jack said with a shrug. "Sometimes, and maybe more often than not, I function by pure reflex without much thought for the consequences. On the spur of the moment, it seemed like the right thing to do in response to her order."

"She *is* the chief," Vinnie reminded him.

"She's the chief here, but not necessarily at 42 West 106th Street," Jack said. "At home, it's supposed to be a bicameral government. Unfortunately, she's starting to bring her work persona home and act as if she is in charge there, too."

"I suppose it is rather unique to be married to the chief," Vinnie said.

"Don't get me started," Jack said. "Instead, let's finish this case, so we can move on to one with a bit of forensic challenge."

CHAPTER 5

Following Laurie's visit into the autopsy room, Jack and Vinnie rapidly completed the autopsy on Sue Passero. As Jack had anticipated, there had been no stroke, since the brain was entirely normal, and he was again worrying about having to complete a death certificate with no obvious cause of death.

Just before they had opened the calvarium to examine the brain, a number of other mortuary techs showed up en masse and began to prepare the other tables for the morning cases. Marvin Fletcher, the mortuary tech whom Laurie favored when she did her weekly teaching case on Thursdays, was the only one who came over to Jack and Vinnie, questioning how they were almost finished with a case so early.

"It's my burden," Vinnie complained with a laugh. "Dr. Stapleton doesn't have a life."

"What's more fun than an early-morning autopsy?" Jack questioned in response. Although it was probably impossible to keep a lid on Sue Passero's identity from in-house chatter, Jack didn't want to be the direct source.

When the case was finished and after Jack had helped Vinnie move the corpse onto a gurney, he ducked into the locker room to grab a white lab coat to put over his scrubs while Vinnie prepared for the suicide case. Aware that Laurie was desperate for all the details about Sue as soon as possible so that she could provide some answers to the family, Jack wanted to get the samples up to Toxicology and Histology, the two departments that worked the closest with the needs of completing the autopsy. As he knew from experience, the fastest way to get something done was to do it himself.

Clutching all the sample bottles to his chest, Jack first walked into Maureen O'Conner's recently remodeled domain. As the Histology Department head, she now had a small private office, which was off the lab itself. From Jack's first days as an NYC ME, he had made a distinct effort to be-friend the red-faced Irishwoman with her broad smile and wonderful brogue. As was the situation with the current case, histology and toxicology often provided the critical information required to solve a difficult case, and the faster the microscopic slides were available, the sooner the case could be completed. All the other medical examiners were willing to wait patiently for their slides to be processed, but that had never been the circumstance with Jack, especially with time constraints. Luckily, befriending Maureen had been easy since she was a remarkably outgoing individual.

"Well, glory be!" Maureen said with her charming accent. "This is the earliest hour I have ever had the pleasure of a personal visit from the famous Dr. Stapleton. To what do we owe this distinct pleasure?"

"I can tell you, but with a condition," Jack said.

"And what might that be?"

"You have to keep it under your hat."

"My lips are sealed, and my curiosity is heightened. What's up?"

"The case involves a very close personal friend of the chief's," he said, lowering his voice. "And she is eager to have any and all information for the family ASAP."

"I'm sorry to hear that," Maureen said, becoming serious. "What is it that you need?"

"Nothing out of the ordinary, other than

sooner rather than later," Jack said. "The friend was a doctor who died yesterday evening sitting in her car in her hospital's garage. Because of the individual's lifelong history of diabetes, it was assumed she'd suffered a cardiac issue. But I just found the heart to be grossly normal, and the coronaries looked remarkably clean. So I need to look at the microscopic sections of the coronary arteries and arterioles to see if they can tell us anything." As he spoke, he separated out the histology sample bottles and arranged them in a line along the front of Maureen's desk.

"We'll get right on it," Maureen said without hesitation.

"When the slides are ready, give a shout, and I'll pop up here to get them," Jack said.

"I will call you myself," Maureen responded, as she leaned forward and began picking up the bottles. "I'll try for late today but most likely it won't be until tomorrow morning."

"I appreciate your help," Jack said.

Next he headed to the top floor, where John DeVries, chief of the Toxicology Department, had his new office. Toxicology used to be crammed into a tiny area of the fourth floor but had moved up to take over both the fifth and the sixth floors when most of the OCME team moved into the new high-rise quarters on 26th Street. Although the windows had not been upgraded and looked their more-than-a-half-century age, the rest of the laboratory looked sleek and modern and was certainly state of the art. John's office, which used to be the size of a broom closet and perhaps had once been one, was now spacious and even had windows and a view. Along with the lab's physical enhancements, John's personality had undergone a considerable improvement. Previously prickly if not downright surly, John was now decidedly amiable, and to Jack the transition had been nothing short of miraculous. Since toxicology was as critical as histology for complicated forensic cases, Jack had tried to push John as much as he had pushed Maureen on multiple occasions, but instead of being helpful as Maureen was and willing to speed things up on critical cases, John had become progressively passive-aggressive or even outright aggressive. On several occasions Jack and John had nearly come to blows.

"Good morning, Dr. Stapleton," John said cheerfully as Jack walked in through the open door to the man's office.

"It's *Jack* to you, Dr. DeVries," Jack responded with a smile. John had a PhD in both chemistry and toxicology.

"*Jack* it is. What can we do for you today?"

He went through a similar explanation with John as he had with Maureen.

"And what are the results you are possibly looking for?" John asked, becoming serious.

"Well, you know better than I," Jack said. "First we need to do a general drug screen. The only positive finding at autopsy was mild to possibly moderate pulmonary edema. The chances of it being any kind of drug overdose in my mind is zero, but I've been surprised in the past, and it should be ruled out."

"Of course," John responded. "That goes without saying. What else?"

"She was a type 1 diabetic, so we need to know as soon as possible and as much as possible about her level of glucose control, insulin levels, and whether any ketoacidosis or hyperglycemia was present when she had her terminal event."

"Certainly," John said agreeably. "You are giving us a vitreous sample?"

"Absolutely," Jack said. He pointed to the specific sample bottle.

"Good," John said. He quickly glanced through the other sample bottles, nodding as he did so. "What's this?" he asked, picking up one merely labeled INJECTION.

Jack bent over to take a look. "Ah, yes, thanks for pointing that one out. That's an en bloc sample of skin and subcutaneous tissue from her last insulin injection site on her thigh. I didn't know if it was something you ever look at in terms of assessing the amount of insulin."

"It's not usual in forensic cases. There are lots of studies on how various insulin preparations are absorbed in the subcutaneous space. Do you think it might have any particular significance in this case?"

"I can't imagine," Jack said. "But I'm finding this case troubling. I'm going to need a cause of death for the death certificate."

"I'll give it some thought," John said.

On his way back down to the autopsy room, Jack stopped in his office and left the rest of the sample bottles. They were going to go down to 421, as the OCME high-rise was called. He personally wanted to give them to the DNA laboratory or Forensic Biology Department head, Naomi Grossman, and explain exactly why he wanted to have the lab search for the cardiac channelopathy mutations. Like with Maureen and John, Jack thought it was important to have a personal interaction with the department head. Otherwise, test results got put off, sometimes for weeks.

With all that accomplished, he was about to descend back down to the basement level where the autopsy room was located to get cracking on the supposed suicide case, but as his hand hovered over the basement button in the elevator, he changed his mind. Instead, he pushed the button for the first floor. He decided to stop briefly in Laurie's office to see if she might be available for a quick chat. Vinnie's comment about her not appreciating his salute was probably correct, and he thought maybe it would be wise to apologize again for leaving at the crack of dawn. There was no doubt he should have at least left a note.

Cheryl Stanford, an aging African American woman who could have retired years earlier and who had been the secretary for the former chief, Harold Bingham, had been kept on as Laurie's secretary. Laurie had pleaded with her to do so, and she had graciously complied, significantly helping Laurie make the transition from medical examiner to chief. The process had not been easy for Laurie, as she had had no administrative training or experience and frankly had not been interested in being an administrator until the job was offered to her by the mayor. It wasn't until all the medical examiners, including Jack, had talked her into it that she had been willing to accept.

As he entered the administration area near the front entrance of the building, Cheryl looked up. It was obvious she was on the phone and in the middle of a conversation, but the moment she saw Jack, she gave him a thumbs-up, meaning Laurie was currently available. He knocked before opening the inner door.

The décor of her office was the antithesis of the previous chief's, as was her personality, considering he had been rheumy and grumpy. Although the physical space was identical, it was as if the room were on a different planet. Instead of being dark and forbidding, it was bright and cheerful. It even had colorful drapes and a couch upholstered in matching fabric. Instead of gilt-framed dark paintings of brooding, overweight men in dark suits, the walls were hung with lively Impressionist prints with narrow, blond wood frames.

"Well?" Laurie questioned. She was sitting behind the large, dark mahogany partners desk, which was the only remnant of the office's previous occupant. Its size emphasized her svelte figure. Spread out in front of her were architectural drawings. "Was there any suggestion of a cerebral hemorrhage?"

71

"Nothing," Jack said. "Except for the history of diabetes, she was the picture of health. I've rarely seen a cleaner autopsy."

"Good grief!" Laurie complained, running her free hand nervously through her hair. "That's distressing. What on earth am I going to tell Abby and the kids?"

"You'll have to tell them that the cause of death is pending, dependent on what's to be found on the histology sections and with the toxicology. At least the kids will understand."

"Unfortunately, Abby already called," she said. "I spoke to him briefly. Like last night, he was emphatic that he didn't want an autopsy done, so I had to explain once more that we are required by law to determine the cause of death, which dictates an autopsy. But I told him that the autopsy was already nearly done and that he would get a call to let him know what was found. Most important, I told him that Sue's body would be available later today to be picked up by a funeral service of his choosing."

"Was he receptive?"

"Not really. He's obviously and understandably beside himself. And then he surprised me by asking if the death certificate will be available when the body is released because he was going to need it ASAP."

"That's curious," Jack said.

"My thoughts, too," Laurie said. "So I asked him why he needed a death certificate ASAP."

"And what was his response?"

"He said that the life insurance company will not release the funds until they have it in hand."

For a few beats, they stared at each other. It was Jack who broke the silence. After clearing his throat, he questioned: "Could we be participating in a B movie here?"

Laurie nodded. "I have to confess the same thought went through my mind until I chided myself for even thinking such a thing. At the same time, I've known how strict a control Sue always maintained over her diabetes day in and day out. If anything, she was fanatical about it. Anyway, I mentioned to Abby that I didn't know that Sue had life insurance. I told him that she and I had talked about life insurance when Nadia and Jamal had decided to go to medical school, but that she had decided against it. His response was to say that they had changed their mind a little over a year ago, considering the debt that they had accepted for the kids' educations, which he said they had been in the process of paying off. He then reminded me that having been a stay-at-home dad and husband, he didn't have a lot of current career options."

"I don't know what to say. It does potentially put a different spin on the case."

She sighed. "Maybe, maybe not. One way or the other, it's clear Abby is going to be pressuring us for the death certificate sooner rather than later, and I'm going to feel obligated to produce it."

"That's going to be a problem. Unless something definitive comes out of Histology, Toxicology, or Forensic Biology, I have no idea what I could put on a death certificate. I've never been comfortable with *indeterminate.* I consider it kind of a forensic cop-out."

"The death certificate can always be amended when new information comes to light."

"That's not my style," Jack said.

"Don't let your imagination run wild," Laurie said, showing a bit of emerging exasperation. "Listen, Sue and I were close and confided in each other. As far as I know, she and Abby got along just fine."

"That may be, but peoples' private life can be far different than what other people suspect. Plus, people evolve and change.

Who knows the mindset of a stay-at-home dad after the kids have left the house, when a career has been abandoned, and aging begins to rear its ugly head."

"Jack, please!" Laurie snapped. "You are jumping to conclusions. Cool it! Besides, you specifically said on the phone that the reason you slunk out of the apartment this morning was to come in here and find yourself a challenging case. Well, here it is! And you have to handle it because I can't." She gestured to the architectural drawings. "We need a new morgue, and the city council has balked on the funding. It's become critical because the lease on this building from NYU Medical Center is running out, and we are going to be literally out in the cold with no autopsy suite. I've got a new mayor who is going to be inaugurated in a little more than a month, and I have to get him on board. What all this means is that you are going to have to carry the ball dealing with Abby by providing him with the death certificate he needs. Are we clear on this?"

He gritted his teeth, desperately trying to keep himself from provocatively saluting again. She was back to giving him orders, and although it was more appropriate in this instance, it still galled him. Yet instinctively he knew another salute would cause a scene, as he was aware of the pressure she was under. She'd been vainly struggling with the pressing need for a new morgue for more than a year, and with the city council dragging its feet, it truly was becoming critical.

"Well?" Laurie questioned impatiently when Jack demurred.

"I'll work on it," Jack said. "I'll make sure the Forensic Biology lab looks into the channelopathy issue, as unlikely as it is, and I've already dropped off the samples to Maureen and John, asking them to fire their respective afterburners."

"Thank you," Laurie said with a sigh of relief. She smoothed out the drawings in front of her, clearly preparing to get back to trying to lower the estimated cost of the building without compromising its mission.

"But I'm not promising anything with the death certificate if nothing positive turns up," Jack said as he headed for the door. "Without a discernable cause of death, I don't have to tell you of all people that the manner of death is moot, and if it ain't a natural death, like a heart attack, which we expected, that leaves only accidental, which isn't likely; suicidal, which is less likely with no note or obvious method; and homicide.

Obviously, the idea she died due to a therapeutic complication, the last manner of death, is a nonstarter, as she wasn't being treated for anything other than her diabetes."

"As I said, you wanted a challenge, so now you have it. Good luck, but get it done! To help you, I'll give Abby a call back shortly because I said I would. I'll tell him that the results of the autopsy are pending and that you will be giving him a call to convey them. I'll also mention that you will be the one to provide the death certificate and will arrange for the body to be released to the funeral home."

"Aye, aye!" he said, being careful to resist making a salute by keeping his hand tightly gripped on the doorknob. Then he left.

CHAPTER 6

Tuesday, December 7, 9:55 A.M.

"Are you convinced now?" Jack asked Vinnie as he held the narrow wooden dowel alongside the head of the woman lying supine on the autopsy table. Her name was Sharron Seton, and she was suspected of having killed herself the night before. The dowel was lined up with a stellate gunshot entrance wound in her left temple, indicating the muzzle of the gun had been held against the skin when it discharged, and Jack had found the location of the bullet in the right mandible beneath one of her lower cuspids. In Jack's experience and for most medical examiners, suicide with a handgun invariably entailed contact with the gun's barrel, either against the temple or in the mouth.

"I'm convinced even if he isn't," Lou Soldano said when Vinnie hesitated to respond. Lou was lieutenant commander detective, a rank called LCD by those in the know. He had arrived while Jack was talking with Laurie in her office. He'd come in because Sharron Seton was the wife of Detective Third Grade Paul Seton, who worked under Lou, and Lou had gotten a call with the terrible news that Paul's wife had killed herself. As the caring commander of a group of homicide detectives, Lou had wanted to get what information he could to help his young team member, but what he was learning was certainly not good news.

Lou Soldano was a distinctly masculine, quintessentially Southern Italian–appearing man who was getting a bit long in the tooth and past his pension age, meaning that by continuing to work, he was losing money over the long haul. But he didn't care. Being a police officer completely defined him. There was no way he could imagine retiring, and as a particularly dedicated detective, he was frequent visitor to the OCME. Early in his career he had learned the value of forensic pathology in solving homicide cases, probably more than anyone else in the entire NYPD. And as a hopeless workaholic who had trouble sleeping more than a few hours, Lou frequently went out into the field on night homicide calls, and when he did, he would often follow the body to the

79

morgue to observe the post. This appreciation of forensics led him to meet Laurie when she'd joined the OCME, and for a short time they had even seen each other socially. But it didn't work out, more to do with what they admitted was a cultural difference than anything else. When Jack arrived on the scene as a medical examiner, Lou had found him to be especially copacetic, particularly appreciating Jack's speed as well as his sarcastic humor. When Jack and Laurie became an item, Lou was a great advocate, and when they eventually married, he became one of their closest friends.

"Obviously the path of the bullet means the gun was angled from above the head and posterior to the midline," Lou said. "That doesn't compute."

"Exactly," Jack said. "Try to do it." Jack formed his left hand into a gun by extending his index finger and thumb while keeping the rest of his fingers balled into his palm. In this fashion he tried to position it in a way that could align with the path of the bullet. "It's impossible," he said. "There's no way this could have been a suicide. Zero!"

"I get it," Vinnie said. "I'm just dumbfounded people can be so damn stupid. I mean, you don't have to be a rocket scientist to stage a goddamn suicide, especially if you are a police detective."

"It's probably more indicative that there wasn't a lot of planning," Jack said. "Then again, we shouldn't jump to conclusions other than this wasn't a suicide. I suppose it could have possibly been an intruder. Any sign of a break-in?"

"No, none," Lou said with a shake of his head. "The only people in the apartment at the time of the shooting were Paul and Sharron. That's been established. Paul told me that he'd been sleeping in the guest room because he and Sharron had a bad argument and that he came running when he heard the gunshot. Obviously, that was not true from what you have demonstrated here. But to be honest, I'm not terribly surprised. When the boys from the precinct arrived on the initial nine-one-one call from Paul, Paul's father was already there, and he lives in New Jersey. That means Paul had called him long before placing the nine-one-one call, which in my book raises a red flag. I just didn't want to believe it."

"It raised a red flag for the MLI, Janice Jaeger, as well," Jack said. "She brought up the same facts in her report along with emphasizing the deceased was naked. All in all, it's a good demonstration why all suicides need to be medical examiner cases."

"Yeah, well, it's goddamn depressing," Lou said. "Paul Seton is a promising detective. Two lives ruined in an instant of insanity! What a tragedy!" Lou let out a long sigh behind his mask and face shield.

"Misery loves company," Jack said with an equivalent sigh. "Obviously this case is going to end up being a major murder trial, which is going to involve me, and I hate court cases." All medical examiners invariably worked closely with the District Attorney's Office and were frequent participants in trials, which is why the OCME was so careful about chain-of-custody issues. Most medical examiners appreciated the legal role they were required to play, and some of them enjoyed the participation. Jack wasn't one of them. Going to court and sitting for hours on end while lawyers bickered and tried to bully him wasn't his idea of time well spent. It also kept him out of the autopsy room. In the end, he'd come to resent the court experience.

"But being dragged into court isn't the worst of it," Jack continued. "I was counting on this case to be a forensic challenge and keep me occupied for a couple of days, which it would have been if the husband had an ounce of criminal caginess. Instead, it's turned out straightforward and simple. That's not what I wanted. I'm in desperate need of a diversion from my own rather tumultuous home scene."

"Uh-oh," Lou said with concern. "What's up at home?"

"Don't get me started," Jack said. "At least not until this case gets done, and we're away from prying ears."

"Ha ha!" Vinnie voiced derisively. "As if I'd give a flying crap."

Lou was a good enough and close enough friend that Jack had confided in him on numerous occasions to get his opinion about issues involving Laurie, as he had insights about her that Jack had learned to respect. There had even been a time years ago that the two had conspired to try to prevent her from marrying a man they were convinced was a two-faced, unprincipled, shady arms dealer who would have made Laurie's life a misery.

"You bum," Lou mockingly complained. "Now I have to stick around longer than I'd planned."

After the retrieval of the slug from the mandible, which was handled with great care for ballistics purposes, the rest of the case went rapidly, as it involved an entirely healthy thirty-three-year-old woman. There was little conversation until Jack slit open the uterus, at which point there was a silent pause.

"Is that what I think it is?" Lou questioned finally. He bent down to look a little closer.

"Afraid so," Vinnie said.

Jack picked up a metal ruler to measure. "Almost two and a half centimeters. That, my friends, is about a ten-week-old fetus."

"Good grief," Lou commented. "That compounds the tragedy. I wonder if they knew. Paul never let on his wife was pregnant."

"He might not have known, but she undoubtedly did," Jack said. "One way or the other, it's certainly not going to help his case."

"Nor should it," Lou said with a shake of his head.

For the rest of the autopsy, there was little talk. The discovery of the fetus was unsettling. By the time they were finished, the autopsy room was in full swing with all the tables occupied. A low-level din of multiple conversations prevailed, punctuated intermittently by the sound of power tools, particularly the vibrating saws used to open the craniums.

"If you and Lou want to talk, I'll finish up here," Vinnie said as soon as Sharron Seton was sewn up and thereby returned to a semblance of normalcy, at least outwardly. The internal organs had been returned to the body cavity inside a large plastic bag, except for the brain, which was in a jar filled with formalin.

"You're being uncharacteristically gracious," Jack teased. Normally Jack made it a point to help with the post-autopsy chores, as did most of the medical examiners, as it speeded up the schedule considerably. When things went smoothly, the day's cases were usually done around noon.

"I'm assuming we're done for the day," Vinnie added.

"That would be my guess," Jack said, as he waved to Lou to follow. On the way out of the room, Jack stopped briefly at Jennifer's table and reintroduced Lou. They had met previously, but Jack was intent on keeping Lou feeling welcome.

"Any more cases for me today?" Jack asked her.

"You are all done. Sorry that your supposed suicide case wasn't as challenging as you had hoped. Word has it that it was rather cut and dried."

"It's not your fault," Jack assured her. He wasn't surprised she already knew. It was just another indication among many that the grapevine at the OCME was alive and well. As a rule, there were few secrets. "Maybe I'll be more lucky tomorrow."

"I'll try my best," Jennifer kidded, and Jack responded with a thumbs-up.

Jack also stopped at the table of his old office mate, Dr. Chet McGovern, so Chet could say hello to Lou as well. Back when Jack and Chet shared an office, Chet had met Lou on innumerable occasions when Jack and Lou had collaborated on various cases. Chet responded by introducing both Jack and Lou to Margaret Townsend, one of the two new senior NYU pathology residents who were rotating through the OCME to get a hands-on taste of forensic pathology. They had arrived at the beginning of the month and would stay on until the new year.

Jack and Lou then pushed through the swinging doors leading out into the main hallway. After appropriately disposing of their personal protective gear, they ended up sitting at either end of the bench that ran between the lockers in the changing room. Both were still dressed in scrubs.

"Okay, you've kept me in suspense long enough," Lou said. "Out with it! What's got you bummed out on the home front?"

"Before I get into that," Jack said, "do you

remember Dr. Sue Passero? She and her husband were at that Halloween costume party Laurie and I had three years ago. I remember introducing you two."

"Of course I remember her," Lou said. "She came to the party as the Giants running back and looked the part. Now that you have reminded me, I think the Giants could have used her this year. Kidding aside, what's with her?"

"She did appear very athletic, and I happen to know that she worked out regularly and was a vegetarian. Yet despite all that, she suffered a terminal event last night in her car in the MMH parking garage. She was autopsied this morning, and at Laurie's specific request, I did it."

Lou shook his head in dismay. "That couldn't have been pleasant."

"It wasn't."

"Good God!" Lou moaned. "Having someone that's fit suddenly kick the bucket is a shock and a reminder we are all living on borrowed time. I do remember her looking as healthy as a goddamn horse. Or is it healthy as an ox?"

"Either one works," Jack said, waving off the distinction. "And you are right, the autopsy proved it. Even though she did have diabetes, which often affects the heart, I found no pathology, nothing. Of course, there's the outside chance microscopic sections might offer some explanation, but I sincerely doubt it, as carefully as I went over the heart. To be honest, I've never had a case quite like this, and it's bothering me big-time, especially because of Laurie's connection with the woman and her family."

"I'm sorry to hear all this," Lou said. "But why are you telling me? Are you suspecting foul play here or something in that vein?"

"Laurie spoke to the husband by phone this morning who, I might add, was suddenly against an autopsy, supposedly because he was Muslim, which was completely new information to us even though his wife and Laurie were good friends. We even had socialized all together maybe a dozen times, and his being Muslim never came up once. And on top of that, he told Laurie that he wants to get the death certificate ASAP for a life insurance claim."

"Okay," Lou said, rolling his eyes before looking back at Jack. "Suddenly I see how those wheels are turning in that overly inventive brain of yours. So, you are suspecting foul play here on the husband's part. Am I right, or am I completely off base?"

"Well . . ." Jack fumbled for words because now that he was giving vent to his thoughts, he realized how much he was jumping to conclusions on very little evidence. Lou had mocked him in the past when he tried to play detective — and warned him on multiple occasions not to do so. Here was yet another instance.

"You've been watching too many run-of-the-mill TV dramas! If you want to know what I think, here it is. Whatever is bothering you at home is making you look for a diversion and playing detective has been your method in the past. I mean, listen to yourself! You're telling me a woman with diabetes died in her car with no signs of trauma and you are suspecting the husband. Please! I mean, what could be involved here? Some kind of mysterious poison or possibly carbon monoxide somehow? Well, correct me if I'm wrong, but your Toxicology Department will be looking into all that stuff. Am I right?"

"You are right," Jack said, feeling embarrassed. What Lou was saying was all true.

"And if the husband was guilty, would he offer the life insurance information right off the bat? I don't think so."

"Okay, you are right. I'm sorry I brought it up."

"Don't be," Lou said. "There's a lesson to be learned here. As I have reminded you time and time again, playing detective is dangerous and not for amateurs, and you are exactly that: a goddamn amateur when it comes to homicide investigation. Hell, just looking at you is a reminder of the danger. That chipped front tooth and that hairline scar, if I remember correctly, came from your playing detective a number of years ago. Am I right?"

"Okay, okay!" Jack repeated, holding up his hands as if to ward off Lou's derision. Lou was entirely correct. The scar and the chipped tooth had come from Jack investigating a conspiracy pitting one major managed care company against another by starting outbreaks of infectious disease in the other's primary hospital. "I get the message."

"Fine and dandy," Lou said. "You're a forensic pathologist and a damn good one. Leave it at that. If and when you have any suspicions about criminal and particularly homicidal malfeasance, you call me. Understood?"

"Understood," Jack said.

"All right, let's hear about what's really bothering you. Let me guess. It's either your mother-in-law and her anti-vax stance, Emma's autism, or JJ's possible ADHD. Which is it?"

"All three," Jack said. He then explained the latest developments, and Lou dutifully listened, nodding in support whenever appropriate.

CHAPTER 7

Tuesday, December 7, 10:57 A.M.

Hefting his bike up onto his shoulder, Jack climbed the short flight of stairs next to the unloading bay at the OCME high-rise building on 26th Street just four blocks south of the outdated old building. Before ducking inside, he paused for a moment to look out over the expansive parking area where Laurie was hoping to build the new morgue building. Currently it was where many of the refrigerated trucks were parked that had been dispersed to the city's hospitals during the Covid pandemic to store the rapid increase in citywide deaths. Like everyone at the OCME, Jack was eager for the new morgue to be built. It was going to make it easier for everyone. Traveling back and forth was a major inconvenience, as Jack was currently demonstrating, although using the bike at least made it quick. What he was eager to do was get Sue Passero's tissue samples to the Forensic Biology lab to analyze the DNA for any cardiac channelopathy mutations. He could have had a junior staffer take them over, but for hopes of speeding up the process he knew it was best to deliver the samples personally, like he'd done with Maureen in Histology and John in Toxicology. The adage *the squeaky wheel gets the grease* was alive and well at the OCME, as Jack had proved to himself time and time again.

Samples for DNA analysis were received on the fifth floor, and to get there he used one of the many elevators. As he rocketed skyward, he couldn't help but compare the experience with the ancient equipment at the 520 building, particularly the painfully slow back elevator. In seconds, he was where he needed to be. The fifth floor was also home to the MLI Department, as well as the neighboring Communication Department, both of which operated on a 24/7/ 365 basis. With floor-to-ceiling interior glass dividers, Jack glanced into both areas as he passed down the hallway, heading east.

Because the chain-of-custody concerns were particularly important for DNA work, there was a complicated procedure for all samples to be signed in, and Jack followed the rules to the letter. He knew that on the fifth floor, the DNA would be extracted from the samples. When that was completed, the samples would go up to the sixth floor for amplification. Following that, the samples would be moved to the seventh floor for post-amplification and sequencing. He couldn't help but feel proud that the NYC Department of Forensic Biology was the largest public DNA crime laboratory in the world, occupying three floors.

After Sue Passero's samples were on their way, Jack took the time to go into the office of the Forensic Biology Lab's department head, Naomi Grossman. As busy as she was, he had to first deal with her secretary, Melanie Stack. Since the secretary was particularly outgoing and friendly, it was hardly a burden. Besides, she knew Jack from some of his previous visits when he'd been championing other cases he'd deemed emergencies.

"She's available," Melanie said cheerfully, gesturing toward the open door into the inner office.

Naomi Grossman, whose defining physical characteristic was a nimbus of remarkably curly hair surrounding a wide oval face, wasn't quite as outgoing as her secretary but was similarly friendly. "Okay, Dr. Stapleton," she said with an equally broad smile.

"What is it you need ASAP on this occasion?"

"Am I that pushy?" he questioned in a self-mocking fashion.

"Infamously so," Naomi answered.

"Well, now that you mention it, there is something."

Jack explained what he needed and why. Naomi listened and then said, "It's interesting that your request involves channelopathies, because there has been increased interest in them of late in the literature, genetically speaking. Why is there an issue of speed for the results? Something I should know?"

"The individual is a very close friend of the chief's," Jack explained. "Laurie has already been in touch with the husband and their two children, who happen to be doctors in training. She's very eager to have an explanation for the woman's death besides her history of diabetes. I did the autopsy, but it was clean, although I have yet to look at the microscopic."

"The heart was grossly normal?"

"Completely."

"Any history of cardiac arrhythmias with the patient?"

"None."

"How about with the family?" Naomi

asked, furrowing her brow.

"Not that we know of."

"I guess you know that the chances of finding a channelopathy under those conditions are extremely unlikely. Most are autosomal dominant, and even if they exhibit variable penetrance, there is usually a positive history."

"I know," he said. "It's grasping at straws, but I'm going to need something for the death certificate."

"Okay, fine," Naomi said. "Are the samples already here?"

"I just signed them in two minutes ago."

"I'll see that it gets done," Naomi said.

"Great," Jack said. "Laurie will be appreciative."

Even though it was only four blocks back to the 520 building, Jack enjoyed the ride. A relatively new bike lane on First Avenue made it easy to avoid wayward taxis and rideshare cars, whose drivers often behaved as if they despised bicyclists. To get the most out of the moment, he put some muscle in the effort like he'd done that morning when he challenged the expensively outfitted riders. Keeping up with the traffic, he completed the journey in seconds. It helped that he hit all four green lights.

After storing his bike and helmet, he used the back elevator to get up to the third floor. Once in his office, he pulled off his corduroy jacket, hung it over the back of his desk chair, and sat down, fully intending to get some serious paperwork done. As usual, the main part of his desk with his computer terminal was stacked high with autopsy folders waiting to be completed and death certificates to be signed. On the L portion of the desk, where his microscope stood, there were equivalent piles of microscope slide trays whose contents were waiting to be studied. As the medical examiner who did the most autopsies, he was always behind, which was a standing joke since he was always badgering colleagues like Maureen and John to work faster.

With every intention of getting to work, Jack positioned the top slide tray next to his microscope and turned on the objective light. He had even slipped the contents of the associated autopsy folder onto the desk when his mind took a U-turn that left him staring ahead with unseeing eyes. What had hijacked his attention was the irony of how the morning's two cases turned out to be the opposite of what he had expected. Thinking that the only clue to questioning whether the suicide case was truly a suicide might be the MLI's noting the deceased's nakedness, he was prepared to use every trick in the forensic book to try to discover the truth, whatever it might be. Instead, the case turned out to be a slam-dunk as a homicide thanks to the startling ineptitude of the husband. As a detective, even a green detective, he should have known better than to shoot his wife in the left temple since he had to know she was right-handed, which Janice Jaeger had determined during her investigation. And he should have made sure the gun was held at a right angle to the long axis of the body and not aimed anteriorly.

Equally surprising was Sue Passero's case, but in the opposite direction. He'd been even more certain it was destined to be boringly routine from a forensic point of view, yet it was turning out to be nothing of the kind.

Jack ran a couple of nervous hands through his hair and ended up supporting his bowed head with his elbows on the desk. He could hear Lou's mocking comments accusing him of watching too many TV crime dramas and knew he was right in that he was jumping to conclusions by even entertaining a manner of death other than natural. At the same time, he had to recognize that the chances of a channelopathy mutation was very unlikely, as Naomi Grossman had reminded him. On top of that he was acutely aware that Laurie was going to be pressing him for a death certificate.

Suddenly he stood up quickly enough that his desk chair skidded across the room on its casters to thump against his bookcase. "Okay," he said with determination as he switched off the lamp on his microscope. "I was looking for a challenge, and, as Laurie said, I've found it. Or, more accurately, it found me!"

With an infusion of energy and direction, Jack leafed through the contents of Sue Passero's autopsy folder, pulling out Kevin Strauss's investigative report. After pocketing it, he grabbed his jacket and left his office. He had made a snap decision. Although it was strict NYC OCME policy that the medical examiners were not to go out in the field for scene investigation, since that was the role the MLIs were trained to do, Jack was going to do it anyway. He understood that if he had questions or needed other specific case-related information, he was supposed to call the involved MLI and have them do it, but the problem was that he was caught in the Socratic conundrum of not knowing what he didn't know, so it was impossible to ask Kevin Strauss for help. From Jack's perspective, it was a simple decision, and it didn't particularly bother him that he was disobeying the rules the OCME chief, his wife, was committed to enforcing.

As he rode down to the basement, using the slow back elevator because it reduced the chance of running into anyone who might question where he was headed, he seriously considered the rather unique situation in which he found himself. Never had he been involved in a case where he was as acquainted with the deceased as he was with Sue Passero, particularly knowing her as a happy, engaged, proud mother and wife as well as an accomplished, well-trained, and knowledgeable internist. Given that such an individual had to be inordinately capable of handling her type 1 diabetes, the idea that her passing could have been accidental, meaning giving herself the wrong dose of insulin or something along those lines, was a nonstarter. Same situation existed for suicide with no history of depression, no note, and no obvious method. What that left was homicide, which seemed equally unlikely because there was no apparent method of murder and there had been no robbery involved. Kevin Strauss had noted in his report that her personal belongings, including a certain amount of cash, were found untouched in her BMW.

He found himself guiltily smiling as he got out on the basement level. He had no idea if a site visit was going to help but was determined to do it. What he did know was that if Laurie found out about it, she'd be fit to be tied. On numerous occasions during Thursday afternoon department-wide staff conferences, she reminded the entire medical examiner team that off-site investigating by the MEs was verboten even though when she was an ME and not the chief, she had chafed under the rule and had violated it almost as often as Jack. Her rationale for her current stance was that the MEs had more than enough work to keep them in-house; most of them — including Jack — were behind on signing out their cases; and, more important, the MLIs were far better at scene investigation since that was what they were trained to do. The MLIs also got along better with the police because they saw each other more as workaday equals. And in contrast to Jack they tended not to ruffle feathers of various influential people like hospital presidents, CEOs, or police brass, which Laurie was well aware that he had a particular proclivity to do since, as she explained it, he didn't suffer fools.

Another reason for her strong feelings was the need to keep the medical legal investigators happy, which wasn't easy, as they were overworked, prideful about the role they played, and resentful about having their autonomy and expertise challenged. When Laurie became chief, she'd had a rude awakening about the difficulty of keeping the number of MLIs needed to handle some forty thousand deaths a year on staff. To qualify for forensic training, an MLI had to become a physician assistant first, which required a lot of training and investment. Since PAs often could get jobs that paid more than what the NYC civil service had to offer, recruiting and retaining them was no easy task, especially since dealing exclusively with death didn't appeal to everyone.

As Jack unlocked his bike, he promised himself that he'd make his site visit as short as possible and also that he'd make an effort to be as diplomatic as he was capable. He wanted to keep his activity a secret, and unless Laurie specifically asked, he wasn't going to volunteer. It seemed opportune that it was nearly lunchtime, so his absence wasn't likely to be noticed. His plan was to be quick about his inquiries, and as soon as he had some sense about what he needed to know, he'd beat it back to the OCME. He would then ask Kevin Strauss or even Bart Arnold, the MLI department head, to follow up and get what was needed.

CHAPTER 8

Tuesday, December 7, 12:02 P.M.

At the corner of First Avenue and 30th Street, Jack waited for the light to turn green. When it did, he crossed the avenue to gain access to the First Avenue bike path on the left side of the road. Because it was lunchtime there were more bikes than earlier, but because it was December, there weren't that many bikes despite the hour, and for safety reasons, he stuck to the bike lanes. He knew Laurie was against his bike riding for reasons of safety, but he persisted. For him cycling was part of his identity, representing a kind of freedom that characterized his new life. Instead of giving it up, he made concessions, like using the bike lanes. Although he knew that if he went out into the street, he'd be able to go faster, he wasn't that concerned about the time. He guesstimated the journey would take about twenty minutes and only five minutes less if he were to ride out in the road with the motorized traffic.

Using the bike lane had its own hazards and required considerable attention. First of all, it wasn't the same all the way to 78th Street, where he planned to turn west to Park Avenue, where the front entrance to the Manhattan Memorial Hospital was located. For the first fifteen or so blocks, there was an isolated bike lane separated from the vehicular traffic, but at 46th Street it changed to be merely a painted lane along the side of the road. Adding to the problem in Midtown, there were more of the electric bike delivery people who flaunted every rule, even to the point of going in the wrong direction. At various times as he headed north, Jack was forced to venture out into the road, keeping up with the cars, taxis, trucks, and buses before returning to the bike path.

When he turned left at 78th Street, the traffic diminished significantly. But here the connected bike path was a mere painted strip running along the street side of parked cars, providing the added danger of someone opening their car door without looking. Even more nerve-wracking were the many taxis and rideshare vehicles, which completely ignored the painted right-of-way by blocking it when picking up or discharging passengers.

Despite the potential hurdles and hazards, including Park Avenue having no bike lane, Jack arrived safely at the front entrance to the Manhattan Memorial Hospital in slightly less than the twenty minutes he'd anticipated. Pulling over to the curb, he dismounted and gazed up at the multistory structure. The entire medical center was an enormous complex of buildings occupying several square blocks of the Upper East Side of Manhattan, stretching all the way from Park Avenue west to Central Park. It served as the flagship hospital of AmeriCare, a large healthcare corporation that owned multiple hospitals and rapid-care clinics around the country.

Jack had an unpleasant history of association with the company, as it had bought the hospital where he'd had his original practice of ophthalmology, precipitating his decision to change from clinical medicine to forensic pathology to avoid the reality of American medicine being taken over by business interests and the profit motive. It was during his training in Chicago for his second medical career as a medical examiner that his entire family, including his wife and two young daughters, had died in a small plane crash after visiting him. Although he had eventually recovered enough to start a second family, he'd never forgiven Ameri-Care.

Using his cable bike lock, Jack secured his bike and helmet to a NO PARKING sign near the hospital's front entrance. When he was done, he again gazed up at the building. He had even had negative dealings with Ameri-Care and the MMH as a medical examiner back before the hospital had changed its name from Manhattan General Hospital to Manhattan Memorial Hospital when it had bought and merged with another smaller NYC hospital. About ten years earlier, on another site visit, he had exposed a hospital employee who was purposely infecting inpatients with serious diseases and causing multiple diagnostically confusing deaths. That experience of playing detective had resulted in the chipped front tooth and hairline scar of his that Lou had made reference to when they'd had their tête-à-tête in the locker room.

Jack had to laugh at the irony that instead of being hailed as a hero at the time for saving lives, which he most surely had, he'd been reprimanded by the then–OCME chief, Dr. Harold Bingham, for going out into the field; branded a persona non grata by the then–MGH president Charles Kelley; and garnered the lasting enmity of the hospital's Microbiology Department head, Dr. Martin Cheveau.

"Such is life," Jack murmured as he got out Kevin Strauss's MLI report and read it over quickly to decide exactly where to start. His first thought was to go directly to administration to put everything on the up-and-up and open doors since the hospital had a new president named Marsha Schechter, hired after the murder of Charles Kelley. But he hesitated, concerned about what kind of person this new president would be. The AmeriCare board had hired Kelley, who Jack had thought was the opposite of what a hospital chief executive should have been, as Kelley had been totally consumed by the business side to the detriment of the patient-care side. In Jack's mind, there was little hope the new president would be any different and instead of being helpful might very well end up complaining to Laurie about Jack's presence. After all, the death of a staff member in the hospital's parking garage was bad publicity and the faster the whole affair was forgotten, the better.

Instead of going to administration and announcing himself, he decided to visit security directly. He wanted to find out what he could about the exact site and circumstance of Sue's death above and beyond what Kevin had put in his investigative report. After that he would go to the Emergency Department and find out what he could about the resuscitation attempt.

Repositioning the required Covid-19 mask he'd taken from a dispenser just inside the front door, he used the stairs rather than the elevator to head up to the Security Department's office on the second floor. As he climbed, he hoped he wouldn't run into Martin Cheveau, since all the hospital's laboratories, including the microbiology lab, were also on the second floor. The man was unhinged enough to possibly cause a scene, which might up the chance Laurie would be notified he was defying orders.

The security office wasn't as physically impressive as the other parts of the renovated hospital. Instead, it was a large single room with six institutional metal desks. The two things that made the space unique were large floor-to-ceiling interior windows that looked out onto the marbled two-story hospital lobby and an entire wall of flat-screen monitors alternately displaying various locations inside and outside the hospital. Most of the people in the room were watching the monitors, although a few were busy typing behind computer screens. All were dressed in nondescript dark suits with ties. No one was wearing a pandemic mask.

Approaching the nearest desk, Jack asked for the Security Department's head and was directed to Mr. David Andrews, whose desk was the farthest away from the entry door. Deciding on the spot to be forthright and businesslike, Jack got out his medical examiner badge and flashed it as he introduced himself. He rarely used his badge but had always been impressed with its effect on most people, since it looked very official and rather like a policeman's badge. David Andrews wasn't all that impressed, even though he asked to look at it more closely. From a framed selfie photo of the man in blue uniform on his desk, Jack got the sense that David Andrews had been a high-ranking policeman before being hired as head of security for the hospital.

"What can I do for you, Doc?" he asked nonchalantly.

"I needed to do some follow-up on the death of Dr. Susan Passero," Jack said. "First I'd like to express my condolences, as I know she was a well-liked and well-respected member of the MMH community."

"She was, indeed," David said.

"Have there been security problems in the hospital's garage?"

"A mild amount. We had two relatively recent muggings, one about two months ago and another five months ago, both occurring during shift changes and both on the first floor. We've beefed up the security presence at the appropriate times and believe it has solved the problem. Why do you ask? I was told Dr. Passero died of a heart attack."

"Her death is under review. I'm just doing some routine follow-up on the investigation by the medical legal investigator." Jack cringed knowing he was offering a little white lie.

"I have to say, the investigator seemed knowledgeable and professional."

"Our MLIs are the best in the business," Jack said. "My being here in no way faults the work he did. Tell me, were you here when this unfortunate event occurred?"

"I was called when the situation was in progress, and I came in immediately. I had left for the day."

"My understanding from the MLI's report is that Dr. Passero was discovered by a nurse named Ronald Cavanaugh, who happened to see the doctor slumped over her steering wheel."

"That's what we were told," David said.

"Ronald Cavanaugh is one of our nursing supervisors. He and another nurse named Barbara Collins were coming on shift and started CPR and alerted the ED. As quickly as possible, the doctor was transported to the ED for a full resuscitation attempt."

"Did you or any of your security people look at the car?"

"Of course. I did myself and gathered Dr. Passero's personal belongings."

"Was there anything amiss with the car?"

"*Amiss.* What the hell kind of word is that?"

"Sorry!" With some difficulty Jack held himself in check. "What I meant to ask is if you noticed anything at all unusual about the vehicle. Anything at all? Was it messy inside? Anything unexpected in it? Did it smell strange?"

"No, not at all. Nothing. It seemed entirely like a normal BMW owned by someone who appreciated it. As far as odor is concerned, it smelled like leather."

"Where is the car now?"

"It's still in the same spot where it was," David said. "At least as far as I know." Then he made Jack jump when he suddenly and without warning yelled out to one of his colleagues, asking if Dr. Passero's car was still in the garage. "There you go," he said to Jack after getting confirmation the vehicle had yet to be moved.

Mildly surprised by this turn of events, Jack asked if he could view it.

"I don't see why not," David said. "But what on earth for?"

"Forensic science encourages the examination of a death scene," Jack said. He was surprised that the question came from a former police officer and again had to hold himself in check from making a reflex sarcastic comment.

"Even when it involves a heart attack?" David questioned.

"Yes," Jack said. "Even then."

"Suit yourself," David said. "Come on! I'll take you."

Before they left the security office, David stopped by the desk of the individual who had yelled out that Sue's car was still in the garage to get the keys.

David grabbed a mask from a dispenser and hooked it over both ears. "We have a valet parking service for our doctors in the morning to expedite their arrival," David explained as he gestured the proper direction out in the hallway. "I made sure we had both the valet set and the doctor's set for whomever was coming to pick up the vehicle."

The route to the garage was rather complicated, as it required passing between and
through several separate buildings but
without having to change floors. Finally,
they reached a pedestrian bridge over
Madison Avenue to get to the high-rise
garage. As they crossed, Jack couldn't help
but reminisce about another extraordinarily
unpleasant experience he'd had at the
MMH more than ten years earlier. He'd
chased a nurse who'd nearly managed to
kill Laurie across the same bridge. Jack
hadn't counted on the nurse being armed,
resulting in a horrendous shootout in the
woman's car. If Lou Soldano had not
showed up in the nick of time, Jack knew he
wouldn't be alive. The episode was yet
another cogent reminder that Lou was
entirely correct that playing detective was a
dangerous pastime for amateurs.

Jack shuddered at the memory and forced
himself to concentrate on the present. Sue's
black BMW was in the doctors' reserved
parking area on the second floor of the
garage, not too far away from the entrance
to the pedestrian bridge and close to where
the unnerving shootout had been.

As they came alongside the car, David
handed Jack the key fob, which he used to
unlock the vehicle. After opening the

driver's-side door, he leaned inside. As David had said, there was a definite smell of leather, suggesting the car was rather new. He tried to visualize Sue slumped over the steering wheel as she had been described. In the center console was an empty paper coffee cup and a mobile phone holder on a flexible rod. Sue's hospital ID hung on a lanyard from the rearview mirror. A recent copy of the *New England Journal of Medicine* with its iconic cover design was on the passenger seat. Jack could imagine Sue leafing through it while stopped at red lights. He knew Sue was one of those individuals who felt obligated to use every minute productively.

"Any startling conclusions?" David asked in a mocking tone.

Once again holding himself in check, he chose not to respond but rather backed out of the front seat and opened the car's rear door. On the back seat was a box of N95 masks, a roll of paper towels, a box of facial tissues, a snow removal brush, and a collapsed umbrella. Noticing that everything was pushed over onto the right side, Jack assumed it was so Sue could reach them from sitting in the driver's seat.

"Okay, thank you," Jack said while handing back the key fob. "Now, if you can point me in the right direction, I'd like to head to the Emergency Department and try to chat with someone who participated in the resuscitation attempt. I'm assuming the two nurses who discovered the doctor aren't currently available."

"That's correct. They both work the night shift, so on the days they are on duty, they come in sometime between six and seven P.M. I don't know if they are scheduled to work tonight."

"Understandable," Jack said.

"Come on. I'll take you to the ED. It's not easy unless you go outside and come in through the emergency entrance."

CHAPTER 9

Tuesday, December 7, 12:45 P.M.

As Jack expected, the Emergency Department waiting area was nearly full of patients. Lunchtime was a frequent time for people to decide to visit, although the vast majority hardly needed the attention of a trauma 1 facility. The problem was that they had no place else to go for basic healthcare needs and the hospital was required to see them by law. Many were there for particularly trivial reasons, like needing a prescription refilled or for a minor symptom that they had endured for days if not weeks. As a result, Jack was forced to wait in line to talk with a triage nurse. He could have forced the issue but decided against it, trying not to make waves. He'd even turned down David Andrews's offer to intercede.

When he got to the counter, he flashed his medical examiner badge and told the nurse he was there on official business and needed to talk with the doctor in charge. The result was impressive. Within a minute or two, Jack was approached by a slight woman with steely eyes and dressed in personal protective gear over scrubs. He couldn't see her expression because of her mask, but despite her size she exuded a competent, no-nonsense, in-charge persona.

"I'm Dr. Carol Sidoti," she said with authority. "I'm the ED shift supervisor. What can I do for you?"

Just as he had done with the security head, Jack introduced himself and told the woman that he was doing a routine follow-up on the unfortunate death of Dr. Sue Passero that had been investigated by one of the OCME MLIs and whose death was under review. He said he'd already done the autopsy but needed to ask a few more questions by speaking with one of the members of the team who had tried to resuscitate the doctor.

"I was in charge of the resuscitation," Carol said. "I'm happy to talk with you. Let's go someplace a little more private. Follow me, please."

Carol led Jack back into the depths of the ED to a square, counter-high command area surrounded by individual emergency bays, most of which were occupied by patients. Gesturing for him to enter one of the multiple entrance points of the central desk, she pushed a free chair toward him and took one herself. Within the area were more than a dozen doctors and nurses working at monitors. Others were coming and going. In the background various monitoring devices beeped constantly. It was a very busy scene.

"Sorry for the pandemonium," Carol said.

"No problem," Jack said, although the level of activity was distracting, especially when a monitor started sounding an alarm and no one seemed to care. He found it strange that Carol felt the location was "a little more private." In Jack's mind it was anything but.

"So . . ." Carol said. "What can I tell you?" In contrast to the security head, who had been mildly passive-aggressive initially, the ED shift supervisor presented herself as wanting to be demonstrably helpful.

"I'm interested in going over what our investigator reported to make sure we have all the details," Jack said. "Our understanding is that the patient was initially discovered by a nursing supervisor, and he and another nurse administered CPR before getting the patient here."

"That's correct," Carol said. "Our night

nursing supervisor Ronald Cavanaugh was involved, which we thought was auspicious."

"What do you mean, auspicious?"

"Ronnie is a competent nurse and conscientious nursing supervisor. To give you an idea, just about every time he's on duty, he makes it a point to arrive at the hospital an hour or so early. One of the things he invariably does is come to the ED merely to check out what's happening, particularly what kind of trauma cases are in process. He does it just to get a sense of what to expect during his shift. He's that dedicated. He's also clinically astute. As part of his responsibilities, he's required to respond to every code in the hospital, which he does with true dedication. Consequently, he's had a lot of experience, probably more than our cardiology residents, when you think about it. And he's had a lot of success with resuscitations. There's no doubt he's saved more than his share of patients."

"I get it," Jack said. "What you meant by *auspicious* was that you thought the chances of a successful resuscitation were a bit higher since he was involved from the get-go."

"Without a doubt," Carol said. "Especially when he told us that his CPR efforts initially had a definite positive effect."

"What was he referring to specifically? Or was it just an intuitive sense on his part?"

"He was being very specific. He claimed that after just a few breaths and a few minutes of chest compression the patient's color improved dramatically."

"I would say that was a good sign," Jack admitted. "Tell me, did you see the patient when she first arrived here?"

"Of course. We had been alerted the code was coming in from the garage, and we were all set up and waiting in one of our trauma rooms."

"How was the patient's color when she arrived?"

"Not too bad, and it pinked up considerably once we got an endotracheal tube in and respired her with oxygen."

"That makes sense. What was the presumed diagnosis at that point?"

"Heart attack for sure, especially after we got back the elevated troponin levels combined with the history of type 1 diabetes. Has it been confirmed?"

"It's still pending," he said. "Curiously enough, we didn't see any evidence grossly, but histology has yet to be seen. We are also looking into a possible channelopathy."

"Now that would be interesting," Carol said. "That might explain why we weren't able to get the heart to beat even with a pacemaker. It was frustrating, considering the patient was a respected hospital staff member who we all knew. I can assure you we pulled out all the stops."

"I can imagine," Jack said. He got to his feet. He felt a bit guilty taking the woman's time as another monitor alarm had begun sounding. He wondered how people could work in such a pressure-filled environment day in and day out. "I want to thank you for your cooperation. It looks like you are busy, and I hate to take any more of your time."

"We're always busy," Carol said. "Especially during this freaking pandemic. If you want any more details, I suggest you talk directly with Ronnie Cavanaugh. He's a personable guy, and I'm sure he'd be happy to talk with you. He's scheduled to be on tonight."

"I just might do that," Jack said. The problem was that the man worked the night shift and obviously slept during the day, meaning a face-to-face meeting would require his coming to the MMH one evening. How to arrange that without Laurie knowing he was out in the field investigating wouldn't be easy.

"If you need anything else, you know

where to find me," Carol said. She also stood and gestured for Jack to precede her out of the desk area.

Chapter 10

Tuesday, December 7, 1:05 P.M.

Once back in the ED waiting room, Jack checked his phone. He wanted to make sure there had been no calls and no texts, as he'd put it on silent mode while he was at the MMH. He was relieved to see he was still in the clear with no one questioning where he was. He also checked the time and moaned when he saw he'd already been away from the OCME for more than an hour and fifteen minutes. Although his absence so far hadn't evoked any attention, he knew it wouldn't last forever and that he'd better get back. The problem was, at least so far, his visit had done nothing to solve the dilemma of not knowing what he didn't know about Sue Passero's passing. There was still one more place that might offer some clues: her private office.

A visit to the information desk solved the minor problem that he had no idea where it was. Within minutes he was on his way to the Kaufman Outpatient Building. He'd been told Dr. Susan Passero's office was located on the fourth floor in the Internal Medicine Clinic.

As he rode up in the elevator, he recognized he was now on more or less shaky legal ground. Up until that point he had been perfectly in his legal right as a medical examiner tasked to investigate Sue Passero's death to check out the scene where she had been found as well as the Emergency Department where she had been declared dead. But now, going up to her office without probable cause, he was pushing the boundaries and legally he should obtain a warrant. But getting warrants was time-consuming, and time was something Jack didn't have if he was going to be forced to produce a death certificate quickly. An added concern was by pushing the legal boundaries, he was also accepting a slightly bigger risk the hospital admin might find out about his presence and flag it to Laurie.

The Internal Medicine Clinic was as busy or busier than the ED as it was now early afternoon. Like clinics in all privately owned hospitals, the doctors were overscheduled as a way of maximizing corporate income. Every day the clinic was in operation, it would get backed up, and as a normal day progressed, the number of people waiting to be seen for supposedly scheduled appointments multiplied geometrically. As had happened in the ED, Jack was forced to wait in line at the clinic check-in desk. When it was his turn, he again flashed his badge and asked to speak to whoever worked the closest with Dr. Sue Passero. The clerk directed him into the scheduling office to talk with Virginia Davenport.

Jack knocked on the door. When no one answered, he repeated with a bit more force. When there was still no answer, he tried the door. It was unlocked, and he walked in. Inside the windowless room were four desks occupied by four women of various ages. All were wearing headphones and parked behind individual computer screens while busily engaged in ongoing scheduling conversations. Like the security office, none of them were wearing masks.

Approaching the nearest desk, he asked for Virginia Davenport. The clerk responded by pointing to one of her coworkers without interrupting a conversation she was having with someone on her phone line.

Approaching this second woman, Jack waited until she had finished a call. She then slipped off her headphones and looked up at him quizzically, making him sense that visitors were not a common phenomenon in the clinic scheduling office. Looking down at her, two things caught his attention: piercingly dark eyes and teeth white enough for him to be tempted to ask her brand of toothpaste.

"Sorry to interrupt," Jack began as he once again held up his badge while introducing himself. He explained he'd like to ask her a few question about Dr. Sue Passero.

"Are you Dr. Laurie Montgomery's husband?" Virginia asked after repeating his name. She was looking at him sideways and with a touch of surprise.

"I am," Jack said. He inwardly grimaced at the unexpected question bringing up Laurie's name.

"I've spoken with your wife on many occasions," she said. "I've arranged lunches and dinners for her and Dr. Passero. What a surprise to meet you."

"Small world," he said, trying to be nonchalant. "Is there someplace we can talk briefly, provided you can take the time? Maybe it would be better if I come back if you are too busy." The buzz of the ongoing conversations was distracting.

"No, this is fine. It's always this hectic. We

can use Dr. Passero's office if that is okay with you."

"That would be perfect," Jack said. Getting to see Sue's office was the goal. He was on a fishing trip with the only questionable justification of checking if she had an insulin source in her office and, if so, if it all looked normal.

After telling her coworkers where she was going and grabbing a mask, Virginia led him out of the scheduling office, through the crowded clinic waiting area, and down a hallway before eventually stopping at an unmarked, closed door. Getting out a ring of keys, she unlocked it and stepped aside to let Jack enter. Following, she closed the door behind her. A sudden, welcome stillness prevailed.

It was a modest-sized room with a window that looked out into an interior courtyard. There was space enough for a nondescript desk, a desk chair, a reading chair, and a small bookcase. On top of the bookcase was a collection of family photos, mostly of Sue's children as they had grown up. On the desk was a monitor and several bookends supporting a number of brightly colored folders, each clasped with a matching elastic. The room was neat and utilitarian.

"First let me express my sincere condolences for Dr. Passero's death," he began as he walked over to the desk.

"Thank you," she said. "It's been a terrible shock to all of us, but particularly to me. I'm the most senior scheduling clerk, and I worked closely with Dr. Passero, essentially functioning as her assistant. It's why I got to talk with your wife as often as I did. She and Dr. Passero were extraordinarily good friends."

"I can assure you that the doctor's passing was a terrible shock to my wife as well," Jack said. "How was Dr. Passero's health in general? Was she having any problems?" He glanced at the labels on the folders. Each seemed to be titled with the name of a hospital committee.

"It was perfect, as far as I know," Virginia said. She sat down on the edge of the reading chair, with her legs demurely tucked to one side. She was dressed in dark slacks and a sweater with a long white lab coat. "She was back to going to the gym three times a week now that it had reopened."

"How about her diabetes?" he asked. "Do you know if that had been stable?"

"As far as I know. She was very careful."

"Did she have an insulin source here?"

"Certainly. It's in the closet behind you."

Jack turned and opened the closet door.

Inside were several highly starched white lab coats on hangers. To the side on the floor was a small refrigerator. He opened it and looked at the vials of insulin. It was obvious all was in order. Even the labels were lined up. So much for any idea that her death could have been due to an accidental mix-up with her medications — not that Jack had seriously considered it, but it was another fact to be checked off his mental list.

Closing the refrigerator door, he caught his breath as he felt his phone vibrate in his pocket. With trepidation he pulled it out and looked at the screen. With a sense of relief, he saw that it was John DeVries, head of the Toxicology Department. "Excuse me," he said to Virginia as he took the call. She motioned she understood.

"I got some news on the Passero case and wanted to get it to you ASAP," John said. "No ketoacidosis, no hyper- or hypoglycemia, meaning no need to check her insulin source or levels."

"What about the general drug screen?" Jack asked.

"My God, you are impossible," John teased. "You're never satisfied. The rest is pending. I'll let you know as soon as we have the answers."

After repocketing his phone, Jack again apologized to Virginia for taking the call, mentioning it involved Dr. Passero. He then asked her if she knew who Dr. Passero used as her GP.

"Dr. Camelia Gomez. She's an internist over at University Hospital who specializes in diabetes. I can get you the doctor's number if you'd like."

"No need. I'm sure I can find it," he said. "Do you know if Dr. Passero had seen her recently?"

"I doubt it," Virginia said. "When Dr. Passero did see her, I usually made the appointment, and the last time I did was probably six months ago."

"Do you mind if I glance through these folders and Dr. Passero's desk drawers?"

Virginia shrugged. "I don't mind. Suit yourself. But why? I can probably answer any questions you might have. What else did you want to know?"

"To be honest, I'm struggling a bit with the exact cause of death," Jack admitted. "I knew it is a long shot coming here, but I thought there could be a slim chance of finding some notes to herself or something that suggested she was worrying about some personal health issues that she was keeping to herself."

"We were told she had a heart attack," Virginia said, looking confused. "Is that not true?"

"It's probably true," Jack said. "Tests are still pending. I just want to make sure I've crossed the *T*s and dotted the *I*s. Laurie is interested in knowing all the details for the family, particularly for the kids, who are now both doctors in their own right."

"Please, look as much as you want," Virginia said. "I did all of Dr. Passero's copying, which was always rather extensive because of her hospital committee responsibilities, and she was a bit old school about having hard copies. I can tell you it's never been about an individual illness or symptoms she might have been worried about. But talking about family, maybe you should know that Dr. Passero's husband has already been here, gone through the desk, and possibly taken some of Dr. Passero's personal items."

He froze in the process of glancing into the center drawer of the desk and slowly let his point of view rise to stare at her. He wasn't sure he'd heard correctly. "Did you say Abraham has already been here?"

"Yes, this morning, rather early, while we were still setting up to open."

"That's curious," Jack said. It was more

than curious in his mind and immediately raised the life insurance issue and its implications. But as fast as the idea occurred to him, he dismissed it. The idea that Abby would take out life insurance on his wife and then murder her was preposterous. Same with the idea that Sue might be involved in some nefarious plot, waiting the desired grace period, and then killing herself in some undetectable way.

After Jack ran his fingers through his hair a couple of times, which he often did as a way to reboot his brain, he asked, "Did you happen to notice if he removed a lot of things?"

"I don't know if he took anything because I didn't see him leave," Virginia said. "But just looking around now that I am in here, it doesn't appear so. I mean, all the kids' photos are still there on the bookcase."

"I noticed the photos when I first came in," he said. He shrugged, wondering why Abby had thought coming to the office to rescue personal items was a priority, especially leaving all the photos. Being involved with death as much as he had been as a medical examiner, Jack was well aware that most people were paralyzed by grief with the passing of a family member, especially a spouse. And why would Abby make the effort to come to the office and yet leave the BMW in the garage?

"To change the subject, let me ask you this," Jack said. "How was Dr. Passero's mood lately? Did she act at all depressed over the last month?"

"Not in the slightest," she said without hesitation. "Dr. Passero was not the depressive type. She was much too busy day in and day out to be depressed. She even insisted on coming in on most Saturdays, and so did I even though the clinic was closed. She did it just to see the patients she couldn't see during the week but felt needed to be seen, and I couldn't let her be here by herself."

"Sometimes depression can be subtle," he suggested. He glanced in each desk drawer in turn.

"I'm aware," Virginia said. "In fact, I'm probably more aware than most people. I have a master's degree in psychology and know a fair bit about depression. If anything, instead of showing any depressive symptoms, Dr. Passero had been fired up of late. I'm not trying to suggest she was manic, but she was, let's say, *very enthused* over multiple committee-related issues and campaigning hard despite how busy she was with her patient load."

"I noticed these folders," Jack said, redirecting his attention to the desk's surface. He slipped a couple out whose labels read COMPLIANCE COMMITTEE and INFECTIOUS CONTROL COMMITTEE. He glanced in each. Both were jammed full of meeting programs and handouts of case histories, as well as copies of emails Sue had sent to fellow committee members on a variety of topics. Glancing at them it was obvious to him that Sue had been a very active member, just as Virginia suggested.

"What exactly was she campaigning for?" Jack asked as he returned the two folders to where they had been. He then pulled out a third that was labeled simply HOSPITAL MORTALITY ARTICLES OF INTEREST. He pulled off the elastic and opened it.

"Mainly two positions she dearly wanted," Virginia said. "First and foremost was the Mortality and Morbidity Task Force, which was a subcommittee of the Mortality and Morbidity Committee, of which she was already a member. The second was becoming a member of the hospital board itself. She'd been trying her darndest to join both for well over a year, and it was frustrating for her."

"Whoa!" he said. He looked up at her. He was surprised. "Dr. Passero was trying to get on the hospital board? That's a steep mountain to climb, especially being one of the frontline workers who actually saw patients." AmeriCare Corporation, the owner of the supposedly nonprofit Manhattan Memorial Hospital, was controlled by a private equity group, which was demanding increased profitability. The fastest way to accomplish that was to raise prices and drastically lower costs by firing a bunch of highly paid nurses, particularly more senior ones. There had been a big article about it in the *New York Times.*

"She knew it was an uphill struggle," Virginia said, "but it didn't deter her from trying. She was horrified by the hospital reducing the nurse-to-patient ratio, believing patient care was suffering. She was intent on reversing the trend."

"There's absolutely no doubt that reducing nursing staff negatively affects patient outcomes," Jack said. "Wow! I can't imagine administration was fond of the idea of her being on the board." This information was putting a new spin on his thinking. He'd always thought Sue Passero was a universally appreciated individual. Apparently, that wasn't necessarily true.

"That's an understatement," Virginia admitted. "There were a few people Dr.

Passero clashed with on a regular basis because of her activism, particularly Peter Alinsky, one of the executive vice presidents in charge of the outpatient clinics who also oversees the Outpatient Reorganizing Committee, another committee on which Dr. Passero was a member. He and Dr. Passero were always exchanging less than flattering emails on all sorts of issues. I know because I printed all of them for her files. And to make matters worse, Mr. Alinsky was also the major opposition to her joining the Mortality and Morbidity Task Force, where he was also a member along with a surgeon and an anesthesiologist who shared his views about Dr. Passero. Alinsky was, in many respects, Dr. Passero's bête noire."

"Wow!" Jack voiced. "This is all new to me. I thought Dr. Passero was a particularly well-liked and highly respected member of the MMH community." He recalled having just heard Dr. Carol Sidoti sing Sue's praises.

"Don't get me wrong. She was adored, truly, but mainly by the clinical community, particularly the Department of Internal Medicine, and, of course, all her patients. From my perspective, she was far and away the most respected doctor. Unfortunately, that didn't necessarily extend to segments of administration, and the feelings were mutual."

"Well, I can understand," he said. "I've never been thrilled by the MMH admin nor its parent corporation, AmeriCare. But getting back to this task force. What is it or what's its role? I've never heard of it. I'm certainly familiar with the Mortality and Morbidity Committee. I even had a stint on one way back when."

"I'm hardly an authority, but according to what Dr. Passero communicated, it's a small committee whose main function is to decide which deaths or adverse outcome cases get presented by the residents to the Mortality and Morbidity Committee itself. Not all of them are presented. Second, it generates the hospital's mortality ratio, which I never could quite understand, to be honest. But Dr. Passero understood it, and it motivated her. She told me it was the statistic used by the hospital along with the M and M Committee to maintain its accreditation, which was the reason she wanted to make sure it was accurate."

"I'm not sure if I have heard of a mortality ratio, either," Jack said. He made a mental note to look it up later while he returned his attention to the folder he was holding, HOSPITAL MORTALITY ARTICLES

OF INTEREST. He pulled out the contents and noticed that they were printouts of various pieces, some from medical journals and others from newspapers or magazines. The first one was the heavily underlined, shocking 1999 report put out by the Institute of Medicine called "To Err Is Human." He remembered it well, as did anyone who had read it, because it revealed the sobering fact that somewhere between 44,000 and 98,000 people died in American hospitals every year from preventable medical errors.

"That's the article that motivated Dr. Passero to get so engaged in her committee work," Virginia said. She stood up from the reading chair. "At least that's what she told me when I came on board. In the ten years I've been here, Dr. Passero has never stopped being a patient advocate. We are all going to miss her terribly. And speaking of missing her, I'd better get back to help my team. Dr. Passero saw more patients than any of the other doctors on the staff and rescheduling them is going to take weeks, if not a month. She is going to be difficult to replace, and she is going to be sorely missed on multiple levels."

"It certainly sounds like it," Jack said. "Do you mind if I stay here a bit longer?"

"Of course not," she said. "Stay as long as

you'd like. I'll be in the scheduling office if you have any additional questions that I can try to answer."

"Thank you," Jack said. "I really appreciate your help."

"Not at all," Virginia said. A moment later she was gone.

CHAPTER 11

Tuesday, December 7, 1:38 P.M.

Taking advantage of being alone, Jack removed his mask and put it to the side. He then went back to leafing through the collection of articles he was holding, recognizing they were enough to depress yet also motivate anyone interested in patient well-being. There were stories of regrettable hospital deaths due to a variety of inexcusable circumstances as well as gross screwups like huge overdoses of medications, medications given to the wrong patient, operations on the wrong patient, or on the wrong organ, or on the wrong limb. It was a litany of hospital horror stories.

Beneath these loose articles was another whole group isolated with a heavy metal clasp. These were equally as shocking and involved stories of a specific category of patient deaths: those caused by medical serial killers. The first article Jack recognized immediately. It was a *New York Times* piece only a little more than a month old about a nurse in Texas who'd killed a few patients in cardiac intensive care by injecting them with air, causing strokes. Other articles were equally horrific, several because of the sheer number of patients involved. One was about a doctor in the UK and another about a nurse in New Jersey, each responsible for hundreds of deaths. As Jack scanned article after article, he realized that he'd had no idea of the extent of the problem, and it begged the question of how many more medical serial killers there might be who hadn't been exposed. The idea of an individual entering a profession to cure people but ending up killing them seemed so unbelievably perfidious. As a doctor himself, it was embarrassing as well as unconscionable.

One case he knew intimately. It was about a nurse named Jasmine Rakoczi. She had been paid to eliminate postoperative patients who carried genetic mutations that made them susceptible to future serious diseases, which would have ultimately cost their health insurance company millions of dollars. This was the same nurse he had recalled with trepidation as he crossed the pedestrian bridge with the head of security and whose exposé Laurie had spearheaded and who had tried to kill Laurie and shoot him.

It was at that point that Jack came across another group of articles bound together with a smaller metal clasp. These seemed to be primarily from psychology journals discussing medical serial killers from the point of view of motive. Scanning the titles, he could see that they discussed issues like mercy killing, where the killers, to some degree, believed they were saving patients from the ravages of terminal illnesses. Others were about hero killers, who purposely put patients in jeopardy so that they could save them and get the associated credit. He even noticed an article about Munchausen syndrome by proxy. Curious as to why Sue Passero might have included this piece, he scanned it rapidly. It involved a nurse who had been convicted of killing several of her foster children over a number of years by creating illnesses requiring multiple hospitalizations where she worked.

Suddenly the door to the hallway burst open, causing Jack to jump, as three people rushed into the office, all wearing masks. The first was a tall, tanned, striking woman with steely blue eyes and sleek, shoulder-length chestnut hair. She was impeccably dressed in a dark blue business suit with an open-neck white blouse. "Are you Dr. John Stapleton?" she demanded with authority, her arms akimbo.

"I prefer to answer to *Jack,*" he said, rescuing his mask and pressing it against his face.

A short man was standing behind the woman. He was dressed in a long white lab coat. Jack could see some culture tubes showing in his pockets among other laboratory paraphernalia, giving Jack an idea of who he was.

"Will you kindly tell me what you are doing in this office unannounced and unaccompanied, going through private hospital papers?" the woman demanded.

"Enjoying a little reading away from the fray," Jack said, but he immediately regretted his response's sarcastic overtone. The last thing he wanted to do was make waves that might get back to Laurie, yet he couldn't help himself. He was put off by the woman's officiousness, and sarcasm was reflexive for him.

"That kind of answer makes me think your concerns were justified, Dr. Cheveau," the woman said to the smaller man. Then to the taller she said, "Mr. Alinsky, I think you should call security as you suggested and have Dr. Stapleton escorted off the premises."

Jack's ears perked up hearing the name *Alinsky,* remembering Virginia describing him as Sue's bane. "I'm here on official medical examiner business investigating Dr. Susan Passero's death," he said. He put the articles he was holding down on the desk and stood, staring at Alinsky while the man stepped to the side with his phone, presumably calling security. Jack had the urge to ask him a few questions.

"Dr. Passero's heart attack occurred in the parking garage," the woman said, turning back to Jack. "She didn't die in this office. Last night we fully cooperated with a medical legal investigator from the OCME. Then a few minutes ago I got word that you had showed up and were here asking questions. I checked with the hospital counsel about this situation and was told that for you to be here at this point, you'd need a warrant and to get one you'd have to have probable cause. At the very least, you could have had the decency to come to Administration to get permission. You probably would have gotten permission, as Dr. Cheveau told me that you provided a significant service to this institution in the past."

"I beg to differ," Jack said. "It was more than a service. I exposed a laboratory assistant hell-bent on spreading infectious diseases to patients, trying to start an epidemic."

"Yes, so I was told, and I give you credit for that," the woman said. "But in the process, according to Dr. Cheveau, you caused serious disruptions to the hospital and to a number of its staff. You are, in Dr. Cheveau's words, a bull in a china shop."

"As if he is an authority on character assessment," Jack said with a roll of his eyes. "Dr. Cheveau was ultimately responsible for allowing his lab tech to get away with lethal shenanigans for months right under his nose. But, be that as it may, who exactly are you?"

"For your information, my name is Marsha Schechter. I happen to be the president of this hospital, having taken over from Charles Kelley, rest his soul."

Jack eyed the impressive-looking woman and wondered if being tall, tan, and aristocratic-appearing was a requirement to be selected as the president of the MMH by the hospital board or by the powers that be at the AmeriCare corporate office. Although opposite genders, Marsha Schechter and Charles Kelley seemed as if they could have come from the same mold.

"I want to be damn certain you do not

cause any disruptions on this occasion," Marsha continued. "Our dealing with Dr. Passero's untimely death is difficult enough for the hospital without it being in any way compounded. Do I make myself clear?"

"I'm certainly not here to cause any trouble," Jack said. "I just want to make sure that we medical examiners are not missing anything."

"What can you possibly mean about not missing anything? Dr. Passero died of a heart attack. Is that not true?"

"The cause and manner of death are still pending," Jack said evasively. As he spoke, he noticed Alinsky had finished with his phone call. Jack looked at him directly and asked him if his name was Peter Alinsky. Although mildly taken aback at the question, he responded in the affirmative.

"Now *that* is a coincidence," Jack said. "Tell me, what did you have against Dr. Passero being on the Mortality and Morbidity Task Force?"

Jack's question must have struck a sensitive nerve because the man appeared stunned. Instead of answering, he glanced over at Marsha for help.

"What the hell does the Mortality and Morbidity Task Force have to do with Dr. Passero's passing?" Marsha questioned irritably with her brow deeply furrowed, seemingly equally as surprised.

"I have no idea," Jack said. "That's why I asked."

"I'm beginning to see why Dr. Cheveau thinks of you as a bull in a china shop," Marsha said with a short, frustrated laugh, clearly losing patience. "Our Mortality and Morbidity Task Force is certainly none of your or the OCME's business. Clearly Dr. Passero's heart attack had nothing to do with the hospital's internal affairs. Is this something you came across while looking at these private papers?" She leaned forward and used a hand to turn some the articles on the desk around to read their titles.

"Indirectly," Jack admitted.

At that moment, David Andrews arrived out of breath along with an impressively large fellow security officer. Both were carrying radios. "What's the problem here, Ms. Schechter?" he managed with his commanding baritone voice.

"We have an intruder here whom Dr. Cheveau happened to see leaving the ED, and I want him escorted off the premises."

"Certainly, ma'am," David said. Without hesitation, he stepped forward and confronted Jack. Meanwhile, out of sight of the others in the room, he rolled his eyes for

Jack's benefit, then gestured toward the door to the hallway.

"It's been a fun party, but I can tell when I'm not wanted," Jack said to Marsha as he started toward the door. As soon as the comment left his mouth, he regretted having made it, knowing that such flippancy could only possibly make the situation worse. Ultimately what he wanted to avoid was provoking an official complaint about his presence, which had happened in the past, but he particularly didn't want it to happen now that Laurie was the chief.

"Watch yourself, Dr. Stapleton. I have eyes and ears everywhere," said Marsha.

Once out in the hall and on the way to the elevators, David asked sotto voce what on earth Jack had done to incite the president's wrath. The other security person followed silently several steps behind.

"I suppose just being myself," Jack said. "Diplomacy is not one of my strong points."

"But what the hell made her come and confront you in person?"

"I suppose because I've had a checkered relationship with the MMH," Jack said. "I've been lionized by some and denounced by others. More important, I had a particularly rocky relationship with the previous president, and it's already not looking good with this one."

"She's an impressive woman," David said. "Supposedly one hell of a businessperson, and I respect her. She runs a tight ship."

"To be truthful, the fact that she showed up surprised me as well," Jack said. In the back of his mind, he'd been confused by the issue. When he combined it with the curious reaction he'd unexpectedly elicited from mentioning the Mortality and Morbidity Task Force, specifically the forceful denial it had evoked of not having anything to do with Sue Passero's passing, he couldn't help but be intrigued. It was the kind of random information that set off alarm bells for him by suggesting the idea there could be some mysterious relationship between Sue's death and this enigmatic committee. And if Forensic Biology, Histology, and Toxicology didn't come up with a cause and mechanism of death confirming it as natural, Jack was going to need some fresh ideas.

"How are you going to get back to the OCME?" David asked as they arrived at the elevator. "I only ask to know where I should take you to exit."

"I came on my bike," Jack said. "I left it near the main entrance. But first I have a favor to ask."

"Bike?" David questioned with astonishment. "Are you serious?"

"Very much so," Jack said. "It's my preferred method of transportation. With no congestion pricing and traffic as it is in this city, and inconsistent subway service, it's by far the best way to get around."

"It's the best way to get you dead," David said. "But what's this about a favor? Please don't put me in trouble with the big boss. My orders are to escort you off the premises straightaway."

"I wouldn't think of coming between you and your glorious leader," Jack said. "All I'd like to do is make a rapid revisit to Dr. Passero's car, where I'm certainly authorized to be. I meant to take some pics of the interior for the record."

Jack had no need of photos of the car, but claiming he did was the only way that came to mind to wrangle on impulse a return to the vehicle. If it turned out ultimately that there was to be no confirmation of Sue's death being natural or accidental from Maureen, John, and Naomi, he was going to want to come back to the MMH to look into the Mortality and Morbidity Task Force issue that had been fortuitously dumped into his lap. With his persona non grata status he was going to need access, so he

151

was thinking of borrowing for a time Sue Passero's hospital ID, which was hanging by its lanyard on the BMW's rearview mirror. Although he knew he'd have to make it a point to steer clear of Marsha Schechter and Dr. Cheveau, the hospital ID, even with the wrong name and photo, would mean his presence would be less likely to attract attention. If he turned the ID photo toward himself, he had reason to believe he might get away with it.

As they rode down in the elevator, David used his radio to have one of his security people meet them in the garage with the BMW key fob. And a little more than twenty minutes later and after a quick revisit to the BMW, Jack was unceremoniously escorted out the hospital's main entrance.

CHAPTER 12

Tuesday, December 7, 2:34 P.M.

Having just made the turn from Second Avenue onto 30th Street, Jack felt his phone vibrate in his pocket. Knowing it was well after two in the afternoon, meaning he'd been gone from the OCME for more than two hours, he felt it wise to see who was calling. Applying his bike's brakes, he pulled to the side of the road at a fire hydrant, then struggled to get his phone out of his hip pocket. As soon as he could, he checked the screen. To his dismay, it was Laurie.

After a brief debate whether he should take the call or wait until he got back to the OCME, which was only going to be a matter of minutes, he took the call. Unfortunately, the moment he did, a siren could be heard with a marked Doppler effect passing behind him on Second Avenue. It provoked Laurie to start the conversation by asking where he was.

"Stepped out for a few minutes," he said evasively. "I wanted to get Sue's samples to the Forensic Biology lab as soon as possible, but I'm on my way back, and I'll be there in minutes." Jack wasn't one to lie, but he didn't have any problem being less than totally forthright if it maintained the peace.

"Thank you for prioritizing the case," she said. "I appreciate it. Anyway, can you stop into my office when you get here? I had another long talk with Abby that I want to tell you about."

"Sure thing," Jack said agreeably.

After repocketing his phone, he made the rest of the journey in rapid time. He stored his bike in the usual location, waved to the security person as well as to the two mortuary techs in the mortuary office, and took the stairs by twos up to the first floor. As per usual, Cheryl Sanford was on her phone with headphones in place. Jack gestured toward Laurie's office door. She nodded and gave the thumbs-up that the coast was clear, and he walked in.

Laurie was just as he'd left her some six hours earlier, sitting behind her massive desk communing with the architectural drawings. Jack plopped himself down on the colorful couch just like he was accustomed to doing.

"First let me assure you that Abby is clearly devastated," Laurie said, raising her eyes to meet his and tilting back in her desk chair. "It was abundantly clear on my second conversation with him, so I'm absolutely certain that our momentary B movie thoughts about an insurance scam of some sort are totally out of the question."

He nodded but didn't respond. Instead, he was thinking about Abby's early-morning visit to Sue's office and wondered if Abby had said anything about that to Laurie during their phone conversation. Although Jack wanted to mention it to her, he didn't know how to do it without revealing he'd been over at the MMH investigating.

"We also discussed at length the need for doing the autopsy," Laurie said. "And when I told him it was already completed, he mellowed on his objection to it and said that he was mostly concerned about making sure the burial gets done within twenty-four hours, which goes along with what I said this morning. So we are okay in that realm."

"That's good," Jack said. He was still puzzling over some way to let her know about the man's rather strange visit to his wife's office.

"We also talked about his being Muslim," Laurie continued. "I told him that we had

had no idea."

"And what did he say?" he asked. In the back of his mind, it was also that discrepancy that was fueling his unease.

"He said he thought people would assume as much since it was common knowledge he'd grown up in Egypt, where the population is more than ninety percent Muslim. He also said that their reticence followed from an agreement he and Sue had made early in their relationship, namely that they wouldn't foist their individual religious beliefs on each other, with her being brought up as a Southern Baptist. They had also decided that they wouldn't force the children in either direction but let them decide for themselves after being exposed to both."

"Hallelujah," Jack said. "I wish the rest of the world could be so reasonable. Did he happen to mention what Nadia and Jamal decided? What a unique opportunity."

"Curiously enough, they are both agnostics. Obviously neither religion won out, at least not yet."

"Interesting," he said vaguely. "To change the subject a little, I've already heard back from John. Toxicology found no ketoacidosis and normal glucose levels. Obviously, Sue's diabetes was under perfect control, just as you suspected."

"I'm not surprised except by the speed of your getting the results. How did you manage to build a fire under John?"

Jack laughed. "It wasn't difficult. He's truly a new man with his relatively new laboratory and a real office. He's a far cry from his previously irascible self."

"Getting back to Abby," Laurie said. "I told him he would be hearing from you straightaway about the results of the autopsy. Cheryl has his mobile number so get it from her and make the call."

"The problem is there ain't much to tell," he said. "After insisting on an autopsy against his wishes, it's not going to sit right for me to tell him his dead wife was found to be perfectly normal."

"Don't make this more difficult than it need be," Laurie said with the first signs of impatience. With all the administrative stresses and strains she was under, it was a frequent occurrence as conversations with anyone dragged on. As the chief she was always dealing with one or more pressing problems from early in the morning until she turned out the light at night. "You figure it out," she snapped. "Just make the call. I also told him you are responsible for releasing Sue's body to the funeral service, and I said you'd be doing it today so that the burial can proceed."

"I don't know if I can release the body," Jack said.

Laurie audibly groaned before leaning forward to rest her face in the palms of her hands with her elbows on the desk. She took a couple of deep breaths while rubbing her eyes with the tips of her fingers. When she looked up at him, her eyes were reddened, and she needed to blink a few times. "I'm not asking for the moon," she said in a tired, restrained voice.

"Maybe not the moon, but it is significant," Jack said. "This morning when we talked about this, I told you I was having trouble with the cause and manner of death and what I was going to put on the death certificate, assuming I don't get something convincing from Maureen, John, or Naomi, which seems more likely than not. Call it experienced forensic intuition. Where does that leave me with the manner of death if it is not natural, accidental, or suicide? I'll tell you where it leaves me . . . homicide!"

"Don't tell me you are still thinking of the insurance issue?" Laurie demanded.

"I haven't totally dismissed it," he admitted.

"Well, you should," she said. "Abby brought it up when he explained about

158

needing the death certificate. He said getting the life insurance was at Sue's insistence to have a backup to pay off the kids' sizable medical training if for any reason her salary became compromised. He said he never thought it would be needed and got choked up when he said she was right."

"All that does make sense," Jack agreed. "But listen, I'm not overly invested in the why or the who, and I won't be until I've figured out the how. I'm consumed by finding out what is the actual cause and mechanism of death, and I'm completely stymied. The only halfway positive finding was the mild pulmonary edema. Given that we both are reasonably confident Sue wasn't using drugs, maybe somebody slipped her something like fentanyl. I know I'm sounding desperate, but you have to see my conundrum because I'm not going to sign it out as indeterminate. That's a cop-out."

"Toxicology surely will find fentanyl if fentanyl is involved," Laurie said impatiently.

"Yes, of course, but that's not my point. My intuition is telling me John isn't going to find it. I'm mentioning it out of desperation, pulling a possibility out of thin air no matter how unlikely, because there is something inherently weird about this case. I can feel it in my bones. The problem comes down to whether I can, in good conscience, release the body. What if new information becomes available and I'm forced to look into something else that I hadn't anticipated and the body is gone?"

"Good gravy," Laurie complained. "You are overthinking this! Tell me, did you take samples of everything, every organ, every fluid, etcetera?"

"Yes, of course."

"Well, there you go. That should cover just about any contingency."

"I wish I shared your confidence."

"Just take care of it!" she ordered with obvious exasperation. "I'd be happy to be more involved, but I've managed to schedule a presentation this afternoon with the mayor-elect and a bunch of his people about why our budget and the new autopsy suite are justified. It's going to be in the main auditorium at 421 an hour from now, and I've just started to prepare."

"Okay," Jack said with a shrug of resignation. He got to his feet.

"As I said earlier, the death certificate can be amended if new information becomes available." Laurie redirected her attention back to her computer screen.

"Yeah, sure," Jack said without enthusiasm. "Good luck with the mayor." As he headed toward the door, he wondered anew why he'd encouraged her to become the chief.

CHAPTER 13

Tuesday, December 7, 2:50 P.M.

Emerging from Laurie's office, Jack practically bumped into George Fontworth, the deputy chief, who'd obviously been waiting for him to leave. They did a little dance to get around each other. To make matters worse, he was clutching a significant number of OCME brochures to his chest.

Jack stopped at Cheryl's desk. She was speaking to someone on the phone but had anticipated his need of Abby's mobile number and produced it without having to be asked. Jack took the slip of paper and mouthed a thank-you. Cheryl responded with another of her thumbs-up gestures without interrupting her conversation.

After making a detour to get a candy bar from one of the vending machines in the second-floor employee lunchroom, Jack went up to his office. There he took off his jacket and sat down at his desk, putting Abby's phone number center stage. He stared at it for a time, wrestled with the idea of calling the man, but ultimately put it off. Instead, as he munched on the candy bar, he called University Hospital, where Laurie's father had been one of the top-notch cardiac surgeons when he'd been alive. Once he got the operator, he identified himself as Dr. Stapleton and asked to speak to Dr. Camelia Gomez.

It took a long time to get the doctor on the line, as Jack had to go through several different clerks at different clinics, each time being put on a lengthy hold. He wasn't surprised, as he was well aware that modern American medicine had devised multiple ways to shield doctors from contact with the outside world. As he waited, he tried to think of how he was going to proceed with the Passero case. He could see Laurie's position as Sue's dear friend and understand her wish to be as helpful to Abby as possible, and he respected it. He also recognized that Laurie was correct in that he had obtained samples of every tissue and fluid he could think of during the autopsy, making it difficult for him to imagine a circumstance that would necessitate a redo. Consequently, he decided to follow Laurie's order and release the body. But the death certificate problem was another issue entirely. He had never signed one out as being *indeterminate,* and he wasn't going to do it now, no matter what Laurie said. For him it was a matter of professional integrity.

Jack's patience ultimately paid off and finally he got to speak with Dr. Gomez. After introducing himself, he told her that Dr. Susan Passero had died the previous evening.

"I'm so sorry to hear," Dr. Gomez said. "That's a shock. What happened?"

Jack said, "The cause of death is still pending, which is the reason I'm calling you. As medical examiners we have the right to subpoena her medical records if necessary."

"Of course. I understand."

"What we need to know is if she ever had had any cardiac issues or symptoms to your knowledge."

"I don't think so," Dr. Gomez said. "But give me a moment to bring up her record in our system."

"Certainly," he said. He could hear a series of keystrokes during a brief pause.

"My memory was correct," Dr. Gomez said. "There were no cardiac issues. She even had an entirely normal ECG recently. In our judgment, Dr. Passero was in fine cardiovascular health. She had absolutely no evidence of diabetic retinopathy, either. We checked that out by an ophthalmology consult and fluorescein study."

"Thank you," Jack said. "That's very helpful."

He disconnected and tossed his mobile phone to the side. He hadn't even thought of asking about the status of her retina. With no retinopathy the chances of her having coronary artery disease were probably close to zero, meaning Histology wasn't coming to the rescue in the search for a mechanism of death. So, only Toxicology and the DNA lab were left, and he wasn't hopeful.

Without another convenient way to put off calling Abby, Jack grabbed his phone and lined up the slip of paper Cheryl had given him so he could read the number. He wasn't looking forward to making the call for many reasons, but by far the biggest was that it reminded him of the worst call he'd ever gotten in his life. It had been a call from a small rural Illinois hospital informing him his wife and daughters had perished in a plane crash after visiting him in Chicago, where he was doing his second residency, this time in forensic pathology.

"Get a grip!" he snapped as the call went through. He almost hoped Abby wouldn't answer, but he did and in a way Jack had not anticipated.

"Thanks for calling, Jack," Abby said right off in a sad, hesitant voice without even saying hello, apparently having Jack's mobile number in his phone. "I can imagine it's difficult, probably reminding you when your first wife and children died." Abby had a slight and refined English accent. Although he'd grown up in Egypt, he'd gone to boarding school in England before coming to the United States for college.

It took Jack a few beats to recover his thoughts. Here was a man undeniably suffering acutely, yet able to empathize with someone else and his experiences. Jack had shared the sad story of his former life one night with both Sue and Abby after several bottles of wine.

"I'm so sorry for Sue's passing," Jack managed.

"It was so unexpected," Abby said, his voice cracking. "I still don't completely believe it. She was so vital, so healthy, so much healthier than I. Why am I the one here and she's gone? It doesn't seem right."

"I know how you feel," he said, but then didn't know what else to say. It was the first time in years that he was at a loss for words. A rush of guilt from having even briefly entertained the crazy idea of Abby involved in some wild insurance scam had him embarrassed and tongue-tied.

"Laurie said that you would be taking care of Sue for us," Abby continued, seemingly unaware of Jack's discomfort. "Thank you for doing that. I'm sure it's not easy but it's appreciated. She also said that you would be arranging to have the body released today, so we can have the burial. We appreciate that as well."

Jack cleared his throat to speak yet his voice still came out in a higher key than usual. "Yes, I will make the arrangements. All you will need to do is select a funeral service and have them call here. They know the ropes."

"I've already chosen a funeral home," Abby said. "I'll call them and let them know. Meanwhile, I hate to cut you off, but Nadia and Jamal just arrived, and as you can imagine, they are very upset. I need to spend time with them."

"Of course," Jack said, again surprised. The unexpected twists of the conversation were disconcerting. "But before you go, I did want to ask you a quick question. When I was talking with Virginia Davenport earlier today, she happened to mention that you had stopped by Sue's office this morning.

Was there some particular reason?"

"Purely for sentimental reasons," Abby said. "Sue loved her work. She was so caught up in it. It was a way of saying goodbye."

"Did you take anything?"

"No, but I know I'll need to do that," Abby said. "We'll be in touch. And thank you again."

It took Jack a moment to realize the call had been disconnected. Slowly he put the phone down. He'd expected Abby to have been particularly interested in the exact cause of Sue's death, if only to justify the autopsy that had been done despite his objections. Yet the question hadn't even come up, making him wonder yet again if an insurance scam wasn't all that far out of the realm of possibility. But then he remembered the sound of Abby's voice when he answered the call as well as the surprising empathy he voiced about Jack's loss of his own wife.

Jack shook his head in frustration. He'd never been caught up in a forensic conundrum in which he was so emotionally involved. He'd wanted a puzzling case as a challenging distraction, but this wasn't what he'd had in mind. Picking the phone up again, he called down to the mortuary office, looking for Vinnie. Marvin Fletcher answered and said he'd find Vinnie and have him call.

Putting his phone back down, he glanced at the imposing stack of autopsy folders next to his monitor and the equally towering group of histology slide trays next to his microscope. He knew he needed to deal with them, but at the moment he felt incapable. Instead, he had an idea, which required putting in a call to the MMH Internal Medicine Clinic in hopes of reconnecting with Virginia. Although it wasn't she who answered the call initially, he got to speak with her quickly, much more quickly than he'd gotten to speak with Dr. Gomez.

"Sorry to bother you again, knowing how busy you are," Jack said.

"It's no bother," Virginia said. "We've finally gotten a handle on the day, dealing with Dr. Passero's absence. What can I do for you?"

"First I'd like to thank you for the help you have already given me," Jack said.

"It was my pleasure."

"I've been thinking about Dr. Passero's committee work," he said. "You mentioned she was really fixated on two goals: being a member of the Mortality and Morbidity

Task Force and the hospital board."

"Very much so. Particularly the task force."

"Do you think she could have been depressed about it since you mentioned she found it frustrating?"

"Not at all. As I said, Sue was the opposite of a depressive type. I think the challenge was stimulating for her rather than vice versa."

"I had planned on looking at the contents of the Mortality and Morbidity Committee file after what you had said. Unfortunately, I had to leave the hospital rather suddenly and get back here to my office."

Jack paused for a moment to give Virginia a chance to respond, to see if his expulsion by Marsha Schechter was part and parcel of hospital gossip. When she didn't react, he continued. "I'm thinking it might be helpful for me to glance through it. Would you be willing to leave the folder down at the information desk with my name on it? I could stop by on my way home this afternoon and pick it up. I could have it back tomorrow if necessary."

"Certainly," Virginia said without the slightest hesitation.

Encouraged by the woman's response, he asked if she could also include the folder labeled HOSPITAL MORTALITY ARTICLES OF INTEREST, and she agreed again without pause. Disconnecting, he felt pleased. He'd decided that getting an idea of Sue's mindset might be helpful although he didn't know exactly why.

Having made the call to Virginia and being reminded of the conversation that he'd had with her in Sue's office, Jack turned on his monitor and googled *death ratio.* It was a term that had come up when Virginia mentioned Sue's abiding interest in joining the hospital's Mortality and Morbidity Task Force. He didn't find much. Mostly the search turned up articles about *mortality rate,* a more general term. But then he came across a specific article about death ratio that had been put out by the Mayo Clinic.

Quickly scanning the piece, Jack learned that *death ratio* referred to a ratio of the number of hospital deaths divided by the expected number of hospital deaths. A value of one meant the hospital was doing as expected. A value of greater than one meant the hospital was not doing so well, and a value of less than one meant it was doing better than expected. When he finished reading, he noticed that there had been no explanation of how the denominator, the expected number of deaths, was determined, although he assumed it had something to do with the expected mortality of each individual illness.

The harsh jangle of Jack's office phone interrupted him. It was Vinnie calling back. Jack told him to go ahead and make the arrangements for Sue Passero's body to be released.

"Will do, Señor Commandant," Vinnie teased. "But, let me ask you, are you sick?"

"I'm not sick," he said. "Why do you ask?"

"Hey, it's three o'clock, and you haven't bugged me, texted me, or nothing for hours." Vinnie laughed. "I thought for sure you had to be on death's door."

"Consider yourself lucky," Jack said, and hung up the phone.

With Vinnie reminding him how late it was, Jack suddenly had an idea. Since he was still suffering from not knowing what he didn't know, despite his visit to the MMH, and since he knew that the evening MLIs arrived at three, he thought it was an opportune time to chat with Kevin Strauss. Although he'd read Strauss's excellent workup on Sue several times, he still thought it might be of interest to talk with the man directly on the outside chance there was something he'd not included, perhaps thinking it was not relevant. With that in mind,

Jack snatched up the office phone once again and punched in the MLI office main number.

CHAPTER 14

Tuesday, December 7, 3:25 P.M.

Just like he had that morning, Jack entered the OCME high-rise through the back receiving bay. Arriving from the rear, he had to pass the double doors of the auditorium to get to the bank of elevators. Believing Laurie was probably in the middle of her presentation to the incoming mayor, he was tempted to poke his head in to get a sense of how it was going, but he resisted. He didn't have time. He'd connected with Kevin Strauss by phone, and Kevin had told him if he wanted to speak with him in person as Jack had asked, he had to hurry. Kevin told him he already had a full plate of investigations on his schedule thanks to an abnormally large number of death calls just prior to his arrival.

On the fifth floor, Jack passed through the bank of floor-to-ceiling glass that separated the Medical Legal Investigation Department from the hallway. It was a large room segmented into cubicles with chest-high dividers and the building's structural columns visible. The number of medical legal investigators at the NYC OCME was just about the same as the number of medical examiners, around forty, although their number varied as the turnover rate was higher.

Although he was a relatively frequent visitor to the Medical Legal Investigation Department, he'd never personally met Kevin Strauss, and he had to ask the location of his cubicle. As Jack wound his way into the room, he saw that most of the evening shift's newly arrived MLIs were on their respective phones. The department was a busy place that served as the gatekeeper for the OCME. Of the seventy to eighty thousand deaths that occurred in New York City every year, about a third of them had to be reported to the OCME because of specific and well-publicized criteria, and every one of those needed to be checked out by one of the MLIs by telephone. Not all of those had to be fully investigated, meaning a site visit, and an even fewer number would be sent in and possibly autopsied, so the MLIs served an important and vital function, which was why they had to be highly trained.

"Kevin Strauss?" Jack questioned as he walked into the cubicle where he'd been directed. A man was sitting at the built-in desk with a sizable list called TELEPHONE NOTICE OF DEATH on his monitor. When Jack first started at the OCME, these had been done on multi-sheet carbon-paper forms. Now it was all computerized. Down the hall in a much smaller room the communication clerks manned the phones 24/7, taking the "death calls" and entering the information along with a case number directly into the OCME's database. Those cases were then distributed among the MLIs.

"Dr. Stapleton?" the man questioned as he got to his feet and fumbled with a mask, trying to get the elastic straps around each ear. Jack guessed he was in his late thirties. He was boyish-appearing with a broad face and pug nose, pale of complexion with medium blond, longish hair.

"Thanks for waiting for me," Jack said. He took the chair Kevin pushed in his direction while Kevin sat back down in his. "I know you're busy, so I won't take much of your time."

"No problem," Kevin said. He swept wayward strands of hair off his face with his hand. "What's up?"

"I autopsied Susan Passero this morning," Jack began. "It was surprisingly clean. No gross evidence of pathology, more specifically no sign of coronary artery disease."

"That's surprising."

"My thoughts as well," Jack said. "Before I go on, I'd like first to commend you on the workup you did. I was impressed that you'd gotten access to the patient's digital health record. Your write-up was first rate."

"It was an easy site investigation," Kevin said. "I wish they were all like that."

"Here's the problem," Jack said. "Unless Histology comes back with a big surprise, which I sincerely doubt, I'm going to be at a complete loss, which is a problem because I'm under some pressure to come up with the death certificate sooner rather than later. There's also the rare possibility of an inheritable cardiac conduction problem, which the DNA people are looking into.

"What I wanted to ask you is if there was any other fact, or even an opinion you might have heard or just randomly thought about, that you didn't put in your report. I know I'm grasping at straws here, but it seems I'm reduced to it. Is there anything that comes to mind . . . anything at all?"

Kevin snapped his head back, trying to

get his hair out of his eyes, but it didn't work, and he was reduced to using his hand once again. He stared at Jack for several beats with glazed eyes. It was obvious to Jack that he was searching his memory banks. Unfortunately, the short pause was terminated by a negative shake of his head, and he said, "I'm sorry, but nothing comes to mind."

"Did you get a chance to talk directly with the doctor who ran the resuscitation attempt?" Jack asked. He wasn't going to name Dr. Carol Sidoti because he didn't want to admit to Kevin that he'd gone to the MMH. He had several reasons. The first was that it might have offended Kevin by his taking it as a negative reflection on the job he'd done. The MLIs knew the MEs were not supposed to do scene visits. Second, it would have raised some eyebrows, being out of the ordinary, and possibly become part of the OCME gossip mill. If that happened, there was a reasonable chance it would get back to Laurie and cause some personal fireworks.

"Yes, but only by phone," Kevin said. "She was the one who called in the death to communications, and I spoke to her briefly. When I got to the MMH, she'd left. I did get to talk with the night ED supervisor,

Dr. Phillips, who told me about what he'd heard and allowed me to read all the ED's notes, including Dr. Sidoti's write-up. What I got out of all of it was that the ED team really pulled out all the stops on the resuscitation attempt and were really bummed it wasn't successful. I didn't mention this in the report, but they tried for several hours and were reluctant to give up. I don't know if that is helpful."

"During your investigation did you get the feeling that Dr. Sue Passero was well liked?"

"Absolutely," Kevin said. "I believe that's why they continued the resuscitation long after it was obvious it wasn't going to work."

"How about with the hospital administration? Did you get any sense of her reputation with them?"

"No, not at all," Kevin said with a shake of his head. "There was no need to talk to the administrator on call."

"What about the two nurses who originally started the resuscitation in the garage? Did you talk with either of them?"

"Indeed I did," Kevin said. "I talked with Ronnie Cavanaugh at length, who's one of the MMH's night nursing supervisors. If you want to talk to anyone yourself about the case, he's the one I'd recommend, and not just because he's the one who initially found the patient slumped in her car. He's a sharp dude. I've dealt with him in the past on quite a few occasions because he's the individual who makes the vast majority of the night-shift death calls from the MMH, most of which don't require our making a site visit because he's so thorough, and he knows what we are looking for."

Kevin's praise of Ronnie Cavanaugh reminded Jack of Dr. Sidoti's equally as complimentary comments as well as her recommendation Jack should chat with him if he wanted any more details. Although at the time Jack had thought trying to meet with him would be difficult since he worked at night, he recalled Dr. Sidoti saying that the man made a habit of coming into the ED an hour or so early. Suddenly Jack had the idea of stopping by there on his way home when he planned on picking up the folders Virginia said she'd leave for him at the information desk. It seemed like a reasonable plan provided the man showed up early enough for Jack to get home around seven.

"You didn't mention the name of the other nurse involved in the initial CPR. Was there a reason?"

"I didn't think it was important," Kevin said. "I got all I needed and more from

Ronnie Cavanaugh. And she didn't stay in the ED during the resuscitation attempt. Her major contribution was to call the ED while Ronnie started the CPR. I can certainly get her name if you think it is important."

"It wouldn't hurt," Jack said. He didn't mention that he already knew her name.

"Well, is that it?" Kevin asked after a pause. "If so, I've got to get my act together here."

"One other question," Jack said. "In your report you described Ronnie as saying he'd seen some improvement initially, but you didn't explain what the improvement was."

"Oh, sorry," Kevin said. "My bad! I should have been more specific. It was that the patient's cyanosis improved. I thought it was an interesting point because it suggested to Ronnie that the resuscitation might work, but probably the brain went too long without oxygen."

"All right, thank you," Jack said, getting to his feet. "If you think of anything else at all, don't hesitate to give me a call, and I'll do the same if I think of any more questions."

"Will do," Kevin said as he also stood. The two men touched elbows, smiling at employing the pandemic method of greeting and saying goodbye.

Leaving the Medical Legal Investigation Department, Jack eyed the bank of elevators but then remembered that Forensic Biology Director Naomi Grossman's office was just down the hall. As desperate as he was, he couldn't help himself from stopping in with the hope of getting some information, even if only preliminary, about the possibility of a channelopathy. What he did get was a chuckle out of Naomi, accusing him of expecting the impossible since he'd delivered the samples only hours earlier. But his visit wasn't totally in vain. It evoked a call from Naomi to one of her laboratory supervisors to remind the team that the case was of particular interest to the chief, Laurie Montgomery. On the same call, she asked that a rapid screening test be done, which wouldn't be final, meaning defining a specific channelopathy, but would merely determine if a channelopathy existed. Jack was ecstatic, believing he'd saved himself days, if not weeks.

Pleased with himself, he descended in the elevator to the main floor and headed back toward the freight receiving dock. This time when he passed the doors into the auditorium, he stopped. Curious about how Laurie was making out and if the presentation to the incoming mayor was still in progress, he pushed open the door and stuck his head inside.

The auditorium was large enough to seat several hundred people, but Jack estimated there were only about twenty or thirty currently, all seated way down by the lectern in the first couple of rows. Since the lights were significantly dimmed, they were mere silhouettes. With so few people, Laurie could have used the conference room in the old OCME building where the weekly Thursday medical examiner meetings were held. But the old conference room didn't have the high-tech audiovisual equipment the new auditorium had, which she was using to full advantage. At the moment, Laurie was in the middle of a professionally made PowerPoint presentation about the enormous benefits the NYC OCME provided to the city.

Careful to avoid making any noise, Jack let the auditorium doors close. He'd seen the presentation a number of times and had participated in creating it. Besides, with so much on his mind, he knew he wouldn't be able to just sit there and listen. Instead, he trusted Laurie would tell him how it all went that evening. Knowing how nervous she'd been, he hoped it was going well.

CHAPTER 15

Tuesday, December 7, 4:12 P.M.

Even the short bike ride from 26th Street to 30th Street gave Jack a chance to partially clear his head. Although he hadn't learned anything by taking the time to go to the high-rise, the effort had helped to at least devise a plan of attack, as he was now committed to meeting with the nursing supervisor, Ronald Cavanaugh, or Ronnie, as he seemed to be known. If Jack wasn't able to run into the man in the Emergency Department for whatever reason, he decided he'd arrange to talk to him by phone at the very least. Although he knew from experience, when you don't know what you don't know, it was far better to interview someone in person, because there had been times when Jack had learned more from an individual's behavior and expressions than from their answers. One way or the other, he was going to make sure he chatted with the man.

After waiting for the traffic light to change, Jack rode across First Avenue and started down 30th Street, passing the OCME on his left. Turning in between several OCME Sprinter vans, he saw something he didn't expect: a nondescript, black Chevy Malibu, which he recognized as Lou Soldano's. Jack saw Lou frequently but not often twice in the same day. Getting off his bike and walking it, Jack came alongside the vehicle and noticed it wasn't empty. Lou was sitting in the driver's seat with his head back, mouth ajar, obviously fast asleep. Although he was surprised to see Lou, he wasn't surprised to see him sleeping. The man notoriously burned the candle at both ends, especially on nighttime homicides, like the Seton case, and frequently took catnaps whenever the opportunity presented itself.

Rather than wake Lou immediately, Jack took his bike inside and secured it. He then came back out to the street. Knowing that sometimes Lou would wake up with a start, ready for combat, he very quietly rapped on the driver's-side window. When Lou didn't stir, he knocked harder. Finally, he pounded against the glass with the base of a closed fist, which finally had the desired effect. Lou straightened up, blinked a few times, then opened the car door.

"What year is it?" Lou asked, trying to be humorous. "Sorry! I was told by security that you'd just gone out, so I took the opportunity for a few winks."

"How am I so lucky?" Jack asked rhetorically. "I usually don't get to see you twice in the same day."

"I know, but I needed to talk with you. Something unexpected came up."

"Like what?"

"This might take a few minutes to explain," Lou said. "What say we head up to your palatial office?"

"Be my guest," Jack said, pointing toward the loading dock.

As they were rising in the slowpoke back elevator, Lou yawned loudly, smacked his lips, and said that he hadn't felt as tired since yesterday. Jack dutifully laughed.

Inside Jack's office, after Lou took off his winter coat and Jack took off his corduroy jacket, Jack shoved his desk chair in Lou's direction. With its casters on the slick floor, it thumped decisively into Lou, who grabbed it and sat down backward, resting his forearms on the backrest. Jack leaned his rump against the L portion of his desk and placed his hands on his hips, staring at Lou expectantly. In his mind, Lou was not acting like himself, and Jack was intrigued.

"Well, what's up?" Jack questioned.

Lou cleared his throat and asked him if he'd given the case that Lou had witnessed that morning any more thought.

"You mean the Seton case?" Jack questioned. "No, I haven't. To be honest, the Sue Passero case has been dominating my mind. Why do you ask?"

"There's been a development you should know about."

"Oh?" Jack said. "And what might that be?"

"A suicide note has turned up."

"Really?" Jack questioned with disbelief. This was unexpected. In his forensically oriented mind, Jack was confident that the death had been a homicide. It was nearly but perhaps not totally impossible for Sharron Seton to have shot herself considering the bullet's path. "I'm rather surprised, to say the least. Has it been authenticated?"

"Yes, preliminarily by a handwriting expert in the crime lab."

"Why wasn't it found during the initial investigation?"

"It was found in the wife's appointment book."

"By whom?"

"The husband, Paul Seton."

"Have you seen it?"

"Yes, I have," Lou said. "It struck me as authentic as well. It seems that Sharron Seton has suffered with depression most of her life, for which she has been treated since she was a teenager. She was on a whole pharmacopoeia of medications that were constantly being adjusted up and down. Apparently becoming pregnant was something she couldn't deal with and said as much in the note. Paul claims he didn't know she was pregnant. All he knew was that her depression had taken a serious turn for the worse of late, and she was refusing to see her therapist, which they had been arguing about, and which was why he was lately sleeping in the guest room more often than not."

"I guess this puts more of an onus on your investigative team," Jack said.

"No doubt," Lou said. "What I'm wondering is if this new information will influence your feelings about the manner of the death and how you will sign it out. Obviously, that is going to be critical."

"Not really," Jack said, groaning inwardly. "From a forensic point of view and the preponderance of evidence I can show, it's a homicide, not a suicide." The writing was on the wall that the case would involve a lengthy trial, reminding him how much he hated trials.

"I think the defense attorney is going to request another autopsy," Lou said. "Does that bother you?"

"Not in the slightest," Jack said. "It's certainly within the defendant's rights. I get the feeling you want this Paul Seton fellow acquitted."

"Obviously," Lou said. "But only if he didn't do it."

"If there was no break-in, he did it or was an accessory," Jack said. "The only other possibility is that he did it in collusion with his wife. Maybe he was convinced it was in his wife's best interests, but she couldn't do it herself."

Lou half laughed and waved Jack off with his hand. "That's creative but unlikely."

"From my perspective, it's at least a possibility, no matter how small the probability. Nonetheless, I'm signing the case out as a homicide, though, suicide note or not. Sorry, my friend."

"That's okay, you have to do what you have to do. I was hoping the suicide note might change your mind. Be that as it may, let's move on as long as I am here. What's the story with the Passero case that had you bamboozled this morning to the point of suspecting uxoricide?"

"What the hell does *uxoricide* mean?"

"Wife killing," Lou said. "When you've been involved with murder as long as I have, you hear all the words for it, even the Latin ones."

"You'll be happy to know, I'm leaning away from the husband," Jack said with a self-deprecating smile. "But I'm still confused. Even after an autopsy, I'm without a cause or mechanism of death, and if anything, the situation is bothering me more now than it did when you and I talked earlier. I have to confess to you and you alone that I even took the time to go over to the Manhattan Memorial to do a little investigating. I talked to the doc who headed up the team that tried to resuscitate her, as well as a few other people."

"Uh-oh!" Lou voiced. "Am I sensing you are back to playing detective? You aren't supposed to be let out of your cage to investigate anything."

"I know it's frowned upon," Jack said with a guilty smile. "And generally, it is not needed because we have such a talented Medical Legal Investigation team."

"I happen to know directly from the big boss that it's more than frowned upon."

"Well, maybe so, but I'm counting on you not to mention it to the big boss," Jack said.

"Besides, the dangerous part of being a detective is when it comes down to *who*, whereas I'm merely caught up in *how*. If, when I figure out the *how* and it points to a *who*, you will be the first to know."

"Excuse me," Lou said. "Now you're splitting hairs. If there is a *who* involved, they're not going to take kindly to you looking into a *how*. Believe me! Good God! How do I allow myself to get into these weird conversations with you? For your own good, stay here in your fortress and keep away from the MMH. I distinctly remember having to save your ass over there. Besides, I happen to know that you have more than enough work to keep you busy 24/7 right here. But let's move on. I've been thinking all day about what you told me this morning about Laurie, the kids, and your mother-in-law. If you want my advice, mothers always seem to know what's best for their children. It's in their genes. Don't make waves!"

"That's easier said than done," Jack responded. "Part of the problem is that Laurie is adapting so well to being chief here at the OCME that she is bringing home the same *my way or the highway* attitude. Under those conditions it is becoming difficult not to make waves."

"Okay, I hadn't considered that. I can see

how that kind of attitude could become a problem."

"But you are probably right. I'm going to take your advice to heart and let things slide on the home front. At least this Sue Passero case is giving me something to occupy my mind."

As Lou got to his feet Jack's mobile rang. When he glanced at the screen, intending to silence the ringer, he saw it was Naomi Grossman. Instead, he took the call. As he did so, he waved to Lou to hold up a moment.

"Well, your persistence has paid off," she said with no preamble.

"What did you find?" Jack asked, his hopes rising.

"Now this is just a preliminary screen, as I told you, and we will be following up with the usual full amplification process. But the rapid screen tells us that there is no inheritable genetic evidence of any channelopathy. None of the usual mutations are present."

As quickly as Jack's hopes rose, they now collapsed.

"I trust that providing this information as fast as we have helps your case," Naomi said. "And, needless to say, we'll get you the full report as soon as it is available, but it is going to be a week or two."

Jack thanked the department head, terminated the call, and tossed his phone onto his desk. He looked over at Lou with a hangdog expression. "That was really my last hope of science providing the *how*," he said. "There's still histology and toxicology, but my intuition tells me that both are going to be negative as well."

"Is it time for me to get involved?" Lou asked.

"Not yet," Jack said. "But maybe soon."

"I'll be waiting," Lou said. "I've got to run, but you stay put here." He waved over his head as he walked out into the hallway and turned toward the elevators.

Jack looked back at the stack of unfinished autopsy folders and then over at the equivalent stack of histology slide trays. He knew he should get some of his looming paperwork done, but after the short talk with Lou and getting the disappointing call from Naomi, he was reinvigorated about the Passero case.

Picking up his phone again, Jack texted Laurie. Undoubtedly, she was at still at 421 continuing her attempt to indoctrinate the incoming mayor. In the message he told her he was leaving for the day so that she wouldn't be looking for him when she returned to the office. When he was finished, he pocketed his phone and pulled on his jacket. From one of the coat hooks on the back of the door, he took down a backpack and put it on. His plan was to stop at the MMH, pick up Sue's folders at the information desk, head to the ED to try to meet up with Ronnie Cavanaugh, and then go home. As he walked down toward the elevators, he mused about how nice it would be to take advantage of the mild weather and get a run in on the basketball court that evening. Some good competitive exercise would do wonders for his patience on the home front.

CHAPTER 16

Tuesday, December 7, 4:55 P.M.
Jack used the same route as he had at midday, yet the ride was far different since the sun had set. It was also rush hour with an increase in vehicular traffic as well as the number of bikes. The congestion was particularly significant all through Midtown and didn't ease up until he was well beyond the Ed Koch Queensboro Bridge. The crosstown traffic was the worst, making him feel particularly thankful to be on his bike, cruising past all of it.

At the front of the MMH, he used the same NO PARKING sign to lock up his bike and helmet. Jack wanted to make his visit to the information booth as quick as possible after apparently having been seen by chance in the lobby earlier that day by Martin Cheveau, resulting in the confrontation with Marsha Schechter. Luckily, when he approached there was no one waiting, and he was able to walk directly up to the counter.

"Hi, I'm Dr. Jack Stapleton, and I believe there should be a parcel waiting for me from Virginia Davenport." As he spoke, he slipped off his backpack and unzipped it.

His comment precipitated a brief questioning conversation between the two women and the one man behind the counter. Then one of the women seemed to have recollection, as she snapped her fingers and bent forward, briefly disappearing from Jack's view. But instead of producing a package, she extended a mere letter-sized envelope toward him, along with a pleasant smile. Confused, Jack took the envelope. Written on it in an elegant cursive was his name and, in the lower left-hand corner, TO BE PICKED UP.

Getting his thumb under the flap, Jack opened the letter and pulled out a note written in the same style. It was short and sweet, merely stating that Virginia was sorry, but when she returned to Sue's office, the committee folders had vanished, and she had no idea where they had gone or who could have taken them. As a final postscript he read: *If you have any questions, I'm here at least until 6:00 p.m.*

Jack cursed under his breath, believing Marsha Schechter was to blame. The missing folders also underlined his sense that things had hardly been copacetic regarding Sue Passero's relationship with the administration and some of her committee co-members. Why else would those folders be taken from her office, particularly the one labeled HOSPITAL MORTALITY ARTICLES OF INTEREST? It certainly didn't contain any private letters or communications.

Whether the disappearance of these folders could in any way be related to her death, he had no idea. He also knew it was associated more with the idea of who, not how, yet if he was going to be denied whatever insight the folders might have provided, he was going to have to come up with an alternative plan.

He thanked the woman, and because of his disappointment, he made a beeline to the doctors' cloakroom, where he intended to get himself a white lab coat and leave his backpack. Doctors who were not part of the salaried staff used the cloakroom to leave their outer coats and don a doctor's coat. Obtaining one was a way for Jack to blend in, which he wanted to do now that he was going to make a quick return visit to the Internal Medicine Clinic. Jack had used this ruse in the past when he'd visited the MMH for investigative purposes. If possible, he wanted to avoid being spotted by Cheveau or anyone from administration or security, particularly any of the those who had interrupted him in Sue's office earlier that day.

Now clothed in a highly starched white doctor's coat plus a hospital-issued pandemic mask, he set out for the Kaufman Outpatient Building. To complete his disguise, he'd added Sue Passero's hospital ID, hanging its lanyard around his neck while being careful to have the photo turned toward himself.

Although the hospital's lobby had been relatively busy, the clinic building was quiet. As Jack rode up to the fourth floor, he was happy to be the only person in the elevator.

As it was now after five P.M. and the clinic supposedly closed, there were far fewer patients waiting, although still a few. At the patient sign-in desk there were none, and the two remaining clerks were seated and chatting among themselves.

"Excuse me," he said, approaching the counter. "I'm looking for Virginia Davenport."

Almost simultaneously the two clerks pointed behind them at the scheduling office where Jack had found her earlier that day. Approaching the door, he briefly debated whether to knock but decided against it, remembering it had been unnecessary earlier. Inside he found her at her desk. The other two scheduling secretaries had apparently left for the day.

"Still at it?" he questioned.

"It's the burden of being the clinic supervisor," Virginia explained. She took off her headphones and then reached for her mask.

"Hold on," Jack said. "Are you fully vaccinated against Covid-19?"

"I am, and boosted, too," she said.

"So am I," he said. "Are you comfortable putting our masks aside if we maintain a bit of distance?"

"I am," Virginia said. "Thank you. I can't wait for this pandemic to be over. Anyway, I assume you got my note."

"I did," Jack said as he pocketed his mask. "And I do have some questions. I was disappointed, to say the least, not to get the folders, particularly the Mortality and Morbidity one. Do you have any idea why they were removed or who might have taken them?"

"No idea whatsoever. To be honest, I wouldn't even know where to start if I was tasked to find them."

"I was afraid that might be the case," he said. He grabbed one of the room's desk chairs, wheeled it over closer to Virginia's desk, and sat down. "First of all, I'm sorry I didn't get to say goodbye earlier and thank you again for your help."

"No need to apologize," she said. "I certainly didn't expect another thank-you. Excuse me, but I notice you're wearing a doctor's coat. Does that mean you might be willing to see some patients for us since we are now shorthanded?" She smiled to indicate she was teasing.

Jack chuckled at the thought. "I don't think you'd want me. It's been a long, long time since I saw live, internal medicine outpatients — not since I was a medical student in the previous century. I also borrowed Dr. Passero's ID." He turned the ID around so Virginia could see the photo.

Virginia leaned forward to look at the photo and smiled anew, shaking her head in the process. "You two don't look very similar."

"True, which is why I'm careful the photo doesn't show," Jack said. "I'm wearing this outfit and using the ID to try to blend in and not be recognized by anybody in administration. MMH presidents and I truly don't get along. After you left me in Sue's office, I was confronted by Marsha Schechter, who had me escorted off the premises by security."

"Oh, my! Why would she do that? Don't

you have the right to be here investigating Dr. Passero's death?"

"I do indeed," he said. "And I could force the issue, but it would take court action and that takes time. With this case, I don't have the benefit of time, as I explained earlier."

"It still seems oddly personal for the president of the hospital to be involved," she observed, wrinkling her brow.

"It *is* personal," Jack said. "No doubt about it. In the past, I offended the MMH Microbiology Laboratory Department head, Dr. Martin Cheveau, by pointing out his administrative incompetence. He probably told her that the previous president and I got along like oil and water. Kelley thought of me as a provocateur par excellence, as I have had a habit of unearthing serious problems over here at the MMH. Dr. Cheveau was with Marsha, along with Peter Alinsky."

"Oh, my goodness," Virginia said. "Maybe that's an explanation of why those folders disappeared, particularly the one with all the Mortality and Morbidity Committee material. There were a lot of letters critical of Mr. Alinsky in that folder. Okay, now it's starting to make sense."

"I'm sensing that you don't expect the folders to reappear," Jack said.

"I don't."

"That's unfortunate," Jack said. "As I mentioned earlier, I'm at a loss to explain the cause of Dr. Passero's death, so I'm interested to learn what I can about her recent circumstances and perhaps her mindset, particularly in relation to her ongoing antagonism with this Alinsky fellow. You said she wasn't depressed, but you described her as frustrated."

"I think that is a fair description," Virginia said. "Dr. Passero was a very strong-willed and dogged individual, and she didn't shy away from making her feelings known. Unfortunately, that rubbed certain people the wrong way, particularly Mr. Peter Alinsky, who I believe is rather chauvinistic as well as headstrong. But that's only my opinion from what I heard from Dr. Passero. She never said any of that specifically. It's just what I deduced."

"I get it," Jack said. "And I remember from our conversation earlier that there was a surgeon and an anesthesiologist with whom she locked horns as well."

"Yes. For sure. It was an ongoing battle with Dr. Carl Wingate, Chief of Anesthesia, and Dr. Henry Thomas, Chief of Surgery. Dr. Passero believed that both were firmly in cahoots with Mr. Alinsky. Both are part of the M and M Task Force, the M and M Committee, and the Outpatient Reorganizing Committee, at least in name. Dr. Passero was under the impression, from my understanding, that they merely rubber-stamped whatever Mr. Peter Alinsky decided."

"Interesting," he said. "What about the emails that were in the folders, which I presume were written to these people? Do you have other copies, or do you know if any exist? What about emails and texts? Didn't Dr. Passero use email?"

"Yes, of course, but she never shared her passwords with me."

"That's too bad," Jack said. He thought for a moment and then asked, "Was Dr. Passero on her own with her committee battles or did she have any support?"

"She had one person who was definitely on her side," Virginia said. "Cherine Gardener."

He perked up with the prospect of a source that might help fill the gap created by the missing folders and letters and electronic communications. "Who is she?"

"She's a charge nurse on the orthopedic floor. She was appointed to the M and M Committee about six months ago. My sense is that she and Dr. Passero came to agree on a lot of issues, particularly about which cases were presented at the committee hearings and maybe more strongly about which cases were not presented. That was another one of Dr. Passero's major gripes: A lot of cases she thought should be brought up but weren't. Cherine also was clearly not a fan of Mr. Peter Alinsky, which I believe particularly endeared her to Dr. Passero."

"This sounds like someone I should chat with," Jack said. "What's she like? Is she personable?"

"I've only spoken with her over the phone but that was on multiple occasions. If you want my honest opinion, my sense is that she is a very good nurse but a private person. I'd describe her as a no-nonsense, serious individual who runs a very tight ship. I think that was the main reason that Dr. Passero was drawn to her and valued her support and opinion. Dr. Passero was also very organized and thorough."

"I get the picture," Jack said. Virginia's description of the woman reminded him of his sixth-grade teacher who had ruled the classroom like a third-world dictator. He wasn't particularly encouraged, but he realized he didn't have too many other possibilities to learn about what had been going on in Sue's life recently. For that, speaking with

Cherine Gardener sounded opportune, especially since she served on the key M and M Committee. Whether she'd be forthcoming was the question.

"I have her mobile phone number," Virginia said. "If you like, I could find out if she is on duty."

"That would be very helpful," Jack said. "Especially if I could possibly have a word with her while I'm here."

She picked up her mobile phone from the edge of her desk and made the call. As she did, she transfixed him with her piercing dark eyes that looked to be all pupil with just a slight rim of dark brown iris. Jack could hear the electronic sound of Cherine's phone ringing and heard when it suddenly stopped. But he couldn't make out Cherine's voice. Virginia introduced herself and there was a short conversation back and forth about Sue Passero's passing and how tragic and what a shock it was. Then Virginia asked if Cherine were in the hospital on duty. "The reason I'm asking," she continued, "is because I am presently talking with Dr. Jack Stapleton, the medical examiner looking into Dr. Passero's death, who happens to be the husband of Dr. Passero's closest friend. He'd like to speak to you for a few minutes if you could spare the time."

Virginia kept staring at Jack as she listened. He could hear Cherine talking but couldn't make out her words. Virginia nodded few times as she listened and then finally said, "Okay, fine! I understand. I'll tell him. Bye!" Then to Jack she said, "She is here on duty and can probably manage to talk with you briefly provided you go right over this minute."

"Okay, terrific," he said. He was mildly surprised and pleased. Virginia's sign-off had suggested otherwise.

"But here's the story," she said. "She's off duty at seven and is about to give report for the shift change. So time is of the essence."

"Got it," Jack said. He stood up and gave the desk chair a shove back where he'd gotten it. "Out of curiosity, is there a way to get over to the main hospital building without having to go through the main lobby to get to the elevators? I'd rather not risk running into Cheveau, Alinsky, or Schechter if at all possible."

"Yes, there is," Virginia said. "Go up to the sixth floor here. There's a pedestrian bridge. Ortho is on the eighth floor in the Anderson Building."

"Oh, perfect," he said. "And thank you again for your time."

"I hope she's helpful," she said. She stood

up as well.

"So do I," Jack said. He got out his mask, put it on, and waved back at Virginia as he hustled out into the main part of the Internal Medicine Clinic.

CHAPTER 17

Tuesday, December 7, 5:42 P.M.
When Jack got up to the sixth floor of the Kaufman Outpatient Building, he understood why there was a pedestrian bridge over to the main hospital. The entire sixth floor was composed of various procedure rooms for such things as colonoscopies and cardioversions, which could be done as inpatient or outpatient. Once in the Anderson Building, he found it simple to locate the main elevators, and within minutes he walked out onto the ortho floor.

As it was now nearing 6:00, the orthopedic floor was busier than he expected, since he'd seen a sign in the hospital's lobby limiting visitation due to the Covid pandemic. Besides visitors, there were also more patients being ambulated after joint replacements than he anticipated since he was aware that elective surgery was still not being encouraged for the same reason. To add to the chaos, Food Service was in the process of delivering the evening meal. All in all, it was a bit more pandemonium than Jack would have liked to see, including at the busy central desk where there were upward of a dozen doctors, nurses, and nurses' aides busily working. From experience, he knew it was the charge nurse who was tasked to monitor it all and keep it all under control. He feared that Cherine Gardener wouldn't be able to manage much of a conversation.

Making sure Sue's ID photo was pointing toward himself to avoid any questions, Jack approached the nearest person at the central desk. He guessed he was a resident as he was dressed in scrubs, including a surgical cap with the usual stethoscope casually slung around his neck. Jack smiled to himself. As he had gotten older, hospital residents seemed to get younger. The youthful man was busy typing into a monitor, seemingly oblivious to the chaos around him.

"Excuse me," Jack said to get the man's attention. "Can you point out Cherine Gardener?"

Wordlessly the man gestured toward the last person in the mix that Jack would have chosen to be her. From Virginia's description of her character, he'd envisioned someone in Sue Passero's league, meaning athletic, muscular, and commanding. Instead, the individual the man had pointed at was a mere slip of a woman, whom Jack estimated weighed a hundred pounds give or take five. The only similarity to Sue was her short, spiky hairstyle that Jack guessed needed very little attention, which was how Sue had explained her preference for the look. Cherine had a lighter complexion than Sue, at least from what Jack could see visible above her mask. She was obviously a charge nurse who was hands-on. As he got closer, he could see she had a sprinkling of freckles over the bridge of her nose and on her temples.

After he waited for her to finish a phone call, he introduced himself. She responded by loudly calling out to one of her nursing colleagues, explaining she was going to be in the chart room for a minute or two. She then waved for Jack to follow her.

The chart room was behind the central desk next to the supply room, and when the door closed behind them, a welcome hush ensued. Although still called the chart room, there were no longer any hospital charts. The MMH, like all modern hospitals, was fully computerized, so the room's name

210

should have been updated to the computer room or data entry room. But, like at many hospitals, the staff persisted in calling it the chart room out of entrenched habit. Inside, three people were typing into monitors, two men and one woman. The only sounds were the clicks from the keyboards, although muffled remnants of the tumult outside at the central desk and hallway could be heard through the closed door. Jack guessed the three were attending surgeons as they were dressed in long white doctor's coats over civilian dress like himself.

"Sorry about the chaos out there," Cherine said as she pointed to a desk chair for him and took one herself a distance away from the other occupants. "It's always like this at this time of day."

"I remember it from when I was in clinical medicine many moons ago," Jack said.

"How can I help you?" Cherine asked, ignoring Jack's comment. "As I mentioned to Virginia, this has to be very short since I'm pressed for time with a full house and report starting in minutes."

As quickly as he could, he reiterated who he was and why he was there. He told her that toxicology and histology results were still pending, but meanwhile he felt the need to investigate a bit more the circumstances around Sue's untimely passing.

"I'm not sure I understand," Cherine said. She knitted her brows and stared back at Jack intently. "What do you mean by 'the circumstances around her death'? I was told she had a heart attack in her car in the garage."

"I'm not completely sure what I mean myself," Jack admitted, sensing the woman's impatience, giving credence to Virginia's description of her as a no-nonsense, serious person. "I suppose I mean her mindset and mood. I understand from Virginia that Dr. Passero was frustrated in her dealings with certain members of the administration about committee assignments and responsibilities. Is there any possibility from your vantage point that she could have been seriously depressed?"

Cherine gave a short, mirthless laugh. "You are right about her frustration, but believe me, she wasn't depressed. Not in the slightest! If anything, she was becoming progressively determined over these last few weeks, and she didn't hide it."

"Are you talking about her wanting to become a member of the Mortality and Morbidity Task Force? Virginia talked about that being important to her."

"Absolutely! There's no doubt in the

slightest," Cherine said. "Dr. Passero was gearing up to make a big stink about being denied an appointment to the task force. She fully intended to force the issue, which is why her death is such an organizational tragedy as well as a personal one. She saw getting on the task force as the only way to initiate much-needed reform, because the task force essentially dictates what the M and M Committee does. The task force picks which cases, out of all the deaths and episodes of adverse outcomes, will be discussed at the committee hearings and which cases will be ignored. And I was going to help her. I've only been a member of the M and M Committee for a bit more than six months, but it's clear to me, as it had been to Dr. Passero for several years, that the committee is hardly equipped to find out which hospital deaths and which adverse patient outcomes could have been prevented by instituting systemic reforms. That's what the committee was intended to do. Instead, it's devolved to be a kind of sham, just going through the motions to fulfill the Joint Commission requirements to maintain hospital accreditation."

Jack was taken aback by the women's vehemence and her emotion. He could see it in her dark eyes and hear it in her voice, which had grown increasingly more strident despite her effort at keeping her volume down. Jack gathered from her obvious passion that she was undoubtedly as much a reformer as Sue Passero apparently had been, meaning the two women could very well have been perceived as provocateurs or agitators. "This is all very interesting," he said while trying to rein in his ricocheting thoughts and orient himself around this new information. He couldn't help but recognize its potential significance if it turned out that a cause and mechanism of Sue's death remained elusive and the idea of a homicide had to be considered. "Virginia alluded to some of what you are saying, but I don't think she is quite aware of the details. She did mention three people who Dr. Passero bumped heads with, namely Peter Alinsky, Dr. Carl Wingate, and Dr. Henry Thomas."

Cherine let out another brief laugh of derision. "She got that right! That's the triumvirate, which was what Dr. Passero and I called them. But it was more than just bumping heads with them. Dr. Passero couldn't abide any of them, and they control who gets appointed to the M and M Task Force. All three of them are serious narcissists. Funny you should mention Dr. Thomas. I was just talking with him on the phone after he finished his final case for the day. He's an orthopedic surgeon, and I'm forced to interact with him pretty much on a daily basis. To give you an idea of what he is like, he called to inform me that his patient is a VIP, and he ordered me to treat him as such. Can you imagine? I'm a charge nurse. I treat all patients as VIPs. The nerve."

"So, he's in Surgery right now?" Jack asked, thinking this might be fortuitous. With what he was learning, it seemed Dr. Thomas was someone he'd love to chat with to get a sense of how the administration felt about Sue Passero's advocacy inclinations.

"Probably," Cherine said. "He was calling from the post-anesthesia recovery room." She then leaned forward and, after a quick glance to make sure the attending physicians weren't paying them any attention, she said in a lowered voice, "I can tell you a major secret that Dr. Passero recently told me, which will surprise you, as it did me. She was worried that a medical serial killer has been active in this hospital over this past year. No, let me correct that: She was more than worried. She was convinced."

The moment Cherine made this revelation, an alarm bell sounded in Jack's mind. All at once, the cache of articles about medical serial killers he had seen in Sue's folder titled HOSPITAL MORTALITY ARTICLES OF INTEREST assumed a new significance. More important, what it said to him was that if there was a serial killer and the killer found out that Sue was convinced of his or her existence, Sue surely would have been courting mortal danger. For Jack, this new information seriously raised the possibility of Sue's death being homicidal.

"When did Dr. Passero tell you this?" Jack asked.

"Four or five days ago," Cherine said. "It was Thursday or Friday. Probably Thursday."

Immediately following dropping her bomb, Cherine intently stared back at Jack as if challenging him to refute what she had just revealed. After clearing his throat to help organize his thoughts, he asked in as calm a voice as he could conjure, "Well, I do find that interesting for lots of reasons. But tell me, did Dr. Passero explain to you exactly why she was convinced there was a medical serial killer on the loose?"

"Oh, yeah," Cherine said decidedly, but keeping her volume low. "She even showed me some data she'd put together from material she'd gathered from the M and M Task Force and the Hospital Compliance

Committee. I was initially quite skeptical, but she was beginning to convince me."

"And you think you're the only person she told about this," he said.

"Yes," Cherine said. "The only other possibility is Virginia Davenport. She and Dr. Passero worked as a team running the Internal Medicine Clinic, but truthfully, I would have been shocked if they discussed this subject. Dr. Passero was not the talkative type about such issues, especially something as serious as this. By any chance, did Virginia mention anything to you that might make you suspect she'd been told?"

"No, she didn't. Not at all, and she gave me the impression of being entirely forthright."

"She's the only one I can imagine might possibly have known," Cherine said. "Over the last few days, Dr. Passero and I discussed who should be told. It wasn't an easy decision. Without hard-and-fast proof, she was afraid to bring it to the attention of the muckety-mucks for fear they would see it more as a publicity nightmare and just try to bury it. Nor did she want whoever was responsible to be forewarned in case the only way to figure out who it was, was to catch the person in the act."

"Did she suspect anyone in particular?"

"No. That was what was the whole problem. She didn't know if the murderer was a doctor, a nurse, an aide, or part of the housekeeping crew. All these people have frequent access to patients."

"Okay, okay," Jack said, his mind racing. "Tell me exactly why she was so convinced a medical serial killer was operating here." He inwardly smiled at his ironic verb choice.

"I can't right now," Cherine said. "It's a complicated story involving hospital data and statistics and policy, and it will just take too long to explain. I'm already late for report as it is, and to be honest, I'm exhausted. But this is the last day of my three-day, twelve-hour shift cycle. I'm off tomorrow, and if you are available sometime during the day after I've had some sleep, I can explain it all then."

"Fair enough," he said, although he was disappointed. He fumbled in his pocket to get out one of his business cards. He circled his mobile number and handed the card to Cherine. "Call when convenient tomorrow. I truly appreciate you talking with me, as busy as you are. Thank you for your time, and I look forward to hearing from you tomorrow."

They both got to their feet.

"I think it is important someone knows,"

Cherine said. "When I heard that Dr. Passero had passed away and after I got over the initial shock, I was at a complete loss of who I was going to approach, for obvious reasons. In a way, you are an unexpected savior."

"It is a role I cherish," Jack said. "It's what we medical examiners do: We speak for the dead."

Cherine nodded and then flew out the door, disappearing in a flash and leaving Jack standing by himself. He turned and looked at the three attending physicians, half expecting they would have expressions of shock from having overheard Cherine's exposé. Instead, they were still engrossed inputting data into the hospital's insatiable computer bank, oblivious to what he had just been told.

Checking his watch and seeing it was now just after 6:00, Jack thought it was time to head down to the Emergency Department in hopes that Ronnie Cavanaugh had shown up before his shift began, as Dr. Sidoti suggested he was wont to do. With the idea there was a possible medical serial killer on the loose, talking with Ronnie and finding out more about Sue's death seemed even more crucial. Yet, as soon as he thought about heading down to the ED, he remem-

219

bered that Dr. Henry Thomas might be serendipitously available for a quick casual chat.

With that thought in mind, Jack hurriedly left the chart room and wended his way back toward the main bank of elevators. Having an idea of what the hospital administration thought of Sue Passero had taken on new significance, particularly from a member of what Cherine had described as the triumvirate. Knowing what he did about the generally cool relationship between the clinical staff and the administrative staff of a chain hospital, Jack wasn't particularly worried about word getting back to Laurie that he was out in the field investigating.

The orthopedics floor was even busier now with more visitors. As he progressed toward the elevators, another thought occurred to him concerning the possibility of a medical serial killer operating in the MMH, and he took out his mobile phone. Using his contacts, he put in a call to Bart Arnold, the OCME Medical Legal Investigation Department head, hoping to catch him before he left for the day. Jack was pleased when the phone was picked up on the second ring.

"I'm glad I caught you," Jack said with no introduction. "I have a favor to ask."

"I've got one foot out the door," Bart said. "What do you need?" Bart and Jack had a superb working relationship, as each appreciated the other's talents. They frequently worked hand in hand on complicated cases. At the same time, Jack wasn't about to tell the man where he was at the moment and what he was doing, for fear he'd take offense. He was understandably protective of the MLI Department prerogatives.

"I'd like you to get me some figures," Jack said. "Do you think it is possible to find out the monthly death rates called in to the OCME from the Manhattan Memorial Hospital over the previous two years?"

"I don't see why not," Bart said. "Can this wait until tomorrow?"

"Truthfully, the sooner the better," Jack said.

"If the team isn't too busy tonight, I'll have someone start looking into it. I imagine I'll have something for you tomorrow. Will that work?"

"Perfect," Jack said.

CHAPTER 18

Tuesday, December 7, 6:14 P.M.

As Jack descended in the elevator, he thought briefly about Lou Soldano's warning not to play detective because it was dangerous. He knew Lou was correct, as evidenced by that horrendously scary shoot-out that Jack had been reminded of when he'd crossed the pedestrian bridge to the MMH's garage. At the time he had definitely been playing detective. Yet in the current situation, he could deny that he was taking any risk since all he was doing was gathering evidence to decide whether a detective like Lou Soldano was needed. Jack still didn't know whether Sue's death was a homicide, but this new information that she had believed that a medical serial killer was on the loose seriously raised its specter. If Sue's death ultimately turned out to be a homicide, the suspected serial killer would have to be a prime suspect. All in all, the nature of Sue's professional world was far different than Jack had originally suspected, especially considering the reputed mutual animus between her and the triumvirate.

He got off on the third floor. He knew exactly where he was going because he'd visited the MMH surgical complex on several occasions when he'd been guilty of playing detective in the past. After pushing through a couple of swinging doors, he immediately turned right, entering the surgical lounge. The room, as he remembered it, was about thirty feet square with windows that faced one of the inner courtyards. The furniture consisted of a couple of well-worn vinyl couches, a handful of unmatched chairs, a number of dictating stalls, and a TV stand. The TV was tuned to the evening news with the volume turned down. At the far end, away from the entrance, was a kitchen nook with a refrigerator and a coffee machine.

With the operative day drawing to a close, the atmosphere was relaxed despite the room being fairly crowded with more than a dozen people all dressed in the same unisex scrubs. Some had hats or hoods, some didn't. No one was wearing a mask, although many had one dangling around their necks. Jack took his off, counting on everyone being vaccinated. Most of the occupants were involved in isolated conversations, probably rehashing the events of the day, which created an overall buzz. A few were reading while others were dictating. From his personal experience as an eye surgeon, he knew that the egalitarian look of the environment was a sham since the OR was one of the most hierarchical domains of the hospital, with the surgeons and anesthesiologists invariably thinking of themselves as the top of the heap.

Making sure Sue's photo was still pointing inward, Jack approached the nearest pair. "Excuse me," he said, interrupting two women. "Can you tell me if Dr. Henry Thomas or Dr. Carl Wingate are available?"

The pair looked at each other questioningly. Then the first said, "I believe I saw Henry go into the locker room," whereas the second said, "I saw Dr. Wingate duck into OR eight."

"Okay, thank you," he said. "Sorry to interrupt."

"No problem," the first individual said. As Jack walked away, he could hear the second person question, "Who the hell is that?" Jack didn't hear the response because he was already nearing the men's locker room door. Without hesitation he pushed inside.

He knew what to expect in the locker room. Surgeons who were involved in long, stressful surgeries, like cardiothoracic surgeons, often took showers, whereas those surgeons who were accustomed to short cases, like eye surgeons, didn't. Orthopedic surgeons were somewhere in between. What Jack was counting on more was that in his experience orthopedic surgeons tended to be a happy, congenial group and easy to talk with.

The locker room was rather crowded, as was the lounge area, but he didn't have any trouble finding Dr. Henry Thomas. The first person he asked pointed him out. Encouragingly, the orthopedic surgeon was whistling softly as he buttoned his shirt while standing in front of his open locker, suggesting his last case had gone well and that he was in good spirits. Jack's initial impression just by watching the man for a few beats was that Henry Thomas was an intense, competitive, probably reasonably athletic individual, not so different from himself. His stature was a bit shorter than Jack's six-foot-one, but stockier, with a threatening spare tire. His eyes were dark and deeply set, and he had a shock of dark brown hair with a bit of salt and pepper over his ears.

"Dr. Henry Thomas?" Jack began, sounding upbeat and cheerful.

Henry stopped whistling and gave Jack a once-over. He then asked in a surprisingly serious, confrontational tone, "Who wants to know?"

Mildly taken aback by this reaction, Jack successfully suppressed his inclination to be sarcastic, as it suggested the man had either a guilty conscience, a wildly inflated ego, or both. Instead, Jack said with a forced smile, "I'm Dr. Jack Stapleton from the medical examiner's office. I've been tasked with looking into the death of Dr. Susan Passero, and I'd like to ask your opinion about the circumstances."

"My opinion?" Henry raised the pitch of his voice as if it were a silly question. "About the circumstances?"

"Yes," Jack said. "We are having some difficulty determining the exact cause of her death, and it's forcing us to look into the whole situation leading up to her demise. I've learned that she was at odds with a few people about her hospital committee memberships here at the MMH."

"Who suggested this?" Henry demanded, obviously taking offense.

"I'm not at liberty to divulge," Jack said. "What I can say is that you were named as

one of the people who feuded with Dr. Passero."

"Who told you this?" Henry demanded
again. He was now clearly angry. "Let me
guess: Cherine Gardener?"

"As I said, I'm not at liberty to divulge
that information."

"Well, let me tell you something about Dr.
Passero. She was one hell of a left-winger
troublemaker, wanting to be on every goddamn committee of this hospital and constantly searching for a reason to get on her
high horse and complain. Her causes were
endless and constantly expanding, like the
oppression of Native Americans, the history
of slavery, the plight of trans people, you
name it. I could go on and on. I tell you,
she was one big pain in the ass and far too
much a part of this goddamn woke culture.
She and Cherine Gardener were out to ruin
this hospital's reputation. Those of us who
care about this venerable institution were
equally committed to putting an end to it
all."

With angry gestures, Henry went back to
dressing, seemingly having had as much of
a conversation with Jack as he could tolerate. Jack watched him. The man radiated
hostility, yet was it enough to drive someone
to homicide? Jack had no idea, but it cer-

227

tainly added to his theory that Sue's work environment and reputation among the staff was far different than he'd imagined from knowing her socially.

When Henry finished dressing, he turned to Jack, who had waited patiently. The man was clearly angry. His face had even significantly reddened. "All I can say is good riddance to Dr. Passero! The MMH is better off without her."

"I did hear that she had a strong desire to join the Mortality and Morbidity Task Force, but that you and other people were opposed to the idea. Would you like to comment on that issue?"

Henry's facial flush deepened. Jack tensed, thinking the man might take a swing at him. But the moment passed. "I'm finished with this conversation," he spat. He slammed his locker door and strode off without looking back.

Jack glanced over at the nearest doctor, also in the process of dressing, who was only about six feet away. He was considerably younger than Dr. Thomas and had obviously witnessed the confrontation between Jack and Henry.

"I couldn't help but overhear your conversation," the younger doctor said. "Don't mind Dr. Thomas! He can be quixotic, to say the least, and often flies off the handle. On the plus side, he's a damned good trauma surgeon and oversees a well-run orthopedic department."

"He seemed rather quick to take offense," Jack said.

"It's his narcissistic style. Don't take it personally."

"Have you heard about Dr. Susan Passero's death?" Jack asked.

"Yes, of course. I didn't know her, but the word is that she was a respected internist. Rather sad, I'd say."

"Dr. Thomas seemed to feel she was a firebrand. Had you ever heard anything along those lines?"

"Can't say I have," the man said, "but then again, I try to steer clear of hospital politics."

"Thanks."

"No problem."

Turning around, Jack headed back out to the lounge. He wondered if he'd see Henry Thomas perhaps having a coffee or talking with a colleague, but he was nowhere to be seen. Jack had in mind to give him one of his cards in case he came to his senses and was willing to have a more reasonable conversation. After checking his watch to make sure he'd still have plenty of time to hopefully meet Ronald Cavanaugh down in the ED, he approached another pair of women conversing near the windows. The courtyard was lighted with hundreds of small, white lights carefully wound around the trunks and out all the branches of the leafless trees, anticipating the upcoming holiday season.

"Excuse me," Jack said. "I'm sorry to interrupt, but I'm looking for Dr. Carl Wingate. A few minutes ago, I heard that he was in OR eight."

"He's out now," one of the women said. "That's him over at the coffee machine." She pointed toward a very heavyset man of medium height dressed like everyone else: in scrubs and surgical hat. His face was full and rather doughy with a bushy mustache. He had just added cream to a freshly filled mug while chatting with a somewhat slimmer colleague.

After thanking the woman, Jack approached. As he got closer, he could see Carl had distinctive red patches on his cheeks just below his eyes, as if he was wearing rouge. Having been reminded of the approaching holiday season by the festive lights in the courtyard, he imagined that Carl Wingate with a white full beard could make a convincing Santa Claus.

"Excuse me, Dr. Wingate," Jack said. "I hate to butt in, but can I have a moment of your time?" After the short and turbulent conversation with Henry Thomas, Jack was more prepared on this occasion come what may. He already had one of his medical examiner cards in hand, and he extended it toward the anesthesiologist. The man took the card with his free hand.

"I'll catch you later," the colleague said, and headed toward the door.

As Carl examined Jack's card, Jack went through the same initial introduction he'd given to Henry Thomas, including the issue and apparent controversy about Susan's hospital committee assignments. As he was talking, Jack's active and forensically creative mind reminded himself of something that he hadn't thought of until that moment. Of all people in the hospital, an anesthesiologist might be the most knowledgeable person concerning the best ways to kill someone in a fashion that would be difficult to detect. In a very real sense, every case of general anesthesia required putting a patient into a near-death state, maintaining them, and then saving them at the end of the procedure.

After examining Jack's card, Carl gestured to give it back.

"No, that's yours to keep," Jack said, holding up his hand, palm out. "It will make it easy for you to contact me if, after our chat, you remember something else you think might be significant."

"I can't imagine that will be the case," Carl said. In sharp contrast with Henry Thomas, he spoke with no discernable change in his demeanor after hearing Jack's introduction. Instead, he merely shrugged, pocketed the card, and then added, "Who have you spoken to so far about Dr. Passero?"

Jack relaxed a degree. Up until that point he'd wondered if Carl was going to react in a fashion similar to Henry Thomas. Jack was relieved when it appeared that wasn't going to be the case. "I spoke briefly with Dr. Thomas," Jack said, watching Carl closely. He purposely didn't mention Cherine Gardener.

"I was told that the doctor had a heart attack," Carl said, maintaining his composure.

"So far there is no indication that was the case," Jack said. "And a preliminary screen has ruled out a channelopathy. At this point, we are proceeding as if it wasn't a natural cause, especially since it has come to our attention that there was some bad blood between her and others on the staff, particularly you, Dr. Thomas, and Peter Alinsky."

For a few beats, Jack remained silent and watched Carl carefully. The only reaction to Jack's potential accusation was a slight quivering of the man's mustache.

"Are you asking me or telling me?" Carl said after a pause.

"I suppose a combination of the two," Jack said. "Is that a fair description of the relationship between you and Dr. Passero? Was there bad blood?"

"Let me say this: Dr. Passero was, in my estimation, a rabble-rouser. Perhaps she had good intentions, but the resulting turmoil she invariably evoked was not in the best interests of this institution. If you have already spoken with Henry, I'm sure he communicated the same message but probably with more vehemence. You'd also get the same message from Peter. The woman might have been a good internist, but she was a pain in the neck about all her trivial and sundry causes and complaints."

Jack nodded. He got the message, but he had to restrain himself from asking if Carl felt the possibility of there being a medical serial killer on the loose was trivial. He would have liked to ask, but he was afraid to because he knew that if it were true, it could be anyone on the staff, from janitors to heads of departments like Carl Wingate. After all, as he had reminded himself, who could be a more efficient serial killer than an anesthesiologist? Instead, Jack said, "I understand there was a particular contention about her wish to be on the Mortality and Morbidity Task Force. Is that true and, if it is, why was she denied a seat?"

"Did you ask Dr. Thomas about this?"

"I did, but he didn't answer. Instead, he abruptly terminated the conversation."

"I'm not surprised. We all found Dr. Passero an insufferable bane, but particularly Dr. Thomas. None of us wanted her on the task force for the simple reason that if she were, she'd gum up the works for the entire M and M Committee. The task force is a purposely small, decisive working panel whose major role is to choose the cases to be presented at the full committee meetings. If she were on the panel, she'd be insisting every death and every patient mishap be presented, which is clearly impossible because there is only so much time for the full committee hearings. If the task force can't do its job, nor can the M and M Committee, and if we have no M and M Committee, we lose our hospital accreditation. And if we lose our accreditation, there can be no Medicare and Medicaid payments. If that happened, we'd be forced to close our doors. It's as simple as that.

"Listen, it's been a pleasure to meet you, but I've got to get back to the OR because there are still several cases going on that I'm supervising." Carl put his full coffee cup down on the counter as if he had lost the taste for it. "If I think of anything else that you should know about Dr. Passero, I have your card, and I'll call."

"I'd appreciate that," Jack said. He was about to pose one last question to inquire about the M and M Task Force in terms of its membership, but without another word nor even another glance over his shoulder, the Anesthesia Department head abruptly headed for the exit and disappeared.

After pausing for a moment, dumbstruck at the precipitous ending to the conversation, Jack followed. His brief tête-à-têtes with both doctors had not been what he'd expected, and he wondered if a conversation with Peter Alinsky would be similar if he dared to try to contact the man. Once out in the hallway and by looking through the windows of the double swinging doors leading into the OR complex, he could see Wingate heading down the central corridor. It was, Jack thought, rather surprising how similar the interactions had been with both doctors, although the anesthesiologist hadn't gotten quite so demonstrably irritated.

He shrugged. He hadn't learned much for his efforts besides that Sue Passero wasn't universally as liked and respected as had been suggested by Carol Sidoti and Kevin Strauss. If a homicide had to be considered, such a fact could very well take on a definite significance in terms of motive, especially with how emotional Henry had grown.

Jack regretted not learning anything new about the medical serial killer issue. Although he had been severely tempted to bring it up with both Henry and Carl, he felt he couldn't, at least not until he had more information. Before approaching anyone with such a horrendous possibility, he would have to have at least some confirmation whether it was true, above and beyond hearing that Sue was convinced it was. He also wanted to have more of an idea of who it might be. From having glanced at the articles in her Hospital Mortality folder, he knew that anyone on the hospital staff, from orderlies to nurses to doctors, had the opportunity to be a serial killer since all had direct access both to patients and the potential means. With the sheer number of articles that Sue had amassed, there were many more medical serial killers than he realized, and those were only the ones who had been caught. Jack shuddered at the idea of how many additional people there might have been over the years who hadn't been exposed simply because hospitals are places where death is anticipated, so it isn't always questioned as much as it ought to be. On top of that was the issue of private equity getting progressively more involved in medicine and wanting to squeeze as much profit as possible out of hospitals by reducing the number of nurses per patient and thereby reducing supervision, making the deed easier for would-be medical serial killers.

Heading toward the elevators while replacing his pandemic mask, Jack tried to get his mind back on track. Although he felt he'd accomplished what he could by taking the time to talk to the two doctors, now it was time to visit the ED in hopes of running into Ronald Cavanaugh. Jack knew he had to return to his primary mission: figuring out the cause and mechanism of Sue's death.

CHAPTER 19

Tuesday, December 7, 6:31 P.M.

As Jack descended in the elevator toward the ground floor, he found himself shaking his head at what a successful diversion he'd managed to find. Since arriving at work that morning and stumbling across Sue Passero's case, the annoying issues on the home front seemed picayune, even a bit egotistic, and certainly manageable, so in one sense he'd accomplished his goal. Yet it was at a definite emotional cost. He'd had many complicated cases in his forensic career, but none had been as emotionally troubling as the one he was now caught up in, especially if his gnawing intuition turned out to be correct. If he was totally honest with himself, he'd have to admit that from the moment he closely examined Sue's heart and was struck by its normality, the fear that he was dealing with the homicide of Laurie's friend was a distinct possibility.

Occupied with these thoughts, he wasn't as attentive as he should have been to his surroundings as he crossed the main hospital lobby on his way to the Emergency Department. It wasn't until he'd practically bumped into his archenemy, Martin Cheveau, that he remembered he was supposed to be vigilant about not being recognized at the MMH, especially having already been officially escorted out of the hospital not that many hours before.

"Jack Stapleton?" Martin questioned in an artificially high-pitched voice. He had his hands spread wide, palms up in total amazement. "What the hell are you doing back here after having been summarily kicked out?"

"I guess it's a kind of addiction," Jack said. "It's such an intriguing place. I just can't stay away."

"You are impossible!" Martin said, angrily changing his tone. "And I can assure you that the president is going to hear about this."

"I would hope she has more important issues to deal with than a civil servant medical examiner legally investigating the death of one of the hospital staff. Besides, I'm almost done, and I'll be on my way, so no need to bother yourself."

Martin sputtered as Jack walked on, heading for the ED. Clearly infuriated, Martin hurried after him. Now, even more angered from being ignored, he said he'd see to it that the president lodged a formal complaint with the mayor's office. Jack winced at this specific threat, knowing it was a possibility, as it had happened in the past. But the damage had been done, and he couldn't think of any way to appease the irate Microbiology Department head.

To Jack's relief, Martin finally gave up as Jack pushed through the swinging doors into the ED. But Jack's relief was short-lived as his phone buzzed, indicating he'd gotten a text. When he looked at the screen, he saw it was from Laurie. Pausing, he guiltily read the message. It said the meeting with the mayor-elect was finally over, and although she had gotten his text, she wondered if he was still in the building.

He texted back he was on his way home and that he looked forward to hearing about how it had gone. He certainly didn't mention where he was now. When that text got a thumbs-up from Laurie, he pocketed his phone and continued on into the ED main waiting room. As he expected, the ED was far busier now than it had been on his earlier visit. He wasn't surprised, knowing that symptoms people had ignored all day often drove them to Emergency around evening mealtime.

Approaching the main desk, Jack was encouraged. He'd planned on having to ask for Dr. Carol Sidoti, but it wasn't necessary. She happened to be there behind the desk, talking with several of the triage nurses. As soon as she broke off her conversation, he called out, "Dr. Sidoti, I decided to follow your advice and try to have a chat with Ronnie Cavanaugh. Have you seen him this evening?"

"Yes, I have," Carol said. "I spoke with him minutes ago."

"Do you have any idea where he might have gone?"

"I believe he went into the ED lounge." She pointed at an unmarked door behind Jack in the corridor that led into the hospital proper. "Since the pandemic started, he's been changing into scrubs for his shift."

After flashing the woman a thumbs-up, Jack headed toward the indicated door. As he pushed into the room, he thought about how much things had changed with emergency medicine since he'd been a resident. Back then it had been called the emergency room and was one large room with curtained-off bays. More important, it had been manned by medical and surgical residents. Now it was called an Emergency Department or ED and was comparatively enormous, divided into separate areas depending on the degree of emergency involved. Emergency medicine had become a specialty in and of itself, composed of highly trained, board-certified emergency medicine doctors, like Carol Sidoti. Residents now merely pitched in to help. In a hospital the size of the MMH, the ED was almost a separate hospital under the same roof, with its own imaging and laboratory facilities as well as overnight beds so patients could be observed for twenty-four hours without having to go through the entire hospital admission process.

In contrast to the surgical lounge, the ED lounge at that time of day was deserted. It also had no windows as it was in the middle of the ED. The furnishings, however, were similar with a couple of nondescript couches, the same variegated mixture of chairs, and a small kitchenette. A flat-screen TV had the evening news on but no sound. In hopes of finding someone, Jack pushed into the men's locker room and immediately saw a muscular, angular man pulling on a scrub top who he estimated was in his mid-thirties. He was already wearing the scrub pants.

"Ronald Cavanaugh?" Jack questioned.

"None other, but I prefer *Ronnie*." He smiled. His voice was a pleasant baritone. To Jack's ear he had a mild Boston accent.

"*Ronnie* it is," Jack said. He eyed the man, who was of equivalent height. To Jack, he looked as Irish as his name suggested with dark brown hair, narrow blue eyes, an upturned nose, high cheekbones, and a prominent, round chin. His complexion was on the pale side and mildly flushed, as if he'd just stepped in from the cold. A small scattering of tiny pockmarks on his cheeks suggested he'd had a bit of acne as a teenager.

Jack introduced himself while handing Ronnie one of his cards. He asked if he could have a moment to talk about Dr. Susan Passero's death.

"No problem," Ronnie said after glancing at Jack's business card. "Provided it doesn't take too long. My shift starts at seven on the dot, but since I've already taken report from the day shift supervisors, I'm golden until then." He then picked up a mask he'd placed on the bench seat that ran down between the lockers and held it up in the air. "Want me to put on my mask?" he asked cheerfully.

"Not if you are vaccinated and boosted," Jack said.

"I am indeed," Ronnie answered. "Of course."

"Same here," Jack said, removing his mask as well.

"Where would you like to chat, here or out in the lounge?" While Ronnie spoke, he gestured at the long bench. It was a similar setup as in the surgical locker room.

"Here is fine with me," Jack said.

The two men straddled the bench, facing each other about six feet apart. Ronnie had gone back to studying Jack's card.

"You know, your name rings a bell," Ronnie said. "And now I remember why. I read about you in the *Daily News* a couple of years ago. You were involved in exposing a pathologist over at NYU who'd murdered his girlfriend. Am I remembering correctly?"

"I played a minor role," Jack said. "The real hero was a pathology resident."

"What I particularly remember is that you play pickup basketball and exclusively use your bike to get around the city. Is all that true?"

"Yes," Jack said simply.

"I played a lot of basketball when I was in

the navy," Ronnie said. "It's great exercise but tough on the knees."

"You were in the navy?" Jack asked. He didn't want to waste time talking about himself.

"Yes, I was and retired as IDC, independent duty corpsman, on a fast-attack nuclear submarine out of Groton, Connecticut," Ronnie said proudly. "Going into the navy was the best decision of my life. It's where I got my initial medical training. The service even helped me get my veterans bachelor of science in nursing degree. But getting back to the issue at hand, I have to tell you that in the four years I've been here, you are the first medical examiner I've met. I'm accustomed to dealing with your field people on all the ME cases. It slips my mind what they call themselves."

"Medical legal investigators," Jack said.

"Right!" Ronnie responded. "And I assume you know that last night I talked at length about Dr. Passero's death with Kevin Strauss. He's someone I've dealt with many times before, mostly on the phone, since it is invariably me as the night nursing supervisor who calls in ME cases. He's a sharp fellow and certainly knows his stuff."

"I'm aware that you met with him," Jack said. "And I have spoken with him about the case. I have to say, he was similarly complimentary about you."

"We worker bees appreciate each other," Ronnie said with a laugh and a wave of dismissal. "I'm not looking for compliments. My point here is that I don't think there is anything I can add to what I told him. I'm sorry if I can't be more helpful."

"You might be correct," Jack agreed. "But we know more now about Dr. Passero's case than we did last night. A full autopsy has been done, but no evidence of any cardiac pathology was found, meaning we have no cause and mechanism of death as of yet. The heart and the coronary arteries appeared entirely normal on gross inspection. Although histology is still pending, I doubt it is going to shed any light on the situation."

"Really?" Ronnie questioned. "That's a shock." His narrow eyes narrowed further, and his brow creased dramatically. "A completely normal heart? How can that be? I thought for sure it was a heart attack. So did everyone in the ED, especially knowing she had diabetes."

"We were surprised as well," Jack said, "which is why I am here."

"This is totally unexpected," Ronnie said. "What about a stroke or a channelopathy?

We were never able to get a heartbeat, which I think I mentioned to Kevin Strauss."

"There was no sign of a stroke, and a channelopathy has been preliminarily ruled out," Jack said. He was impressed. He remembered Carol Sidoti describing Ronnie as clinically astute as well as personable, and Kevin Strauss calling him a sharp dude, and Jack now had to agree on all accounts. It was encouraging and a relief after the not-so-pleasant conversations with the two doctors. Jack was about to continue by asking Ronnie exactly how things unfolded minute by minute in the garage when he held up. Ronnie had momentarily closed his eyes and cradled his head in both hands, letting out a plaintive sigh while massaging his eyes. Respectfully, Jack waited. It was apparent that Ronnie was struggling.

A moment later, Ronnie dropped his hands, blew out a deep breath, and looked directly at Jack with watery eyes. "Sorry about this," he apologized. "I'm not being very professional, but I'm afraid I'm in uncharted emotional territory for me. I've never tried to resuscitate a friend and a colleague, and, let me tell you, dealing with it ain't easy, especially since it wasn't successful. I've been involved in more than my share of code blues, as it is incumbent on me to attend every code that occurs when I am on duty. And I have become pretty successful at handling them. Actually, I can say *very* successful. But the one time it really counted, I couldn't make it happen."

"I'm sorry to make you relive it," Jack said. "But I'm sure you can understand the possible importance. In forensics, it is critical to have a cause and mechanism of death, and at the moment, we're at a loss."

"Of course I understand. But I do have to admit that I find talking about this difficult. Sue was one hell of a marvelous doctor, and she really appreciated us nurses as the ones who are in the trenches supplying the hands-on care of the patients. And I can tell you that type of recognition is not universal with all doctors. On top of that, she was also just a warm and gracious person. I'm going to miss her, as will a lot of other people."

"Are you saying you were friends, as well as colleagues?" Jack asked with a bit of surprise. Such information was akin to the surprise he felt learning about the animosity of Thomas, Wingate, and Alinsky, just in a more positive direction.

"Oh, of course," Ronnie said. "If she needed anything at night with one of her inpatients, she always called me directly on my mobile. She even invited me not too long ago to her home over in Jersey where I met her husband, Abby, and their two children."

"That's somewhat of a coincidence," Jack said. "My wife and I were also friends of hers, and we've been to her home in Fort Lee as well, and she and her husband have been to our home here in the city."

"I'm not surprised," Ronnie said. "She was friends with just about everyone except some of the MMH muckety-mucks."

"That's interesting to hear you say. And I'd like to discuss that more, but first I'd like to concentrate on the details of when you first found Sue in the garage."

Ronnie checked his watch, a gesture that wasn't lost on Jack, who asked, "How are you doing with the time?"

"Not bad. I have another ten minutes until I have to clock in."

"All right, I'll try to speed things up," Jack said. "Take me back to when you arrived last night in the garage. Did you see anyone or any vehicles out of the ordinary? Take a moment to think back."

"I don't need to think about it," Ronnie said. "Last night when things had quieted down, I went over it in my mind. But it was just like normal. I always arrive about an hour before the shift change, which is earlier than most night-shift people, so there was no incoming traffic. I'm allowed to park my Cherokee in the doctors' reserve section on the second floor near the pedestrian bridge, provided I make a point of leaving just after seven in the morning. That's why I happened to catch Sue slumped over her steering wheel. I'm familiar with her BMW since we had occasionally run into each other. When I saw her car, I thought: *Wow, Sue's sure leaving late tonight,* and then I happened to catch her silhouette."

"Do you remember seeing anyone else around you or her car at that point?"

"Not around her car," Ronnie said. "I did hear someone coming along behind me, which turned out to be Barbara Collins from the GYN floor. She was the one I ended up flagging down to lend a hand."

"Okay. What happened next?"

"I stopped and watched Sue for a second. I couldn't see her all that well, but it suddenly dawned on me she wasn't moving. Wondering if she was having car trouble, I hustled over to her driver's-side window. That's really when I could see she was probably unconscious."

"Okay," Jack said. "What did you do then? Try to remember everything. Was she moving at all, like clutching her chest or completely still?"

"I didn't wait to see if she was moving," Ronnie said. "I rapped on the glass, though *pounded* on it is probably more accurate. She, of course, didn't budge, so I tried the door, which was unlocked. In the next second, I could tell she was in extremis, as she tumbled out of the car into my arms. I yelled for Barbara as I laid her on the pavement. Sue wasn't breathing, had no pulse, and her color was strikingly pale around her mouth and her conjunctivae were slate blue. Without hesitation, I started CPR with chest compressions."

"I understand you told Kevin Strauss that Sue's color definitely improved."

"Yes, and I told the ED docs the same. Almost immediately her cyanosis pinked up rather dramatically. I was very encouraged, which only made the final outcome that much more difficult to accept. On other code blues that I've been on, when something like that happened, it usually was a harbinger of a positive outcome. Why it wasn't in this case is probably going to haunt me forever." For a moment Ronnie stared off into the near distance. He sighed again before redirecting his attention to Jack. "Sorry," he said.

"No problem," Jack said. "I can appreciate it's not been easy for you. Tell me, did
the ED people get to the scene in short
order?"

"Oh, yeah," Ronnie said. "While I was doing the chest compressions and the mouth-
to-mouth at a thirty-to-two ratio, Barbara
called the ED, and they were there in
minutes, including several nurses and a doc.
They also brought oxygen and an ambu
bag, and Sue's color improved even more.
We had her down in one of the trauma
rooms in under five minutes, continuing the
CPR all the way. There they started a serious resuscitation attempt and, believe you
me, they tried their darndest."

"That was my impression when I talked
with Dr. Sidoti," Jack said. "How are we
doing with the time?"

Ronnie checked his watch once again.
"Not bad. I've got another five minutes."

"Okay, good," Jack said. "Before I leave
you alone, I'd like to go back to your curious statement regarding Sue's being friends
with everyone except some of the MMH
muckety-mucks. Can you elaborate on
that?"

"Sure," Ronnie said. "It's common knowledge that a relatively small number of
higher-ups thought Sue was a troublemaker

bent on tarnishing this institution's good name. Recently, they'd become a bit desperate, since there was a rumor she might get on the hospital board. The irony is that from my perspective, and most other people's, she was more concerned about the hospital's reputation than just about anyone, which was the motivation for her activism. She practically wanted to be on every hospital committee, and when she served on one, she really took it seriously, in contrast with most doctors."

"When you say higher-ups, I assume you are talking about the triumvirate of Thomas, Wingate, and Alinsky," Jack said, feeling like he had to speed up the conversation to get more in before Ronnie had to leave. Normally he made it a point not to lead people when he was doing a forensic interview.

Ronnie's jaw slowly dropped open in surprise at Jack's comment, and then he snickered. "Whoa! You have been busy! I'm getting the impression you have talked about all this with more people than just your medical legal investigator."

"I'm committed," Jack said. "It's why I'm here, trying to get all the information I can if it turns out I can't come up with a cause of death. This is actually my second visit here today. Earlier I'd checked out her car and spoke with Virginia Davenport, who was quite helpful."

"Virginia will be a good source for you since she and Sue worked together closely but only vis-à-vis Outpatient Clinic affairs," Ronnie said. "I was going to suggest someone else who you would find more interesting for your purposes, but I'm getting the impression there's no need. I'm sensing that you've already spoken with Cherine Gardener. Am I right?"

"I did talk with Cherine Gardener," Jack said, surprised that Ronnie had guessed. "How did you know?"

"I knew as soon as you used the term *triumvirate.* It was a private and somewhat derogatory moniker that just Sue, Cherine, and I used as a kind of code for the three people you named. But we used it exclusively just among ourselves."

Jack's ears perked up with the idea that the triumvirate of Thomas, Wingate, and Alinsky had spurred a triumvirate of Sue, Cherine, and Ronnie, meaning that perhaps Sue had shared her concerns about a medical serial killer with Ronnie as well as Cherine. The problem was how to find out. He was in the same bind he'd felt with Thomas and Wingate and didn't know how to proceed.

"Was Cherine helpful?" Ronnie asked.

"Shockingly so, although she could only spare a few minutes from her duties," Jack said. "But she's off tomorrow and has offered to get in touch with me to give me all the details she didn't have time to explain. She did say that Sue was gearing up to make a big production about being denied a seat on the Mortality and Morbidity Task Force. I assume this is something you know about."

"In intimate detail," Ronnie said with another half laugh. "When I have more time, I can tell you all the ins and outs about that. It's all rather involved, with oversized egos in jeopardy, if you get my drift."

"When will you have some free time?" Jack asked.

"I'm working tonight, obviously. Then I have three nights free. We could arrange something maybe Wednesday or Thursday during the afternoon. I don't need much sleep. I'll send you a text, so you'll have my number."

"That would be terrific," Jack said. "In terms of getting together, the sooner the better. In the meantime, are you the only nursing supervisor on the night shift?"

"That's an affirmative," Ronnie said. "There used to be two of us, which worked a lot better than just one supervisor. But a bit over a year ago, AmeriCare, in their infinite wisdom, cut us back to a single night nursing supervisor at the same time they reduced the nurse-to-patient ratio from one-to-five to one-to-eight. It's all about saving money, if you know what I'm saying. But the reality is that it's made my job nearly impossible. At night, I'm it! I'm where the buck stops for just about anything that happens because there is no administrator on duty. There's one on call, but they hate to be called, so everything that happens in this whole damn hospital falls on my shoulders."

"That sounds stressful," Jack said. "Do you work exclusively nights? Is it your choice?"

"It *is* my choice," Ronnie said. "I mean, I complain about it, as do the other night supervisors because it's stressful, but we like there being no administrators here with their big egos. Also, there's not so many private doctors around demanding this and demanding that. They can be as bad or worse than the administrators."

"You said earlier that you speak often with Kevin Strauss. Why is that the case? Are you often involved in reporting medical examiner deaths?"

"Absolutely," Ronnie said. "I'm called in on every death. It's why I'm so familiar with what constitutes a medical examiner case and what doesn't. When it is a medical examiner case, I'm invariably the one who calls it in to your people."

"The private physician or the staff physician isn't involved?"

Ronnie gave a short laugh. "Rarely! As I said, being the night nursing supervisor, the buck stops on my desk. Whether it's a patient falling out of bed or kicking the bucket at three o'clock in the morning, I'm the one who handles it from A to Z."

Ronnie again glanced at his watch and, seeing the time, he got to his feet. "Uh-oh! Sorry, but I have to break off this chat to clock in. We can continue tomorrow or Thursday, your choice. I'll give you a call tomorrow when I wake up, and we can arrange it. Ciao!"

"One last quick question," Jack said. "I've heard that the M and M Task Force was a small committee. How small, and by any chance do you know everyone who sits on it?" Jack remembered from Virginia that Thomas, Wingate, and Alinsky were members.

"It's very small," Ronnie said as he slammed his locker and spun the combination dial. "It's only four of us."

"Wow, that *is* small!" Jack marveled. "And you said 'us.' Are you on the committee?"

Ronnie gave another short laugh. "I'm not only on the committee, but for all intents and purposes, I *am* the committee. The other members are the triumvirate, but they are members in name only. I have to do everything myself and just get their rubber stamp of approval. I'm the one who plans and schedules the full M and M Committee meetings, which is a royal pain in the butt. And it was why I was heavily championing Sue Passero's appointment. She would have helped and carried her weight, which I can't say for the three other muckety-mucks."

Brandishing Jack's card to indicate he'd be in contact, Ronald Cavanaugh started for the door. Jack reached out and grabbed his arm, pulling him to a stop. Ronnie looked down at Jack's hand on his forearm with a quizzical expression. It was as if the gesture caught him totally unawares. "I really have to go," he said. "I make it a point never to be late, something I learned in the military."

"Of course," Jack said. He let go of the man's arm. "But I heard that the M and M Task Force was also responsible for generating the death ratio. Is that true?"

"Supposedly," Ronnie hurriedly said. "But actually, the death ratio is generated by the hospital computer on a regular basis with all the daily input vis-à-vis hospital deaths. The task force just approves it for the Compliance Committee to indicate that the M and M Committee is keeping an eye on it."

"How has the death ratio been running, say, over the last year?" Jack asked, trying to get in one last question despite Ronnie's need to leave. With the idea of a possible active medical serial killer on the loose, it suddenly occurred to him that the statistic would be particularly telling and might have been what had convinced Sue.

"The death ratio has been terrific," Ronnie said as he pulled open the door to the hallway. "In fact, during this year it's fallen to less than point-eight-five, which is damn good for an academic medical center that deals with referrals of difficult cases from other hospitals. In fact, it's the best in New York academic centers, including Columbia, Cornell, and NYU. Ciao! I'll call you sometime tomorrow afternoon." In the next instant the door closed, and the nurse was gone.

For a few minutes Jack remained where

he was, straddling the bench, marveling that the diversion he'd managed to find was getting progressively more complicated. He'd learned a lot from Ronnie and would undoubtedly have to learn more if he ended up having to pursue both Sue's death as a homicide as well as the serial killer issue, especially if they were somehow related, with a putative serial killer feeling that Sue had to be eliminated to keep from being exposed.

Going back over the conversation with Ronnie, he regretted not having brought up the medical serial killer issue to get his take on the possibility, as integrated as he was in the MMH world. The reason he didn't was the same reason he didn't bring it up with Wingate or Thomas: Everybody was a suspect. But if Sue, Cherine, and Ronnie had been an opposing triumvirate, it seemed only reasonable they would have shared such a momentous and serious concern. At the same time, he couldn't be sure Ronnie knew about it, as it had only been four or five days, with an intervening weekend, since Sue had told Cherine her theory, and Cherine had been adamant she was the only one Sue had told. And now Jack had learned that the mortality ratio for MMH had been going down over the past year. How could there be statistical evidence of a very active medical serial killer, meaning deaths of people who weren't supposed to die? Cherine had suggested Sue's belief was based on statistics, but if Ronnie was right about the mortality ratio going down, it seemed far-fetched indeed.

With a sigh, Jack got to his feet. There was no doubt Ronnie and Cherine had been the two most fruitful sources so far, and he was certainly glad he'd made the effort to come back here. Yet despite what he'd learned, he couldn't help but admit that he still didn't know what he didn't know. The key issues were going to have to wait until tomorrow, when he hoped to learn from Cherine exactly what statistics had made Sue convinced a serial killer was on the loose, and he'd find out if histology and/or toxicology were going to provide a cause and mechanism for Sue's death.

Leaving the ED, he headed back toward the main lobby with the hopes he wouldn't again run into Martin Cheveau or Alinsky or, worse yet, President Schechter. As it was now almost seven, he thought the chances were slim but not impossible. And as he rounded a corner his worst fears were realized. Beyond the crowd waiting for an elevator he caught a glimpse of the hospital president, Cheveau, and several black-suited security guards coming rapidly in his direction. Immediately reversing direction, Jack hustled back toward the ED, fearing that he'd hear his name called out. Thankfully, that didn't happen, and he was able to exit the ED through its entrance. To avoid another scene, he then hurried around the hospital to retrieve his bike at the front.

CHAPTER 20

Tuesday, December 7, 7:25 P.M.

After traversing most of a darkened Central Park, Jack exited on the West Side at 106th Street and rode the distance to his brownstone. There he hefted the bike up onto his shoulder and climbed the stoop. When he reached the top, he turned around to gaze wistfully over at the small park across the street with its illuminated basketball court whose lights he'd paid to have installed. A game was in progress, and even from that distance he could make out the identities of a number of the players. He felt a definite tug to join, as he loved to play, but regretfully it wasn't to be. He had decided on his way home that he was going to do a bit of research that evening on medical serial killers and wanted to get to it in short order. He would have preferred to have Sue's folder, so he'd be sure to read the specific articles she favored. Obviously he couldn't, but he guessed he'd be able to find on the internet most of the articles she'd printed out. He was also interested in calling Abby to see if he had any knowledge of Sue's trials and tribulations at the hospital, and if she had ever spoken of the possibility of a serial killer stalking its halls. He doubted it, though, because Sue had said on several occasions that she had a hard-and-fast rule not to bring home any work-related issues.

Once inside, Jack put his bike in the utility room he'd created when they renovated the building. He hung it by its front wheel next to his son's bike. Also stored in the room was the sporting equipment that he and JJ used in Central Park on weekends and occasional summer evenings when it stayed light until almost nine. He put his empty backpack in one of the cubbies that lined the opposite wall.

He then started up the stairs. Their apartment occupied the top three floors. On the lower three floors they had fashioned six rental units, which paid most of the expenses of the building, including a sizable portion of the mortgage. Jack considered his buying the mid–nineteenth century structure a number of years ago one of the best decisions of his life. As he climbed, his quadriceps complained because of the exercise from riding the bike all day. Just like that morning, on the way home he'd had the opportunity to aggravate a few very serious bicyclists by challenging them speed-wise as they rode around the northern portion of Central Park.

Once inside the apartment he could hear *PBS NewsHour,* which Dorothy watched religiously every night. The sound drifted down the open stairway from the fifth floor where the kitchen, dining room, living room, family room, and study were located. The fourth floor, where he was now passing, had the guest suite and Caitlin O'Connell's apartment. Caitlin was their long-term nanny, whom they adored and couldn't live without since both Jack and Laurie worked every weekday from early morning until early evening.

As the fifth floor progressively came into view, he saw his mother-in-law parked on the couch in front of the TV. JJ and Emma were sitting at the table with JJ playing *Minecraft* and Emma watching. It was a reassuring sight, particularly because it was evidence of the great strides Emma was making in dealing with her autism. Her case was still being handled by the board-certified behavior analyst organization that Dorothy had originally found, which was providing daily behavioral, speech, and physical therapy. As Jack neared the top of the stairs, he could see Caitlin in the kitchen, who he guessed was cleaning up after making the kids and Dorothy their evening meal.

"Hi, everybody," he called out, but only Caitlin returned his greeting. Undeterred, Jack went over to the table to kiss the tops of the children's heads and give each a hug. Both made an effort to resist contact, as they were concentrating on the structure JJ was making. Jack didn't take it personally and made it a point not to interfere since he was pleased to see Emma's concentration and interaction with JJ.

"There's some pasta in the fridge, if you are interested," Caitlin called out from behind the kitchen island.

"I think I'll wait for Laurie," he responded as he turned his attention to Dorothy. As usual at that time of the day her thin form was clothed in her black velvet robe with matching mules. "Hi, Nana, anything interesting on the news?" he asked in a cheerful tone to make social contact and possibly a bit of conversation.

"This newest Covid variant is spreading like wildfire," Dorothy said in her high-pitched voice, without taking her eyes off the TV screen. "It's terrible." She was always particularly caught up in and enthralled with bad-news stories of any sort.

"It is a very transmissible variant," Jack said. Then he bit his tongue so as not to add: *All the more reason to get the goddamn vaccine.* For a beat he waited to see if there would be any more interaction, but, like the children, Dorothy ignored him.

Feeling like he'd at least made an effort at being sociable, he walked down the short corridor and went into the study. He sat down on his side of the used leather-topped partners desk he and Laurie had recently found online and booted up his laptop. While that was in progress, he pulled out his phone and placed a call to Abby. Knowing that the burial was to be that evening, he expected to have to leave a voicemail and was surprised when Abby picked right up.

"I'm glad you called," Abby said without preamble. "I was just about to call you and apologize for cutting you off earlier this afternoon."

"No need to apologize," Jack said. Once again, he was mildly caught off guard. He never expected an apology. "I was hesitant to call, knowing you and the kids would be busy with the burial."

"We're all done," Abby said. "I have to give credit where credit is due. The funeral home was terrific and accustomed to Muslim traditions, which they followed to the letter. I'm glad to say that Sue has already been put to rest, Allah bless her soul. So thank you for releasing her body so quickly."

"You're welcome," he said, not knowing what else to say. He tried to block memories of his own struggles back when his family perished. It had been the most difficult time of his life.

"The kids, my parents, Sue's sister, and I are here as a family celebration of Sue's life."

"That's terrific," Jack said. "Being with family is important after such tragedy. Listen, I won't take much of your time, but, if you don't mind, I'd like to ask you if Sue had been talking at all with you recently about everything that was going on at the hospital with her committee responsibilities and such."

"She didn't like to talk about hospital affairs or any of her patients," Abby said. "At the same time, I know she was frustrated of late about getting another committee assignment, but I don't know the details. Nor did I want to know, because I knew she really wouldn't want to explain it fully."

"I remember her saying she didn't like to bring hospital business home," Jack said, "so I'm not surprised. But there is one specific issue I'd like to ask you about, but please keep it just between you and me."

"Of course," Abby said. "What's on your mind?"

"Had she said anything to you at all about being convinced that someone at the MMH was hurting patients rather than taking care of them?" He had to smile at his own attempts at evasive language, avoiding the inflammatory term *medical serial killer.*

"Heavens, no," Abby said. "What makes you ask that?"

"It would take too long to explain," Jack said. "I'll let you get back to your family."

"What about the death certificate?" Abby said. "I spoke to the insurance agent, and she said the sooner they got that documentation, the sooner they can fulfill the terms of the policy."

"I'm working on it, for sure," Jack said. "We have to wait for a couple of tests to come back."

"Okay, I understand," Abby said. "My best to Laurie."

After saying goodbye, he slowly put down his phone. Having learned nothing from Abby, he was becoming even more curious as to what Cherine Gardener was going to tell him tomorrow, especially after hearing from Ronnie that the hospital's death ratio had been trending downward and not upward. What kind of statistics would point to a serial killer if the mortality ratio was going down? It didn't seem to make much sense.

With the computer ready, Jack googled *medical serial killers,* and as he expected he got more than twelve million results in a third of a second. He picked a number with headlines he recognized from Sue's collection and quickly read them. In one of the first, he found a quote that spurred his imagination — "Although rare, they are more common than most of us imagine" — followed by the recent assertion that on average thirty-five medical murders happen every year in the United States alone. On Wikipedia, he found a lengthy list of medical serial killers and the number of deaths they had been convicted of causing, although almost all of them admitted to far more. Reading on, he found a number of articles about the motivations and psychology of the killers. All in all, it was disturbing reading, even for someone accustomed to death like Jack was.

In the background, Jack heard Laurie's cheerful voice calling out a hello to everyone as she came up the open stairs to the fifth level. He was tempted to turn off the computer and go out into the kitchen to welcome her, but at that exact moment he'd stumbled across an interesting article associating some medical serial killers with a condition known as Munchausen by proxy, where individuals, in this case medical personnel, derived some gain from causing illness in others. As he read on he learned that the gain could be direct, by making the diagnosis and providing the cure, which resulted in acclaim from colleagues, or less direct, by causing the death of the individual and thereby supposedly saving them from the misery of going through a protracted dying process if they were considered terminally ill.

He shook his head in dismay, recognizing that the old adage *it takes all kinds to make a world* was certainly a truism. Yet it was difficult to believe people could be so screwed up. He couldn't help feeling this way, despite having studied a bit of psychiatry in medical school, which had exposed him to the entire spectrum of human mental disorders.

"There you are," Laurie said brightly, bursting into the room. "Why aren't you out there joining in? Come on, this is family time!" She came over to Jack and gave him a forceful hug and then playfully messed his hair to indicate she was not really finding fault with him being in the study. She seemed in a particularly good mood.

"You seem happy," he remarked as he patted his hair back into a semblance of normal.

"I am," Laurie said. "I feel like the presentation George and I gave to the mayor-elect went superbly. It was obvious from his questions that he was duly impressed with what we have been able to accomplish, and he's certainly not in the mood to curb our budget. I'm convinced his background in law enforcement is what saved the day, and I'm optimistic he's going to support the new morgue building lock, stock, and barrel. Now it's just the city council I have to convince to come up with the funding, not that that is going to be a walk in the park."

"Bravo," Jack said.

"My word," she said, leaning over to look more closely at Jack's laptop screen. "What on earth are you reading about? Medical serial killers and Munchausen by proxy?"

"It's been an interesting day for me, too," he said. "Maybe not as successful as yours. I've been on the phone a bit." Jack was not one to lie, but he thought that being cagey was not a sin. He wasn't about to admit to having been over at the MMH twice that day for fear of changing Laurie's mood, yet he was eager to share what he'd learned and get her take. He was nostalgic about how they used to bounce ideas off each other before she had ascended to being the chief. Back then, she'd been as eager as he to go out into the field on difficult cases.

"What have you learned about medical serial killers and Munchausen by proxy?" Laurie asked. She folded her arms and leaned her backside against the desk, staring down at Jack. She was clearly intrigued.

"Some medical serial killers are thought to suffer from Munchausen by proxy," he said.

"Okay," she said. "I suppose that makes sense. But what made you motivated to read such an article?"

"I learned something particularly surprising today," Jack said. "Apparently Sue had recently become worried that there was an active medical serial killer at the MMH, particularly over the previous year."

"Good gravy! Really?" Laurie questioned. "How did you learn this? From Abby?"

"No, from an orthopedic charge nurse Sue was friends with. They both served on the Mortality and Morbidity Committee and took their positions seriously, becoming more or less comrades in arms. So much so that it created, should we say, ill feelings from some of the higher-ups, who thought of them as provocateurs or co-conspirators. As you know, hospital politics can get vicious, particularly when it involves narcissistic docs and narcissistic administrators, of which there are far too many."

"Yikes," Laurie said. "What was Sue's suspicion of a medical serial killer based on? Any idea?"

"That I don't know yet," he said. "The nurse I was speaking with was on duty and couldn't say much other than to suggest it had something to do with statistics. But later I learned that the hospital's mortality ratio has gone down, which argues against there being any serial killer or certainly not an active one. She's off tomorrow and has promised to get in touch with me. So I hope to learn more specifics then."

"Well, I'll be eager to hear what you find out," she said. "If it is true, it's critical to find out who it is and put a stop to it. I envy you getting to work on such a case rather than jousting with the city council. It reminds me of when I exposed Jasmine Rakoczi. What a horror if it turns out that the MMH has yet another medical psychopath."

"I couldn't agree more," Jack said. "I can also imagine how much you miss the challenges of being an ME and doing forensics. In fact, maybe you should think about stepping down from being the chief and rejoin us plebeians. I'm serious." Jack would like nothing better than to have Laurie back as a colleague, both at the OCME and at home.

"Don't think it doesn't cross my mind on occasion," Laurie said wistfully. "But I accepted this challenge, and by God I'm going to see it through. Who are you working with on this? Kevin Strauss? Didn't you say he was the MLI on Sue's case?"

"He's the one, and I went down to 421 to talk with him directly. I wanted to make sure there weren't any nuances that hadn't made it into his write-up. I also have Bart Arnold pulling together some statistics on the number of ME cases coming out of the MMH over the last couple of years to see if it's risen, and if so, how much. I hadn't heard any red flags like that, have you?"

"I haven't."

"It's all very interesting, and I wonder if none of it would have come to light had Sue not passed on."

"Well, keep me informed," she said. She straightened up to head back out to the kitchen. "Do you think you should let Lou Soldano know about the possibility of a medical serial killer at the MMH? You remember how critical he was in the Rakoczi debacle."

"It's a little early for that," Jack said. "I've only been told Sue was convinced with no idea why yet, or even if it was based on anything specific. But it is interesting you bring up Lou's name because I saw him today and hadn't for some time. He came over to observe the post on a supposed suicide of the wife of one of his junior detectives."

"I can't help but notice you used the word *supposed*. Did you find reason to think otherwise?"

"For sure," he said. "I'm about ninety-nine-point-nine percent certain it was a homicide, and with no break-in, it was most likely perpetrated by the aggrieved husband. It's a sad situation, made worse by the woman being pregnant. Understandably Lou is taking it hard, as he is fond of his detective."

"I can imagine," Laurie said. She then clapped her hands, indicating her wish to change the subject. "That's quite enough shop talk! Instead, let's have some dinner and family time?"

"Sounds good," Jack said. He turned off his laptop. "But first let me say that Lou had a couple of suggestions for me. He reminded me I shouldn't play detective, but, more important, he advised me against making waves here on the home front."

"Bravo!" she said with another clap. "I think both are fabulous suggestions that you should follow."

"I'm glad you approve," he said. "So, I'll resign myself to your mother staying here as long as she likes and verbally give her credit for truly helping with Emma, and I'll also make a concerted effort not to get into any more arguments with her about vaccines. Regarding Emma, I'll stop advocating her trying schooling in the near term until there is concerted agreement on it. With that said, I do still oppose the Adderall issue for JJ although I'm not against a second professional opinion. What do you say?"

"I'd say that is significant progress," Laurie said. "Three cheers for Lou. Now if you would throw in a moratorium on commuting on your bike and finding a different sport than pickup basketball, I'd be willing to sign a truce."

Jack looked up at his wife with dismay until he caught her smile, indicating she was teasing about the bike riding and the basketball playing, even though she was against both. He laughed. "Okay, you got me! Very funny!"

"I have one more question," she said. "Have you spoken again with Abby? What's the status there?"

"I did speak with him not ten minutes ago," he said. "All is well. The burial took place within the twenty-four-hour period. He and his children and Sue's sister were having a kind of wake."

"Oh, dear." Laurie groaned. "I feel so guilty about not being there for my friend."

"I'm sure Abby understands. It's one of the difficulties of having a funeral service so quickly."

"I suppose," Laurie said. "Did he mention the death certificate?"

"He did, and I reiterated that I'll be checking the histology and toxicology tomorrow."

"Did he seem fine with that?"

"He did," Jack said.

"Okay, thanks for handling it all," Laurie said. "I certainly couldn't have done the autopsy. But be that as it may, let's try to enjoy some family time."

CHAPTER 21

Tuesday, December 7, 8:51 P.M.

"Okay, Mama," Cherine Gardener said to her mother, whom she called on a regular basis, especially since the pandemic started two years ago. Since then, she'd made it a point to do her mother's grocery shopping online, having the items delivered from the nearest Kroger. Although Cherine had tried to get her mother to join the twenty-first century, she'd resisted and had refused to learn how to use a computer or even a smartphone. Getting her to use a mobile phone at all had been a major undertaking. "I'll call you tomorrow night, but you call me if the groceries don't arrive, okay?"

It was always a little hard for Cherine to terminate a call, and she could tell her mother was lonely. Destiny lived in the Church Street neighborhood of Galveston, Texas, in the same apartment Cherine had grown up in. It was not a good area, which was why Destiny rarely ventured out and usually only to see her other daughter, Shanice, and her three children. For a number of years, Cherine had tried to get her mother to move up to New York, but with grandchildren nearby, it had been a losing proposition.

Cherine had been in New York for a bit more than five years, having been recruited by MMH from University of Texas Medical Branch Hospital, where she had worked since graduating from the School of Nursing there. She was the first person in her family as far as she knew who had gone to college. It hadn't been easy coming from a single-parent household. Her father, a merchant marine, left on a trip when she was four and never returned. From an early age, she'd been determined to be a nurse, having been introduced to the profession by her mother, who'd been a nurse's aide.

Professionally Cherine couldn't be happier, as she loved being a nurse even during the pandemic when so many of her colleagues complained bitterly about the working conditions and the stress. As a testament to her commitment, she was also enrolled in a Master of Science in Nursing program at Columbia, which she had every intention of completing, despite the effort of working while doing it. And although exhausted after twelve-hour shifts three days in a row, she intended to study that night and had her materials and laptop spread out on her kitchen table.

Cherine lived on the third floor of a converted brownstone on the west side of Manhattan that had two apartments on each level, one in the front and one in the rear. Cherine's unit was in the rear facing a warren of backyards now populated by leafless trees. In the spring, summer, and fall it appeared verdant. Now too much trash, including discarded tires, could be seen.

Working twelve-hour shifts and studying most of the time she was off, Cherine didn't know anybody in the building on a personal level; just enough to say hello in the rare instances she ran into someone in the hall. The stairs, particularly the first flight, were rather grand, serving as evidence of the days when the building was a single-family mansion. The hospital had helped her find the apartment, and Cherine thought of it as luxurious living. Although the rent was high, she made what she considered a good salary as a charge nurse. Despite sending money regularly to her mother, she was also able to save a significant amount as well as pay her bills.

After putting away the dishes she'd washed after eating the takeout she'd brought home, she was about to sit down to start her coursework when her door buzzer sounded. Jumping at the raucous sound since it was such a rare occurrence, she rushed over to the intercom unit next to the refrigerator. As she did so, she glanced at the time. It was after nine o'clock, making it even more unusual. She could feel her pulse in her temples.

"Cherine?" questioned a male voice after she'd said a quick hello.

"Who is it?" Cherine asked nervously, wondering if she should have even responded.

"It's Ronnie Cavanaugh. I'm sorry to bother you so late, and I would have called but I never got your mobile number. My bad. Anyway, I need to talk with you briefly. It's important."

"I thought you were working tonight," Cherine said.

"I was," Ronnie said. "But I needed to talk with you, and I was able to convince Sarah Berman to come in and take the shift by offering her a two-nights-for-one trade. I tried to catch you up on the ortho floor, but you had already left."

Debating what to do, Cherine looked

down at herself. As per usual, the first thing she'd done on coming home was take a shower. It was a ritual started when the Covid-19 pandemic exploded. At that moment she was dressed in jammies with a robe, entirely unfitting for company, even with someone she knew as well as Ronnie Cavanaugh. "Okay, but I'm not dressed. Give me a minute."

"No problem," Ronnie said. "I'm sorry for the hour, but it is important."

As quickly as she could, Cherine dashed into her bedroom, stripped off her night-clothes, and pulled on a pair of jeans and a hooded sweatshirt. After re-spiking her hair with a large comb in front of the bathroom mirror, she went back to the intercom panel and pressed the button, asking if Ronnie was still there.

"I'm here," Ronnie responded.

"I'm in 3B," she said as she pressed the door release button and held it in for a moment, which she had learned was necessary. Even though she was two floors up, she could hear the heavy front door close as it jarred the whole building. Walking to the door to the hallway, she again checked herself in the mirror over a small console table. Satisfied she looked reasonably presentable, she waited, but didn't have to wait long. When there was a knock, she released the dead bolt and the chain lock and opened the door.

Ronnie was dressed in a navy-issued pea-coat over hospital scrubs as well as a navy wool watch cap. He again apologized for the late hour and for arriving uninvited as he pulled off his coat and hat and placed them on a chair by the door.

"It's okay," Cherine said. "Can I get you anything to drink? I have some OJ."

"No, I'm fine. This won't take long. Where should we sit?"

With the kitchen table occupied by her course materials and computer, Cherine gestured toward the couch, which was a sleep sofa that she had been planning to use if she'd been successful in getting Destiny to move to New York. While Ronnie made himself comfortable, she turned around one of the chairs from the table.

"How did you find out where I lived?" Cherine asked.

"I looked it up in admin records in the computer," Ronnie said.

"I thought that was supposed to be confidential."

"Not for night nursing supervisors," Ronnie explained. "We have full access. We even have all the administrators' addresses and phone numbers, including the president."

"I guess that's understandable," Cherine said. "Anyway, you are here. But what's so important it couldn't wait until tomorrow?"

"I wanted to talk about Sue's passing," Ronnie began. "She's going to be sorely missed, particularly by you and me as we fight to make the M and M Committee live up to its obligations. Anyway, before I started my shift, I was interviewed by a medical examiner named Jack Stapleton. He's looking into Sue's death because he thinks she might not have had a heart attack as everyone assumed."

"Oh, yes, I talked to him briefly this afternoon just before report. He told me the same thing about Sue. It's curious and surprising."

"I know you spoke to him because he told me about it. When I asked him if you had been helpful, he answered in the affirmative, describing it as having been shockingly helpful. He used that word, *shockingly.* Afterward, I started to wonder what you could have told him that made him describe it that way, and I could only think of one thing you might have said. And I'll tell you why I'm thinking as I am. Early yesterday morning, when I was going off shift, I happened to run into Dr. Passero in the garage.

Whenever we ran into each other, we'd chat briefly about M and M issues. This Monday's conversation was different. She took me aside and then told me something in strict confidence that I truly found shocking. I'm wondering if it was the same thing that you told this Jack Stapleton, which would mean that Dr. Passero had confided in you as well. I'm sorry to beat around the bush like this, but I don't know what else to do. I don't want to burden you with something if I don't have to. I just want to know if you and I are privy to the same information, and if we are, what we're going to do about it. I've been worried about what I was going to do and who I was going to tell the minute Sue was pronounced dead in the ED."

Cherine stared at Ronnie when he finally paused in his monologue, but for a moment she didn't respond. She was coming to realize that Dr. Passero must have decided on impulse to tell him about her belief a serial killer existed. It was the only thing that came to her mind that was truly shocking. Cherine knew that Dr. Passero had gotten the data that had convinced her from him, so in many respects, it made a lot of sense. As nursing supervisors, Ronnie and his colleagues knew more about the hospital's internal affairs, petty interpersonal squabbles, and rumors than most of the staff, as it was part of their job to handle all the problems that arose involving staff members or patients.

"I'm not sure what to say," Cherine confessed.

"I understand," Ronnie replied. "It's why I'm struggling as well. What I'm referring to is rather serious, and I don't want to burden you with it if you don't already know. Let me try to be slightly more direct: Did Sue tell you anything recently that you found shocking?"

"She did," Cherine said, making up her mind that she and Ronnie were indirectly referring to the same disturbing issue. "She told me that she was worried a very active medical serial killer had been murdering patients over the last year at an increasing rate and had the data that strongly suggested it."

"Okay," Ronnie said, letting out a breath. "It's good to know I'm not alone. What exactly did you tell Jack Stapleton?"

"Not much. We only spoke briefly as I was about to have report. I only got to say Dr. Passero was convinced that it was so."

"Did you explain at all why she was convinced?"

"No, there wasn't time. But I'm off tomorrow. He gave me his card. I'm going to call him in the morning and arrange a meeting. He impressed me. I think he can help us."

"I do, too," Ronnie said. "Maybe he can get a real look at some of the cases that made Dr. Passero suspicious and either prove they were murders or disprove it once and for all."

"That's a good point," Cherine said. "You are right. He is a medical examiner. Maybe he can even find out why they hadn't been medical examiner cases in the first place, which is what Dr. Passero questioned."

"That's another great question," Ronnie said. "You are right! He's the perfect person to get involved. I also like not having to go to Dr. Thomas or Dr. Wingate."

"I agree," Cherine said, feeling relieved herself. She didn't realize how keyed up she was from having an unexpected visitor, even someone she knew. "I certainly wouldn't like to mention it to them. No way. In fact, I wouldn't put it past either one being the guilty party if it turns out Dr. Passero was correct. I'd only say this to you because of how often the three of us talked about them. They are both such self-centered odd ducks. I can never understand why people with their personalities ever go into medicine in the first place."

"I couldn't agree more," Ronnie said.

"What do you think? Is there a medical serial killer, much less an active one?"

"I don't think so," Ronnie said. "As you know, the mortality ratio, which is used for hospital accreditation, has been going down."

"But Sue told me you were the source of the material that made her think as she did. She briefly explained some of it to me, but we were in a rush at the time. What all did you give her?"

"I just gave her a bunch of raw data, but it wasn't complete, so she was just looking at overall rates without factoring in which deaths were expected. You know as well as anyone that as an academic medical center we get far more serious cases than a regular hospital."

"I see," Cherine said. She nodded a few times. "That makes sense to me."

Ronnie then cleared his throat before adding, "You know, that offer of OJ is sounding better and better. That is, if you don't mind."

"I don't mind at all," Cherine responded.

"Might you have a little vodka to go with it?" Ronnie said. "I could use a shot. I need to calm down."

"Sorry, but I don't have any vodka," Cherine said as she got to her feet and started for the refrigerator.

The second Cherine turned her back, Ronnie silently leaped to his feet, skirted the low coffee table, and lunged after her.

CHAPTER 22

Tuesday, December 7, 9:31 P.M.

As on edge as Cherine was with having her normal schedule interrupted unexpectedly, she sensed sudden movement behind her and started to turn around when Ronnie collided with her. He had intended to throw a dark blue pillowcase over her head as he had done with Sue Passero, but Cherine saw it coming and ducked to the side. Abandoning the sack, Ronnie tried to envelop her in a bear hug, but Cherine straight-armed him. Knocking her arm to the side, Ronnie lunged forward, essentially tackling her and causing both to collide with the kitchen table, sending books, pencils, dishes, and computer flying to create a gigantic clatter.

Cherine was a slight woman, but lithe and strong. She was also in relatively good physical shape.

Although Ronnie had thought subduing Cherine would be easy considering her comparative size, he was shocked at how fiercely and successfully she now was able to resist his attempts to subdue her. Several times when he thought he had her pinned, she squiggled partially free. She also let out a scream that rang in Ronnie's ears and infuriated him, forcing him to use one hand to slap over her mouth. In the next instant they collided against a rickety secondhand bookshelf filled with a combination of books and knickknacks that also crashed to the floor, creating even a bigger clatter than the upending of the kitchen table.

Even with his hand firmly clasped over the lower part of her face, she was able to make significant but muffled noises. Eventually, with some effort, he was able to get her pinned in the angle created by the wall and the floor. At that point, just when he was sensing success, she managed to get a small part of his palm inside her mouth and bit down on it as hard as she could.

"Goddamnit!" he spat, yanking his hand free and losing a tiny bit of skin in the process. As she started another scream, he slapped her hard enough to bounce her head off the wall. Even though now for the moment she was only moaning and not screaming, he reclasped his hand back over her mouth. At the same time, he reached down with his free hand while pressing his full weight on top of her to pull out of his pocket a syringe he'd loaded with a carefully calculated dose of succinylcholine. All he wanted to do was paralyze her for the time necessary to stop her breathing long enough to kill her, yet small enough to be rapidly metabolized. In Ronnie's armamentarium, succinylcholine and potassium chloride were his go-to agents, since they were all but impossible to detect after the fact.

Using his teeth to remove the syringe's cap, Ronnie jammed the needle through Cherine's jeans into the side of her buttock and pressed the plunger. Putting the syringe and its cap to the side, he now waited while keeping her pinned to the floor. It didn't take long. He could feel the resistance drain out of her. An arm and a hand that she had been using to flail against his side went limp, as did her whole body. Rearing back and taking his hand off her face, he looked at her. She stared back at him with eyes that reflected terror. She knew what was happening.

A moment later, he rolled over, sat up, and got to his feet. When he looked down at her he could see her eyes were now glazed and she wasn't breathing. She was also turning blue with cyanosis. He snapped up the syringe and replaced the cap. After putting it back into his pocket and picking up the pillowcase, he rapidly glanced around at the mess the apartment had become. After all the crashing noises, ruckus, and particularly Cherine's semi-scream, he wanted to get the hell away ASAP in case a neighbor decided to investigate or call 911. Yet he also wanted to make completely sure there was no evidence of his visit. When he was convinced, he pulled out of his pocket a small plastic bag containing powdered cocaine laced with fentanyl. He'd added the fentanyl himself, so he knew it would be lethal. He sprinkled some of the powder into her nostrils before placing the bag on the coffee table in full view.

Rushing over to the door, he donned his coat and hat before using the pillowcase to open the door to avoid leaving any fingerprints. He'd been careful not to touch anything in the apartment during his visit. After glancing up and down the stairs to make sure they were clear of any of the tenants, he stepped out into the hallway and closed the door, again with the pillowcase. Pulling his cap low over his ears, he descended the first flight of stairs and then the second, all the while fearing he'd run into someone. Luckily it didn't happen. It wasn't until he'd pulled open the heavy front door that he heard someone from a floor or two above call out, "Hey, what's going on in 3B?"

The next instant Ronnie was outside, thundering down the granite stoop, and then heading west in the direction of his Cherokee. Luckily there was no one in the immediate area he had to worry about seeing him. He moved quickly but resisted the temptation to run, reasoning that running might attract more attention if anyone happened to be looking out their window. Keeping himself at a fast walk, he put distance between himself and what he called ground zero. It wasn't until he arrived at Columbus Avenue, where there were lots of people going about their business, that he allowed himself to slow down and relax to a degree.

Thinking back on what had transpired, he shook his head in dismay. It certainly hadn't gone as smoothly as planned, yet at least it was over. The one thing he had to give himself credit for was that he had been correct in worrying that Cherine knew about Sue's recent fears of the existence of a medical serial killer. Although Sue had implied she'd talked to no one about it when she had confided in him, she obviously had.

"God," he whispered to himself as he walked. His anxiety was reverting to anger. "When it rains, it pours." Up until the moment Sue had gotten active on the M and M Committee, demanding this and demanding that, insisting on getting onto the task force subcommittee, everything had been running perfectly, essentially like clockwork. He'd been totally confident the secret of his behind-the-scenes activities was his alone, and he'd had no fear of being discovered or even suspected. He didn't have to be a rocket scientist to know that if Sue had succeeded in being appointed to the task force, all the effort he'd expended getting Thomas and Wingate to let him do the work of the subcommittee, which they merely rubber-stamped, would have been put in jeopardy, particularly Ronnie's insistence that the only data given over to the Compliance Committee once a month was the death ratio and not the raw data including of the total unadjusted number of deaths.

A half a block south on Columbus Avenue was where Ronnie had found a parking spot for his beloved flat-black Cherokee. Using his key fob, he unlocked the vehicle as he approached, and the SUV responded by switching on its interior lights to welcome his return. For him the vehicle was like family, and he took care of it as such. He'd even had an artist paint some flames extending back from the wheel wells. Climbing in behind the steering wheel he first reached over and put his SIG Sauer P365 pistol in the glove compartment. It was his second-favorite possession, which he used frequently at a pistol range not too far away from his apartment and in the woods surrounding his hideaway up in the Catskills. He'd had the gun in one of his jacket pockets on his visit to Cherine's just in case he needed it, which he certainly hadn't expected. Still, he thought it best to be prepared, come what may.

Straightening back up in the driver's seat, Ronnie peered out the front windshield with unseeing eyes as his mind went back to musing about his suddenly worrisome situation and how he'd gotten to where he was currently. He'd always had a soft spot for those people unlucky enough to be diagnosed with incurable, deadly diseases, particularly patients with cancer that had metastasized. As doomed individuals, they were ripe for modern medicine to experiment on, torture, and mutilate needlessly with all sorts of harrowing drugs and horrendous surgical procedures knowing full well it was not going to be curative. As a regular floor nurse, Ronnie had had limited opportunities to save these people from their fate, the same fate his foster mother had suffered, for fear of being exposed by a medical system that had evolved to protect its rights to do what it pleased. It hadn't been until he'd risen to the role of nursing supervisor that he was able to help a significant number since the role gave him access to the whole hospital and the freedom to roam at will. But the biggest boost to his avowed crusade was when AmeriCare decided, in its infinite wisdom, to save money by reducing the night-shift nursing supervisors from two people to a single individual, meaning, to Ronnie's delight, there was suddenly no one supervising the supervisors.

On his first night as the sole supervisor, Ronnie was able to save four people from a frightful and painful fate. It was up to him to decide after a death whether it was expected. If it was expected, which was what he always determined, it contributed to the denominator of the mortality ratio, hence making the hospital appear better. Also, it was up to him to declare if a death was a medical examiner case, and he made sure that none of the people whom he had saved from being tortured by the profession were ME cases. But even if they had been ME cases, it wouldn't have mattered since Ronnie invariably used for the coup de grâce one of the drugs that the patient was already being given, like insulin or digitalis, but in a lethal amount. Over time Ronnie had amassed an entire pharmacopeia of drugs and had them stored in one of his private drawers in the nursing supervisor's tiny office.

As he got better and better at his personal crusade, something interesting occurred to him one night five months ago in the beginning of July, when he arrived at the bedside of one of his beneficiaries after a code blue had been called. He was required to respond to all the code blues, but on those he was responsible for causing, he never wanted to be the first to arrive to avoid any chance at suspicion of having caused the emergency. On this occasion, when he dashed into the room after an appropriate wait, he couldn't help but notice that the rather green, new residents, all of whom had just started their graduate training and who had already arrived at the bedside, were seemingly at a loss of what to do. As he was wont to do in such circumstances, Ronnie took control.

Since he knew what the problem was in this instance from having caused it, he also knew what would reverse the situation immediately, and before he really thought about what he was doing, he barked out an order for the appropriate antidote.

Later he silently lambasted himself for what he had done, as the hospice patient had been revived and the heart returned to a normal sinus rhythm. As he was preparing to leave, several of the new residents came up to him and congratulated him on his clinical astuteness and willingness to take charge. Ronnie had been surprised at the compliments and also taken aback at how much he enjoyed them. He had been even more amazed at how much it had raised his credibility as a nurse par excellence.

As a result, Ronnie had begun to expand his covert activities to include nonterminal patients if a situation presented itself. As he did this, his clinical reputation had soared. He liked this so much because it ameliorated the mild inferiority complex he'd always had from having gotten his nursing training from the military and a community college rather than a fancy Ivy League university and academic medical center. Although a few of these patients ended up dying, the downside was more than worth the results. He even started to be treated as a clinical equal by some of the attending physicians.

Ronnie started his Cherokee, and it responded with a roar, as he'd customized his muffler to sound like a McLaren 720. Pulling out from the parking spot into the traffic, he headed south with the intention of working his way over to the Queensboro Bridge and then on to his apartment in Woodside. As he drove, he found himself getting angry all over again at Sue Passero and her incessant meddling and how much damage she'd managed to inflict on his world. What had started merely as her complaining about which cases were being presented at the full M and M meetings had morphed into her insistence to get a task force appointment. Although Ronnie had been able to convince both Dr. Thomas and Dr. Wingate it was a bad idea, it had become obvious to Ronnie that Sue was not going to give up, especially after she'd managed to get from him by his own carelessness some of the raw death rate data that showed a rather steep increase in the number of hospital deaths over the year without an associated increase in the severity of the general admissions. Of course, that had been a giveaway to his extensive efforts to eliminate the unnecessary suffering of a hundred or so patients being kept alive without regard for their quality of life or the pain and disfigurement they endured. Now, in retrospect, he realized that he should have shut her down way back when rather than acting as if he were on her side.

As unsettled as Ronnie felt, at least he could give himself credit for ridding himself of both Sue and Cherine before they could do too much damage. He also gave himself credit for cleverly learning that the ME, Jack Stapleton, had been told of Sue's suspicions, although thankfully without getting any of the corroborating evidence. The previous night when things had quieted down around three, he'd made the effort of getting into Sue Passero's office using a housekeeping passkey. There he'd been able to easily find the facts and figures Sue had put together from what he had unsuspectingly provided. For his convenience, he'd come across the incriminating papers in a folder right on top of her desk conveniently labeled MOR-TALITY AND MORBIDITY COMMITTEE. After taking and destroying them, he had thought he was back in the clear until the unexpected meeting with Jack Stapleton and learning that Cherine had known and had agreed to meet with him the next day to spill the beans.

Cursing with a series of particularly offensive expletives he'd learned in the navy, Ronnie pounded his steering wheel several times in frustration. The outburst and the physical activity calmed him, and he was able to regain his composure and think more clearly. He was even able to see a bright side: The situation had awakened him to the reality that he needed to be more careful in the future, perhaps even to the point of cutting down on proving himself with saves, despite how much he enjoyed those episodes. The reason, of course, was that those deaths, if they occurred, were more difficult to pass off as expected, meaning they'd be added to the numerator, thereby raising the mortality ratio. It was also harder to declare them non-ME cases.

Ronnie felt himself smiling as he drove up the ramp leading to the top level of the Queensboro Bridge with its impressive view of lower Manhattan and the burgeoning development of the opposing side in Brooklyn. The situation as he saw it was not unlike the efforts that had to be undertaken to keep a viral outbreak like Covid-19 from becoming an epidemic or even pandemic. Cases had to be diagnosed quickly, isolated, and removed before the disease spread.

He'd been able to take care of Sue Passero and Cherine Gardener with comparative ease, although Cherine had been a bit more difficult than expected. That left only Jack Stapleton. There was no question in Ronnie's mind that the pesky ME had to be eliminated soon, before a possible contagion erupted.

The problem was that Stapleton was not a member of the MMH community, which limited Ronnie's access to him. On the plus side, he knew that the man wanted to meet with him again and that he foolishly used his bike for traveling around New York City. Like many medical personnel, Ronnie was aware that there were almost twenty thousand bike and vehicle collisions each year with a score or more deaths. It almost seemed as if the man was asking to be eliminated by tempting fate.

Reaching out with his right hand, Ronnie patted the dash of his Cherokee, which he often did because he liked to treat the vehicle as a pet. As he did so he murmured, "You and I will take care of this pest for good tomorrow."

CHAPTER 23

Wednesday, December 8, 7:08 A.M.

As Jack rode down 30th Street alongside the OCME, he saw something he didn't expect. Once again, Lou Soldano's black Chevy Malibu was parked between two ME Sprinter vans. Having seen him twice yesterday, he didn't think he'd have the pleasure of seeing him again although Jack knew the supposed suicide of his detective's wife was weighing on his mind.

After locking his bike in its usual location, he took the stairs heading up to the first floor. He'd arrived later than he had the day before, and in a completely different mindset. Lou's advice about how he should handle the problematic issues on the home front had been spot-on.

Also affecting Jack's mood was that he had a forensic case that engrossed him, and one that he was fully motivated to make significant progress resolving. Although it had only been twenty-four hours, he hoped both Maureen in Histology and John in Toxicology were going to come through. Of the two, John was the more questionable, which he fully recognized. At the same time, he was prepared to tell the man that he would be satisfied with a preliminary screen like he'd gotten from Naomi.

After passing the SIDS office, Jack entered the ID room, where Jennifer was again going through the night's cases. As he expected from seeing the Chevy Malibu, Lou was there but fast asleep in one of the club chairs. Since Jack was arriving almost a half hour later than he had the day before, Vinnie was also already occupying the other club chair, hiding behind his newspaper. Most important, he'd already made the coffee in the common pot, and Jack immediately headed in its direction. He was eagerly anticipating a cup, as much for its warmth as for its stimulant effect. The bike ride that morning had been nippier than it had been the day before when it had been unseasonably springlike.

"I had in mind taking a paper day today," he called out for Jennifer's benefit as he poured the coffee. "Unless the lieutenant commander has other ideas." A *paper day* in ME lingo meant a day spent completing previously autopsied cases by collating all the material, looking at the histology slides, and signing out death certificates. It was in lieu of doing any additional autopsies.

"Hallelujah!" Vinnie voiced with alacrity from behind his newspaper. Jack was forever making him start cases way before he'd had a chance to go over the sports pages and earlier than any other ME insisted on starting.

"Is that going to be a problem for you if I don't take any cases?" Jack asked Jennifer while ignoring Vinnie. He added a bit of sugar and cream to his mug and began to stir.

"Not at all," Jennifer said. "It looks like there's only going to be dozen or so autopsies today. As far as I am concerned, you're in the clear if you'd like."

"I'd like," he replied. "Any particularly interesting cases I'll be missing?"

"No, except maybe the one Detective Soldano is here to observe." She picked up one of the autopsy folders from the desk and held it aloft, thinking that Jack might want to see it. "I haven't looked at it yet, but he did say before he fell asleep that he hoped you'd be the one doing it."

Jack groaned. He was one hundred percent eager to get right back to work on Sue

Passero's case and had been since he'd woken up that morning. Overnight he'd given the whole complicated situation a lot of thought, and he'd come to one potentially meaningful conclusion. The fact that Ronnie Cavanaugh had described Sue as being cyanotic when he first found her in the garage and that the cyanosis had improved when he started his CPR made Jack mull carefully over the physiological details in extremis situations. With deadly heart attacks, it's the heart that is struggling, but whatever blood the faltering organ is able to pump around the body is fully oxygenated because the lungs are functioning fine, at least initially, so the deceased's coloration is generally rather normal or, if anything, pale. When cyanosis occurs and is evident, particularly in a woman of color where cyanosis is not as apparent as it is in a Caucasian person, it means the lungs are not doing their job oxygenating the blood. That's what happens with an overdose, severe asthma, drowning, or even strangulation. Obviously, Sue did not have asthma and had not been strangled as there had been no bruising around the neck and, more important, the basic neck dissection he'd done had been normal. Of all the other possibilities, the most probable statistically was certainly an overdose despite how unlikely he'd originally thought it. What all this suggested to Jack was that he had to rethink the whole situation, particularly in regard to toxicology, which was surely going to provide the answer of the cause and manner of death. At this point, he was reasonably certain John was going to confirm the death was an overdose.

All these thoughts rocketed around inside his brain as he stared over at Jennifer, who was still holding up the folder. "What kind of case is it?" he asked hesitantly.

"I don't really know," Jennifer said. "It's listed as a probable overdose by the MLI, which seems a little strange with Detective Soldano involved."

Jack groaned again. Because of his friendship with Lou, he accepted that he didn't have a lot of choice whether to do the case, especially if Lou asked him directly. But he wasn't excited about it, and it wasn't just because of his eagerness to get back to work on Sue's case. There was also the issue that he'd done hundreds of overdose autopsies over the last several years, as there had been a virtual epidemic of them, meaning there was minimal forensic challenge. At the same time, if Lou was involved, there had to be a twist, and that idea intrigued Jack to a degree. Resigned and with coffee in hand, he walked over to the desk and took the folder from Jennifer.

Slipping out the contents, he rifled through it until he was able to come across the MLI's workup. Like Sue Passero's case, it had been written by Kevin Strauss. He was about to read the relatively short write-up when his eye caught the name at the top of the form. It was Cherine Gardener.

"Shit!" Jack blurted. Like the previous day when he came across the name *Susan Passero,* his seeing the name *Cherine Gardener* was an utter shock. "Sorry for my outburst," he added for Jennifer's benefit. He even held up his hand as a kind of apology. He was rather old school when it came to expletives and frequently criticized mortuary techs who used colorful language. As loud and out of character as Jack's utterance had been, even Vinnie lowered his *Post* to peer at him, dumbfounded.

"What's wrong?" Jennifer asked. She was as surprised as Vinnie.

"I think I know this person," he said. "God! Two days in a row." His eyes scanned the page for identification details, learning that the deceased was a nurse at the Manhattan Memorial Hospital. Unfortunately, all that confirmed for Jack that the deceased was the Cherine Gardener he feared it to be.

"How did you know her?" Jennifer asked. "Another friend?"

"No, she wasn't a friend," Jack said, scanning the workup again as he spoke. "Curiously enough, I just met her yesterday afternoon for the first time. I can't believe this. She was a nurse at the MMH who was supposed to call me sometime today, so we could get together to finish a conversation we were having about Passero's case."

"You met her at the MMH?" Jennifer questioned. She frowned.

"Yeah," he said, trying to sound casual but covertly wincing as he realized he'd just made a regrettable faux pas by admitting he'd been out investigating. In an attempt to recover he added, "I stopped there briefly on my way home last night just to pick up some paperwork that was left for me."

"And you happened to run into her?" Jennifer asked quizzically.

"That's what happened," Jack said, wincing yet again as his explanation sounded pathetic, even to him.

"Well, that's quite a coincidence," Jennifer said. She shrugged.

"It sure is," Jack agreed quickly as he went

back to Kevin's workup. All he could do was hope his loose talk didn't find its way to Laurie's ears.

"Do you want to change your mind and do the case?" Jennifer asked.

He didn't answer right away but waited until he'd reread the workup more carefully. "Sorry," he said again when Jennifer's question registered. "Yes, I guess I'm going to have to do the case whether I want to or not."

"Fine and dandy," Jennifer said. "But tell me, does reading the MLI's workup give you an idea of why Detective Soldano is here?"

"Yes and no," Jack said. "At least not entirely. It seems it wasn't run of the mill."

"How so?" Jennifer asked. In her experience, a case had to be significantly consequential for a lieutenant commander detective to be involved.

"Well," he said while looking back at the workup to come up with a synopsis, "the patrolmen who responded to the original nine-one-one call ended up calling the precinct detectives and the crime scene unit following an unsuccessful attempt with the Narcan because the apartment was in shambles, as if there had been a struggle. Anyway, it was out of the ordinary."

"Were there signs of a break-in?"

"Nope, no break-in, and a bag of white powder was found on the coffee table. More important, one of the building's tenants said she heard what might have been a scream although she wasn't entirely sure. What she was positive about was hearing crashing noises, explaining the apartment's disarray and debris scattered about the living room. Another tenant said they saw a man leave the building who seemed to be in a hurry and who didn't turn around when she called out to him. That's it."

"It sounds a bit suspicious," Jennifer agreed. "But it still doesn't explain why a detective of Detective Soldano's rank is here to observe the autopsy."

"That's my feeling, too," Jack said. "Luckily it's going to be easy to find out, which I will do right now."

With the reconstituted autopsy folder under his arm and his coffee mug in his hand, he walked over to Lou Soldano's sleeping form and gave his shoulder a gentle shake. Jack had to do it a second time to get the man to lift his eyelids. When Lou finally did, it was obviously a struggle requiring quite an effort.

"Why can't I sleep this soundly when I am at home?" Lou questioned. He took off his glasses and rubbed his eyes with the tips of his fingers hard enough to create squishing noises. When he was done, he sat up straighter and looked up at Jack, who had waited patiently. The whites of Lou's eyes were beet red.

Jack held up the autopsy folder. "I heard you are here about this Cherine Gardener case, which confuses me. I read the MLI workup, and he signed it out as an overdose. What gives? Why are you interested? What's up?"

"My gut tells me it wasn't a run-of-the mill overdose," Lou said. "Same with the responding detective who called me last night. But I have to confess up front, we homicide detectives, maybe me more than anyone else, are getting sick and tired of the uptick in homicides this pandemic is bringing to our fair city. Before the pandemic big strides had been made lowering the rate, but now it's getting out of control, which we're all taking as a personal insult. So maybe we are more sensitive than we should be, especially in a case like this where some rank amateur might be trying to camouflage his dirty work by making it look like an overdose. If that's what we're dealing with here, I want to know ASAP. Will you help?"

"When you ask so nicely, how can I say

no?" Jack questioned as he playfully slapped Lou on top of his head with the autopsy folder. "Okay, but let's get it over with so you can get your ass home and get some real sleep, and, more important, so I can get back to yesterday's case."

Walking over to Vinnie, who was still hidden behind his newspaper, Jack snapped the tabloid out of his hands and plopped the autopsy folder in his lap. "Let's go, big guy! Let's knock this one of the park."

"I knew it was too good to be true that you'd be taking a paper day," Vinnie whined. With a sudden lunge, he grabbed his paper back and then calmly pretended to go back to reading it. Jack snapped it away for the second time. On this occasion, he rolled it up into a tight tube and smacked Vinnie over the head with it before dropping it into his lap. Both laughed while Jennifer rolled her eyes.

Chapter 24

Jack held the door to the stairwell open for Lou. They had delayed leaving the ID area so Lou could help himself to a quick cup of coffee. Vinnie had gone ahead to get everything ready for the autopsy. While Lou downed his needed shot of caffeine, Jack thanked him for his advice about not making waves at home, saying that he'd taken Lou's suggestions and was feeling a lot better about everything. Lou was pleased, saying he wished he had followed his own advice years ago. He'd been divorced for more than a decade.

"Any more news on the Seton case?" Jack asked as he followed Lou down the stairs.

"Yes and no," Lou called over his shoulder. "The handwriting experts at the crime lab finished their analysis, confirming their initial impression it had been written by the deceased. Have you thought more about the

316

case? Does a final confirmation that the suicide note is for real influence how you are going to call it?"

"Of course I've thought about it," Jack said. "But I'm sticking to my guns that the probability is overwhelming it was a homicide. But I have come up with another idea. Are you interested?"

"Let's hear it," Lou said.

"You said Paul's father was already at the Setons' apartment when the patrolmen arrived, which you rightly questioned because of the timing. What if the father were involved in a collusion between himself and his son? For that matter, what if it was a collusion between all three of them, sort of like Agatha Christie's classic *Murder on the Orient Express*?"

"Well, I have to give you credit for being creative," Lou said as he held the door to the basement level open for Jack, "but, Mr. Hercule Poirot, we've already confirmed that Paul called his father first before calling nine-one-one, and the father was at his home in New Jersey. We still don't know why Paul called his father first, and it is a bit suspicious, but the father couldn't have played any role in the actual shooting."

It was Jack's turn to hold the locker room door open for Lou. As Lou passed, he asked, "How are you doing with your Sue Passero case? Are you keeping out of trouble?"

"Interesting you should ask," Jack said. He got scrubs for both of them and handed a set to Lou. "I'm leaning toward Sue being also an overdose. I'll find out for sure today."

"Well, that's surprising, to say the least," Lou said. "She certainly didn't strike me as someone who might use drugs."

"I couldn't agree more," Jack said. "But I have something more interesting to tell you. I spoke in person with this Cherine Gardener yesterday, who we are about to post."

Lou stopped unbuttoning his shirt. He'd already hung up his jacket and tie in the locker Jack had provided for him years before. "Are you trying to pull my leg?" he asked, staring intently at Jack.

"I wish," Jack said. "I spoke with her in the late afternoon, and I was anticipating speaking with her again today. I was almost as shocked to see her name on the autopsy folder as I was seeing Sue's yesterday."

"This is big-time strange," Lou said. "Especially with my gut telling me that this Gardener woman wasn't an overdose like we are supposed to think, even with a bag of powder conveniently in plain sight. The disarray of the apartment tells a different

318

story unless, of course, she was in some kind of drug-induced psychosis. But we're not seeing that like we used to, not with this fentanyl involved. What I can also tell you, with a high degree of confidence, is this woman was no druggie. It probably isn't in your MLI's workup, but we've substantiated that she's been a mainstay frontline healthcare worker through this pandemic, working extra shifts and taking a master's degree course in nursing at the same time. Does that sound like an addict to you?"

"Hardly," Jack said as he got into his scrubs. If Jack was wrong about Sue, and both deaths were homicides, the chances that they were related, probably by being carried out by the same person for the same reasons, went up considerably, as did the possibility that a medical serial killer was on the loose at the MMH. This all stood to reason except for the fact that it depended on too many *if*s.

Lou went back to changing into the scrubs that Jack had handed him. "Where were you supposed to talk with Cherine Gardener today?" he asked.

"That hadn't been decided," Jack said. "She was going to call me. She was scheduled to be off today, and I was going to suggest she come here."

As Lou knotted the strings to the scrub pants, it was obvious his mind was in high gear. Jack's was, too, as he debated how much of what he was thinking he should say.

"And where did you speak with her yesterday?" Lou suddenly asked. "Don't tell me! Let me guess — you went back over to the MMH despite my warning not to." He closed the locker and spun the combination wheel.

"I merely stopped in on my way home to pick up some papers," Jack said, trying to sound casual. "That's when I spoke with her, and she told me some rather interesting things, namely that the MMH was a kind of hotbed of intrigue and animosity."

"That doesn't sound good or safe," Lou said. "That's my point. Did any of this intrigue and animosity involve Sue Passero?"

"Absolutely. She and Sue and another nursing supervisor were partners, so to speak, all serving on the Mortality and Morbidity Committee and allied against three hospital higher-ups."

"God, what a name for a hospital committee," Lou said after he repeated the title. "Leave it to the medical profession to come up with a name like that to scare the bejesus out of us poor potential patients. But, never mind! More important, why the hell did you go over there when I advised you not to do so for your own good? Obviously, you were playing detective again." He sighed loudly and shook his head. "You, my friend, are impossible."

"I wasn't there that long, and I was still involved only with the *how*," Jack said, trying to excuse himself. "The problem is, if I'm wrong about Sue's death being an overdose, I'll be back to square one, at a loss for explaining the cause and mechanism."

"That might be true," Lou snapped, "but the only way you are going to solve such a mystery is by staying here and taking advantage of all the technological wizardry you guys have at your disposal. You certainly are not going to solve it by heading out and gallivanting around the city, snooping in the Manhattan Memorial Hospital, talking to God knows who, and putting yourself at risk like you have in the past."

"Maybe you are right," Jack said. "Okay, I'll stay here." He didn't want to get into an argument, which he knew he would ultimately lose, nor did he even want to broach the serial killer possibility. There was a certain risk to visiting the MMH, Jack accepted that, but up until that point he didn't think there was any other way of understanding what was going on, whether Sue's worry that a medical serial killer was involved had any validity, which was now his main concern. If there actually was a serial killer, calling in the cavalry at this point, meaning Lou, would probably cause the guilty party to go underground.

Jack felt strongly that he needed just a wee bit more time, maybe even a single day, to find out the source of her beliefs. Since he wasn't going to have the opportunity to learn the statistical details Cherine had alluded to, at least he had another source waiting in the wings . . . Ronnie. Jack was now counting on Sue having told Ronnie as much as she had told Cherine. On the positive side, using Ronnie as a source rather than Cherine would undoubtedly provide more details about the members of the triumvirate than Cherine would have because he worked closely with them, and from Jack's perspective they all had to be what he called persons of interest.

"Does Laurie know anything about you going over there?" Lou asked as he took the personal protective gear Jack handed him.

"No, and I'd prefer you don't spill the beans," Jack said. "Give me one more day, okay? Then if you feel obligated to expose me, fine!"

"Hell!" Lou complained. "You guys are always putting me between a rock and a hard place, and this is a good example. If I tell her, you'll be pissed. If I don't tell her and something god-awful happens, she'll be pissed. I lose in both directions."

"One more day," Jack repeated. He held up his index finger to emphasize his point. "And I'll be extra careful and try to stay out of the MMH."

"Shit. Being friends with you guys is a fool's errand," Lou said while throwing up his hands in a kind of surrender. "All right, one more day, but only if this Cherine Gardener isn't an obvious homicide like my gut is telling me."

"Fair enough," Jack said. He was relatively confident that was going to be the case.

Chapter 25

Wednesday, December 8, 8:31 A.M.
Cherine Gardener's X-ray was on the view box, and it was normal, meaning there was no unexpected bullet someplace, which had happened on rare occasions in the past. Her mildly cyanotic, nude body was stretched out on the autopsy table with her head on a wooden block. Her eyes stared unseeing at the ceiling. Running water flowed along her sides and with a mild gurgle disappeared at the base of the table. Although Jack was all too familiar with the sight, seeing her made him pause. Perhaps not with the same degree of discomposure he'd felt with Sue Passero the day before or what he felt autopsying the pathology resident a few years earlier, but he did hesitate for a moment, lamenting the fragility of life. Having directly spoken with her the day before made her passing somehow personal and for a moment reminded him of the death of

his first family.

"Okay!" Jack said to reorient his brain away from his emotional centers to his more analytical regions. He was standing on Cherine's right side, whereas Lou and Vinnie were on her left next to each other. "Do both of you see what I see right off besides her cyanosis?"

"I imagine you are referring to what looks like a small bruise on her cheek," Lou said.

"Exactly," Jack said. Using a digital camera, he took several photos. He had already photographed the white powder visible in her nares.

"She was found lying against the wall," Lou said. "I suppose she could have gotten that when she collapsed."

"No doubt," Jack said. "But it should be noted anyway."

"Could she have been strangled?" Lou asked.

"Doesn't look like it," Jack said. "Invariably bruising is seen around the neck, particularly if a ligature was used. But to be sure, we'll do a brief neck dissection and check the hyoid bone." He inspected her scalp, then opened her mouth to look at her gums and teeth.

"Wait a second," Vinnie said. He bent over for a closer look at something that had caught his eye. "What's that?" He pointed into the left side of Cherine's mouth.

Against her cheek and her lower molars was a small errant piece of tissue where the coloration and texture were different than the surrounding mucosa.

"Hand me some forceps," Jack said. He took the instrument from Vinnie and snagged the two-millimeter piece of tissue.

"What is it?" Lou asked.

"I haven't the slightest idea," Jack said. "For all we know, it could be possibly left over from her dinner, but who knows. Specimen jar, please."

Vinnie picked up one of the many specimen jars he had positioned on the instrument tray, opened it, and Jack added the small piece of tissue. "Histology will tell us what it is," Jack said.

After the head, Jack examined the hands and fingernails before doing a careful full-body inspection. Neither he nor the others found anything of significance. This continued until the body was rolled onto its right side. It was Lou who saw the tiny imperfection first.

"Is this something?" he asked, pointing toward a mere millimeter-round blemish on the lateral side of the left buttock, which was otherwise unremarkable. The spot was darker than the surrounding skin and appeared like a slightly convex period at the end of a sentence.

Both Jack and Vinnie bent over to look. "It's hard to say," Jack voiced. He tried to wipe it off with one of his gloved fingers. It didn't budge. "But it is worth taking a peek. Hand me a scalpel, Vinnie."

With scalpel in hand, Jack took a two-centimeter circular plug of skin that included subcutaneous adipose tissue and muscle. After slicing the sample into two pieces by cutting through the surface imperfection, he put each in separate specimen jars that Vinnie held out. Remembering all the injection sites on Sue's thighs and abdomen from insulin injections, Jack thought there was a chance that it, too, represented an injection site, especially since there was a tiny but visible amount of subcutaneous hemorrhage, but he didn't say anything as it could have been many other things as well, most likely a small nevus.

When the external exam was over, they started the necropsy. By then there were other mortuary techs scurrying about bringing bodies in and making preparations for other cases. The three people at table eight ignored the commotion.

Once Jack had Cherine's body completely

open, he began what he announced was probably the most important part of this particular autopsy, namely taking all the fluid samples of blood from the heart, urine from the bladder, and vitreous from the eyes for toxicology. When that was done, he started removing the organs, beginning with the heart. To his surprise, he detected a slight degree of aortic stenosis. After opening the vessel, he pointed out the valvular pathology to Lou.

"Could that have killed her?" Lou asked.

"I can't imagine," Jack said.

"Would it have become a problem as she got older?"

"I doubt it," Jack said. "It's mild, and even if it did become symptomatic, it is a condition that can be treated without much trouble since valve replacement and open-heart surgery have come a long way in recent years."

The next organs were the lungs, and as Jack removed the left lung from the chest cavity, he gauged its weight by lifting it up and down in his hand. "Okay. My guess it's a bit heavier than expected considering her size, which suggests a fluid-filled lung. Of course, that points toward it being a drug overdose." Jack put the lung onto the scale hanging over the table. "Yup," he added, looking at the digital readout, "that's certainly on the high side considering her size and habitus. But let's confirm." Taking the lung from the scale and putting it on a wooden tray, he used a butcher's knife to make multiple slices into it. Fluid immediately ran out onto the surface to form a puddle. "There you go! Pulmonary edema, a sine qua non of a drug overdose."

"Really?" Lou said, sounding either exhausted or depressed. He shrugged. "Well, maybe I was wrong. I suppose it isn't the first or last time, but I'm surprised. I was so sure."

"We can't be certain it was an overdose until toxicology confirms it," Jack said. "There are a few other things that can cause it." He was thinking about how much the lung in front of him looked like Sue's, which reminded him of his thoughts last night about Sue's cyanosis and what it had suggested to him. There was no doubt in his mind that all the same thoughts applied equally to Cherine, as she looked as cyanotic as Sue had or more so. Jack glanced up at Vinnie, wondering if he'd recognized the same thing, but Vinnie didn't give any indication he was thinking anything besides his normal impatience to get the case done. Looking back down at Cherine's open body, now missing its heart and one lung, Jack couldn't help but wonder if whatever had killed this woman was the same as what had killed Sue. Could they possibly have shared the same drug? After all, they were collaborators and apparently friends.

"Yeah, sure, other things can cause it," Lou said. "The important thing here is that it's not looking anything like a homicide. Far from it. I don't know what I was suspecting, but I thought there'd be something to explain the supposed muffled scream and the guy departing. Maybe it was a drug dealer, but we'll probably never know. Anyway, with that said, I need some shut-eye big-time. If you two gentlemen will excuse me, I think I'll mosey on home."

"Good idea," Jack said. "Meanwhile on my end, I'll try my darndest to get Toxicology to give us some answers ASAP to confirm or disprove a drug overdose."

"You do that," Lou said. "And thanks for letting me observe you guys. It's been a pleasure as always." He started to walk away but hesitated and then returned. He looked directly at Jack and pointed a finger. "And remember! One day! You are a superb medical examiner, but you are a piss-poor detective. So be careful!"

"Aye, aye, sir," Jack said while giving a

partial salute.

"I wish I could count on that," Lou mumbled loud enough for both Jack and Vinnie to hear. Then he left.

"What did he mean by 'one day'?" Vinnie questioned, watching Lou pass down behind all the autopsy tables, most of which were now occupied. "And what does he mean you are a poor detective?"

"Beats me," Jack said.

CHAPTER 26

Wednesday, December 8, 9:17 A.M.

Juggling an armload of specimen bottles just as he had the day before, Jack got off the elevator on the sixth floor and managed to walk into John DeVries's empty office in Toxicology without dropping any. Carefully he unloaded them, separated the toxicology specimens from those destined for Histology, and then arranged the toxicology bottles like toy soldiers in single file, front and center on John's desk. Just as he was finishing, John walked in.

"Ah, more care packages!" John declared humorously. He was dressed in a laboratory coat, which he took off and hung up on an antique coat-rack. "What do we have here?"

"Probably nothing particularly interesting. It's a female nurse with a preliminary diagnosis of overdose. A bag of powder was found at the scene, which tested positive for fentanyl."

"But you bringing the samples up here yourself tells me you suspect otherwise," John said. He twisted the bottles around to line up the labels, telling him the source of each.

"You're getting too sharp in your old age," Jack quipped.

"I wish that were the case," John said. "Okay, enough flattery. What's the story here?"

"Detective Soldano was thinking the patient was a victim of homicide, considering aspects of the scene and some testimony. He felt so strongly that he even came in this morning to observe the post. As he explained to me, he's taking the uptick in homicides personally and was convinced this was another one disguised as an overdose. Unfortunately for him, the post didn't back him up."

"I remember Detective Soldano," John said. "You brought him up here one day and introduced us."

"I did because he's a big fan of forensics and particularly toxicology," Jack explained. "Anyway, the autopsy, as I said, has seemed to confirm it was indeed an overdose with mild pulmonary edema being the only pathology. But because of his interest and because of the demographics of the case, he and I would like to know right away if it indeed was an overdose."

"Why is it that so many of your cases are toxicological emergencies?" John questioned with a laugh. "All the other MEs seem to be content with the usual week to two-week delay in getting final results."

Jack laughed in response. "I suppose that is a good question. I guess it's because I take my job speaking for the dead seriously."

"I can certainly vouch for that," John said. "But it is a little late to help them since they are already dead."

"It's to prevent more deaths," Jack explained. "That's really what we MEs and you toxicologists ultimately hope to do."

"Well said," John remarked. "What's this bottle labeled 'skin lesion'?"

"Good thing you pointed that out," Jack said. "I meant to explain it. It is a sample of a skin lesion, which is probably a small nevus, but since this case reminded me of yesterday's, it occurred to me it might be an injection site. I'll know once Histology makes some slides. If it is an injection site, it's going to be key to know what had been injected."

"Fair enough," John said. "So, you'll let me know what Histology tells you?"

"I will," Jack said. "Now, what can you

tell me about results from yesterday's case?"

"It's only been twenty-four hours," John said, rolling his eyes. "Everything is still pending except the general screen, which was negative."

"No!" Jack blurted. After all the thinking he'd been doing about cyanosis and the physiology of extremis, he'd been progressively sure Sue had taken a lethal drug, which he assumed had been fentanyl as it had become so common in causing overdoses because of its potency.

"You are surprised?" John questioned. "Why? You told me yesterday you thought the chances of the case being an overdose were zero. Obviously, you were correct, so why the surprise now?"

"Because I had rethought everything since I spoke to you, especially that the deceased had been cyanotic and had such characteristic pulmonary edema. The main reason I'd been against the idea was having known the woman personally and, I thought, relatively well, but when it comes down to it, who knows anybody well? Damn!" Jack added with growing emotion. "Now I have to go back and rethink everything all over again. Jesus H. Christ!"

"Sorry to be the bearer of bad news," John said.

"Don't be silly, it's not your fault," Jack said, while his mind churned with a kaleidoscope of thoughts relating cyanosis, pulmonary edema, and the associated physiology. Suddenly, these thoughts dovetailed in the curious associative fashion that only the human mind can do. As a result, the name *Carl Wingate* popped unbidden into his consciousness, and Jack knew why . . . the man was not a fan of Sue or Cherine, was an odd duck in his estimation, but, more important, he was an anesthesiologist, and anesthesiologists used a drug called succinylcholine on a daily basis. Succinylcholine, or SUX as the medical profession frequently called it, paralyzed people almost instantly with just a tiny amount, and unless the anesthesiologists or anesthetists breathed for the patient, the patient would become cyanotic and die.

"All right, thanks for stopping by," John said agreeably as he started to pick up the specimen bottles. "I'll have the techs run a general drug screen on this new case. If I crack the whip again, I should have at least a preliminary reading by this time tomorrow."

"Wait a second!" Jack said. "I've just had another thought. What's the status of detecting succinylcholine? Has that improved of late?" Like any ME, Jack knew that detecting the powerful drug was inordinately difficult because the body very quickly degraded it into compounds that were indigenous to the human body. He also knew that Histology might have something to contribute even if changes weren't pathognomonic or specific for succinylcholine poisoning.

John paused picking up the sample containers and smiled. "Sounds like you have been reading some recent detective stories. Yes and no, as far as success in detecting it goes. There have been some successes in several recent legal cases by looking for specific metabolites with high-performance liquid chromatography–mass spectrometry, but it isn't easy and often fails and can be challenged in court. Do you have reason to suspect it in either of these cases?"

"Maybe both," Jack said, warming to the idea, as Sue certainly had had an injection and even Cherine might have had one combined with both having some degree of cyanosis as well as mild pulmonary edema.

"We can certainly try," John said. "But that will take real time, probably at least a week, provided I can afford to put someone on it right away."

"Let's give it a whirl," Jack said. He

remembered when he had been talking with Lou earlier in the locker room, the thought had passed that if both Sue's and Cherine's manner of death were homicides, which they certainly would be if succinylcholine was involved, it probably would have been caused by the same person, raising the specter of a medical serial killer. Succinylcholine certainly wasn't something available at the local pharmacy.

"Okay," John said. "We'll get on it, but don't be pestering me. Let me call you, okay?"

"Fine," Jack said agreeably. With his mind in overdrive, he was eager to plan what he was going to do during the single day that he had promised Lou. First off, he needed whatever slides were ready, and then he was going to set up a meeting with Ronnie Cavanaugh. There was no doubt in his mind that he was making significant progress on what was becoming one of his more interesting cases out of an inordinately large repertoire.

After quickly but sincerely thanking John for his help and saying goodbye, Jack took the remaining specimen bottles and made his way to Histology.

"Ah, my favorite ME," Maureen said with a big smile as Jack came into her office. Her cheeks were noticeably redder from the cooler weather.

"Ah, you say that to all the MEs," he said, pretending to be dismissive.

"You are wrong!" Maureen said with a laugh. "You're the only ME who visits us, which I love. It makes us feel appreciated. And now it appears you are bearing gifts."

"More work, I'm afraid," Jack said. Just as he had the previous day, he lined up the specimen bottles on Maureen's desk. There were quite a few more than he'd dropped off in Toxicology, which was the reason he usually made his visits in reverse order, but he'd wanted to give John as much of a head start as possible.

"I've got slides from yesterday's case right here for you," Maureen said. She turned around in her swivel desk chair to take a slide tray off the countertop behind her. As soon as Jack was finished unloading the specimen bottles, he took the tray from her.

"I appreciate getting this so soon," Jack said.

"I hope Dr. Montgomery isn't too devastated by her friend's death," Maureen said, becoming serious.

"She's okay," he confided. "Luckily she's got a lot on her plate to keep her mind occupied."

"I've made it a point to keep that little bit of information private."

"I'm sure the chief appreciates it," Jack said.

"What's the story on these new specimens? Any specific staining requests?" Maureen glanced at the labels.

"No," he said. "But I would appreciate getting slides on this particular specimen ASAP." Jack found and lifted the specimen bottle containing the slice through the potential nevus or injection site, handing it to Maureen. "Whatever is found histologically will influence what John does up in Toxicology."

"Okay," Maureen said agreeably. "I'll put someone on it right away." She placed the bottle apart from the others.

"Okay, thanks, Maureen," Jack said. He raised the slide tray she had given him. "And thanks for this. The chief thanks you, too."

Exiting the Histology Department, he made his way down to his office using the stairwell to avoid having to wait for an elevator. He put the slide tray that Maureen had just given him next to his microscope before hanging up his jacket on the hook behind his door. Plopping himself down in his desk chair, he pulled out his phone and clicked on Bart Arnold's name, whom he had called the day before at 6:03 P.M. As the call went through, Jack put his mobile on speaker and placed it on his desk. Then he stripped off the rubber band from around the Sue Passero slide tray and lifted its cover. The numerous slides were arranged in two vertical columns with their origins carefully labeled. He lifted out several from the heart. He'd look at the lungs second and then the rest.

"Bart Arnold here," Bart said.

As Jack introduced himself, he turned on his microscope light and fitted one of the slides onto the mechanical stage with the stage clip. "Have you had a chance to look into the monthly death rate that we've gotten from the Manhattan Memorial Hospital over the previous two years?" Jack was now running the objective down with the coarse adjustment wheel to practically touch the slide.

"Yes, Janice Jaeger was able to spend some time on it last night in the wee hours of the morning because things were slow."

"Great," Jack said. He truly appreciated Janice Jaeger's thoroughness. "What did she find?" He put his eyes to the microscope's oculars and peered in while backing up with the fine control. Out of the visible blur, sudden pink images emerged of cardiac cellular structure.

"The number of cases referred to the OCME was pretty uniform during the first year," Bart said. "Then it started to change. At first it was a relatively slow change but then picked up speed."

"Ouch! I was afraid of that," Jack said. He sat back, questioning how such a fact could jibe with the hospital's reported decrease in the mortality ratio. Obviously, it couldn't, and although indirect, more deaths lent weight to Sue's concern about a possible medical serial killer. "Exactly how much has it gone up?"

"Gone up?" Bart questioned. "It hasn't gone up. It's gone down, and it's gone down considerably."

Stunned almost as much as he'd been up in John's office learning Sue's drug screen had been negative, Jack tried to adjust to this information that was the opposite of what he'd expected. Although deaths being referred to the OCME from the MMH going down didn't necessarily eliminate the chances a medical serial killer existed, it certainly and significantly reduced them, especially when it confirmed the mortality ratio, which had also gone down, meaning the two statistics did indeed jibe.

"Are you still there?" Bart questioned when Jack failed to respond.

"Yeah, I'm here," he said. He felt oddly depressed, as if everyone was working against him. First Cherine died, then John threw him a curveball, and now Bart. It was as if facts and circumstance were mocking him. Of course, he knew such thoughts were ridiculous, but he couldn't help but feel them at least for the time being.

"Is there anything else you'd like us to do?" Bart asked. "Would any breakdown of the various causes of death help you?"

"No, but thank you," Jack said. "I'll be back to you if I think of anything."

"We're here when you need us," Bart said, and then he hung up.

Jack leaned farther back, causing his desk chair to creak, and stared up at the blank ceiling, thinking it was symbolic of his current state of mind. He'd started the day in a fit of excitement, feeling as if he were on the edge of solving the whole mystery, and now he seemed no better off than he'd been the day before when he'd finished Sue's rather unremarkable autopsy.

Tipping forward again, he eyed his microscope and the open tray of histology slides. He reminded himself that he'd originally thought there was a chance that histology would add some important information. With that thought in mind, he wheeled forward and returned to staring into the microscope's oculars.

For the next several minutes, Jack carefully scanned multiple sections of the heart. As had been suggested by the totally negative gross examination of the organ, the microscopic sections were also boringly routine. There were a few pockets of errant red blood cells, but he reasoned they were probably artifact due to the slicing of the samples with the microtome. More important, the cellular structures all appeared completely normal, as did the cardiac capillaries and coronary arteries. There was only a tiny bit of possible thickening in one artery cross section, but he knew it wasn't any more than what might be seen in an adolescent's heart. There was absolutely nothing that would have supported a diagnosis of a heart attack.

Next he looked at the sections of the lungs. Except for some extra fluid, which was expected with pulmonary edema, and a few extra red blood cells, they were unremarkable. Same with the rest of the organs of the body.

When he was finished looking at the slides, he closed the tray, returned the rubber band around it, and put it aside. He felt unnaturally becalmed, which for Jack in his current life was a totally foreign mental state. He was accustomed to constant action and, if anything, a strong tailwind pushing him to greater efforts. It was a lifestyle and mindset he'd developed to pull out of the paralyzing depression the loss of his first family had caused. As a result, Jack had become averse to standing still or, as he called it, vegetating. He found himself lamenting that Ronald Cavanaugh worked the night shift because it meant he'd probably be sleeping all day.

Glancing at his watch, Jack tried to imagine what time he might hear from the nurse, as he distinctly remembered him saying he'd call sometime today. Since Ronnie's shift went from 7:00 P.M. to 7:00 A.M., it stood to reason that he'd sleep at least to the middle of the afternoon, so it probably wouldn't be until 3:00 or even 4:00. He sighed. As keyed up as he was, he was at a loss for how he was going to weather the wait. His line of sight moved to the stack of autopsy folders and the unexamined trays of slides on his desk. He could easily spend the hours completing multiple cases, and he probably should, but he realistically doubted he'd be able to concentrate, and if he couldn't concentrate, he reasoned that he might not perform at the level he required of himself.

Instead of signing out cases, Jack picked up his phone and stared at the text Ronnie had sent him during the night: Here's my number. I look forward to continuing our conversation. He typed out a reply. Thank you for your contact. I look forward to continuing our conversation as well. I'm available as soon as it is convenient for you.

Only a moment after Jack had hit the send button, his phone rang, making him start. In a mild panic he looked back at the screen, wondering if in some weird technological way Ronnie was responding instantly. But it wasn't Ronnie calling. It was Laurie.

Jack let his phone ring for several cycles just to allow his brain to readjust, then answered.

"Where are you?" she demanded. Her tone was insistent, angry, and incriminating.

"I'm back at the St. Regis for more French toast," he said, but then regretted it just as he'd done yesterday. The problem was that such sarcasm had become reflex over the years as a kind of defense mechanism. Often it was effective, but with Laurie it rarely worked, and he knew it would only serve to aggravate her more than she clearly already was. Sometimes he was his own worst enemy.

"I'm not even going to respond to that," Laurie said. "Are you in the pit?"

"No, I happen to be up here in my palatial office. You sound a bit out of sorts."

"I *am* out of sorts!" she snapped. "Get your ass down here! I want to talk with you! You, my friend, are again in the doghouse."

"Can we put it off for an hour or so? I'm expecting the pope to stop by shortly." Jack winced, knowing he was undoubtedly making the situation worse. But he couldn't help himself. She was pushing his buttons, acting like the Laurie he'd come to dislike: boss Laurie.

"Get down here!" she yelled before disconnecting.

"Now what?" he questioned as he tossed his phone onto the desk and went back to staring up at the ceiling. He wanted to give himself a moment to let his irritation subside. He tried to think of what she was now angry about, but he couldn't imagine unless it was about his playing detective. That morning everything had been hunky-dory. He'd even managed a pleasant conversation with Dorothy, who had gotten up uncharacteristically early.

When he felt he was reasonably under control and able to deal with whatever it was that Laurie was upset about, he grabbed his jacket. As he walked down the hallway to the elevator, he put it on. He didn't rush.

CHAPTER 27

Wednesday, December 8, 10:30 A.M.
Arriving at the administrative office, Jack approached Cheryl's desk. As per usual, she was on the phone with headphones fitted with a small microphone. Although she wasn't at the moment speaking, it was clear to him that she was listening, as she was also scribbling some notes. When Jack was about to pass, she raised her left hand and motioned with a thumbs-down, meaning Laurie was currently occupied, and he'd have to wait.

For Jack, waiting under such circumstances was like adding insult to injury, but he dutifully went over to the outer-office couch and sat down. Luckily, he didn't have to wait long. Within minutes her office door opened, and the deputy chief, George Fontworth, emerged. His expression was glum.

"Is she in a bad mood?" Jack questioned, getting to his feet as George passed.

"The worst," George whispered back. "Good luck! You are going to need it. Something happened that has made the incoming mayor's support a little rocky. She wouldn't tell me what it was."

"Jesus H. Christ," Jack mumbled. He looked over at Cheryl, who now gave him a thumbs-up. Progressively curious as to why he was being called on the carpet, he walked into Laurie's cheerfully decorated domain. In sharp contrast to the décor, her expression was somber as she drilled Jack with her intense blue-green eyes. Her flushed cheeks reflected the bright red silk dress she was wearing. She was standing behind her large desk, leaning forward on her fingertips with her arms straight. It was apparent she had been again closely examining the morgue architectural plans, which were still spread out on the desk.

"I got a most disturbing phone call a few minutes ago from a member of the mayor-elect's transition team," Laurie said while straightening up. She folded her arms in a way that reminded him of his hard-nosed sixth-grade teacher.

"Oh, good," Jack said brightly. "Were they calling to compliment you anew on your presentation yesterday?"

She shook her head. "Always the wise

guy," she said irritably. "Quite the opposite! The person I spoke with said that she had gotten an angry call from Marsha Schechter, who was a big donor to the campaign and has the incoming mayor's ear. Schechter called to lodge an official complaint that a medical examiner by the name of Jack Stapleton had been caught at the hospital, going into locked offices without permission, and, worst of all, looking into hospital papers that he had no clearance to be reading and was escorted off the campus. Is all that true?"

"No, it is not!" he said with authority.

"It's not?" Laurie questioned, momentarily taken aback.

"I never got to look at the hospital papers, much less read them," Jack explained.

She rolled her eyes and waited a beat before responding to try to calm herself down. "Okay, smart aleck. The critical fact here is that you went over to the MMH one time. Is that true, yes or no?"

"I did not go one time," Jack said.

"No?" Laurie again questioned with equal surprise.

"I went twice," Jack confessed. "In the early afternoon and in the late afternoon." He was now as irritated as Laurie for unfairly being attacked for doing his job.

"Oh, God!" she exclaimed. "You are impossible. You know you are not supposed to go out on site visits. It's been a major policy here for years, which I am now responsible for enforcing. Can you imagine, just once, what kind of message it sends to everyone if I allow my husband to break such an established rule? On top of that, what if I lose the mayor's support for the new morgue building over something like this?"

"Oh, come on," he complained. "The mayor isn't going to stop supporting the OCME because I irritate the MMH president. That's absurd."

"Is it?" Laurie questioned. "That's not what the caller from the transition team suggested, and I'm not interested in testing it. No way! And you understand the bind I'm in vis-à-vis the MLI situation. If they find out I'm allowing our MEs to chip away at their prerogatives, the attrition rate is going to balloon. They have become rightfully proud of their role."

"Yeah, well, do I need to remind you that you were a frequent violator of this rule when you were a mere ME? We both trained at programs that encouraged site visits. It can be critical, and you know it."

"We both know that neither of our training programs had what we have here," Laurie said. It was apparent her anger was lessening but still palpable. "They didn't have the kind of medical legal investigators who are highly trained to do forensic field-work. And I happen to know that on Sue's case Kevin Strauss was assigned, and I also know he is more than capable of doing whatever needs to be done. If you want something from the field, ask him to do it."

"The problem with Sue's case is that I didn't know what I didn't know, so I didn't know what to ask him to do," Jack said. "Listen, I still don't have a cause and mechanism for Sue's death, which you insisted I handle. This morning I went back to believing it had to have been an overdose despite you and I not being able to imagine she'd be using drugs. But then, just an hour ago, John DeVries threw that idea out the window by telling me her toxicological screen was negative. Then I looked at the histology. It was essentially clean. So where am I now? Nowhere! I'm reduced to grasp-ing at straws. To give you an idea of my desperation, I just had a conversation with John about looking for any possible evidence of succinylcholine because one of the muckety-mucks who I found out hated her guts is an anesthesiologist. After all, she did have multiple insulin injection sites. What if one of those injection sites had been SUX, not insulin?"

"Good grief," she said. "Are you really convinced Sue's death was a homicide?"

"No!" Jack snapped. "I'm not convinced of anything. Well, that's not quite true. The only thing I am convinced of is that had I not gone over to the MMH, I wouldn't have gotten wind about Sue's concern about an active serial killer. Who the hell knows whether that's at the bottom of all this malarkey? The long and short of it is that I need a cause or mechanism or a manner of Sue's death. One way or the other, I have to come up with something."

"Oh, right," Laurie said. In her fury following the call from the mayor's transition team, she had forgotten about the Jack's mentioning the possible existence of a medical serial killer at the MMH. After admitting the issue had slipped her mind, particularly after Jack had told her the hospital mortality ratio had gone down, she added, "Any more news about that scary possibility?"

"Not really," he admitted. "I just spoke with Bart, who had Janice Jaeger gather the number of monthly deaths that have been reported to us from the MMH over the last two years."

"And?" Laurie asked.

"The numbers have fallen, not risen, consistent with the falling mortality ratio."

"That's hardly confirmatory," she said. "In fact, it's the opposite. When are you going to be meeting today with the charge nurse who told you about it and find out what statistics were responsible for Sue's suspicions?"

"That's another weird, unexpected curveball," Jack said. "The orthopedic charge nurse, whose name was Cherine Gardener, died last night. I just posted her this morning."

Laurie's mouth dropped open and the fire in her cheeks faded. "You're joking," she said hesitantly. Slowly she sank down into her desk chair with her forearms resting on the desk. She appeared stunned.

"I wish I were joking," Jack said. Following her lead, he retreated to the colorful couch and sat. After waiting a beat to give Laurie a moment to digest what he had just told her, he added, "Needless to say, I was flabbergasted, and frankly disappointed, when I saw her name on an autopsy folder. It shocked me almost as much as seeing Sue's name yesterday. I'm hoping this isn't becoming a daily habit." He chuckled sarcastically.

"It's not a joking matter," Laurie said. "Good grief! Could this death be related in some horrid way with Sue's passing?"

"Obviously that was one of my first concerns," Jack said. "Especially having learned that both Sue and Cherine were seen as partners in crime by some of the MMH higher-ups. But at this point, I'm tending to believe it is just an unfortunate coincidence. With Ms. Gardener, there is evidence it was an overdose and not just because there was typical pulmonary edema, which there was. In contrast with Sue's death scene, a bag of suspicious powder was found in Cherine's apartment that tested positive for fentanyl. Some of the powder was also visible in her nostrils."

"But the timing is so suspect."

"Agreed," Jack said. "So here again the burden is on John, who will have the last word."

"Oh, God!" Laurie complained while gesturing with her hands. "As if I don't have enough to worry about. I'm glad that you are on top of this. What is your sixth sense telling you?"

"To be honest, my sixth sense is reminding me of my favorite Shakespeare quote: 'Something is rotten in the state of

Denmark.' However, at the same time I'm also cognizant of my reflexive hatred of AmeriCare and hence to the administration of its flagship hospital, the MMH. I'm not sure I can be my usual analytic self, but I'm trying. On the positive side, another nurse was in cahoots with both Sue and Cherine and at odds with the same hospital heavy-weights. I already got a chance to speak with him briefly. He's an impressive fellow, and he was helpful to an extent under the time constraints. He works the night shift, so he's undoubtedly sleeping at the moment. But he said he doesn't need much sleep, so I'm expecting a call at any time. My hope is that Sue had been as open about her medical serial killer suspicions with him as she had been with Cherine, which I have reason to believe was the case. When I spoke with him, I tried to find out if he knew anything about it without flat-out asking him, but I wasn't successful because we ran out of time. Hopefully, that won't be the case today, so if he knows about it, I'll be able to find out. Of course, I'm also hoping he doesn't end up here for an autopsy like Cherine." Jack let out a short, mirthless laugh. "To be truthful, I'm getting para-noid."

"That's understandable," Laurie said. "I

hope your talk with this second nurse is fruitful. It sounds promising. But let's talk about how to proceed in a general sense. Last night, I asked if it was time to let Lou know about this possible serial killer issue, but you said that it was a little early. Do you still feel that way? With even the slightest possibility of Sue's and Cherine's deaths being related, I think it's better to be safe than sorry. Your thoughts?"

"Lou is already on board," he said. He inwardly winced since once again he wasn't being entirely up-front. He had purposely not mentioned anything about a potential serial killer to Lou, fearing that Lou's tactics would undoubtedly spook a serial killer, if there was one, making it more difficult if not impossible for Jack.

"Did you talk with him this morning?" Laurie asked.

"I certainly did! He was here when I arrived, which surprised me. I hadn't seen him for almost a month, and then he shows up two days in a row. He had come in to observe the post on Cherine."

"Really?" Laurie questioned. "Why on earth was Lou interested in observing an overdose? They're sadly a dime a dozen these days."

"Interesting you should ask," Jack said. "It

initially confused me, too, because Kevin Strauss had unequivocally signed it out as an overdose. When I asked Lou, he admitted his concern was based more on a gut feeling than a rational one, worried that the death was a homicide gussied up to look like an overdose. But the idea wasn't based on much."

"Like what?" she asked.

"The woman's apartment was in disarray, as if there had been a struggle of some sort, and one tenant thought there might had been a scream. But that was it. Lou admitted his suspicions probably had more to do with his taking personally the uptick in homicides during the pandemic. Halfway through the autopsy, he pretty much had changed his mind to agree with Kevin's assessment. Everything pointed toward an overdose. One way or the other, though, we will know tomorrow from John."

"Did Lou say what he might do between now and then?"

"No, he didn't," Jack said. "Not specifically. But he did agree to give me one more day to see what I could find out before calling in the cavalry."

"You mean your upcoming meeting with the nursing supervisor?"

"Exactly," he added. "I am going to put

pressure on him to talk today. If there is time, I'd like him to come here."

"All right," Laurie said. "But I want you to promise not to cause any more aggravation with Schechter. Can I at least count on that?"

"Absolutely! Scout's honor," Jack said, giving a reassuring smile and a thumbs-up. "There is one administrator who I'd love to talk with, who was apparently Sue's nemesis. Well, along with two doctors, including the anesthesiologist I mentioned who I did get to talk with briefly, but I will avoid talking with the administrator. If by speaking with the nightshift nursing supervisor again, I get even the slightest hint of an active serial killer, I'll let Lou and his team take over. He and his detectives can talk to this administrator, who I'd describe as a person of interest along with the two doctors."

"You said you spoke to Kevin Strauss about Sue's case. Did you happen to tell him that you'd been over at the MMH making a site visit?"

"Of course not," Jack said. "I was careful to avoid it. Interestingly enough, Kevin encouraged me to talk with the night nursing supervisor. Kevin was complimentary about the man, saying he'd worked with him on numerous occasions. I can understand why. Ronnie is clinically astute and personable, just how he was described to me."

"Do you think I should call Bart Arnold and let him know this is a special situation, in case he or one of his MLIs get wind of your visiting the MMH?"

"I don't," he said. "I think it is better to let sleeping dogs lie. I've been careful to avoid anyone knowing and will continue to be."

"All right," Laurie said with a sigh and a wave of dismissal as her line of sight reverted down to the architectural plans. "Keep me informed."

"Will do," Jack said. He got to his feet and started toward the door, feeling he was being summarily dismissed.

"Just a minute!" she called out. "Hold up. I'm sorry I got so mad at you. I'm under a lot of pressure. Your seemingly cavalier disregard for one of the explicit rules set me off, especially if you doing so is going to ruin what progress I made yesterday with the mayor-elect. I understand now that wasn't the case."

Jack stopped and turned around. "I appreciate you saying that. I'm sorry I got mad at you for getting mad at me. You did, after all, ask me to take Sue's case. Of course, neither of us had any idea it was going to be so involved, and I truly had to bend the rules to have gotten where I am."

"I appreciate the effort you are making but want to make absolutely certain you understand the varied pressures I'm under."

"I do," he said. "You are trying to keep this variegated ship afloat in the rough seas of New York City politics, which ain't easy. There are so many competing demands. But for the life of me I can't understand why you are willing to do it, knowing how much you liked forensics, how much effort it took to become an ME, and how much satisfaction it gave you. I couldn't do what you are doing, nor would I want to."

Laurie came out from behind her massive desk, and she and Jack met in a spontaneous and warm embrace, holding each other tightly for a few beats in recognition of the appreciation, respect, and affection that they shared and which had continued to mushroom over the years despite the strains of their children's medical issues.

As they separated, yet still holding hands, Laurie said, "I do miss being an ME and the opportunity to speak for the dead as you are continuing to do. Medical forensics is a true calling. But now I see this job as speaking to the living, which in many ways is equally as challenging and rewarding. A lot of people in high places in this city do not understand the tremendous service and value of the OCME, which can more than justify its considerable budget. It's my role to change that misunderstanding while keeping everyone here happy and motivated and working as a team. As you rightly said, all of this ain't easy. It's like juggling a dozen balls all at the same time."

"Touché," Jack said. "Very well expressed. Being the chief is still not my cup of tea, but I'll accept it is yours when you explain it so eloquently. Accordingly, I will proceed with my inquiries with the utmost tact to avoid any possibility of making your job more difficult. It was pure coincidence that I ran into Marsha Schechter, and I will make damn sure it doesn't happen today."

"Thank you, sweetie," Laurie said. "And definitely keep me actively in the loop and Lou, too, particularly if anything whatsoever hints a medical serial killer is involved. Promise?"

"Promise!" he said. "One way or the other, I'll fill you in as soon as I talk with Ronnie this afternoon, and then we decide how to proceed."

"Be careful," she advised.

"I'm always careful," Jack said with a laugh.

"Yeah, right," Laurie responded with a disbelieving shake of her head.

CHAPTER 28

Wednesday, December 8, 2:50 P.M.

Ronnie woke up with a start, worried that he'd overslept. He snatched up his phone, clicked it on, and then sighed with relief when he saw the time. He'd not overslept. Tossing his phone back on his night table, he lay back on the pillow and tried to relax while he bemoaned the state of turmoil his life had become because of one meddlesome doctor. At the same time, he had to congratulate himself for having managed to deal with the situation so far with such admirable dispatch, even though the episode with Cherine Gardener hadn't been as smooth as he would have preferred. As he thought back to the struggle he'd had with the puny nurse, he couldn't quite believe how strong and defiant she'd been despite her size.

When he'd gotten home the previous evening, he'd been so worked up knowing the problem wasn't quite over that he had to go out to calm himself down. He'd driven over to a sports bar and had a few beers and mindlessly watched a replay of the Knicks game, all the while thinking about Jack Stapleton and how big a threat he might turn out to be. Ronnie also congratulated himself for having cleverly learned that the medical examiner had been told of Dr. Passero's serial killer worry but hadn't been told why. When Ronnie combined that with his mentioning to the man that the MMH's mortality ratio had been trending downward, he felt relatively confident the crisis wasn't super critical, just critical, meaning he was reasonably safe as long as he got rid of the man that afternoon. What was going to help was that Stapleton was expecting Ronnie to call today to set up a meeting. It was Ronnie's plan to arrange the meeting that afternoon.

After closing the sports bar around 3:00 A.M., Ronnie had gone back to his apartment in Woodside. Still somewhat keyed up, he didn't try to sleep. Over the years, he'd become totally adapted to working the night shift and normally didn't go to sleep until around 9:00 or 10:00 A.M. Instead of sleeping, he used his laptop to google *Jack Stapleton* and learn as much as he could about the man, particularly where he lived and where he worked, and, most important, getting confirmation that he used his bike to get around New York City. Ronnie couldn't believe his luck. Such a habit made it seem as if Stapleton was asking to be killed.

By 5:30 Ronnie had made himself some eggs and bacon, and by 6:15 he was back in his beloved Cherokee heading for Manhattan. To facilitate his plan, he had to be certain about Stapleton's habits. Accordingly, well before 7:00 A.M., Ronnie had pulled over to the side of First Avenue just shy of 30th Street, where he could see the OCME building to his right as well as west up 30th Street to his left. Like a lot of buildings in the city, the OCME was surrounded by scaffolding without any evidence of any construction, making him wonder why it was there.

Not too long after sunrise at 7:07, Ronnie had been rewarded by seeing a bicyclist appear in the distance up 30th Street sporting a lime green helmet and dressed in a corduroy jacket with scarf and gloves. As he watched, the man had come streaking toward him, outpacing the vehicular traffic, and then came to a stop at the traffic light. At that point, Ronnie pulled a car-length forward such that the bicyclist would have to cross within feet of him, giving him a chance to make absolutely sure it was Jack Stapleton.

When the light had changed, the bicyclist pedaled across the avenue, and Ronnie had gotten a good look at him. There had been no doubt whatsoever: It had indeed been Stapleton. Satisfied with his accomplishment, Ronnie had driven back to his apartment in Woodside on 54th Street just off Northern Boulevard. The main reason Ronnie lived where he did was because the apartment came with a detached garage reached by a rear alleyway. Once the car was safely put to bed, Ronnie had gone inside and done the same for himself.

"Okay!" Ronnie said as he tossed off his covers and stood up in the chill of his bedroom. He was ready for his day to begin and had a lot to do before he called Stapleton. He didn't want to call too early, as he wanted to control where the meeting happened and limit Stapleton's options. It was Ronnie's intention to insist on meeting again at the MMH back in the ED MD lounge, although the exact location didn't matter. All that mattered was that the meeting would be not at the OCME but at the hospital. Ronnie's plan was simple. He intended to make sure Stapleton did not make it all the way to the MMH but instead would have a terrible, fatal accident on the way.

After making himself some breakfast, it was still too early to call Stapleton. Ronnie wanted it to be late enough to claim there wouldn't be time for him to meet and get from the OCME to the MMH before the start of his shift at 7:00 P.M. To fill the time, Ronnie decided to reaffirm his avowed crusade of saving people from the clutches of the medical profession and pharmaceutical industry, both of which selfishly profited mightily from abusing and torturing mortally ill patients. To do that, he got a step stool out of his closet and a screwdriver from his tools and sundries drawer in the kitchen. After placing the stool under the HVAC vent in his apartment's hallway, which connected his kitchen and bedroom from his living room, he climbed up and removed the sheet metal screws. Allowing the grille to rotate downward, he was able to reach up inside the duct and retrieve a dog-eared ledger. Leaving the grille open, he carried the ledger into the kitchen and sat at the built-in table. Along with the Cherokee and the SIG Sauer pistol, the ledger was a favorite possession, which he perused regularly to celebrate his accomplishments.

Over a period of almost six years, which included two years at a hospital in Queens, where he'd first worked after getting his nursing bachelor's degree before moving to the MMH, he'd kept a careful record of all the mercy killings he'd been able to accomplish. It had started out slowly, as the opportunities had been few and far between, but then had sped up once he'd become a nursing supervisor. The pace had magnified dramatically once he'd become a solo supervisor. Over the last year, he was impressed with how many people he'd saved from an ongoing frightful existence. Each entry had the name, the diagnosis, the horrid treatments they'd endured, the date, and the agent he used, which was usually just an overdose of a medication the patient was prescribed.

As Ronnie's eyes went down the list, he could recall just about all the patients quite clearly. He could even remember conversing with many of them, hearing their sad stories of the tortures they had endured and commiserating with them. All at once, he came to Frank Ferguson, whom he remembered distinctly since his case was a mirror image of Ronnie's foster mother, Iris. She had been a nurse and a stimulus for Ronnie to become a nurse. She had also been a chain-smoker who had developed throat cancer. At the time, Ronnie had been an impressionable preteen and had been horrified when she was transformed from an attractive woman into a ghoulish caricature of herself, both physically and mentally, such that she could have starred in a gruesome antismoking campaign advertisement. It also marked the time that Ronnie and his younger foster brother started becoming chronically sick, requiring innumerable hospitalizations, which Ronnie was later to realize had been caused by Iris plying them with inordinate amounts of salt, which ultimately killed his brother. Ronnie had been able to escape by aging out of foster care and joining the navy.

The last two entries in the ledger were from four days earlier, when Ronnie had used insulin to put an end to the tortures of two men, one with colorectal cancer and another with prostate cancer. Both had had metastatic disease and multiple surgeries. They were numbers ninety-three and ninety-four. It was a comfort for Ronnie to know they were now in a better place.

For a few minutes, Ronnie toyed with the idea of adding the names of Sue Passero and Cherine Gardener to the ledger entries, as their deaths added to the crusade by making sure it continued. But ultimately he decided against it, for the same reason he had never added to the main section of the ledger any of the inadvertent deaths that had occurred when he'd failed to save a patient whom he'd put in jeopardy to get the credit. Instead, he added their names at the back of the journal, where he'd merely listed the inadvertent deaths.

Feeling totally rededicated to his cause, Ronnie closed the ledger and returned it to its hiding place in the HVAC duct. After repositioning the grille and replacing the sheet metal screws, he checked the time. There was still a half hour before he believed it would be appropriate to call Stapleton and adequate time for him to prepare the Cherokee for the afternoon's activities. With that job in mind, Ronnie went out the back door, unlocked the garage, and entered. His first order of business was to remove his license plates, which he stored in the back of the Cherokee, and replace them with old, outdated New York plates that he'd found in the garage when he moved in. Once that was done, he opened a can of water-based black paint and painted over the orange flames radiating from behind each wheel well. He hated to do it because they added so much to the SUV's allure, but he was confident it would wash off easily. He didn't want his car to stand out that afternoon. He also had a lever inside the car, which, when switched, would redirect the entirety of the exhaust into the car's mufflers, significantly reducing its growl. He intended to flip that lever well before making any contact with his target.

When he was finished with the Cherokee, Ronnie went back into the apartment and returned to the kitchen table with his phone and Stapleton's business card. It was now quarter to four in the afternoon, around the time when he'd deemed it appropriate to make his call. For a few minutes, he just sat there and tried to imagine what kind of argument Stapleton might try to make to insist on having their conversation at the OCME. Ronnie could remember telling the man that he was off Wednesday and Thursday, so that information might resurface, but if it did, Ronnie meant to tell him that had changed. In order to get Sarah Berman to agree to come in last night on the spur of the moment, Ronnie had to offer working both Wednesday and Thursday for her. Of course, he was not going to say anything to Stapleton about having made a trade.

When he felt he was as ready as he was

ever going to be, Ronnie placed the call. As it went through, he relaxed as much as he could. The fact that the call was picked up on the second ring wasn't lost on him. The man had obviously been waiting. That was a good sign, suggesting to him that he was in the proverbial driver's seat.

"Thanks for calling," Jack said. "I was getting a little nervous you might have forgotten."

"Not a chance," Ronnie said brightly. "Sorry. I slept longer than I usually do for some reason."

"You must have needed it," Jack said. "No harm done, but I'm looking forward to continuing our conversation, and the sooner the better. Are you available now?"

"Yes and no," Ronnie said. "I was supposed to be off tonight, but I have to cover for one of the other night supervisors who was originally scheduled. Unfortunately, that means I have to be at the hospital around six. Sorry about that."

"That's fine," Jack said. "Of course, I understand schedules change. But it's not quite four. There's still a couple of hours. How about getting together before you have to clock in?"

"I suppose that might work," Ronnie said. "But I wouldn't want to risk meeting somewhere else and take the chance of being late because of traffic. If you want to meet up today, it will have to be at the MMH."

"That's not a problem for me," Jack said without hesitation. "Where exactly and what time?"

"How about meeting again in the doctors' lounge in the Emergency Department, say, at five-thirty? There's never anyone in there late in the afternoon, so we'll have the place to ourselves just like yesterday. And that should give us plenty of opportunity."

"Fine with me," Jack said. "Actually, I prefer the ED to the hospital proper."

"Is it difficult for you to get there at that time of day?"

"Not at all," Jack said. "It only takes about twenty minutes, traffic or no traffic. It's on my way home."

"How was your meeting today with Cherine Gardener?" Ronnie asked. He'd not planned on posing the question for obvious reasons, yet the idea of doing so suddenly presented itself out of pure curiosity.

"That didn't happen," Jack said.

"Oh," Ronnie commented. "Why was that?"

"She has yet to call me," Jack said.

Ronnie nodded. He was impressed with

Jack's speedy and appropriately vague retort.

"While I have you on the line," Jack said, "let me ask you a general question about your role on the M and M Task Force, since I've been thinking a lot about what you told me. When you get the mortality ratio from the computer, would it be possible for you to also get the monthly gross death rate?"

"That's an interesting question," Ronnie said, also speaking without hesitation despite alarm bells going off in his mind. The fact that Stapleton was merely asking the question underlined why Ronnie needed to get rid of the man. Seeing the raw monthly data was what had pushed Sue Passero over the edge and started the whole current ruckus. "Honestly, I don't know because I've never tried to download the monthly gross death rate. But if I had to hazard a guess, I'd say no. The hospital admin is very chary about raw unadjusted data. The only person who might have access, if it is available, would be the senior vice president chief compliance and ethics officer."

"Well, maybe you should just try next time you're logged in," Jack suggested.

"I'll do that," Ronnie said. "Now I better get a move on to get ready for work."

"See you at five-thirty," Jack said before

disconnecting.

For a few minutes Ronnie just sat there, staring off at nothing. The whole situation reminded him of playing with dominoes as a child. You tip over one, and a whole line falls over until the last one tips. He hoped to hell that Jack Stapleton was going to be the last domino, and he could relax and get back to normal.

After checking the time and knowing he wanted to be in position outside the OCME before 5:00, Ronnie slid out from the table's built-in bench seat and went into the bedroom. From his night table, he retrieved his cherished SIG Sauer P365. From habit, he checked the magazine despite knowing it was fully loaded. The mere act of checking made him feel more confident he was prepared for any eventuality. Although Ronnie was at peace with himself vis-à-vis his crusade, he was well aware that not everyone agreed with his methods, and he was a fatalist about what would happen if he were to be exposed. Long ago, he'd decided he'd never let that happen, which was why he'd prepared his hideaway in the Catskills, where he kept another identity that he'd fashioned with the help of the dark web. It included all the appropriate IDs of a former navy nurse his age who'd died a few years earlier. His general plan, if worse came to worst, was to flee first to his hideaway and then disappear completely, probably to Florida or maybe Texas.

When all was ready, Ronnie went out into the garage and revved up the Cherokee. A few minutes later, he was on his way along Northern Boulevard heading toward Manhattan.

CHAPTER 29

Wednesday, December 8, 4:20 P.M.
With a definite sense of satisfaction, Jack
put the newly completed death certificate in
his outbox and moved its associated autopsy
folder and rubber band–sheathed slide tray
to the distant corner of his L-shaped desk,
along with three other sets. With nothing to
do concerning the Sue Passero case until
his upcoming meeting with Ronald Cavanaugh or until John completed his full
toxicology evaluation, Jack had turned to
signing out the stack of cases he had pending on his desk and had already completed
four. Since he didn't have to leave until a
bit after 5:00 for his 5:30 rendezvous, he
picked up the next case in his considerable
to-be-completed stack when his mobile
rang. Checking the caller, he saw it was Lou.

"Are you checking up on me, Daddy?"
Jack asked facetiously.

"Yeah," Lou answered. "How did you

guess? Are you behaving yourself?"

"Totally," Jack said. "I'm working my butt off here in the safety of my cocoon-like office punching out old cases."

"Actually, I'm calling to compliment you," Lou said. "But I hesitate because I don't want you to get a big head."

"Try me!" Jack laughed.

"You were right about the Seton case," Lou said. "Paul broke down and confessed, but it's complicated. According to Paul, the whole sordid affair supposedly involves some crazy-ass therapist guru who had everyone convinced suicide was the right thing to do, including Sharron and her mother. Paul admits he was the one who screwed everything up, claiming he was so nervous that he did everything wrong. I have no idea how it is going to ultimately play out. Your *Murder on the Orient Express* analogy wasn't so far from reality. How the hell did you even think of it?"

"Only because the forensics spoke for themselves," Jack said. "It certainly wasn't a typical suicide, considering all the factors, particularly the bullet's trajectory. It was the only way to tie it all together if the suicide note was authentic."

"Well, I give you full credit," Lou said. "But let me ask you, what the hell are you doing working on old cases after you talked me into allowing you one more day to play detective on the Sue Passero case? The way you were talking, I thought sure you had something definite up your sleeve."

"I did. For sure. I was planning on having a second go-round earlier with another of Sue's colleagues who was tight with both Sue and Cherine. Unfortunately, he didn't call me until just a few minutes ago when he woke up. He works the night shift and sleeps during the day. We're going to meet up at five-thirty. It should be rewarding, especially since he's a knowledgeable guy."

"Okay," Lou said. "Where is this going to happen?"

"He's working tonight and he's paranoid about being late, so he's insisting we get together over at the MMH. On the plus side, we're going to have our tête-à-tête in the Emergency Department, so I don't need to go into the hospital proper, where I'm somewhat a persona non grata."

"Thank God for small favors," Lou said. "What about the toxicology confirmation of this morning's case, have you gotten it?"

"It hasn't even been eight hours," Jack said. "Good God! You're more impatient than I am."

After a few more back-and-forth teasing

comments, they terminated the call. With a bit of time remaining before he needed to leave to head uptown, Jack went back to try to sign out one more case. Luckily it was an easy one and only required confirmation by his looking at a handful of the slides, which he accomplished easily. With that out of the way, he turned off his microscope, pulled on his corduroy jacket, and headed down to the basement to get his bike. A few minutes later, with his helmet and gloves on and his scarf knotted around his neck, he climbed on his Trek and set off up 30th Street toward First Avenue.

CHAPTER 30

Wednesday, December 8, 5:04 P.M.

Suddenly Ronnie sat bolt upright. He'd been impatiently waiting for Jack Stapleton to appear, sitting in his idling Cherokee double-parked on the right side of First Avenue just south of 30th Street, nearly the same location where he'd been that morning while watching for him. The traffic was heavier at 5:00 P.M. than it had been at 7:00 A.M., and on several occasions cars and taxis had pulled up behind Ronnie when the traffic light had been red, expecting him to drive forward when it turned green. When he didn't, there had been lots of horn blowing and then choice epithets when the cars had finally pulled out and driven around.

Also different than ten hours earlier was that it was now dark and Ronnie was in a completely different mental state. Early that morning he'd been a calm observer, whereas now he was mentally hyped up in anticipation of ridding himself of the danger that Stapleton represented to his ongoing crusade. He felt a definite and pleasurable excitement, not too dissimilar to how he felt just prior to administering the coup de grâce to one of his suffering patients. As he'd sat there, waiting, he'd given a passing thought to immediately running over Jack right there at the intersection, as Jack would most likely have to wait for the light to cross over to the First Avenue bike lane that ran north on the west side and present himself like a sitting duck. But ultimately Ronnie decided that plan was far too risky since it involved colliding with Jack and running him over directly in front of too many witnesses. On top of that was the concern that Ronnie would undoubtedly be forced to stop at the next intersection due to the rush hour traffic congestion, which might cause unknown consequences.

"Finally!" Ronnie voiced as he watched Jack pedal up 30th Street and come to a halt at the intersection to wait for the traffic light to change, exactly as Ronnie had envisioned. In anticipation of action, Ronnie pressed on the Cherokee's accelerator a few times with the transmission in neutral just to be rewarded with the purr of the engine, proclaiming it was ready to do battle. Ronnie had flipped the lever earlier so that the mufflers were fully engaged, and the engine was significantly quieter so as not to cause undue attention.

From that point on, Ronnie did not have a specific plan of attack because he wasn't sure if Jack would come out of the relative safety of the bike path, which was busy, as was the avenue. Contrary to the avenue, the traffic on the bike path wasn't as directionally consistent, with occasional electric delivery bikes going in the reverse direction. If Jack did venture out into the vehicle traffic, Ronnie thought it might offer a good opportunity to run him over, or, if that failed, to give Ronnie the opportunity to pull alongside and shoot him at close range through the open window. Since that was a distinct possibility, Ronnie had his beloved pistol conveniently ready on the passenger seat with a round in the chamber.

As Jack pedaled across the avenue only ten or fifteen feet directly in front of Ronnie, he was able to even see Jack's expression thanks to a nearby streetlight. From Ronnie's vantage point, it seemed as if Jack was smiling.

"Smile now, you fool," Ronnie said. He truly couldn't believe someone would be insane enough to commute to work on a bike considering all the crazy taxis and ride-share drivers, and especially only wearing a corduroy jacket. Although the temperature had been unseasonably moderate over the previous week, it was December, which meant winter in New York City. In Ronnie's mind it was crazy, but he wasn't about to look a gift horse in the mouth. If Jack weren't a dedicated bicyclist, Ronnie would have been at a loss for how to get rid of him short of merely shooting him as he came out of work or his house.

When the traffic light finally turned green for Ronnie, he gunned his Cherokee and jumped out ahead of the traffic. His idea was to cross over the five lanes so that he'd be driving alongside the parked cars that separated the bike lane from avenue traffic. Unfortunately, Ronnie had to slow down almost immediately because cars and buses were taking their time leaving the traffic light at 33rd Street. By then, he could see that Jack was already beyond 33rd Street, moving much faster than the vehicular traffic.

Ronnie's heart skipped a beat. This was a situation he'd not anticipated, and he couldn't let Jack get too far ahead. The idea of Jack arriving at the MMH before him would be anathema. As a result, Ronnie switched into his super-aggressive driving mode and the Cherokee responded in kind, allowing him to weave in and out of the traffic. In desperation, he even resorted to using the dedicated bus lane for short spurts, risking being pulled over by traffic police. Ronnie thanked his lucky stars that he wasn't. He was also thankful that Jack wore a lime green helmet and had a flashing red LED rear bike light, making him stand out even from a block away. Within ten blocks, Ronnie had managed to close the gap and out of the corner of his eye he could see that he was currently traveling abreast of him, but it was a struggle to maintain with the amount of traffic Ronnie had to contend with.

The next thing he knew, a new problem had emerged. The lane of traffic he was in was vectored into a tunnel that he'd forgotten about near the United Nations building, whereas Jack's bike lane stayed up in the open air. For several blocks while he was underground, Ronnie lost sight of him. When he emerged, he didn't see him. Assuming that Jack had to wait for several traffic lights that were avoided by the tunnel, Ronnie moved over to the left-hand side of the avenue and slowed down, again evoking lots of horn honking and angry gestures from irate drivers. Finally, Jack appeared in Ronnie's rearview mirror, along with a clot of other bicyclists that Jack quickly outdistanced. Since the location was now Midtown, more electric delivery bikes were going in both directions and the congestion had become more obvious.

By 54th Street, Jack apparently gave up on the bike lane, and Ronnie saw him suddenly dart out into the traffic. Ronnie allowed himself a smile as it was the change he'd hoped would happen. Now with him out in the road, things were looking rosier. Ronnie even lowered his driver's-side window and moved his SIG Sauer into his lap. He also switched off the pistol's safety.

At the light at 57th Street, Ronnie was a mere two cars behind Jack, who had moved up during the red light to the edge of the intersection. Sensing an opportunity, Ronnie's pulse began to race as he waited for the light to change. His plan was to pull into the dedicated bus lane and then come alongside him, shoot him, then dart forward and make the first left-hand turn to disappear into Midtown traffic.

Unfortunately, the light seemed to take forever to turn green, and just before it did, a city bus came east on 57th Street and turned north into the bus lane. When the light turned green for Ronnie and all those people waiting with him, including Jack, the bus lane was no longer available. Accordingly, Ronnie had to stay in line while ahead Jack had upped his speed to stay a little ahead of the traffic, aided by the avenue dipping downhill to go under the approaches to the Queensboro Bridge.

"Shit, shit, shit!" Ronnie cried as he pounded the steering wheel in frustration. His simple plan had been thwarted by the damn bus because just beyond the Queensboro Bridge, the right-hand lane of First Avenue was backed up by a line of cars waiting to turn east toward the FDR Drive. Slowed to a near crawl and feeling momentarily helpless, he watched as Jack gained on him by slaloming through the mostly stalled traffic.

As soon as he could, Ronnie broke free of most of the congestion beyond 64th Street. By then he couldn't even see Jack for certain, at least not until he'd raced ahead a number of blocks by weaving in and out of traffic and even running a few lights. Finally, near 70th Street, he came abreast of Jack, who had returned to the bike lane running along the left-hand side. Since the area was a bit less commercial and more residential, there were far fewer double-parked delivery trucks, which made travel easier both on the street and in the bike lane.

Slowing to match Jack's pace, Ronnie hazarded a glance down at the speedometer and was impressed Jack was maintaining close to twenty-five miles per hour. As the two of them hurled northward by catching the synchronized traffic lights, Ronnie came to understand that the only way he was going to accomplish what he needed to do was to move over in the left lane and time it correctly that he and Jack would start across an intersection of a westbound cross street at the same moment. At that point Ronnie would suddenly swerve into the cross street and either impact Jack directly or, if he were slightly ahead, allow Jack to impact him. Either way, at that speed, Jack surely would be gravely and almost assuredly mortally injured, which was the goal of the whole operation.

Ronnie tensed as the two of them rapidly bore down on 83rd Street. In an attempt to gauge the upcoming collision as carefully as possible, he increased the Cherokee's speed slightly, moving a bit ahead of Jack. He reasoned the Cherokee would have to travel a smidgen farther than Jack's bike as it made the turn if they were to collide as planned.

At the exact moment of entering the intersection, Ronnie yanked the car's steering wheel hard to the left and braced himself against the corresponding g-force that threatened to throw him into the passenger seat. There was an accompanying high-pitched screech of the tires bitterly complaining about the same g-force while the entire car tipped precariously and threatened to roll. Ronnie yanked the steering wheel in the opposite direction as the image of Jack and his bike loomed ahead with everything happening in a fraction of a second and a blink of the eye.

The Cherokee jolted as Ronnie fought with the steering wheel to straighten the vehicle toward the opening between the cars parked on either side of 83rd Street. After an initial shuddering thump, Jack's body went airborne before it collided with a thud against the windshield — causing Ronnie to duck by reflex — and left a swath of blood as it caromed off the right side. Almost simultaneously, Ronnie felt a second shudder and heard a crunching sound as the Cherokee crushed the bike, undoubtedly reducing it to a mass of twisted and broken carbon steel.

Hitting the brakes, Ronnie slowed the car

greatly to regain control and allow a more careful and calm drive west along 83rd Street. He was surprised that he found himself trembling as he switched on the windshield fluid and wipers to wash the blood away. Glancing up into the rearview mirror, he could see both Jack's body sprawled out in the street along with the twisted remains of his bike. With a distinct sense of relief, he didn't see any people who might have witnessed the supposed accident.

Coming up to Second Avenue, Ronnie began to slow, but he wasn't going to come to a full stop. If the traffic light was still red when he got there, he planned to inch out into traffic and turn left as soon as he could. His interest was to get out of the area, although now with the bloodstain mostly washed away and no apparent witnesses it wasn't critical. But luckily the light turned green before he got to the intersection, and he was able to continue straight ahead. When he got to Third Avenue and another green light, he turned right, and only then did he allow himself to begin to calm down. It had all happened so fast that he hadn't realized how very tense he'd become.

Taking the next left-hand turn onto a relatively quiet residential block, Ronnie drove about halfway down to the next avenue, where he pulled over to the curb at a fire hydrant under a convenient streetlight. Leaving the car idling, he sprang out with glass cleaner and paper towels. His first order of business was to check the front of the car for damage, and except for a few minor scratches, which would be easy to rectify with the touchup paint he had back in his garage, it looked pristine. Feeling relieved, he then saw to the windshield. It took only a few moments to make sure it, too, was completely clean and bloodless. He then quickly went around, sprayed, and wiped off the water-based paint he'd used to cover the flames extending back from the wheel wells.

With his beloved Cherokee essentially back to normal, Ronnie took a moment to listen to the sounds of the city. He half expected to hear the undulations of an ambulance siren, but he didn't. Vaguely, he wondered if Stapleton's body had been discovered.

With a progressive sense of calmness after the excitement, Ronnie opened the back of the Cherokee. With a screwdriver he'd put in the storage area, he made short work of replacing the license plates. When he was done, he put the soiled paper towels and the outdated plates in a trash can. Climbing back into the driver's seat, he felt elated. It was as if a new day had dawned and a heavy weight had been removed from his shoulders. His pit stop had taken a mere five minutes but had confirmed for him that his car was none the worse for wear. More important, he felt as if he'd tipped over the last domino, effectively eliminating the growing existential threat that Sue Passero, Cherine Gardener, and Jack Stapleton represented. As he pulled out into the street on his way to the MMH, he reached out with his right hand and patted the Cherokee's dash. "Thank you, my buddy," he said. "You and I make one hell of a team."

Chapter 31

Wednesday, December 8, 5:49 P.M.

Ronnie was feeling chipper and whistling under his breath as he emerged from the Emergency Department's doctors' lounge dressed in a fresh white doctor's coat over scrubs. He was a bit early, but he didn't think it mattered. He walked out into the main waiting area and surveyed the scene. It was moderately busy, as was normally the case at that time of day. A handful of triage nurses and clerks stood behind the main desk and a half dozen or so patients were lined up waiting to check in. Respecting the taped markers on the floor, they were maintaining the social distancing required by the Covid-19 pandemic.

As he approached the main desk, Ronnie scanned the personnel, looking for Dr. Carol Sidoti. She wasn't to be seen, so he approached one of the clerks and inquired after her.

"I'm not sure where Dr. Sidoti is," the clerk said. "She's either in the back or in her office."

Of those two suggestions, the closest was the emergency-physician supervisor's hole-in-the-wall cubby next to the security office. Ronnie rapped on the door in passing, thinking that at that rather busy time, the supervisor would undoubtedly be in the thick of things in the acute care center of the ED. He was surprised to hear Dr. Sidoti call out, "Come in." Ronnie was already several steps away and had to return. Leaning inside while holding the door ajar, he found the svelte, wiry woman at the built-in desk using a hospital monitor.

"Hey, Ronnie!" Carol said. "You're early. Don't you have a life?"

Ronnie laughed. "The MMH is my life," he said.

"I know what you mean," Carol agreed. "Especially during this damn pandemic. It's going to be touch-and-go whether we'll be able to recover our lives when it is over."

"How's the evening looking?" Ronnie questioned. "Anything cooking surgery-wise that I should know about? And how's the bed situation?" Frequently the night nursing supervisor had to find beds for the ED if the hospital was near capacity. On occasion it was Ronnie's most difficult job. He could have called the bed manager, but Ronnie preferred to hear it directly from the ED, who more often than not due to the pandemic had patients lined up in the halls waiting for in-patient beds and or Covid PCR results.

"No problem bed-wise, at least currently. And as far as surgery is concerned, we've got nothing cooking at the moment. But, and this might be a big *but,* I just got a heads-up from an ambulance paramedic that a serious bicycle accident is on its way in."

"Oh?" Ronnie questioned. He experienced a minor jolt, realizing that the serious bike accident could very well be Jack Stapleton, and if it was, it meant the man might unfortunately still be alive. Ronnie had expected to run over Jack like he had the bike instead of catapulting him up into the air, but as hard as Jack had hit the windshield, Ronnie had been relatively confident that a fatal outcome had been achieved anyway. Inwardly Ronnie groaned. At the same time, he realized he should be thankful the ambulance was headed to the MMH ED. If by some miracle Jack had survived the collision, having Jack as a patient meant Ronnie could finish the job if need be, pretty much at his convenience. "How serious is the case, did you get an idea?"

"Very serious, from the sound of it," Carol said. "Vital signs are okay, but the patient is unconscious with a head injury. On top of that, there's a compound right lower leg fracture and a probable hip fracture."

"Well, that certainly sounds like surgery is in the cards. I'll check the ortho beds when I get upstairs."

"My guess is that you should check on the neuro beds. On the other hand, with that much general trauma, he'll probably end up in the surgical intensive care unit."

"Agreed," Ronnie said. "So, it's a male?"

"I believe the paramedic said *he,* and most of the serious bike accidents we see are male, but I'm not one hundred percent sure."

"Did they mention where the accident occurred?"

"Yes, they did. It was at the corner of First Avenue and Eighty-Third. Why do you ask?"

"Just curious," Ronnie said. He nodded. Obviously from the location alone, the incoming patient had to be Jack Stapleton! And recalling the sound of him hitting his windshield, Ronnie was impressed the man was still alive. It was as if he were a cat with nine lives.

"Let me finish here," Carol said, gesturing toward the monitor in front of her.

"Of course," Ronnie said. "Sorry! I'll hang around and check out this patient to have a better idea of what his needs are going to be."

"Be my guest," Carol said.

Ronnie wandered back into the interior of the ED and poked his head into the nearest trauma 1 bay. It was dark and deceptively quiet with all its high-tech equipment at the ready. He knew the scene would be changing dramatically and soon, and indeed he didn't have long to wait. At the moment he was surveying the room, he became aware of the distant undulations of an ambulance siren. As he listened, it slowly gained volume.

Walking a short distance farther down the hallway, Ronnie gazed out at the ED's empty concrete receiving bay, which didn't stay empty long. With its siren trailing off, an ambulance soon burst into view, and after making a rapid three-point turn, it backed up to the dock. Before it came to a complete stop, its rear doors swung open and two paramedics piled out onto the platform. Silently and without a second's hesitation, they pulled out a gurney with a patient strapped into it, raised it up, and then came bursting through the swinging doors with one pushing and the other pulling. As the gurney came abreast of Ronnie, he looked down at the face of the patient. It was, as he'd fully expected, Jack Stapleton. The man was easy to recognize despite a large abrasion on the right side of his face below his closed eyes. Most of his clothes had been cut off. Around his neck was a high cervical collar, and enclosing his right leg was an inflatable cast. At the foot of the gurney was Jack's lime green bicycle helmet with its right side partially crushed in.

The paramedics rapidly wheeled the gurney down the hallway and into the same trauma room Ronnie had just been viewing. Ronnie followed. Already the lights were on and several nurses in protective gear were waiting. In a well-orchestrated series of movements, Jack was unbuckled and transferred onto the examination table in the center of the room. Carol Sidoti and several other doctors swept in and began their evaluation as Jack was connected to an ECG machine, a blood pressure cuff, and an oximeter. At the same time, one of the paramedics gave a running explanation of all that had been done at the scene and en route while the other paramedic handed over Jack's wallet to one of the ED social workers, who set off to make sure the police had notified the next of kin. Clearly, permission was going to be needed for the necessary emergency surgery.

To make himself useful, Ronnie got a large-bore catheter and started an intravenous line on the side opposite the IV the paramedics had started in the field. Everyone in the ED knew Ronnie and were fully aware of the specialized battlefield medic training he'd gotten in the navy, so no one was surprised when he pitched in to help. He wanted a particularly good IV line as he was already thinking ahead to how he was going to make sure that Jack didn't survive his hospitalization. Knowing he'd need something that acted rapidly and with great surety, he had already decided on using potassium chloride intravenously, and he planned on using it that very night no matter whether Jack ended up on the ortho floor, the neuro floor, or the SICU.

Ronnie had used potassium chloride to great success on a number of occasions, as it caused a rapid cardiac arrest that couldn't be reversed unless treated almost immediately with a heavy dose of a very specific neutralizing drug called sodium bicarbonate, but that almost never happened because hyperkalemia, meaning too much potassium, was never suspected unless the patient had chronic kidney disease or a specific endocrine disorder called Addison's disease. Interestingly, Ronnie had used potassium chloride on the case five months earlier, when he'd inadvertently barked out the order for sodium bicarbonate when the newbie residents were at a loss about what to do. It ended up saving the patient, at least until the next night, when Ronnie rectified the situation with an overdose of another surefire agent that the patient had been prescribed: digitalis.

By the time Ronnie had the IV going and it had been determined the patient was stable, it was time for preliminary X-rays of the skull, right hip, and right lower leg. At that point, everyone momentarily crowded out of the room save for the X-ray technician. As Ronnie had walked out of the room, he took the bike helmet to look at it more closely, believing with mixed emotions it was what had kept Jack alive. One of the paramedics, seeing Ronnie with the helmet, approached.

"We had to bring that helmet along," he told Ronnie. "If there was ever an argument for wearing one of those blasted things, this was it. He must have landed on his head, with the way it is broken there on the right side."

"That's what it looks like," Ronnie agreed. Under his breath he cursed the freaking thing since it alone was most likely responsible for forcing him to have to finish the job in the hospital. Jack Stapleton, unfortunately, whose injury stemmed from an accident, would have to be considered a medical examiner case, and Ronnie couldn't do anything about it. On the positive side, from a forensic viewpoint, potassium chloride was a perfect agent as it couldn't be detected, so he wasn't overly concerned. The only potential problem that Ronnie would have to solve was that the lethal effects of injecting potassium chloride intravenously were almost immediate, meaning the timing and the circumstances had to be taken into careful consideration. Ronnie was aware of this reality all too well, as he'd had more than enough experience in dealing with it. What was going to make it a bit more of a challenge was that Jack would undoubtedly end up in the surgical intensive care unit, where nursing supervision of each patient was significantly more than it was in a private room.

CHAPTER 32

Wednesday, December 8, 6:25 P.M.
Cheryl Stanford knocked sharply on Laurie's office door and, contrary to usual protocol, opened the door before Laurie had a chance to respond. At that moment Laurie was finishing up another meeting with the deputy chief, George Fontworth, and was taken aback by the interruption.

"What is it, Cheryl?" she questioned, annoyed, as she glanced over at her secretary, who she thought had left for the day. Laurie was already late leaving and was eager to finish up and get home herself, as she liked to arrive home around 6:00 to spend time with the children instead of after 7:00, which was looking probable that evening.

"There's a call on line one," Cheryl said.

"Take a message, Cheryl! I'll call whoever it is first thing in the morning."

"I think you need to take the call, Laurie," Cheryl said. "It's the emergency room at

404

the Manhattan Memorial Hospital. They need to talk with you immediately."

"What about?" she asked as her heart skipped a beat. Despite her question, she already knew the probable answer but didn't want to admit it.

"I'm afraid it is about Jack," Cheryl said, confirming Laurie's fears. "There's been an accident."

"Good grief!" Laurie managed as she noisily exhaled. She glanced briefly at George with raised eyebrows as if expecting some kind of miraculous help but then quickly snatched up the desk phone, pressed the button for line one, and blurted a nervous hello.

"Is this Laurie Montgomery?" a pleasant voice asked.

"Yes. What is it?"

"Is your husband named John Stapleton?"

"Yes! Is he all right?"

"He's being evaluated as we speak. He's been in a bike accident and will require surgery. We need you to come to the Emergency Department as soon as possible."

"I'm on my way," Laurie said. "How is he?"

"As I said, he is in the process of being evaluated. We'll know more when you get here, and you can speak with the doctors.

Can you give me an idea of when you might arrive?"

"Twenty to thirty minutes," Laurie said.

"Very well. My name is Pamela Harrison. I'm a social worker, and you can ask for me directly."

"Thank you," Laurie said. "I'll be there as soon as I can."

She dropped the phone into its cradle and looked over at George. For a moment, she was at a loss for words, feeling extremes of concern and anger. "Damn!" she finally voiced. "I've been afraid of this call for years."

"How is he?" George asked.

"She didn't say, nor did she probably even know. She was a social worker, not a doctor or nurse. Obviously, I have to get to the MMH pronto. But before I go, I'd like to ask you to officially take over the reins of the OCME. I have absolutely no idea of what I will be facing nor how long I'll be detained, but I don't want to have to worry about what's going on here. Can I count on you?"

"Of course," George said.

"Please notify the operator and whoever is on call."

"Absolutely! I'll do both right away," George said. "Good luck and don't worry about anything here. I'll handle whatever comes up."

"Thank you," Laurie said. Then to Cheryl she said, "Get me a ride to the Manhattan Memorial Hospital ASAP."

Cheryl disappeared as Laurie got out her winter coat. George helped her on with it.

"I've warned Jack about an accident like this until I've been blue in the face," she said. "I've even pleaded with him. All to no avail. Now all I can do is hope it is not as bad as it could be."

"I'm sure he'll be just fine," George said, trying to be upbeat. "I've never known anybody in better physical shape than Jack, and he certainly knows how to ride a bike."

"He does have that going for him," Laurie agreed.

Five minutes later she climbed into an Uber, and she was on her way. The one good thing about it being already almost 7:00 was that the rush hour traffic had begun to abate, and she made good time on her travel northward. While she was in the car, she used the time to call home and talk with both Caitlin and her mother, telling them that she would be late and that she was on her way to the MMH Emergency Department because Jack had had a bicycle accident. Although she admitted she didn't know his actual condition, she tried to sound upbeat with them as George had tried to be with her. The problem was that being a medical examiner she'd seen too many bike accidents. Laurie also talked with JJ and apologized for probably not being able to say good night before he had to get into bed. She told him that she was going to be with Dad at the hospital because he had taken a spill and had to get fixed up.

As soon as the driver pulled up to the ED entrance, Laurie was out, and she dashed up a short flight of steps and through a sliding glass door, accepting a fresh Covid mask just inside, which she quickly put on. Eschewing joining any of the several lines in front of the sign-in desk, she rushed directly up to the counter and asked loudly if Pamela Harrison was available.

"I'm Pamela Harrison," a rather young-appearing woman said. To Laurie she looked more like a high school student than a college graduate social worker.

Laurie introduced herself, mildly out of breath from her efforts.

"Oh, yes," Pamela said. "Dr. Sidoti would like very much to talk with you." Without another word, the woman came out from behind the sign-in desk and waved for Laurie to follow her. Cutting through the part of the ED where ambulatory patients had their initial vital signs taken before being returned to the waiting room, Pamela led her on a shortcut directly to the trauma 1 room where Jack was located.

"If you don't mind, would you wait here for a moment?" Pamela said at the room's threshold.

"Of course," Laurie said. She could see a bevy of people arranged around the examination table in the middle of the room. She assumed it was Jack who was demanding their attention, but from where she was standing, she couldn't see any part of him. Several flat-screen monitors built into the wall showed X-rays while another apparently was displaying his vital signs, but Laurie couldn't make out the details. Reassuringly, the steady beep of a normal-sounding pulse filled the room. Since there didn't seem to be any tension in the air and from the mere fact that she was being led directly to the room, Laurie felt the first stirrings of optimism.

Laurie watched as Pamela tapped the shoulder of one of the figures in the center of the room. When this individual turned, Pamela pointed in Laurie's direction. Despite the personal protective gear, Laurie could tell it was a slender female. The woman nodded, and, breaking away from the group, she walked directly over to Laurie.

"I'm Dr. Carol Sidoti," she said. "I understand you are Dr. Laurie Montgomery, Dr. John Stapleton's wife."

"That's correct," Laurie said. "How is he?"

"I'm pleased to say he is stable with normal vital signs. At the same time, I have to be honest and warn you that he's suffered a major trauma, including a concussive head injury, and has not yet regained consciousness. He's also sustained a non-displaced right femoral neck fracture and a compound fracture of his right fibula. On the positive side, he has seemingly not experienced any spinal or internal injuries in his chest or abdomen."

"Any idea of the extent of his head injuries?" Laurie asked. She looked around the ED doctor, wishing she could rush over and check out Jack herself.

"Our portable X-ray capabilities aren't as good as those obtained in our image center, but so far, we haven't seen any skull fractures. We have a neurology consult pending and an orthopedic trauma consult is in progress."

"I'm a physician myself," Laurie said. "A

medical examiner, to be more specific."

"So I hear," Carol said. "In fact, I've been told you are the chief medical examiner for the City of New York. It's a pleasure to make your acquaintance. I'm sorry it is under these circumstances. I understand the patient is also a medical examiner."

"Yes, all true," Laurie said. "I'm impressed you are so well informed, and so fast."

"We have a talented social service team," Carol said.

"I'd like to see my husband," Laurie said, again looking over at the group huddled around the examination table.

"Of course," Carol said as she turned and led the way. Approaching the group, she called out. "Excuse me, everyone, this is Dr. Montgomery, the patient's wife."

Several of the ED nurses moved aside, making way for Laurie to approach the table. Her first image of Jack wasn't as bad as she expected. The only obvious sequelae she could see was an abrasion on his right cheek and a pneumatic splint covering his right lower leg. Other than that, his color was good, and he appeared as if he was sleeping. He had intravenous lines running into both arms.

"This is Dr. Henry Thomas," Carol said, gesturing across the table at the man occupying center stage. He was dressed in short-sleeve scrubs revealing muscular, moderately hairy arms and sporting both a surgical mask and cap. "He runs our Orthopedic Trauma Department. We're lucky to have him so quickly. By coincidence he had just finished a case when your husband was brought in, so we prevailed upon him to come right down here."

Laurie and Henry exchanged greetings, after which Henry said, "Your husband needs surgery straight off following a neurological clearance. Both fractures have to be internally stabilized. As for the hip, an argument could be made for a replacement considering your husband's age, but personally I'd favor stabilization provided there's not too much displacement, which there doesn't appear to be on X-ray, nor any compromise on the blood supply to the femoral head. Also provided the bone quality is good, which I imagine is the case since your husband looks like an active individual."

"Very active," she said. "Maybe too active. Let me ask you a question, if I may. What do you think of the idea of him being transferred for the surgery over to NYU? I had surgery there a couple of years ago and had a good experience." Laurie hadn't

412

planned on asking such a question until the moment she did. The issue popped into her mind when she felt some relief at seeing Jack's overall condition despite his still being unconscious. All at once the issue of Sue Passero's passing and Jack's talk about a possible medical serial killer at the MMH had come into play in her overworked brain.

Henry paused for a moment. It was not a question he was expecting. He cleared his throat, giving him more chance to think and overcome the mild challenge to his ego. "It would have to be against strong medical advice," he said. "Personally, I believe it would be assuming an unacceptable risk, especially since your husband is unconscious. But beyond that, a delay in taking care of the fractures doesn't serve any purpose and could be detrimental."

"Okay," Laurie said, feeling slightly embarrassed to have even brought the issue up. "How are you going to decide on what to do with the hip?"

"I believe I should be given the opportunity to decide when I get to see the injury up close in the operating room and can access the bone quality and blood supply issues."

"Fair enough," Laurie said. She felt mildly uncomfortable from having brought up the transfer issue, especially after rethinking the medical serial killer idea. She distinctly remembered Jack saying that the hospital mortality ratio had been going down, as had hospital referrals to the OCME, which made the idea of a serial killer moot. Besides, she wondered, why would a medical serial killer be attracted to Jack? Until she remembered that he had been scheduled to speak to someone that very afternoon about Sue's suspicions.

"Excuse me, Dr. Montgomery," Pamela said, interrupting Laurie's thoughts. "If you are finished here for the time being, would you mind following me? We need your signature on admission and informed consent papers."

"Of course," Laurie said, but before following Pamela she looked across at Henry. "Thank you for seeing my husband and for patching his leg back together."

"You are welcome," Henry said.

"I will be waiting to hear exactly what you find." Then, turning to Carol, Laurie said, "And thank you for all that you have done. I'm very appreciative to the whole team. And I'll be particularly interested to hear what the neurological consult has to say."

"Of course," Carol said. "But my shift was over at seven, and I'll be leaving. But I'll let my replacement, Dr. Vega, know."

"Thank you all," Laurie called out as she followed Pamela out of the trauma room.

Chapter 33

Wednesday, December 8, 8:15 P.M.

"Laurie?" a soothing, dulcet voice asked. Laurie was sitting in the ED waiting area, which was much less crowded after the evening rush had slowed. Hearing her name, she looked up from reading emails on her mobile phone into the eyes of a woman in full personal protective gear including a reflective plastic mask. "It's me."

Laurie stood up as Colleen Benn removed the plastic mask. The two women greeted each other warmly. "Thanks so much for coming down to say hello," Laurie said.

After signing all the admission papers for Jack, Laurie had retreated to the waiting area, and as she had calmed down, she'd remembered one of the hospitalists whom Sue Passero had introduced to her on several occasions, as Sue and she were frequent coworkers plus good friends. Wondering if the woman who Laurie remembered as being particularly friendly was on duty, she had called the hospital's central switchboard and had her paged. To Laurie's pleasant surprise, she'd called Laurie's cell phone after only a few minutes.

"What on earth are you doing here?" Colleen asked. She then gestured for Laurie to sit back down while she took the seat right next to her.

"My teenage-mindset husband who insists on riding his bike all over Manhattan took a nasty spill this afternoon."

"Oh, God!" Colleen lamented with a shake of her head. "Men will be boys! How is he?"

"He's still kicking, thank goodness," Laurie said. "But he's unconscious from an apparent concussion and has two fractures in his right leg, which are going to need to be surgically repaired. They are waiting for a neurological consult before going ahead with the surgery."

"How awful. I'm so sorry."

"I keep reminding myself it could have been worse. But anyway, how are you?"

"Coping. With some difficulty, thanks to the pandemic. I'm wondering if my kids will remember me when this is all over considering the number of shifts I've been forced to take. I've been practically living here. When

I get home, I have to change clothes in the garage and shower in the guest room."

"I can imagine," Laurie said. "You front-line healthcare workers have been carrying the burden for all of us. Thank you."

"You're welcome. I guess your team has been equally busy."

"Unfortunately, yes," Laurie said. "Bringing up an unpleasant subject, I suppose you are aware of Sue Passero's unfortunate death."

"Oh, gosh, yes! Such a tragedy for the whole hospital. I still can't believe it. She was so damn healthy and vital and a true contributor to this institution. It was a shock."

"You spoke with her often, didn't you?"

"For sure. Sometimes every day, at least when I wasn't working the night shift like I am this week. Even then, she'd call me often. She frequently had patients in whatever intensive care unit I was covering. She was such a conscientious doctor."

"Did she by any chance say anything to you recently about being worried there might be a medical serial killer active here at the MMH?"

"A serial killer? You mean someone killing patients on purpose?"

"Exactly."

"What a strange question."

"Unfortunately, it's not as strange as it sounds. A dozen or more years ago, I was responsible for figuring out that a medical serial killer was operating here. It was a nurse being paid handsomely to kill off certain postoperative patients."

"Good God! Really? That's terrible. I never heard anything about it, as it was certainly before my time."

"I'm not surprised you haven't heard about it. For the obvious reason it was a PR nightmare. The hospital administration tried to put the kibosh on the story as soon as it was uncovered, and they were reasonably successful. The reason I'm asking the question now is because my husband had been told that Sue recently came across some kind of statistic that suggested to her there might be another such killer."

"If she was concerned, she never mentioned anything to me," Colleen said, with a shake of her head. "Wow! I certainly hope it is not the case."

"Excuse me," a voice said, "are you Dr. Montgomery?"

Both Laurie and Colleen looked up into the masked face of a doctor in a long white coat. A telltale percussion hammer protruded from one of his pockets, indicating his specialty. Laurie answered in the affirmative.

"I'm Dr. Fredricks. I'm a neurology consult. I've examined Dr. Stapleton. He's suffered a concussion and remains unconscious. On the positive side his cranial computed tomography is entirely normal, as is his neurological exam, including being responsive to what we call noxious stimuli, all of which is encouraging. I have cleared him for emergency orthopedic surgery to stabilize his fractures, and he is on his way upstairs to the operating room. I was told to tell you that Dr. Thomas, the orthopedic trauma surgeon, will be in touch as soon as the case is over."

"Thank you for letting me know," Laurie said.

"You are more than welcome. Do you have any questions?"

She thought for a moment before asking how long he thought Jack might be unconscious.

"It's difficult to know," the doctor said. "But as I said, his neurological exam is normal, including all reflexes and responses to stimuli. I'm encouraged. If I had to guess, I'd say twelve to twenty-four hours, tops, but there is no way to estimate exactly. Any other questions?"

"I guess not," Laurie said.

"Very good. If you do, you can page me. I'll be checking in on him after his surgery."

"Thank you," Laurie said.

The doctor nodded, turned around, and hustled back into the interior of the ED.

"Fingers crossed," Laurie said, looking back at Colleen and trying to make light of the situation.

"That's all positive news, and I'm sure he will be fine," Colleen said, trying to be upbeat. "It will be good to get the surgery out of the way. What are you going to do while you wait?"

"I don't know," Laurie said with a shrug. "I suppose sit here and answer email. I'm afraid it's going to be a long evening. I'm really intent on keeping as close a watch over Jack as I can with even a hint of a potential serial killer here. As soon as it is medically okay, I want to have him transferred."

"Why don't I take you up to the surgical lounge?" Colleen suggested. "At this time of day, it's practically deserted and you'll probably have the place to yourself. There's also peanut butter crackers and coffee. Have you had anything to eat?"

"No, but I'm not hungry in the slightest."

"What do you say? It will be better than

sharing this space with the cast of characters who come into the ED on a nightly basis."

"I can't argue with that," Laurie said.

"Then let's go," Colleen said as she got to her feet. "I'll not be far away. I'm mostly in the surgical intensive care unit for tonight, which is near the surgical lounge, so I can pop in and check on you now and then."

"All right," Laurie said. "I'll take you up on your offer. I appreciate your thoughtfulness."

On the way up in the elevator, Colleen had another suggestion. "If you are planning on being here for a long time and intent on keeping an eye on Jack, which I'm sure I can help happen, why don't we get you a set of scrubs? Not only will you be more comfortable, you'll need to be in scrubs if I can prevail on the charge nurse to let you in the SICU, where Jack will probably end up after being in the post-anesthesia unit. The other benefit of your coming up to the surgical lounge is that you have an entire locker room at your disposal. There's even a shower if you are so inclined."

"Wow! I hadn't thought about that but it makes sense," Laurie said. "This is going to take me back to my residency days."

"Is that a good memory for you or bad?"

"Definitely good," Laurie said, managing a slight smile at the thought despite her general anxiety.

Twenty minutes later she found herself dressed in a white doctor's coat over scrubs sitting on a couch in the surgical lounge all by herself. In front of her was a cup of coffee as well as several unopened individual packages of peanut butter crackers. After Colleen had showed her around the lounge and the locker room, she had gone back to the SICU with the promise of poking her head in occasionally. Laurie had Colleen's mobile number in case she needed to get in touch with her.

Once she was situated, the first thing Laurie did was call home. She had hoped to get Caitlin but got her mother instead as Caitlin had already gone to her quarters once Emma had been put to bed. So as not to worry her mother, she merely said that Jack had been in a bike accident and was having an operation to fix his leg and that she planned on being at the hospital for the time being. Although Dorothy did ask about Jack's condition, Laurie could tell she was preoccupied by whatever it was that she was watching on the TV. Keeping the conversation short, which was mostly her mother complaining that Jack never should have been foolish enough to ride his bike in the city, Laurie got to chat briefly with JJ. He, too, was preoccupied as he had finished his homework and had moved on to playing computer games. Neither seemed overly upset that Jack was in surgery, which was good as far as she was concerned.

With the job of calling home out of the way, Laurie did what had been on her mind ever since she'd heard about Jack's accident: call Lou. As the call went through, she hoped she wasn't interrupting something important. She was always a little reluctant to call Lou in the evening because it was mostly in the evening or the wee hours of the morning that he was the busiest. The moment he answered she asked if he could talk or whether he needed to call her back.

"I'm on a homicide call, but I'm okay for a few minutes," Lou said. "What's up?"

"Jack had a serious bike accident."

"Hell's bells!" Lou groaned. "How is he?"

"It's not as bad as it could be," Laurie said. "But it is still bad. He's in a concussion-induced coma, but from the neurologist I got the sense they are optimistic and expect him to wake up soon or at least within twenty-four hours. Luckily there are no skull fractures. At this very moment, he's undergoing surgery to stabilize two fractures of his right leg."

"That's bad enough. What are the details of the accident?"

"That I don't know."

"Do you know where it took place?"

"They told me, but I can't remember. Someplace on the Upper East Side, not too far away from the MMH."

"That will be the nineteenth precinct. Let me call and find out, and I'll call you back."

Before Laurie could respond, Lou disconnected. She shrugged. She didn't know why he was so concerned about the details of the accident. As far as she was concerned, it didn't make much difference, and it wasn't what she was interested in talking to him about. Putting her phone down, she picked up one of the cellophane-wrapped peanut butter cracker sandwiches and tore it open. Surprising herself, she had become a little hungry.

After two bites, her phone rang. It was Lou getting right back to her.

"Rush hour at the corner of First Avenue and Eighty-Third Street and not a single witness. Can you believe it?" he said quickly. "Only in New York. Anyway, it's assumed it was a hit-and-run because the bike was toast, most likely run over by the car or van or whatever it was."

"Whatever," Laurie said. "At this stage it's not going to help the doctors to know exactly what happened or who was at fault. Besides, as fast as he tended to ride, he didn't need a vehicle to get himself banged up badly. Anyway, why I was eager to talk with you is to get your take on the medical serial killer issue and how probable you think it is. Obviously, I'm concerned with Jack now a patient here."

"What medical serial killer issue?" Lou asked with obvious confusion. "I don't know what you are talking about."

"The medical serial killer that Sue Passero was concerned about," she said. "The one Jack had heard about from the nurse you and he posted this morning, the one who shared committee responsibilities with Sue."

"Jack didn't say boo about any serial killer," Lou said categorically.

"Really?" Laurie questioned with surprise. "That's hard to believe. Jack told me that he had you up to speed with all he was learning over here at the MMH."

"All he said to me was that it was a hotbed of intrigue and animosity, which was why I was trying to dissuade him from going over there playing detective."

"You knew about him coming here?"

Laurie demanded sharply.

"Only after the fact," Lou said. "Well, except for this afternoon, where I guess he was headed when he had his accident. I had spoken with him just before he left the OCME, and he told me he was going. He also said he was going to meet whoever it was in the ED and not in the hospital proper."

"Why didn't you tell me?" she questioned angrily. As tense as she was, every new fact bothered her.

"Hey, I'm not the bad guy here," Lou said. "Jack told me not to tell you."

"And you agreed?" Laurie asked with disbelief. "Thank you very much, Detective Soldano. Some friend you turn out to be."

"Hey, don't blame me! As I told him, being friends with you two ain't the easiest job in the world. At his request, I agreed to go along with his wishes and not tattle by giving him just one more day to look into Sue Passero's case, which was what he asked for. But he certainly didn't mention anything about a medical serial killer being involved in any way or form. Had he said anything like that, I certainly wouldn't have agreed to even one day considering what happened the last time you two were involved with a serial killer at the same hospital."

"All right," Laurie said, trying to rein in her roiling emotions. "I'm sorry I snapped at you. I'm not myself, and I just couldn't believe Jack wouldn't have confided in you about this serial killer idea since he said that you were, quote, 'on board.' "

"Apology accepted," Lou said. "So, tell me what you know about this medical serial killer issue. I don't like to think about the possibility, remembering that crazy Jasmine Rakoczi and the mayhem she caused."

"Honestly, I don't know much," Laurie said, surprised Lou brought up the Jasmine Rakoczi episode. She had also been reluctantly reminiscing in the back of her mind about that frightful experience and how close she'd come to being victimized herself. "All I know is the little Jack had been told, namely Sue was convinced of it. And to make matters worse, he'd heard that Sue thought it was a very active medical serial killer, particularly over the last year."

"Meaning, of course, lots of deaths."

"Obviously," Laurie said testily. "That's what an active serial killer means."

"Hey, don't get impatient with me. You doctors speak your own language that we mortals don't always understand. I just want to be sure I'm getting what you are telling me. Do you have any idea why Dr. Passero felt this way?"

"The nurse that you and Jack autopsied this morning told Jack it had something to do with statistics but didn't elaborate, saying she would tell him today, when she'd have more time. But in the interim, Jack took it upon himself to get what statistics he could, which proved opposite to what he expected if a serial killer was involved. From the MMH, he learned that their mortality ratio, which is what the hospital uses for accreditation, was not only impressively low but had actually gone down over the last year. He also had our Medical Legal Department look at the MMH monthly death rate reported to the OCME and found that stat had also gone down over the previous year."

"Whoa!" Lou voiced appreciatively. "Math has never been my forte, but it seems to me all that argues against there being any kind of a serial killer, particularly not an active one."

"I agree," Laurie said. "But here's the rub. Sue allegedly believed it, and Sue Passero was one of the smartest people and most dedicated doctors that I have known. If she truly believed it, I'd have to give the idea significant credence."

"But her believing it is hearsay," Lou said.

"True," she agreed, "but my impression was that Jack gave the source considerable credence. When I combine that with Jack's concern that Sue's death might have been a homicide, along with your concern the nurse's death was a homicide, I'm feeling very uncomfortable having Jack here in this hospital. So much so that down in the Emergency Department, even with Jack unconscious, I brought up the idea of transferring him over to NYU."

"What was the reaction?"

"I was told by the consulting trauma surgeon it would have been against medical advice, so I let it drop. Jack's immediate needs certainly trumped my hypothetical concerns. But let me raise one other, perhaps distant but nonetheless disturbing, possibility that I suddenly find gnawing at me, especially now that you have raised the possibility the accident was a hit-and-run. What if Jack's accident wasn't an accident, but rather was done on purpose as a kind of attempted assassination?"

For a few seconds Laurie didn't hear a sound from her phone, making her pull it away from the side of her face to look at the screen. When she could see she was still connected, she put the phone back to her ear and waited.

"As I've said, you and Jack can be difficult to be friends with at times," Lou said finally, breaking the silence with an exasperated sigh. "But I have to give both of you credit for being investigatively creative. I see your point despite the substantial *if*s involved, and it's best to be safe than sorry. Where are you in the hospital right now?"

"I'm in an empty surgical lounge. When I was waiting down in the Emergency Department, I contacted one of the intensive care hospitalists here named Dr. Colleen Benn. I had met her through Sue on numerous occasions. Luckily it turned out she was on duty, so she came by to see me and has been extraordinarily accommodating. It was her suggestion I wait here while Jack is in surgery, which is perfect. The only way it could have been better is if she got me invited into the OR itself."

"Are you planning on staying at the hospital all night?"

"Absolutely," she said. "I even turned over the reins at work. I'm going to be here for the duration, until we can transfer him."

"I'll come over and keep you company for a bit when I finish here. The crime scene people are taking their time, which is good, but sometimes they drag it out unmercifully. Where do you think Jack will go when he's finished his surgery? To the VIP section of the hospital?"

"First he'll be sent to the PACU, at least for a while," Laurie said. "Then, according to Colleen, he'll most likely be sent to the surgical intensive care unit, particularly if he's still unconscious. Colleen is going to try to get me permission to hang out at the SICU desk, which should work because she's high in the pecking order and happens to be the doctor in charge of the unit for the night."

"I'll tell you what I can do," Lou said. "I'll call back the nineteenth precinct and have them send a couple of uniformed duty officers to stand outside wherever he may be in the hospital, whether an intensive care unit or a private room. They can check everyone going in and out and keep out anyone who doesn't belong."

"I suppose that can appear intimidating," Laurie said. "But not foolproof. The trouble is that a medical serial killer would have access. That's what makes it possible for such an individual to do what they do, and it could potentially be anyone from an orderly to the chief surgeon."

"You're right about the access issue," Lou

said. "But just having the uniformed officers sitting there can be surprisingly effective. Besides, when I come over, I'll clue them in to get maximum effectiveness."

"You're a good friend," she said. "I know Jack will be very appreciative."

"And if anything goes wrong, no matter what it is, call me. The homicide I'm on is fairly close to the MMH, and I can be there in a blink of the eye."

"By the time you come over here, if I'm lucky I'll be in the SICU where you would not be able to come."

"We'll cross that bridge when we get to it," Lou said. "Just be sure to have your mobile with you at all times."

"Will do," Laurie said. After she disconnected, she took a moment to acknowledge how lucky she was to have a friend as loyal as Lou Soldano. It seemed as if whenever she needed him, he was available, and she couldn't help but feel this could be one of those times.

CHAPTER 34

Wednesday, December 8, 11:40 P.M.

"I disagree," Ronnie said, trying to control his impatience. He was talking with a charge nurse named Alan Spallek on a general medical floor. Alan was a heavyset man about Ronnie's age who had also been in the navy but on a surface ship, not a submarine. As evidence of his service, he had a colorful tattoo of a mermaid on his right forearm. Thanks to his military training, he was a no-nonsense nurse who ran the floor like an overly strict chief petty officer. "This patient is not a medical examiner case, period," Ronnie added for emphasis.

"But he fell and had a cerebral bleed," Alan snapped. "That's surely an ME case."

Ronnie, who was sitting in front of one of the monitors at the central desk, pointed to the screen where he had the patient's chart uploaded. "Alan, the man's prothrombin time was six-point-six, which is way out of

434

whack. The man fell because he had a bleed. That's what makes the most sense, especially since you admitted he didn't have a violent fall but rather merely slumped to the floor. He didn't have the bleed because of a fall. I'm telling you, it is not a medical examiner case, period. If I called it in as such, the ME investigator would laugh at me and wouldn't accept it. Take my word! I know what I'm talking about."

"I don't know how you can be so sure," Alan growled. "But fine! It's your call."

"You bet it is," Ronnie said. "Case closed." He stood up and started off, heading for the next problem. As he walked, he took his pulse. It was almost a hundred beats a minute, reflective of the general anxiety he was experiencing, and which had slowly grown as the evening passed. He couldn't stop worrying about Jack Stapleton suddenly waking up from his coma, realizing he was in the MMH, and starting to raise holy hell by carrying on about a serial killer. Even the term itself, *serial killer,* made Ronnie blister. He certainly didn't think of himself as a killer, but rather a merciful savior. The killing was just the means to the compassionate and charitable end.

To add to Ronnie's unease, a half an hour earlier he'd gotten a text message from the administrator on call, saying several police were on the way into the hospital to provide protection for Jack Stapleton and that Ronnie was to cooperate with them whatever their needs might be. When Ronnie asked why the man was being guarded, the administrator said he wasn't told and didn't ask. At first Ronnie was alarmed at the news, but his concern lasted only for a few minutes. In the past when there had been police, usually for guarding prisoners, he remembered they just parked themselves outside the individual's location and that was it. The more Ronnie thought about the development, the more he realized the police would be no problem for what Ronnie had to do. They certainly weren't going to keep him out of the SICU.

But everything added together made Ronnie feel he was like teetering on the edge of a precipice, mostly because for the moment his hands were tied. First, that had been because Jack was in the OR and then in the post-anesthesia unit, both of which were essentially out of bounds for Ronnie. Now, finally, Jack had been moved into the surgical intensive care unit, which was a relief because it was fully in Ronnie's domain. To give himself a leg up, he'd used his control of intensive care bed allocations to be sure that Jack had been given one of the cubicles the farthest away from the SICU's central desk. But still Ronnie had to bide his time, as he knew Jack would be getting a lot of one-on-one nursing attention until he was determined to be stable. At that point Ronnie was confident he would have relatively free rein to do what needed to be done.

The next problem turned out to have already solved itself by the time Ronnie arrived. He'd been called because a patient had taken a fall in one of the MRI rooms in the imaging center. But by the time Ronnie got there, a resident had shown up, examined the patient, determined he had not sustained any injury, and the patient had been taken back to his room. Ronnie made a mental note to check in on the individual when he made his general rounds after his dinner break.

With no other outstanding problems of the bewildering variety that Ronnie had to deal with hour-to-hour or even minute-to-minute, he was now free to make a preliminary check on how things were in the SICU in regard to Jack Stapleton. After a short elevator ride and then coming around a right-angle bend in the corridor, Ronnie's anxiety ratcheted upward. His pulse, already high, inched up at the mere sight of the two uniformed policemen with all their law enforcement paraphernalia, including holstered pistols, sitting on hospital-supplied folding chairs on either side of the double swinging doors to the SICU. Despite knowing that the officers posed no threat to him, Ronnie felt a cold sweat break out on his forehead.

"Evening, Officers," Ronnie said, being as nonchalant as he could manage as he passed.

"Evening, Doctor," the two officers said in unison. Both were on the youthful and probably inexperienced side in Ronnie's estimation, as evidenced by the newness of their equipment, and he sensed they were more nervous being in such an alien environment than he was at their presence.

Without hesitating or showing any identification, Ronnie pushed through the doors. He wasn't challenged, which was a relief. "Some protection they provide," Ronnie whispered snidely, since they didn't even know he wasn't a doctor.

Every night and sometimes on multiple occasions, Ronnie visited all the MMH intensive care units, as allocating intensive care beds was one of his main jobs, even though he'd complained on multiple occasions that the night bed manager should be the one doing it. The job fell to him because he was able to visit the units, whereas the bed manager wasn't. If and when the census was high, it fell to Ronnie to decide which patients, if any, could be moved out to make room for a new, sicker patient. During the height of the pandemic the decision had often been difficult.

The SICU was comprised of sixteen cubicles, eight on each side, and currently was nearly full with only two cubicles vacant. Each patient had their own intensive care nurse, and each cubicle had its own panoply of medical technology with multiple flat-screen monitors displaying various vital signs. Clusters of intravenous bottles hung from poles, and the entire room was filled with a low-volume cacophony of various beeping with occasion brief alarms. In the middle was the central desk, serving as a kind of command post, complete with additional monitors that served as a backup for the monitors in each cubicle. At that moment a couple of staff doctors and a couple of residents were working at computer screens, oblivious to the various comings and goings of nurses obtaining supplies and medications. In command of it all, like a symphonic maestro, was a charge nurse named Patricia Hoagland, along with a clerk named Irene.

Ronnie paused just inside the swinging entrance doors and surveyed the scene. It comforted him that the atmosphere was relaxed, and despite his knowing that the situation could change in an instant, the current relative calmness helped take the edge off his high anxiety. Of the two doctors within the central desk, he was familiar with only one, Dr. Colleen Benn, who was one of the more senior intensive care doctors with whom he dealt frequently. The other woman Ronnie didn't recognize, but it didn't bother him in the slightest nor did the presence of the two residents.

Looking all the way down to the opposite end of the room, he could see the cubicle where he'd assigned Jack Stapleton. Every so often he could catch a glimpse of the nurse busily attending to him, meaning to Ronnie that Stapleton was still in the process of being stabilized after his arrival from the PACU. Ronnie was eager to walk down there to check out the man's status, but he didn't want to make it seem so obvious. Despite having already visited the unit an hour or so earlier to see which beds were available and check on the status of each patient, he made it a point to poke his head randomly into a few of the cubicles to catch the attention of the attending nurse. On each occasion, he simply asked if all was okay and either got a thumbs-up or a quick word of affirmation. He then approached the central desk and got Patricia's attention. She was a particularly friendly, soft-voiced motherly figure, who liked everyone and whom everyone liked, yet despite this affable façade, she was highly organized and ran the unit competently. Ronnie had never had any trouble dealing with her, which he couldn't say about some of the other intensive care unit charge nurses who took themselves way too seriously.

"How's the shift going, Patti?" Ronnie asked, making casual conversation.

"So far, so good," Patti said. "No complaints. Everybody stable. How about for you?"

"The usual number of nursing and nursing assistant no-shows," Ronnie said. "But we had enough coverage in the pool. I suppose you noticed the armed police presence out in the hall."

"I'm aware," Patti said. "Dr. Benn told me. It will keep the riffraff out." She laughed in her characteristic crystalline fashion.

"Talking about Dr. Benn," Ronnie said, "who is the other doctor with her? I've never seen her before."

Patti looked over at Laurie and Colleen. "She's a medical examiner, or so I have been told."

"Really?" Ronnie questioned. Now he was truly interested. "Why is a medical examiner here?"

"She's a friend of Dr. Benn's. She's also the wife of the patient in cubicle eight."

Ronnie's anxiety ticked up a degree. This was something out of the ordinary, and under the circumstances he was not happy about it, considering what he had to do. "Hmmm," Ronnie voiced, pretending to take the news in stride. "Interesting, but it seems highly irregular. Are you okay with it?"

"Oh, yeah," Patti said. "Dr. Benn asked me, and since the woman is a doctor and dressed appropriately, I couldn't see anything wrong with it, especially with Dr. Benn coming in and out. She said she was content to sit here within the central desk and wouldn't interfere in any way. Are you okay with it?"

"I suppose so," Ronnie said with a shrug after giving the situation a bit more thought. If the woman agreed to stay within the central desk area, it didn't seem to him that it would make any difference. "It's all right. I just would have preferred to have been given a heads-up. I am supposed to be in charge of this institution during my shift and to do that I need to know what's going on."

"Would you like to talk with Dr. Benn? I can ask her to come over. Or would you like to meet the woman?"

"No, no! It's not necessary if you are okay with it," Ronnie said. "This is your domain."

"Fair enough," Patti said. She then turned back to respond to the clerk who had shouted a question to her about a stat lab result.

After the short conversation with Patti, Ronnie did what he'd come to do, namely head down to cubicle eight to check out the newest arrival. Walking in, he looked up at the monitors. Blood pressure and pulse and oxygenation were all entirely normal. The nurse was Aliyah Jacobs, a woman whom Ronnie knew rather well as a particularly competent intensive care nurse and who never minded being moved around from unit to unit depending on need, which Ronnie appreciated and took advantage of frequently. One of the major aspects of his job was to make sure staffing was adequate for the night shift, which could be a challenge with people calling in sick, particularly in the ICUs.

"How's your patient?" Ronnie asked. He noticed with satisfaction that both IVs were still running, particularly the large-bore catheter he'd put in down in the ED. He intended to use that IV line later.

"He's rock-solid stable," Aliyah said. "The hip incision site looks fine with minimal discharge, and the circulation of his foot is fine with the temporary plaster cast on his lower leg. More important, he's also moving more, suggesting he's going to come back and join us in the not-too-distant future."

"Excellent," Ronnie said, giving Aliyah a thumbs-up although he was not happy about the idea of Jack emerging from his coma. That threat alone argued for his acting sooner rather than later. Skirting the right side of the bed, Ronnie walked up to its head and looked down at Jack Stapleton. His cheek abrasion had been cleaned up, and he looked hardly worse for wear despite the violence of having been propelled airborne by a collision with the Cherokee at twentysomething miles per hour and slamming into the windshield before tumbling off and falling into the street. Ronnie couldn't help but be impressed despite feeling irritated the man seemed to have nine lives. At the same time, nine lives or not,

Ronnie was confident the potassium chloride was going to solve the problem in spades.

"We're low on ortho beds," Ronnie said. "So he'll probably have to stay here even if he wakes up."

"That's fine," Aliyah said. "Once it's apparent he's stable, I can help on a couple of the other patients who are more demanding. There's a couple of sickies in here."

Ronnie flashed Aliyah another thumbs-up, feeling even more appreciative of her work ethic, and then walked out of the cubicle. As he passed the central desk, he briefly locked eyes with the visitor. He nodded in acknowledgment, but Dr. Stapleton's wife did not respond. He shrugged. He didn't care one way or the other.

Leaving the SICU, he also nodded to the two police officers, both of whom nodded back. *So much for their contribution,* Ronnie thought with derision. Yet their presence did unnerve and bother him to a point, particularly since they were armed, in contrast to himself. Making a snap decision to bolster his nerves, he decided he could use the sense of security and the calmness his SIG Sauer P365 pistol could engender.

Since the hospital was currently problem free and because the pedestrian bridge over to the high-rise garage was only one floor down, he ducked into the stairwell and headed down. A few minutes later, when he arrived at the Cherokee, he slipped into the passenger seat. After giving the Cherokee's dash a loving pat, he opened the glove compartment and pulled out his prized pistol. Although he knew it wasn't necessary, he checked the magazine to make sure was full. It was. He then slipped the gun into the right deep pocket of his doctor's coat before stepping back out of the SUV and locking it up.

As he recrossed the pedestrian bridge, he could feel the pistol gently thumping against his thigh. The weight of it calmed him dramatically by reminding him it was there, just as it had the night before on his visit to Cherine's apartment. It didn't matter that the chances of needing it were minuscule in either situation.

Once back in the hospital proper, he reflexively checked his phone to make sure he'd not gotten any calls or texts about hospital problems that required his immediate attention. Since he was still in the clear, he wanted to take advantage of the time to do what was certain to be one of the most important jobs of the evening, namely preparing the potassium chloride for the coup de grâce.

Using the elevator to get up to the sixth floor, he entered the nursing supervisor's tiny office adjacent to the general medical unit. Locking the door to avoid any possibility of being interrupted, he used a key to open his private drawer in an old-fashioned, upright metal file cabinet. Inside was the entire pharmacopeia of medications that he had amassed over four years for the express purpose of supporting his crusade. The potassium chloride, or KCl, had come from the ED, as had the collection of syringes, although the syringes he could have gotten anywhere.

With appropriate aseptic care, even though he knew it really didn't matter, Ronnie used multiple vials of concentrated, sterile KCl to nearly fill a 50ml syringe. As he held up the syringe and tapped the side to eliminate any air bubbles, he smiled, knowing he had probably enough concentrated potassium chloride to do in an elephant, much less a human.

Once Ronnie was finished, he replaced the plastic cap on the needle and then deposited the syringe in the depths of his left pocket. After relocking the file cabinet drawer, he left the office. As he walked, he could feel the pistol on the right side and the syringe on the left, and the sensations made him feel wonderfully calm and more in control than he'd felt all evening.

CHAPTER 35

Thursday, December 9, 1:10 A.M.

For a brief second, Laurie nodded off and caught herself with a start to keep her torso from tipping forward and falling off the desk chair. Although there was plenty of activity in many of the SICU's cubicles, Jack's had been calm for more than an hour. His assigned nurse had been off helping her colleagues who needed an extra hand, returning to check on Jack every ten to fifteen minutes.

Laurie stood up for a moment and stretched and took a few deep breaths. Patti Hoagland, the charge nurse, had seen the brief episode and stepped over. It seemed that nothing escaped her notice.

"Dr. Montgomery," Patti said. "Clearly you are rightfully exhausted. I have a suggestion. You could lie down in one of the empty cubicles, if you'd like. Your husband is remarkably stable, and we'll be keeping

449

an eye on him as usual. We can certainly let you know if there is any change whatsoever. What do you say?"

"Thank you, but if it is okay, I'll just move around a little bit and maybe have a bit more coffee."

"Of course. Please, help yourself."

Laurie grabbed the mug she had been given earlier and took advantage of Patti's offer. She went into the room that jutted off from the central desk area. It was where all the drugs, fluids, and other paraphernalia were stored, along with a coffee machine. For the most part, she had followed to the letter Patti's dictum that she remain seated at her assigned spot within the central desk, and it felt good just to get up and move around. After pouring herself yet another cup of black coffee, she made a beeline back to her seat. She didn't want to take advantage of Patti's good graces. In front of Laurie was a monitor that had been set up for her that displayed Jack's vital signs and ECG. The mesmerizing regularity of the cursors continuously sweeping across the screen had been partially responsible for her drifting off.

All in all, the evening had gone smoothly so far. Jack's surgery had taken a bit less than the two hours originally estimated, and the surgeon, Dr. Henry Thomas, had come into the surgical lounge, where Laurie was waiting. It was his feeling that the procedure had gone well, and he explained that he used three screws to repair the femoral neck fracture since there was no displacement, the circulation had not been compromised, and the quality of the bone was, in his words, rock solid. With the compound fibula fracture, he'd thoroughly cleaned and debrided the area and reconstituted the fibula with a steel plate and screws and closed the wound without a drain. It was his professional opinion that Jack would do well and ultimately have no limitations or sequalae from either fracture.

Following the surgery, Jack had spent just a little more than an hour in the PACU, and Colleen had been a big help. She'd managed to get Laurie permission to make a brief visit. Jack had appeared quite normal. Even his color was good. As Laurie was leaving the PACU, she was truly thankful that things had gone well and just wished he would wake up.

When he had been transferred from the PACU to the SICU, Colleen had again come through, getting the charge nurse to agree that Laurie could continue her vigil in the SICU provided she remain seated within the confines of the central desk and not get in the way, stipulations that Laurie had agreed to without question. Colleen made it a point when Laurie first arrived to introduce her to the charge nurse, Patti Hoagland, the clerk Irene, and Jack's assigned nurse, Aliyah Jacobs, as well as to the surgical residents who were covering for the night.

After Laurie had been in the SICU for ten or so minutes, watching from a distance as Jack was being connected to all the appropriate monitors, Irene came over to her and said that there was a Detective Soldano to see her out in the hallway. Feeling a little embarrassed she was taking advantage of the charge nurse's good graces by having a visitor, Laurie quickly pushed out through the double swinging doors. Lou was there with two uniformed officers whom he introduced. As anxious as she felt, she didn't even commit their names to memory and told Lou she had to get right back inside. Lou said he understood but suggested that she try to find out who it was Jack had been on his way to meet at the MMH. Nervous and upset, Laurie responded that she wasn't there to play detective. All she wanted to do was keep watch over Jack until he woke up and then arrange to have him transferred.

Lou nodded, and encouraged her to feel free to call him at any time during the night if anything untoward happened. Laurie had promised she would and then retreated through the swinging doors to regain her designated observation location.

Laurie didn't sip this latest cup of coffee, but rather gulped it down in keeping with its sole purpose as a delivery vehicle for caffeine. Her hope was the stimulant would not only keep her awake but also keep her reasonably alert. She'd been startled and embarrassed by nearly falling out of her chair. After putting the empty mug down, she went back to watching the monitor, trusting that she wouldn't find the cursors quite so hypnotizing despite their reassuring but monotonous regularity.

For the most part, the evening had been a welcome bore. There were only two minor interruptions that had made Laurie sit up and take notice. The first occurred when a man dressed in scrubs and wearing a surgical cap and surgical mask suddenly came into the SICU and without checking in at the central desk walked directly into Jack's cubicle. Luckily Colleen had been there next to her at the time, typing into a monitor, so Laurie had been able to ask her who this newcomer might be. Colleen had been happy to investigate and returned to tell Laurie that he was the orthopedic resident on call who was merely checking Jack's hip incision as well as the circulation in Jack's foot below the temporary plaster cast.

The only other interruption to her numbing routine was when another male came into the unit who was dressed similar to her with a long white coat over scrubs and who Laurie initially thought was a doctor. He'd poked his head into several of the cubicles before approaching the central desk to chat briefly with Patti. Then, to Laurie's surprise, he went directly to Jack's cubicle and disappeared inside. Again, thanks to Colleen, Laurie was able to learn the man was the night nursing supervisor, who was responsible, among other things, for juggling all the intensive care beds. In response to her question of what he might be doing in Jack's cubicle, Colleen, with a shrug, had guessed he was checking if Jack could be transferred out. But whatever he had been doing, it had taken only a minute or two, and when he had emerged, he'd headed toward the unit's exit. As he had passed the central desk, he'd nodded at Laurie as if he knew her.

"How about something to eat?" Colleen suggested as she returned from one of the cubicles, interrupting Laurie's musing. "I'd be happy to pop down to the cafeteria and bring you something back. What do you say?"

"Thank you for your offer," Laurie said. "You're too kind. You have been such a help, but I'm really not hungry."

"Fine and dandy," Colleen said. "But if you change your mind just yell."

"Will do," Laurie said as she felt her phone buzz in her pocket. She'd turned the ringer off even though she wasn't expecting any calls, especially since she had turned over the reins of the OCME to George. Thinking it was probably her mother, unable to sleep and wondering about Jack, she looked at the screen to check. It wasn't her mother but rather Lou Soldano. Being careful to speak in low tones, she answered.

"How's Jack doing?" Lou asked. He sounded chipper, like it was the middle of the day and not the middle of the night.

"He's stable and in that sense doing fine. The problem is that he still hasn't awakened although I've been told he's moving more, which I guess is a good sign."

"How come you are whispering?" Lou asked. "I can barely hear you."

"It's a busy place with a lot of sick patients, and I'm trying to stay out of the way and not interfere."

"Oops, sorry. But I wanted to hear how he was doing and also let you know I'm again in the neighborhood. In fact, I'm right around the corner. The nineteenth precinct has had another homicide, so I'm here to make sure it is handled correctly. If you need anything, even just some moral support, give me a buzz. I can be there in minutes."

"Thank you, Lou. That's good of you and thanks for calling."

"No problem. Oh, one other thing. The two officers who I introduced you to went off shift, but there's two new ones as replacements. I understand they are a little long in the tooth, but I've been assured they are competent, good guys."

"Perfect," Laurie said, despite feeling they were not really needed.

"Remember to call if you need me."

"I will," she insisted. "And thanks."

After Laurie had disconnected, she guiltily looked over at Patti, but Patti was engaged in a heated discussion with one of the nurses. Either she hadn't heard that Laurie had taken a call, or she didn't mind. Feeling lucky either way, Laurie pocketed her phone and turned her attention back to the monitor in front of her. As had been the case for hours, everything was normal. She was also pleased at feeling distinctly much more awake after the coffee.

Chapter 36

Thursday, December 9, 2:37 A.M.
As Ronnie left the Emergency Department, he felt his pulse quicken. It was now or never as far as Jack Stapleton was concerned. Earlier he'd been interrupted. Within minutes of having filled the syringe with the potassium chloride up in his office, a trauma code had been called, meaning a case had arrived in the ED with the patient in extremis from a bad motor vehicle accident. As with all codes called in the hospital, Ronnie had to drop whatever he might be doing and respond.

The condition of the relatively young male patient had been extremely poor as he had not been wearing his seat belt and had gone through the windshield on impact. As such he had arrived barely alive. Although he had a pulse initially, his heart soon stopped, requiring CPR as well as an emergency thoracotomy. Despite multiple units of blood and a full, lengthy resuscitation attempt, the patient was ultimately declared dead. At that point, Ronnie, along with one of the ED doctors, had to face the family, always a difficult task that had never gotten easier for Ronnie no matter how many times he had to do it.

When Ronnie had been finally finished with the case, the first thing he had done was use one of the ED monitors to check Jack Stapleton's status. With some relief, he discovered there had been no documented change, and the man was still in the SICU, unconscious.

Getting off the elevator on the third floor, Ronnie rounded the bend and headed down the hallway toward the SICU. As he approached, he could see that the two officers had been changed. Now sat two significantly older white-haired Caucasian patrolmen who seemed much more at home in the hospital. The thinner of the two was tipping back precariously in his metal folding chair as he engaged his partner in an animated conversation replete with exaggerated Italianate hand gestures. Although they were in full uniform, both had removed their hats, which were on the floor beside their seats. As Ronnie neared, they quieted down, and the one who had been leaning back tipped forward with a thump.

As he had done earlier, Ronnie merely nodded an acknowledgment at the two officers and tried to breeze by. He was surprised when the stockier officer, whose name tag read DON WARE, stuck his hand out, bringing Ronnie to a halt as if he had hit up against a locked turnstile.

"Excuse me, Doctor," the officer said. "May we see your ID?"

Rolling his eyes, Ronnie lifted the ID that was hanging around his neck and showed it to the officer. As he did so he said, "I'm not a doctor. I'm the nursing supervisor."

"Excuse me," the other officer said. His name tag read LOUIE AMBROSIO. "Do you have business in the unit?"

"Of course I have business," Ronnie said with demonstrable exasperation, as it were a ridiculous question. The gun in his pocket was close to the officer's hand and he knew he'd be hard put to explain it, despite having a license to carry. "I told you I'm the nursing supervisor. I have business in the entire hospital."

The two officers exchanged a glance and then a mutual shrug.

"Thank you, Doctor," Don Ware said as he retracted his restraining arm.

"I'm the nursing supervisor, not a doctor," Ronnie snapped as he pushed through the doors.

Once inside, Ronnie stopped to get himself under control. He knew he was tense and the minor interaction with the officer had demonstrated it. But glancing around the interior of the SICU was reassuring, and he calmed quickly. Most of the activity of nurses caring for their assigned patients was within the cubicles in the opposite end of the room from Jack Stapleton's, which was definitely opportune. Looking in the other direction, he could see no activity in Jack's cubicle, suggesting Aliyah Jacobs was elsewhere, lending a hand to her colleagues, as she had been doing the last time Ronnie had checked.

Directing his attention toward the central desk, he could see that Patti was involved in an animated conversation with several nurses while Irene was busy with paperwork along with one of the surgical residents. Farther down, Dr. Benn and Jack's wife were situated behind separate monitors, seemingly preoccupied.

As he would often do, Ronnie started going into each cubicle for a brief check on the status of each patient while working his way down toward Jack Stapleton's. As he passed the central desk, Patti interrupted her conversation to acknowledge Ronnie. In response, Ronnie stepped over to the counter.

"I trust you've been informed about the aneurysm case going on in the OR," Ronnie said. "It will be coming here to take one of your empty beds."

"I did hear," Patti said. "No problem."

Ronnie gave her a thumbs-up and went into the next cubicle as Patti returned to her conversation.

Coming out of the cubicle right next to Jack's, Ronnie looked back at the central desk. No one was paying him any heed. It seemed that the timing and the circumstances couldn't be better. Reaching into his pocket, he fingered the syringe, and then in a blink of an eye stepped out of sight into Jack's cubicle. Without hesitating, he quickly moved up along the right side of the bed, and with the flow controller he shut off the large-bore IV that he had inserted in the ED. Rapidly taking down the saline container, he pulled out the syringe from his pocket and removed the needle cap with his teeth. After plunging the needle into the container's port, he used both hands to rapidly distribute the entire contents of the syringe into the saline. He then rehung the saline bag and opened the flow controller completely to allow the IV to run at a rapid rate. He was confident the bag would empty rapidly.

It had all taken mere seconds. In the next instant, he was back out into the main part of the SICU with the empty syringe in his pocket. Resisting an urge to run, he moved as nonchalantly as possible past the central desk. To his relief, no one paid him any heed, other than Irene, who gave him a passing glance. Reaching the swinging doors, he pushed through, once again interrupting the two policemen's spirited conversation, which he now could tell was about the travails of the Knicks.

With a slight, condescending nod, Ronnie walked past the police and proceeded down the hall. As he got farther away, he had the nearly irresistible urge to shout *hurray* and punch the air with his fist in celebration, but he did neither. Instead, when he reached the elevator lobby, he calmly pressed the button, knowing full well that within minutes he would be called for a code in the SICU.

CHAPTER 37

It didn't take Laurie long to start feeling sleepy again despite the additional coffee. The stultifying boredom of watching the unchanging cursors trace across the monitor in front of her was like a narcotic. The only relief was when Colleen would occasionally come and sit down next to her and chat for a few moments before making an entry into the hospital computer on a patient's status like she was doing at that very moment.

To try to engage her mind and keep awake, Laurie thought about Lou's phone call and how she wished she could take him up on his offer to come to the hospital to keep her company. Lou was truly a long-term, dear friend whose well-being was a concern for her since he lived alone and his entire world revolved about his job. Thinking about Lou reminded her of his mentioning Jasmine Rakoczi, the serial killer she had exposed so many years before, back when Laurie was single and even had had a crush on the chief medical officer of the MMH. She shook her head at the thought of the psychotic woman since the whole situation had been such an ugly experience on so many levels and had come very close to killing her after she had killed the chief medical officer.

"Okay, that's done," Colleen said, interrupting Laurie's musings. Colleen stood up and stretched by extending her arms over her head. "I think I'm going to make a quick run to the cafeteria for some fruit or maybe even something naughtier. Can I bring you something? Anything at all? What about a banana? You must be starving."

"A banana would be great," Laurie said.

"Anything else? A piece of pie? Ice cream?"

"A banana is fine," Laurie said, but then her attention was caught by a slight change in Jack's ECG as it traced across the screen. The T wave, a graphic representation of the repolarization of the heart's ventricles after a heartbeat, suddenly began to grow. Laurie could tell because a rapidly fading shadow of the previous beat still existed on the monitor over which the new beat was surcharged.

"A banana it is," Colleen said as she leaned back over the desk to log out of the computer she'd been using. "I'll be back in a jiffy."

As Colleen started to leave, Laurie reached out and stopped her by grabbing her arm.

"What do you make of this?" Laurie questioned, pointing at the fading image of a T wave.

"Make of what?" Colleen asked. She paused and bent over Laurie's shoulder to get a closer look at the monitor.

"I'm years away from my clinical residency," Laurie confessed. "But suddenly there seems to be a change in the T waves, or am I hallucinating?"

"Hmmm," Colleen said. "I think you're right. What on earth could be causing that?" Both women straightened up and looked across the divide into the open door of Jack's cubicle. All was quiet. Aliyah wasn't to be seen although not all the cubicle's interior was visible. To see better, Colleen took a few steps along the desk counter but immediately returned. "I don't think anybody is in there. Any further changes in the ECG?"

"The T waves are gradually getting taller and steeper," Laurie said. "It seems to be

466

progressive." In the back of her mind, she was trying to remember what she knew about T waves, but it was all a hazy, distant memory, and under the stress of the moment her mind wasn't working well. She looked up at Colleen, whom she knew was an expert since watching and monitoring ECGs was part and parcel of her daily job.

"It could be an early sign of ST elevation," Colleen said, but she clearly wasn't convinced. "But that is hardly the case. If anything, the ST segment seems to be going down. Hmmm. I'll head in there and see if anything has changed with the ECG leads."

"Wait!" Laurie said, her heart beginning to race. She had the premonition something was wrong, something major. "The ECG is changing. Now it looks like the P wave is flattening. What on earth could that mean?"

"That happens in atrial flutter or atrial fibrillation, but the pulse seems to be slowing slightly, which doesn't make sense. Yikes! What the hell is going on? I'm going in there and I'll let Patti know. We need a cardiologist ASAP."

With her eyes riveted to the monitor, Laurie watched as Jack's heart rate slowed further until the entire ECG complex began to spread out. Then, to her horror, it degraded into a chicken scratch sine wave and the alarm went off, indicating a cardiac arrest.

The entire SICU erupted in response, with everyone not necessary to keep someone else alive rushing into Jack's cubicle, while Patti placed an emergency code call to bring the circulating cardiac resuscitation team on the run.

With great restraint, Laurie kept her seat. She wanted to rush into Jack's cubicle as well, but she knew she wasn't supposed to leave the central desk. She also knew she wasn't as prepared or as knowledgeable as the nurses and doctors who were already there, so it wasn't as if she could really help, and might be in the way. As she sat there with her heart racing, she had the crushing feeling that she had failed Jack. Her whole effort had been to watch over him, but somehow she'd fallen short with no idea how. This thinking reminded her of Lou's request to call him if anything untoward happened. Although there couldn't be anything more untoward than what was occurring at the moment with Jack's heart in arrest, she wasn't going to call him, since there was nothing Lou could do. But thinking of Lou reminded her again of Jasmine Rakoczi and how she had tried to kill Laurie when Laurie had been a patient.

"My God!" Laurie shouted. Instantly all sorts of connections and associations coalesced in her brain. After the Rakoczi event, she had read a lot about the forensics of potassium chloride poisoning and how it was a near-perfect way for a medical serial killer to carry out their gruesome goals. After death, all the body's cells that had been hoarding potassium in life let it out, so the dead body was essentially flooded with potassium, making the detection of an externally lethal dose having been administered impossible. Part of that reading was about the physiology of sudden high potassium and what it did to the ECG.

With sudden comprehension of what was happening, Laurie leaped up so fast her chair careened across the central desk area on its casters to crash into the counter on the opposite side. Laurie ran toward the opening out onto the main part of the unit. Almost simultaneous with her emergence, the swinging doors into the unit burst open and the resuscitation team came rushing in, pushing the crash cart with a defibrillator, medications, and supplies needed to treat a cardiac arrest.

Laurie and the resuscitation team arrived simultaneously at Jack's cubicle, which was nearly filled with various personnel. The team surged ahead, pushing people aside. Laurie, who desperately wanted to get to Colleen, saw that she was on top of the bed kneeling alongside Jack's right side and doing chest compressions. On the opposite side, Aliyah was using an ambu bag to respire Jack in concert with Colleen's efforts. As the resuscitation team quickly and wordlessly took over both the chest compressions and the respiration efforts while also preparing the defibrillator, Patti, who had seen Laurie arrive, forced her way through the throng to get to Laurie's side. For her part, Laurie was trying to reach Colleen while desperately calling out her name over the raucous sound of the monitor's alarm.

"Dr. Montgomery!" Patti yelled sternly while grabbing Laurie's arm and pulling her to a halt. "You can't be here. You must leave this instant!"

Laurie knocked Patti's arm to the side with shocking force, catching Patti completely by surprise. Laurie then barreled through two intensive care nurses who were talking while looking at the monitor. Laurie reached Colleen and forcibly yanked her wrist to get her attention.

"I know what it is!" Laurie yelled, catching Colleen by surprise. Colleen was watching the placement of the defibrillator paddles.

"Clear!" the leader of the resuscitation team yelled before discharging the machine. Jack's body lurched from the shock. Everyone including Colleen turned their attention to the monitor, hoping the ECG cursor, when it reappeared, would show a heartbeat.

"Colleen!" Laurie yelled in frustration. "It's potassium chloride!"

Colleen turned to her. "What?"

"Restart the compressions!" the team leader shouted when the cursor popped back onto the screen and traced a straight line. Now Jack's heart was no longer fibrillating. It was at a standstill with no electrical activity whatsoever.

"I remembered those specific ECG changes!" Laurie yelled to Colleen. "The peaking of the T waves and the disappearance of the P wave is diagnostic. It's the first signs of hyperkalemia! Jack's been poisoned with potassium chloride. Tell them to start treatment for hyperkalemia immediately! Please! Every second counts."

Frantically Colleen looked from Laurie's tortured face to Patti, who had come up behind Laurie and was trying to pull Laurie from the cubicle. Colleen then looked back at the resident who was doing the chest compressions. She was torn with indecision. Laurie was making a certain amount of sense, but hyperkalemia was a rare problem causing cardiac arrest and mostly seen with serious kidney disorders, not healthy men.

"Tell them to use bicarbonate and whatever else helps!" Laurie shrieked, again knocking Patti's arm away. At that point, Laurie noted the intravenous was going full tilt into Jack. Breaking off from both Colleen and Patti, she pushed her way up to the head of the bed and stopped the IV using the flow controller. Patti had pushed after her and roughly grabbed Laurie's arm, angrily ordering her to leave at once and threatening to call security. But Colleen, who'd recovered from her sensory overload, came up behind Patti and intervened. "Hold on, Patti! I think Laurie has a point. The ECG changes we witnessed are pathognomonic of hyperkalemia. I think she's right!"

"Could someone turn off that freaking alarm!" the resuscitation team leader yelled over the sound, as he prepared for a second defibrillation attempt. A second later, the cubicle fell into comparative silence as Jack's body again heaved in response to the second shock.

"All right, Bruce, listen up," Colleen yelled out to the team leader when the cursor continued to trace a flat line on the monitor. "We are going to treat this case as severe hyperkalemia. I want you to use sodium bicarbonate, along with calcium gluconate, and at least twenty units of regular insulin along with a fifty-gram dose of glucose. Also let's get a stat electrolyte study. And somebody take down those two IV bottles and replace them with saline. Any questions?"

"Why do you suspect hyperkalemia?" Bruce questioned, looking confused. He was a senior medical resident in the last year of his internal medicine residency and lower in the hospital hierarchy than Colleen, who was a staff hospitalist.

"We happened to be viewing the ECG when this problem first started," Colleen explained. "We witnessed the changes in real time as the heart's conduction system went awry."

"All right, team," Bruce said while piling the defibrillator paddles on top of the machine to get them out of the way. "You heard the lady, let's get to it."

As the resuscitation team fell to work, one of the on-call anesthesiologists showed up and deftly intubated Jack so that the respiring could be done with more certainty and a respirator could be used if necessary. With Colleen's encouragement, Patti reluctantly agreed to allow Laurie to stay in the cubicle while Patti left to return to the central desk.

As the minutes ticked by and no change was seen on the ECG monitor, Laurie again fell into despair, wondering how this could have happened, as she'd been there watching. She chided herself despite having no idea what she could have done differently. Looking at Jack, she wished she'd followed her initial inclination and had him transferred when the idea occurred to her when she'd first arrived in the Emergency Department.

When the stat electrolyte results came back, Patti rushed back to the cubicle herself to report them to the resuscitation team rather than using the audio system. After she'd called out the results, she added it was the highest potassium level she had ever seen in her career.

"My God," Bruce responded. "That's the highest I've ever seen as well. Good grief! With such a level I'm afraid we're pissing on a forest fire here with this sodium bicarbonate and the rest. I suggest we get a surgical resident down here pronto and set up either peritoneal dialysis or, better yet, extracorporeal dialysis."

"Do it!" Colleen said. She looked at Laurie. "It's clearly what's needed."

Laurie nodded. She felt suddenly weak.

"How are you holding up?" Colleen asked, noticing her pallor.

"Not well," Laurie admitted. "I think I'll go back to my spot at the desk. I need to sit down."

"Good idea. Please do," Colleen said. "I'll stay here and keep you informed of any changes. I promise."

"Okay," Laurie managed. She was beside herself with guilt and overwhelming anxiety. She turned around and started out of the cubicle. As there were still almost a dozen people jammed into the tiny room, people had to make way for her by stepping aside. She excused herself as she worked her way toward the exit.

Abruptly Laurie stopped in her tracks. She found herself staring at a man dressed in a white coat over scrubs who looked disturbingly familiar despite his Covid mask. Instantly she recognized him as the man she earlier had thought was a doctor when he'd come into the unit and briefly ducked into several of the occupied cubicles before doing the same into Jack's. Attentive to all the comings and goings, she'd asked Colleen at the time who he was and learned that he wasn't a doctor but rather the nursing supervisor who was responsible for allocating all the beds in the hospital's intensive care units. She particularly remembered him because he'd nodded to her on his way out as if they knew each other. But far more important than that remembrance was that Laurie suddenly recalled she'd seen him a second time, apparently doing the same reconnoitering. What made this second sighting so disturbing and provocative was that it had preceded the first signs of trouble appearing on Jack's ECG by minutes. He'd been the last person to enter Jack's cubicle.

All these thoughts went through Laurie's brain in milliseconds, igniting a firestorm of emotion. All at once and without an ounce of doubt, she knew in her heart that this man was the serial killer Sue Passero feared existed, and it was he who was responsible for Jack's impending death.

"It was you!" she screamed. "You were the source of the potassium chloride!"

In a sudden, uncontrollable fury, Laurie launched herself at Ronnie with her fingers of both hands outstretched like cats' claws, aimed at his neck. In her animal rage, she wanted to throttle him.

Shocked at this unexpected attack, Ronnie reared backward, trying to keep himself away from her hands while partially parrying her arms. Still, she was able to make contact with the base of his neck, scratching downward. Several nurses on either side of Laurie, equally shocked at her attack, tried to come to his assistance by grabbing her, but she was unstoppable. She lunged forward again and leaped at Ronnie with her hands outstretched. The nurses managed to sweep Laurie's legs from under her, causing her to ram into Ronnie like a torpedo. As Laurie fell, she tried to grasp at anything with her hands as they slid down the front of his white coat. What they encountered were the two pockets, and, in an attempt to break her fall, she grabbed on, ripping both open and spilling out their contents.

As Laurie hit the floor, so did the empty 50ml syringe and the SIG Sauer P365, causing a collective gasp from all those people not directly participating in the resuscitation attempt and witnessing this sudden eruption of violence. Such a blowup, along with the appearance of a pistol within the sanctity of an intensive care unit, was a shocking and unexpected anathema. The two nurses who had essentially tackled her let go of her and took a step back in bewilderment.

Laurie scrambled to her feet and in the process snatched up both the pistol and the syringe and held them aloft. "Here's proof!" she yelled. "This man is a killer!"

Ronnie was equally as shocked as everyone else, but in a far different way. When he had arrived at the code, which he'd timed to be sure the resuscitation team would already be there, he'd remained in the background to be available in case he was needed. Although he'd been mildly disconcerted when the decision was made to treat hyperkalemia early in the course of the cardiac arrest, he'd still been relatively confident enough potassium had already been delivered. But then, seemingly out of the blue, had come the surprise of his life. And now, facing this wild woman, he instantly knew he was facing an existential crisis despite his careful planning and faultless execution.

In milliseconds, it was utterly obvious to Ronnie that his carefully organized life was collapsing around him, and he had to react right now. There was no time to dither or argue or deny the obvious. He had to initiate his well-prepared escape plan by getting the hell out of the hospital. No doubt, the syringe still had potassium chloride residue in its chamber, which would be easy to verify.

Reaching out with determination, Ronnie grabbed his SIG Sauer, and with all his strength, he tore it out of Stapleton's wife's raised hand. Then he turned and charged out of the cubicle, roughly pushing people to the side.

Laurie reacted with similar impetuosity and, stuffing the empty syringe in her scrub pocket to preserve the evidence, she followed him, dashing out of the cubicle and running full tilt along the chest-high countertop of the central desk.

"Dr. Montgomery!" shouted Patti, who was within the desk and who happened to be on the phone with security. "Stop!"

But Laurie paid no heed. She could see that Ronnie had reached the swinging doors and had burst out into the hallway while still holding the pistol in full view.

"Dr. Montgomery!" Patti yelled out yet again.

Laurie wasn't thinking, just reacting. The last thing she wanted was for this serial killer to get away, and, pistol notwithstanding, she wasn't going to allow it. As she, too, burst out of the SICU, she confronted the two policeman who were seemingly confused about what was happening. Both had leaped to their feet as Ronnie had dashed past. One of the chairs had tipped over as evidence of how surprised they'd been. To the left down the corridor, she could see Ronnie's rapidly diminishing figure as he was continuing his flight.

"Stop him!" Laurie yelled, pointing after him. "He's a killer, and he's got a gun!"

The two policemen took off down the hall in pursuit. One of them yelled "Stop!" but Ronnie ignored them. Laurie followed but slowed as she pulled her phone out. Coming to a near halt, she placed a call to Lou. As the call went through, she resumed her pursuit of the policemen and Ronnie as rapidly as using the phone would allow. Ahead, all of them had disappeared into a stairwell.

"What's up, Laur?" Lou said without preamble.

"I've exposed a killer!" Laurie shrieked. "The two policemen are after him. He's armed." She reached the stairwell and pulled open the door.

"Good grief," Lou said. "Where are you?"

"I'm in a stairwell," she managed. She was getting progressively out of breath. As she plunged down the stairs, she saw the door to the second floor was just settling into its jamb. "They went out onto the second floor. They must be heading for the pedestrian bridge to the parking garage."

"I'm on my way," Lou said. "I'll be there in minutes. And I'll call in backup. Stay out of it, Laurie!"

Laurie disconnected as she pulled open the door to the second floor. From having accepted a ride home from Sue on several occasions, she knew the route to the pedestrian bridge. Running again, she reached it and crossed over to the parking garage, where she yanked open the door. Her hope was to see the policemen had nabbed the killer but what she saw instead were the two officers hunkering down behind the parking valet's podium with their guns drawn. The tall, thin officer frantically motioned for her to go back, but ignoring him, she bent over and joined them, squatting down behind the podium.

"You shouldn't be here!" Louie snapped. "The bastard fired at us."

"I'm not surprised," Laurie said. "I think he's killed a lot of patients, and I have personal reasons to want to be sure he is caught. Where the hell is he?"

"He's behind that gray Mercedes," Don said. He pointed across the lot to a car parked alongside a wall. "We returned fire, and he ran behind that Benz."

"What are you going to do?" Laurie asked. She tried to look. The lighting in the garage was not the best, and there were long areas of shadow.

"Keep your head down," Louie demanded.

"We're going to wait for backup like we are supposed to do," Don said. "They should be here very shortly. When we called for backup, we were told that it was already on its way, which surprised us. When he went into the SICU, this dude told us he was the nursing supervisor. We thought he was a doctor."

"I was told he *is* the nursing supervisor," Laurie said. "More important, he's also a killer and probably a serial killer."

"Jesus Christ." Don moaned. "We thought this was going to be a cushy detail, not a goddamned firefight."

"When you said you have personal reasons to want him caught, what did you mean?" Louie asked.

"I'd rather not say at the moment," she responded. She didn't want to think about it. Instead, she took out her phone and placed another call to Lou. He answered on the first ring.

"I'm almost there," he said. "Two minutes. Where are you and where is the killer? Do you know?"

"I'm in the parking garage," Laurie said.

"And he is, too. I'm with the two officers. There has been gunfire. They have him pinned behind a gray Mercedes on the second floor."

"Tell them not to do anything stupid and that backup is on its way."

"Don't worry! They seem appropriately conservative."

"Good," Lou said. "And it goes for you, too." He disconnected.

For a few minutes, the three people huddled behind the valet podium were silent as they kept their eyes on the gray Mercedes, then all at once they jumped. Behind them the door to the pedestrian bridge burst open and four hospital security men in black suits, talking loudly among themselves, came running into the garage.

"Good God," Louie said exasperatedly as he again frantically waved for the new arrivals to take cover.

"What's going on here?" one of the new arrivals demanded.

"We've got a homicide suspect who fired at us cornered behind that Mercedes across the way," the first officer snapped. "So get the hell down!"

The moment he spoke, a hail of gunfire erupted and one of the arriving security people cried out as he was hit in the leg and fell to the pavement. Everyone else ducked. It was Laurie who spotted the killer, who had run out from behind the Mercedes to take advantage of the commotion caused by the security peoples' arrival.

"He's escaping!" she cried. The two officers hesitantly stood up and then ran out into the roadway, aiming their guns. But the killer disappeared behind a black Cherokee. The security people, still hunched over, crowded around their fallen comrade to lend a hand while one of them called down to the ED to send help.

In the next instant, the Cherokee shot backward with its wheels sending a high-pitched screeching that reverberated around the confines of the garage. Then the SUV powered forward with equal squealing, heading away down the inclined ramp. The smell of burnt rubber permeated the air. In response, the two patrolmen each fired several shots at the departing Cherokee but didn't try to pursue. Don pulled his radio off his shoulder and used it to let his precinct operator know the suspect was fleeing and described the vehicle.

Still holding her phone, she called Lou.

"I'm in sight of the parking garage," Lou barked.

"He's in a black SUV with flames painted

on it, heading for the exit from the second floor!" Laurie yelled back. "He shot one of the hospital security people."

"Ten-four!" Lou said, and disconnected.

Gripping the steering wheel with both hands, Lou turned his Malibu sharply to the right into one of the MMH's garage entrance/exits and crashed through the black-and-white-striped wooden gate. On the other side of the gate area, he pulled into an open slot and then rapidly backed out, completely blocking the roadway. Leaping out of the vehicle, he pulled out his service pistol from his belt holster and then hunkered down behind his car with a view up the ramp over his car's front hood. A flat black SUV appeared at the top of the ramp with screeching tires while making a 180-degree turn to come into view. Accelerating, it came at Lou, closing the gap rapidly.

Realizing the man was not going to stop, Lou dove out of the way at the last second, hitting the pavement hard with his right shoulder. Behind him he heard the thundering crash of glass and metal as the SUV rammed the Malibu and then drove it back to smash against the exit stanchions, where both vehicles finally came to a smoking halt.

Leaping up, Lou raced the few steps to

bring him near to the SUV's driver's-side door while he yelled for the driver, who he could see despite the tinted windows, to come out with his hands held high. Lou waited a beat and then repeated his order, yelling even more loudly. He was holding his service pistol in both hands out in front of him, pointed at the indistinct profile.

The car door suddenly flew open, and a man came into view, gun in hand, trained on Lou. Reacting by reflex honed over the years, Lou shot the man three times. Still the man managed to discharge his weapon, but it was after having taken a round in his chest and his aim was off, and the bullet harmlessly ricocheted around the garage.

Lou watched as the man tumbled out of the SUV onto the pavement. His gun skidded off several feet. Lou pulled out his phone, calling the nineteenth precinct for help, and then the ED. Despite his experience, his hands were trembling.

Laurie had heard the gunshots as they echoed in the garage and hoped that they were from Lou's gun and not the killer's. She also now heard multiple police sirens in the distance as they converged. After the SUV had left, she'd rushed over to see if she could help the injured security man and had assisted in the placement of the man's belt as a tourniquet around his thigh to stanch the bleeding. Now he was being taken away on a gurney brought up from the Emergency Department. She was about to head back upstairs to the SICU when her phone rang. As she expected, it was Lou.

"Are you okay?" Laurie demanded. The sounds of the approaching police sirens were even louder coming through her phone.

"Yeah, I'm okay," Lou said. "But the suspect isn't. I had to shoot the son of a bitch before he shot me. How about you? Are you okay?"

"I'm okay, but Jack isn't. The man you shot tried to kill him the same way that horrid Jasmine Rakoczi tried to kill me, with potassium chloride."

"Good God," Lou said. "How is he?"

"I don't know, and I'm scared to find out," she said. "But I have to get back to the SICU. When I left to chase the bastard, Jack's condition wasn't good. He'd had a cardiac arrest from the potassium he'd been given."

"Don't tell me that," Lou said with alarm. "You're scaring me."

"I'm terrified, too," Laurie said. "I can't believe it happened right under my nose. I was supposed to be watching over him to keep him safe. I'm furious with myself for not having had him transferred and for not keeping him safe when I didn't."

"Oh, come on, Laur! Don't fault yourself! I'm sure you did the best you could and better than anyone else could have done. Minding Jack is a Herculean job. Listen, as soon as I wrap up here, I'll come up and keep you company." The sounds of the sirens reached a crescendo and then rapidly trailed off, suggesting multiple squad cars had arrived.

"It would be nice to have your company and support, but I'm afraid it is out of the question. The only reason I've been permitted in is thanks to one of the senior hospitalists, who I met through Sue and who has taken pity on me. And they might not let me return since I caused a hell of a commotion. I'll have to see."

"All right, I understand," Lou said. "I won't push, but good luck all around. I've got to go, but keep me informed. Please!"

"Okay, will do," Laurie said, even though she wasn't sure she'd have the strength if the news wasn't good. She then pocketed her phone as she made her way to the exit door and then over the pedestrian bridge.

Once in the hospital, she used the elevator

to go a single floor since she felt weak-kneed after the ordeal. Getting out on the third floor, she struggled with ambivalence. On the one hand she wanted to rush back to the SICU to find out how Jack was doing, while at the same time she was nervous that the news might not be what she wanted to hear.

She walked down the long hallway to the double doors leading into the SICU. The two chairs that had been occupied by the police remained. One was still tipped over on its side. After taking a deep breath for fortitude, Laurie pushed inside and then stopped just beyond the doors. From where she was standing, she could see the usual activities in a number of the cubicles, but, more important, she could see that Jack's cubicle was still a center of activity. The cardiac crash cart was positioned by its entrance, which at least meant that the resuscitation team had not given up.

Glancing at the central desk, she saw it had returned to a semblance of normal. The clerk and several resident physicians were sitting in front of monitors making entries into the hospital's central computer data bank. Patti Hoagland was standing in the center of it all and on the phone. The person Laurie most wanted to see, Colleen Benn, wasn't in sight.

Laurie hesitated, unsure what to do. She questioned if she should just ignore everyone and proceed down to Jack's cubicle as if she was entitled to be there or instead approach the central desk, get Patti's attention, and perhaps apologize for the commotion she'd caused.

Laurie didn't deliberate for long. Almost immediately Patti caught sight of her, and despite continuing her conversation with her mobile phone to her ear, she enthusiastically waved for Laurie to approach the desk. Relieved of having to make a decision, Laurie complied. As she neared, she had no idea what to expect.

"Dr. Montgomery," Patti said once she was off the phone. "I was just talking with one of the administrators who has been in contact with security. Your suspicions about Ronald Cavanaugh seem to have been right. I won't ask you how you knew because I'm sure you are anxious to know about your husband's status. Colleen is still with him, and I'm sure she's eager to talk with you." She pointed toward Jack's cubicle.

"Thank you. I'm sorry for having caused such a scene," Laurie said.

"No problem! You were justified, and we as an institution are shocked, saddened, and frankly embarrassed to say the very least. But please, don't let me hold you up. I know Colleen wants desperately to talk with you." Patti gestured toward Jack's cubicle again.

Laurie started in its direction, fearing for the worst but hoping for the best. She knew the term *desperately* could be interpreted either way. As she rounded the crash cart and stepped into the space, she could see the CPR was still being maintained. There was also another piece of equipment in the room, which was attached to blood-filled tubing that ran into Jack's right arm. Laurie assumed it was an emergency dialysis machine despite having never seen one.

Colleen saw Laurie and joined her. "I think we are making progress," Colleen said.

"Is that a dialysis machine?" Laurie asked while pointing.

"It is indeed," Colleen said. "We've pulled out all the stops and started extracorporeal dialysis and peritoneal dialysis simultaneously. We're already seeing a sharp drop in potassium level and even a little bit of electrical activity in the heart. I wouldn't be at all surprised if we see significant electrical activity in the next few minutes. I don't want to be premature, but I do believe we are over the hump. The fact that you recognized the signs of hyperkalemia so fast, I believe, saved the day."

"That's nice of you to say," Laurie said. "Are you being sincere or just trying to be optimistic for my benefit?"

"Absolutely sincere," Colleen said. "And since resuscitation was started so early, there was zero period of hypoxia. During the whole time we've been in here, the oxygen saturation has been in the nineties, so there won't be any problem there, either."

"Hey, look at this, everyone!" the resuscitation team leader yelled enthusiastically. "We've got relatively normal-looking electrical activity."

"Just a minute," Colleen said to Laurie before hurrying back to look at the ECG. After studying it for a moment she called out, "I'd say that looks pretty damn good. Hold up on the CPR!" Then, to the person doing the respiring, "Do we have a pulse?"

"We've got a pulse, and a good one," the resident who had been using the ambu bag said, feeling for the carotid pulse in Jack's neck.

"Is he breathing?" Colleen asked.

The same resident put her hand over the tip of the endotracheal tube to feel if there was air going in and out. "Yes, he's breathing."

"Fabulous," Colleen said. "Go ahead and

remove the endotracheal tube. Also, let's run another stat electrolytes. We need to see exactly where the potassium is before we stop the dialysis."

Laurie advanced into the room and looked down at Jack. Despite the abrasion on his cheek, he looked remarkably normal. She felt enormous relief although she knew she'd feel even more if he would only wake up.

EPILOGUE

Saturday, December 11, 2:45 P.M.

Lou Soldano parked his new Malibu at a fire hydrant, tossed his NYPD placard onto the dashboard, and got out. He was just a few doors down from Laurie and Jack's brownstone on West 106th Street. Carefully he picked up the large manila envelope he had on the passenger-side seat and got out. The weather was rather nice, but it was a bit cold, so he raised the collar of his coat and pulled the lapels together under his chin. He then made his way to their stoop and climbed the ten steps up to the front door.

After ringing the buzzer, he heard Laurie's voice asking if it was he. "It's me," Lou said into the small microphone. A moment later the heavy front door buzzed open, and Lou entered and started up the stairs. As an inveterate smoker for most of his life from teenage years on, he wasn't looking forward

494

to the five flights, and he took it slowly. He'd been trying to quit smoking for years and did it on a regular basis but always relapsed to the point it had become the hackneyed joke that quitting smoking was easy because he did it all the time.

He had called Laurie and Jack earlier that day because he had something he wanted to show them that he thought they would find very interesting even though also depressing.

By the time he got to the fourth floor, Laurie was waiting for him, holding the apartment door ajar. After Lou had taken off his coat and she had hung it in the sizable closet, they hugged.

"Great to see you," Laurie said, finally letting go.

"Likewise," Lou said. "How's the patient?"

She laughed. "He's being a pain in the ass, to tell you the truth. He's so demanding." Laurie laughed again to indicate she was at least partially kidding. "He's already saying he wants to get out to buy a new bike, if you can believe it. He's also already pestering the doctor about when he can play basketball."

"That sounds like Jack," Lou said with a chuckle. "I brought a Covid mask if you want me to wear it. Jack has told me your mother isn't vaccinated."

"True, but she rarely ventures out. Have you been exposed lately?"

"Not that I know of."

"Then the mask is up to you. We're all up to date with the vaccine, including the kids."

"I'm fine going maskless," Lou said. "I'll say hi to Dorothy from afar." He then followed Laurie up the next flight to the kitchen level, where he said hello to the kids, Dorothy, and Caitlin. Then it was time for the final flight up to the top floor where the bedrooms were, including the master bedroom and the kids' rooms.

"I don't know how you people live like this," Lou complained halfway up. He was out of breath.

"It would be good for you, old man," she said. "It would probably get you to finally stop smoking."

"Yeah, I'd stop smoking because I'd be dead," Lou joked. "Changing the subject, I have to say, Emma is making real progress. I was pleased to see she actually seemed to relate to me, which was a first."

"She is doing gangbusters," Laurie agreed. "The team my mother has put together and supervises on a daily basis is doing wonders. I have to say, we're thrilled."

Laurie led Lou a short distance down the sixth-floor hallway and into the bedroom, where Jack was lying on the bed against a bank of pillows. His injured right leg in a pneumatic cast was elevated on an additional pillow. Lots of newspapers and a few forensic medical journals were scattered about. The TV was tuned to CNN but muted.

"Hey, buddy," Lou said, coming into the room and bumping fists with Jack. "How are you?"

"Not too bad, considering," Jack said.

"I wanted to personally thank you for finally waking up," Lou said. "You had us worried there for a while."

"Twelve hours' rest was all I could manage out of the concussion," Jack said. "On the positive side, I'm glad I missed all the excitement of the CPR. Ironically enough, the broken rib I got from that ordeal has pained me more than the two leg fractures."

"What makes me marvel is how you complain about my smoking by telling me how dangerous it is and yet you have persisted in riding a bike around the city."

"And which I plan to get back to as soon as possible," Jack said.

"That is a verboten subject," Laurie stated categorically.

"That reminds me," Jack said. "Thank your crime scene people for finding a bit of my bike's paint on the front of the Cherokee. That bastard tried to do me in twice. What a loser."

"*Loser* isn't a strong enough word," Lou said. "Wait until you see this."

Opening the manila envelope, he extracted Ronnie's dog-eared ledger in a clear plastic evidence bag, which he opened in turn. He then handed the well-worn notebook to the couple. Laurie had joined Jack by sitting on the edge of the bed.

"What the hell is this?" Jack asked. He pushed himself up into a more upright sitting position.

"Open it and you'll see," Lou said. "Our crime scene people found it up in an HVAC duct in the hall ceiling of Ronald Cavanaugh's apartment in Woodside, Queens. It's the main evidence for our investigation."

With Laurie holding the ledger's cardboard back cover and Jack the front, they opened it and, starting at the beginning, carefully glanced at a number of pages.

"Jesus H. Christ!" Jack murmured. "Are each of these entries patients that Cavanaugh knocked off?"

"That's what the investigators believe," Lou said. "They have already started checking with the Manhattan Memorial Hospital to get individual histories, and it's proved to be the case. Can you imagine being in AmeriCare's shoes when all this goes public? I shudder to think of the lawsuits that are going to emerge. But, hey, it was the AmeriCare bigwigs who decided to save money by reducing the night nursing supervisor to one instead of two. This bastard had the run of the hospital."

"Couldn't happen to a nicer organization," Jack said sarcastically as he turned yet another page.

"Here's the other problem," Lou said. "None of these patients that have been checked so far were medical examiner cases. That's why the OCME never got a chance to question the deaths. And the reason was simple. The way the system works is that the night nursing supervisor decides which deaths are medical examiner cases and which ones aren't, and Ronnie Cavanaugh sure as hell wasn't going to send any of his victims to the OCME and let you guys figure out what had happened. He was also the one who decided the death was what they call an *expected death,* meaning each one tended to lower the MMH's mortality ratio, making the hospital ironically look progressively better the more he killed."

"It's tragic," Laurie said with a shake of her head. "How many total did he kill?"

"You'll see," Lou said. "The last two entries, which occurred only days ago, were numbers ninety-three and ninety-four."

"Good grief," Laurie said. "What a travesty. He makes Jasmine Rakoczi, who we thought was the devil incarnate with about a dozen victims, seem like an amateur."

"And the ninety-four patients were just his mercy killings," Lou said. "Take a gander at the next-to-last page of the book. There's another list."

"The cover of this ledger looks like it has seen better days," Laurie said as she and Jack followed Lou's suggestion.

"That's interesting that you noticed," Lou said. "The investigators posit that Cavanaugh handled it on a regular basis. The thought is that he considered it a kind of trophy of his accomplishments and leafed through it maybe as often as every day. It must have been like his devil's bible."

"What a freaking creep," Jack said. "Your having to kill him was a service to humanity, but it's a double tragedy in a weird way. He was a prolific killer, but it was also my impression from speaking with him and from what I had been told by one of the emergency medicine doctors that he was a terrific nurse when he wanted to be. He was certainly smart enough and had gotten good nursing training in the navy."

When the page in question was revealed, both Laurie and Jack audibly sucked in a breath. There was a list of twenty-three names. The next to last was *Susan Passero,* which caught Laurie's eye, whereas Jack noticed not only *Susan Passero* but also the final name, *Cherine Gardener.*

"What on earth is this list?" Laurie managed.

"The investigators have only checked a handful of these cases so far, but here's what they believe. In contrast to the front of the book, where all the cases could be considered mercy killings, meaning the victims had serious medical disease, mostly advanced cancer of one form or another, this latter list, except for the last two entries, seem to be cases that should be called hero victims. Ronald Cavanaugh, at some point, branched off from his mercy killing to purposely put various patients in jeopardy by using some toxic medication or overdose purely to get the credit and prestige of being the one to make the diagnosis of what was ailing them and save them in the process. Unfortunately, it didn't always work out as planned, and that list are the failures, or the patients who died. How many times he tried this hero hoax and with how many patients, we'll probably never know. All we know is twenty-one times the chosen victim didn't get enough antidote or didn't get it soon enough."

"God! What a fiend!" Laurie spat. She closed the book, took it out of Jack's hands, and quickly gave it back to Lou as if handling it made her feel complicit. "Where do these people come from? Are they born that way or are they made to be that way?"

"You doctors are better equipped to answer that question than we lay ignora-muses," Lou said as he repackaged the ledger. "But the investigation into Ronald Cavanaugh's background has shown a bit of light and seems to point more toward the made route. His parents were killed in an auto accident when he was four, and he was taken in by his maternal grandmother. Unfortunately, she ended up passing away when Ronald was eight, and he ended up in the New York State foster care program. Ronald and another boy two years younger were taken in as foster children by a nurse. Everything seems to have been hunky-dory until the nurse, thanks to a cigarette habit, came down with mouth or throat cancer that required aggressive treatment. From then on things went downhill, and years later she was diagnosed with Munchausen by proxy."

"Good gravy," Jack said.

"I think a better expletive than *good gravy* is called for," Lou said. "Anyway, I just learned about the syndrome yesterday. It's big-time weird. But the long and short of it is that Ronald and his foster brother suffered and were constantly in and out of the hospital with myriad complaints, all of which the foster mother was causing using various medications she'd give them, including table salt. Hell, I had no idea table salt could put you in the hospital."

"If you eat enough of it, it can be fatal," Laurie said.

"Somehow Ronald Cavanaugh survived even though his foster brother didn't, and he aged out of the system at eighteen and joined the navy, where he seems to have done okay for himself."

"He did," Jack agreed. "He became an independent duty corpsman on a fast-attack nuclear submarine."

"Good God," Lou voiced. "Now maybe I understand. Being on a submarine underwater for months at a time would have driven me bonkers."

Suddenly Lou's mobile rang in his jacket

pocket. Pulling it out, he looked at the screen briefly. "Sorry," he said to Laurie and Jack. "I've got to take this." He then walked toward the window that faced out onto 106th Street and began speaking in low tones.

Laurie looked down at Jack. "I cannot believe it," she said with a shake of her head. "This whole mess is much worse than I ever could have imagined. What a disaster for so many families and even the MMH. That beast Cavanaugh killed one hundred and seventeen people, and that's what we know of. There could have been more."

"All I can say is that I'm really, really glad he didn't kill one hundred and eighteen," Jack said. "And you had an enormous role in preventing it. So, if I haven't expressed it enough or adequately already, let me say again with true sincerity that I thank you for being there when I needed you."

Laurie felt some tears of joy threaten to surface, which she wanted to avoid since she considered demonstrative emotionalism one of her weaknesses. To avoid a scene, she merely bent over and gave him a strong, heartfelt hug.

"Ouch," Jack complained good-naturedly. "You're forgetting my broken rib."

"Sorry," Laurie said. She straightened up

and gave him a loud kiss on the cheek and then mussed his already disarranged hair. "There was a time that fateful night when I truly thought that I had failed in keeping watch over you. But, needless to say, I'm enormously thankful that everything turned out as it has, for all of us."

"Unfortunately, I've got to run," Lou said, interrupting Laurie as he hustled back from where he'd been standing at the window. He was still holding his phone. "But before I go, I have to give you two enormous credit for exposing and ridding the city of this awful man. You guys are quite a forensic team, which I have to admire even if it frequently makes being your friend difficult. Nonetheless you both deserve a medal for what you've done. Bravo!"

"Let's give credit where credit is due," Laurie said. "We wouldn't have been able to do what we did without Sue Passero and her commitment as a caring physician. She's the one who deserves the lion's share of the credit. If it hadn't been for her and her ultimate sacrifice, Ronald Cavanaugh would still be merrily carrying on and probably would have continued for years to come."

"Hear, hear!" Jack and Lou voiced in unison while nodding enthusiastically.

REFERENCES

Appelbaum, Eileen, and Rosemary Batt. "Private Equity in Healthcare: Profits Before Patients and Workers." Center for Economic and Policy Research. December 14, 2021.

Scheffler, Richard M., Laura M. Alexander, and James Godwin. "Soaring Private Equity Investments in the Healthcare Sector: Consolidation Accelerated, Competition Undermined, and Patients at Risk." School of Public Health, University of California, Berkeley. May 18, 2021.

ABOUT THE AUTHOR

Robin Cook, M.D., is the author of more than thirty books and is credited with popularizing the medical thriller with his groundbreaking and wildly successful 1977 novel, *Coma.* He divides his time between Florida and Massachusetts. His most recent bestsellers include *Charlatans, Host, Cell,* and *Death Benefit.*

The employees of Thorndike Press hope you have enjoyed this Large Print book. All our Thorndike, Wheeler, and Kennebec Large Print titles are designed for easy reading, and all our books are made to last. Other Thorndike Press Large Print books are available at your library, through selected bookstores, or directly from us.

For information about titles, please call:
   (800) 223-1244

or visit our website at:
   gale.com/thorndike

To share your comments, please write:
   Publisher
   Thorndike Press
   10 Water St., Suite 310
   Waterville, ME 04901